CW01508750

ETIDORHPA

OR

THE END OF THE EARTH.

THE STRANGE HISTORY OF A MYSTERIOUS BEING

and

The Account of a Remarkable Journey

AS COMMUNICATED IN MANUSCRIPT TO

LLEWELLYN DRURY

WHO PROMISED TO PRINT THE SAME,

BUT FINALLY EVADED THE RESPONSIBILITY

WHICH WAS ASSUMED BY

JOHN URI LLOYD

WITH MANY ILLUSTRATIONS BY

J. AUGUSTUS KNAPP

—

EXTENDED EDITION

—

First published on 1895, enlarged in 1901.
This edition: 2019
Nighttime Editions

ISBN: 9798538305285

Nighttime Editions
2019
For contact and other books published:
https://nighttimeeditions.wordpress.com

I am the man

"I AM THE MAN"

CONTENTS.

FOURTH INTERLUDE

THE NARRATIVE CONTINUED

FIFTH INTERLUDE

ILLUSTRATIONS

FULL-PAGE

HALF-PAGE AND TEXT CUTS

INTRODUCTION AND BIOGRAPHIC NOTE ON THE AUTHOR

John Uri Lloyd (April 19, 1849 – April 9, 1936) was born in Bloomfield, upstate New York, United States. Son of teachers Sophia Webster and Nelson Marvin Lloyd. In 1853 his family relocated to Florence and Petersburg in northern Kentucky, near Cincinnati, Ohio. From an early age, he showed himself enthusiasm about science, particularly chemistry; this is how, at age 14, he took an apprenticeship with chemist William J.M. Gordon, then he would study with George Eger.

His younger brothers, Nelson Ashley Lloyd and Curtis Gates Lloyd also studied chemistry, in 1886 the three brothers bought the Merrel and Thorpe Company, renaming it as Lloyd Brothers, Pharmacist, Inc.

Lloyd was a very influential chemist and pharmacist at his time, writing for several publications as well as publishing his own studies in several books. He was an entrepreneur, investigator, writer, professor as he was also inventor, he patented the "Cold Still extractor" which was used from the 1940s to the 1970s to extract ingredients from plant materials and to distill volatile oils, perfumes, and essences from natural materials. Another invention was the first buffered alkaloid (made with hydrous aluminum silicate), called Alcresta.

His studies contributed to the development of pharmacognosy, ethnobotany, economic botany, and herbal medicine. He was part of Eclectic medicine, a branch of American medicine that made use of botanical remedies along with other substances and physical therapy practices. He was awarded the "Ebert Prize" by "The American Pharmacists Association" on three occasions (1882, 1891, 1916).

He was an avid book collector and people started to send him copies for his library, this is how he affirms to have received the manuscript which forms Etidorhpa. With this collection ever-growing, he founded, together with his brothers, the "Lloyd Library and Museum" in 1919, dedicated mostly to works in botany, pharmacy, natural history, medicine, scientific history, and visual arts. This institution is still open and is considered one of

Cincinnati's hidden treasures. Also to note that Lloyd's house in Cincinnati was added to the "National Register of historical places" in 1973.

Proving to be a true eclectic he also wrote fiction, being this, Etidorhpa, his first published work, it first appeared in 1895 and was re-edited several times and later translated to German and Swedish, in modern times (after 2000) was translated to Portuguese and Spanish (this one by yours truly). Lloyd wrote more fiction in a realism vein, but this, Etidorphpa, is the one that transcended the most, traveling thru time as a cult book, of speculations about its veracity and its fiction, as a study about its scientific affirmations as much as its metaphysical hypothesis, and at the same time this is also an early science fiction story, about mystery and exploration in all the senses of these words, offering a multi-layered interpretation.

My first edition of this book was the Spanish translation that I made, but watching the different English versions available I decided to make my own, I rearranged the extras (Etidorhpa is left intact), the contents page and made some small corrections, I also added an article about the "real" I-am-the-man (the main protagonist).

The extended parts of this edition are chapters XLIV, XLV, and XLVI, which were originally included in a 1901 edition at the end of the book, here I decided to put them where they would have originally belonged. I also added a couple of alternative illustrations (pg. 267 and 309) that were present in different editions of Etidorhpa. Besides, a new appendix about the incomplete sequel of this work.

I hope you enjoy this reading and find it as thought-provoking as I did.

Lisandro Cottet

ASCRIPTION.

To Prof. W. H. Venable, who reviewed the manuscript of this work, I am indebted for many valuable suggestions, and I call not speak too kindly of him as a critic.

The illustrations, excepting those mechanical and historical, making in themselves a beautiful narrative without words, are due to the admirable artistic conceptions and touch of Mr. J. Augustus Knapp.

Structural imperfections as well as word selections and phrases that break all rules in composition, and that the care even of Prof. Venable could not eradicate, I accept as wholly my own. For much, on the one hand, that it may seem should have been excluded, and on the other, for giving place to ideas nearer to empiricism than to science, I am also responsible. For vexing my friends with problems that seemingly do not concern ill the least men in my position, and for venturing to think, superficially, it may be, outside the restricted lines of a science bound to the unresponsive crucible and retort, to which my life has been given, and amid the problems of which it has nearly worn itself away, I have no plausible excuse, and shall seek none.

JOHN URI LLOYD.

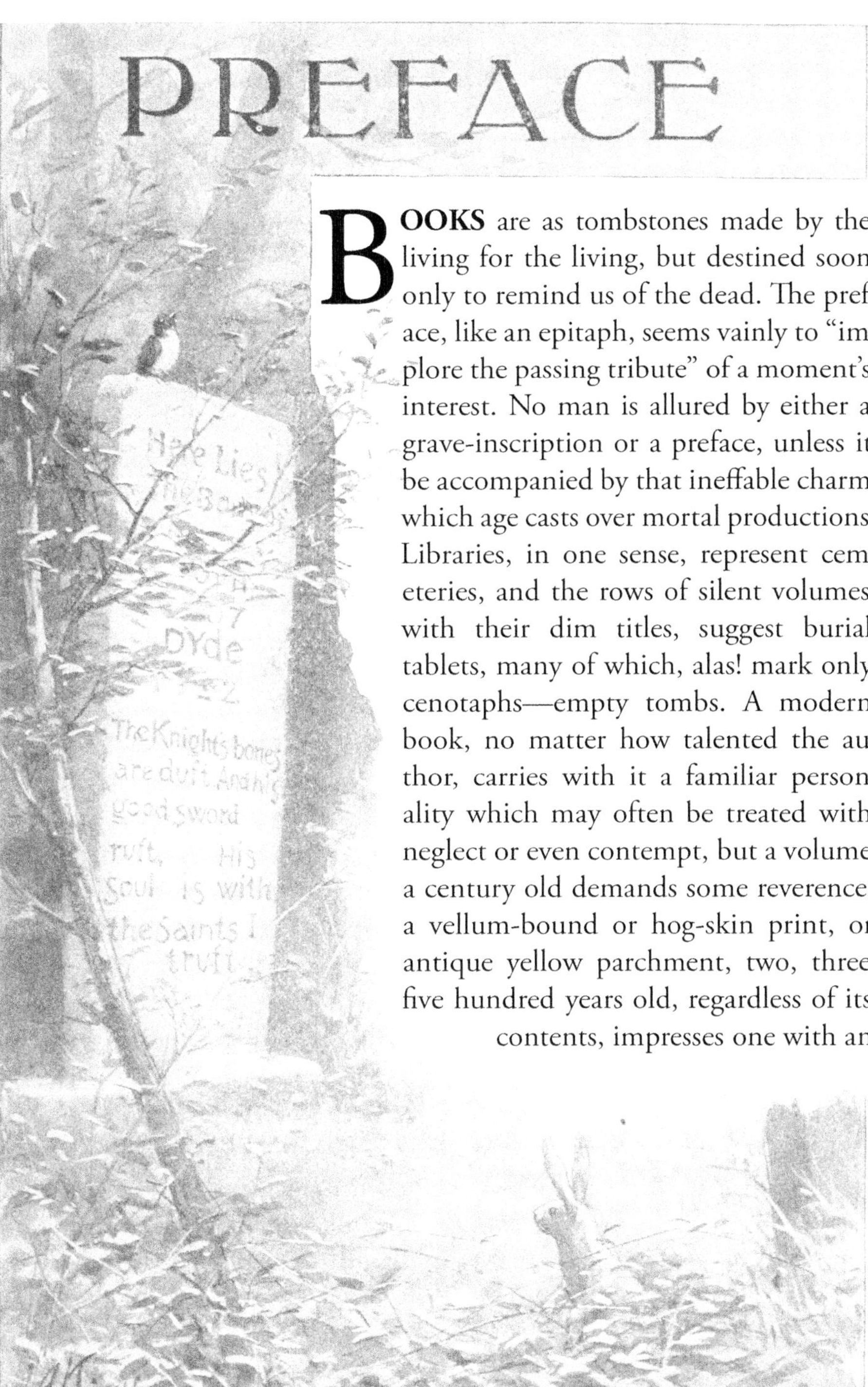

PREFACE

BOOKS are as tombstones made by the living for the living, but destined soon only to remind us of the dead. The preface, like an epitaph, seems vainly to "implore the passing tribute" of a moment's interest. No man is allured by either a grave-inscription or a preface, unless it be accompanied by that ineffable charm which age casts over mortal productions. Libraries, in one sense, represent cemeteries, and the rows of silent volumes, with their dim titles, suggest burial tablets, many of which, alas! mark only cenotaphs—empty tombs. A modern book, no matter how talented the author, carries with it a familiar personality which may often be treated with neglect or even contempt, but a volume a century old demands some reverence; a vellum-bound or hog-skin print, or antique yellow parchment, two, three, five hundred years old, regardless of its contents, impresses one with an indescribable feeling akin to awe and veneration, —as does the wheat from an Egyptian tomb, even though it be only wheat. We take such a work from the shelf carefully, and replace it gently. While the productions of modern writers are handled familiarly, as men living jostle men yet alive; those of authors long dead are touched as tho' clutched by a hand from the unseen world; the reader feels that a phantom form opposes his own, and that spectral eyes scan the pages as he turns them.

"THE STERN FACE . . ACROSS THE GULF."

The stern face, the penetrating eye of the personage whose likeness forms the frontispiece of the yellowed volume in my hand, speak across the gulf of two centuries, and bid me beware. The title page is read with reverence, and the great tome is replaced with care, for an almost superstitious sensation bids me be cautious and not offend. Let those who presume to criticize the intellectual productions of such men be careful; in a few days the dead will face their censors—dead.

Standing in a library of antiquated works, one senses the shadows of a cemetery. Each volume adds to the oppression, each old tome casts the influence of its spirit over the beholder, for have not these old books spirits? The earth-grave covers the mind as well as the body of its moldering occupant, and while only a strong imagination can assume that a spirit hovers over and lingers around inanimate clay, here each title is a voice that speaks as though the heart of its creator still throbbed, the mind essence of the dead writer envelops the living reader. Take down that vellum-bound volume, —it was written in one of the centuries long past. The pleasant face of its creator, as fresh as if but a print of yesterday, smiles upon you from the exquisitely engraved copper-plate frontispiece; the mind of the author rises from out the words before you. This man is not dead and his comrades live. Turn to the shelves about, before each book stands a guardian spirit, —together they form a phantom army that, invisible to mortals, encircles the beholder.

Ah! this antique library is not as is a church graveyard, only a cemetery for the dead; it is also a mansion for the living. These alcoves are trysting places for elemental shades. Essences of dis-enthralled minds meet here and revel. Thoughts of the past take shape and live in this atmosphere, — who can say that pulsations unperceived, beyond the reach of physics or of chemistry, are not as ethereal mind-seeds which, although unseen, yet, in living brain, exposed to such an atmosphere as this, formulate embryotic thought-expressions destined to become energetic intellectual forces?

I sit in such a weird library and meditate. The shades of grim authors whisper in my ear, skeleton forms oppose my own, and phantoms possess the gloomy alcoves of the library I am building.

"THE PLEASANT FACE OF ITS CREATOR . . . SMILES UPON YOU"

With the object of carrying to the future a section of thought current from the past, the antiquarian libraries of many nations have been culled, and purchases made in every book market of the world. These books surround me. Naturally many persons have become interested in the movement, and, considering it a worthy one, unite to further the project, for the purpose is not personal gain. Thus, it is not unusual for boxes of old chemical or pharmacal volumes to arrive by freight or express, without a word as to the donor. The mail brings manuscripts unprinted, and pamphlets recondite, with no word of introduction. They come unheralded. The authors or the senders realize that in this unique library a place is vacant if any work on connected subjects is missing, and thinking men of the world are uniting their contributions to fill such vacancies. Enough has been said concerning the ancient library that has bred these reflections, and my own personality does not concern the reader. He can now formulate his conclusions as well perhaps as I, regarding the origin of the manuscript that is to follow, if he concerns himself at all over subjects mysterious or historical, and my connection therewith is of minor importance. Whether Mr. Drury brought the strange paper in person, or sent it by express or mail,—whether it was slipped into a box of books from foreign lands, or whether my hand held the pen that made the record,—whether I stood face to face with Mr. Drury in the shadows of this room, or have but a fanciful conception of his figure,—whether the artist drew upon his imagination for the vivid likeness of the several personages figured in the book that follows, or from reliable data has given fac-similes authentic,—is immaterial. Sufficient be it to say that the manuscript of this book has been in my possession for a period of seven years, and my lips must now be sealed concerning all that transpired in connection therewith outside the subject-matter recorded therein, And yet I can not deny that for these seven years I have hesitated concerning my proper course, and more than once have decided to cover from sight the fascinating leaflets, hide them among surrounding volumes, and let them slumber until chance should bring them to the attention of the future student.

"SKELETON FORMS OPPOSE MY OWN."

These thoughts rise before me this gloomy day of December, 1894, as, snatching a moment from the exactions of business, I sit among these old volumes devoted to science-lore, and again study over the unique manuscript, and meditate; I hesitate again: Shall I, or shall I not? —but a duty is a duty. Perhaps the mysterious part of the subject will be cleared to me only when my own thought-words come to rest among these venerable relics of the past—when books that I have written become companions of ancient works about me—for then I can claim relationship with the shadows that flit in and out, and can demand that they, the ghosts of the library, commune with the shade that guards the book that holds this preface.

JOHN URI LLOYD.

PREFACE TO THIS EDITION.

(In reference to the 1897 edition)

The foot-note on CHAPTER XXIV, with the connected matter, has awakened considerable interest in the life and fate of Professor Daniel Vaughn.

The undersigned has received many letters imparting interesting information relating to Professor Vaughn's early history, and asking many questions concerning a man of whose memory the writer thinks so highly but whose name is generally unknown.

Indeed, as some have even argued that the author of Etidorhpa has no personal existence, the words John Uri Lloyd being a nom de plume, so others have accepted Professor Vaughn to have been a fanciful creation of the mystical author.

Professor Daniel Vaughn was one whose life lines ran nearly parallel with those of the late Professor C. S. Rafinesque, whose eventful history has been so graphically written by Professor R. Ellsworth Call. The cups of these two talented men were filled with privation's bitterness, and in no other place has this writer known the phrase "The Deadly Parallel" so aptly appropriate. Both came to America, scholars, scientists by education; both traveled through Kentucky, teachers; both gave freely to the world, and both suffered in their old age, dying in poverty—Rafinesque perishing in misery in Philadelphia and Vaughn in Cincinnati.

Daniel Vaughn was not a myth, and, in order that the reader may know something of the life and fate of this eccentric man, an appendix has been added to this edition of Etidorhpa, in which a picture of his face is shown as the writer knew it in life, and in which brief mention is made of his record.

The author here extends his thanks to Professor Richard Nelson and to Father Eugene Brady for their kindness to the readers of Etidorhpa and himself, for to these gentlemen is due the credit of the appended historical note.

J. U. L.

PROLOGUE.

My name was Johannes Llewellyn Llongollyn Drury. I was named Llewellyn at my mother's desire, out of respect to her father, Dr. Evan Llewellyn, the scientist and speculative philosopher, well known to curious students as the author of various rare works on occult subjects. The other given names were ancestral also, but when I reached the age of appreciation, they naturally became distasteful; so, it is that in early youth I dropped the first and third of these cumbersome words, and retained only the second Christian name. While perhaps the reader of these lines may regard this cognomen with less favor than either of the, others, still I liked it, as it was the favorite of my mother, who always used the name in full; the world, however, contracted Llewellyn to Lew, much to the distress of my dear mother, who felt aggrieved at the liberty. After her death I decided to move to a western city, and also determined, out of respect to her memory, to select from and rearrange the letters of my several names, and construct therefrom three short, terse words, which would convey to myself only, the resemblance of my former name. Hence it is that the Cincinnati Directory does not record my self-selected name, which I have no reason to bring before the public. To the reader my name is Llewellyn Drury. I might add that my ancestors were among the early settlers of what is now New York City, and were direct descendants of the early Welsh kings but these matters do not concern the reader, and it is not of them that I now choose to write. My object in putting down these preliminary paragraphs is simply to assure the reader of such facts, and such only, as may give him confidence in my personal sincerity and responsibility, in order that he may with a right understanding read the remarkable statements that occur in the succeeding chapters.

The story I am about to relate is very direct, and some parts of it are very strange, not to say marvelous; but not on account of its strangeness alone do I ask for the narrative a reading; —that were mere trifling. What is here set down happened as recorded, but I shall not attempt to explain things which even to myself are enigmatical. Let the candid reader read the story as I have told it, and make out of it what he can, or let him pass the page by unread—I shall not insist on claiming his further attention. Only, if he does read, I beg him to read with an open mind, without prejudice and without predilection.

Who or what I am as a participant in this work is of small importance. I mention my history only for the sake of frankness and fairness. I have nothing to gain by issuing the volume. Neither do I court praise nor shun censure. My purpose is to tell the truth.

Early in the fifties I took up my residence in the Queen City, and though a very young man, found the employment ready that a friend had obtained for me with a manufacturing firm engaged in a large and complicated business. My duties were varied and peculiar, of such a nature as to tax body and mind to the utmost, and for several years I served in the most exacting of business details. Besides the labor which my vocation entailed, with its manifold and multiform perplexities, I voluntarily imposed upon myself other tasks, which I pursued in the privacy of my own bachelor apartments. An inherited love for books on abstruse and occult subjects, probably in part the result of my blood connection with Dr. Evan Llewellyn, caused me to collect a unique library, largely on mystical subjects, in which I took the keenest delight. My business and my professional duties by day, and my studies at night, made my life a busy one.

In the midst of my work and reading I encountered the character whose strange story forms the essential part of the following narrative. I may anticipate by saying that the manuscript to follow only incidentally concerns myself, and that if possible I would relinquish all connection therewith. It recites the physical, mental, and moral adventures of one whose life history was abruptly thrust upon my attention, and as abruptly interrupted. The vicissitudes of his body and soul, circumstances seemed to compel me to learn and to make public.

ETIDORHPA.

CHAPTER I.

"NEVER LESS ALONE THAN WHEN ALONE."

MORE than thirty years ago occurred the first of the series of remarkable events I am about to relate. The exact date I cannot recall; but it was in November, and, to those familiar with November weather in the Ohio Valley, it is hardly necessary to state that the month is one of possibilities. That is to say, it is liable to bring every variety of weather, from the delicious, dreamy Indian summer days that linger late in the fall, to a combination of rain, hail, snow, sleet, —in short, atmospheric conditions sufficiently aggravating to develop a suicidal mania in any one the least susceptible to such influences. While the general character of the month is much the same the country over, showing dull grey tones of sky, abundant rains that penetrate man as they do the earth; cold, shifting winds, that search the very marrow, —it is always safe to count more or less upon the probability of the unexpected throughout the month.

The particular day which ushered in the event about to be chronicled, was one of these possible heterogeneous days presenting a combination of sunshine, shower, and snow, with winds that rang all the changes from balmy to blustery, a morning air of caloric and an evening of numbing cold. The early morning started fair and sunny; later came light showers suddenly switched by shifting winds into blinding sleet, until the middle of the afternoon found the four winds and all the elements commingled in one wild orgy with clashing and roaring as of a great organ with all the stops out, and all the storm-fiends dancing over the key-boards! Nightfall brought some semblance of order to the sounding chaos, but still kept up the wild music of a typical November day, with every accompaniment of bleakness, gloom, and desolation.

Thousands of chimneys, exhaling murky clouds of bituminous soot all day, had covered the city with the proverbial pall which the winds in their sport had shifted hither and yon, but as, thoroughly tired out, they subsided into silence, the smoky mesh suddenly settled over the houses and into the streets, taking possession of the city and contributing to the melancholy wretchedness of such of the inhabitants as had to be out of doors. Through this smoke the red sun when visible had dragged his downward course in manifest discouragement, and the hastening twilight soon gave place to the blackness of darkness. Night reigned supreme.

Thirty years ago, electric lighting was not in vogue, and the system of street lamps was far less complete than at present, although the gas burned in them may not have been any worse. The lamps were much fewer and farther between, and the light which they emitted had a feeble, sickly aspect, and did not reach any distance into the moist and murky atmosphere. And so, the night was dismal enough, and the few people upon the street were visible only as they passed directly beneath the lamps, or in front of lighted windows; seeming at other times like moving shadows against a black ground.

As I am like to be conspicuous in these pages, it may be proper to say that I am very susceptible to atmospheric influences. I figure among my friends as a man of quiet disposition, but I am at times morose, although I endeavor to conceal this fact from others. My nervous system is a sensitive weather-glass. Sometimes I fancy that I must have been born under the planet Saturn, for I find myself unpleasantly influenced by moods ascribed to that depressing planet, more especially in its disagreeable phases, for I regret to state that I do not find corresponding elation, as I should, in its brighter aspects. I have an especial dislike for wintry weather, a dislike which I find growing with my years, until it has developed almost into positive antipathy and dread. On the day I have described, my moods had varied with the weather. The fitfulness of the winds had found its way into my feelings, and the somber tone of the clouds into my meditations. I was restless as the elements, and a deep sense of dissatisfaction with myself and everything else, possessed me. I could not content myself in any place or position. Reading was distasteful, writing equally so; but it occurred to me that a brisk walk, for a few blocks, might afford relief. Muffling myself up in my overcoat and fur cap, I took the street, only to find the air gusty and raw, and I gave up in still greater disgust, and returning home, after drawing the curtains and locking the doors, planted myself in front of a glowing grate fire, firmly resolved to rid myself of myself by resorting to the oblivion of thought, reverie, or dream. To sleep was impossible, and I sat moodily in an easy chair, noting the quarter and half-hour strokes as they were chimed out sweetly from the spire of St. Peter's Cathedral, a few blocks away.

Nine o'clock passed with its silver-voiced song of "Home, Sweet Home"; ten, and then eleven strokes of the ponderous bell which noted the hours, roused me to a strenuous effort to shake off the feelings of despondency, unrest, and turbulence, that all combined to produce a state of mental and physical misery now insufferable. Rising suddenly from my chair, without a conscious effort I walked mechanically to a book-case, seized a volume at random, reseated myself before the fire, and opened the book. It proved to be an odd, neglected volume, "Riley's Dictionary of Latin Quotations." At the moment there flashed upon me a conscious duality of existence. Had the old book some mesmeric power? I seemed to myself two persons, and I quickly said aloud, as if addressing my double: "If I cannot quiet you, turbulent Spirit, I can at least adapt myself to your condition. I will read this book haphazard from bottom to top, or backward, if necessary, and if this does not change the subject often enough, I will try Noah Webster." Opening the book mechanically at page 297, I glanced at the bottom line and read, "Nunquam minus solus quam cum solus" (Never less alone than when alone). These words arrested my thoughts at once, as, by a singular chance, they seemed to fit my mood; was it or was it not some conscious invisible intelligence that caused me to select that page, and brought the apothegm to my notice?

Again, like a flash, came the consciousness of duality, and I began to argue with my other self. "This is arrant nonsense," I cried aloud; "even though Cicero did say it, and, it is on a par with many other delusive maxims that have for so many years embittered the existence of our modern youth by misleading thought. Do you know, Mr. Cicero, that this statement is not sound? That it is unworthy the position you occupy in history as a thinker and philosopher? That it is a contradiction in itself, for if a man is alone he is alone, and that settles it?"

I mused in this vein a few moments, and then resumed aloud: "It won't do, it won't do; if one is alone—the word is absolute—he is single, isolated, in short, alone; and there can be no manner of possibility be any one else present. Take myself, for instance: I am the sole occupant of this apartment; I am alone, and yet you say in so many words that I was never less alone than at this instant." It was not without some misgiving that I uttered these words, for the strange consciousness of my own duality constantly grew stronger, and I could not shake off the reflection that even now there were two of myself in the room, and that I was not so much alone as I endeavored to convince myself.

This feeling oppressed me like an incubus; I must throw it off, and, rising, I tossed the book upon the table, exclaiming: "What folly! I am alone—positively there is no other living thing visible or invisible in the room." I hesitated as I spoke, for the strange, undefined sensation that I was not alone had become almost a conviction; but the sound of my voice encouraged me, and I determined to discuss the subject, and I remarked in a full, strong voice: "I am surely alone; I know I am! Why, I will wager everything I possess, even to my soul, that I am alone." I stood facing the smoldering embers of the fire which I had neglected to replenish, uttering these words to settle the controversy for good and all with one person of my dual self, but the other ego seemed to dissent violently, when a soft, clear voice claimed my ear:

"You have lost your wager; you are not alone."

I turned instantly towards the direction of the sound, and, to my amazement, saw a white-haired man seated on the opposite side of the room, gazing at me with the utmost composure. I am not a coward, nor a believer in ghosts or illusions, and yet that sight froze me where I stood. It had no supernatural appearance—on the contrary, was a plain, ordinary, flesh-and-blood man; but the weather, the experiences of the day, the weird, inclement night, had all conspired to strain my nerves to the highest point of tension, and I trembled from head to foot. Noting this, the stranger said pleasantly: "Quiet yourself, my dear sir; you have nothing to fear; be seated." I obeyed, mechanically, and regaining in a few moments some semblance of composure, took a mental inventory of my visitor. Who is he? what is he? how did he enter without my notice, and why? what is his business? were all questions that flashed into my mind in quick succession, and quickly flashed out unanswered.

The stranger sat eying me composedly, even pleasantly, as if wait-

"AND TO MY AMAZEMENT SAW A WHITE-HAIRED MAN."

ing for me to reach some conclusion regarding himself. At last I surmised: "He is a maniac who has found his way here by methods peculiar to the insane, and my personal safety demands that I use him discreetly."

"Very good," he remarked, as though reading my thoughts; "as well think that as anything else."

"But why are you here? What is your business?" I asked.

"You have made and lost a wager," he said. "You have committed an act of folly in making positive statements regarding a matter about which you know nothing—a very common failing, by the way, on the part of mankind, and concerning which I wish first to set you straight."

The ironical coolness with which he said this provoked me, and I hastily rejoined: "You are impertinent; I must ask you to leave my house at once."

"Very well," he answered; " but if you insist upon this, I shall, on behalf of Cicero, claim the stake of your voluntary wager, which means that I must first, by natural though violent means, release your soul from your body." So, saying he arose, drew from an inner pocket a long, keen knife, the blade of which quaveringly glistened as he laid it upon the table. Moving his chair so as to be within easy reach of the gleaming weapon, he sat down, and again regarded me with the same quiet composure I had noted, and which was fast dispelling my first impression concerning his sanity.

I was not prepared for his strange action; in truth, I was not prepared for anything; my mind was confused concerning the whole night's doings, and I was unable to reason clearly or consecutively, or even to satisfy myself what I did think, if indeed I thought at all.

The sensation of fear, however, was fast leaving me; there was something reassuring in my unbidden guest's perfect ease of manner, and the mild, though searching gaze of his eyes, which were wonderful in their expression. I began to observe his personal characteristics, which impressed me favorably, and yet were extraordinary. He was nearly six feet tall, and perfectly straight; well proportioned, with no tendency either to leanness or obesity. But his head was an object from which I could not take my eyes—such a head surely, I had never before seen on mortal shoulders. The chin, as seen through his silver beard, was rounded and well developed, the mouth straight, with pleasant lines about it, the jaws square and, like the mouth, indicating decision, the eyes deep set and arched with heavy eyebrows, and the whole surmounted by a forehead so vast, so high, that it was almost a deformity, and yet it did not impress me unpleasantly; it was the forehead of a scholar, a profound thinker, a deep student. The nose was inclined to aquiline, and quite large. The contour of the head and face impressed me as indicating a man of learning, one who had given a lifetime to experimental as well as speculative thought. His voice was mellow, clear, and distinct, always pleasantly modulated and soft, never loud nor unpleasant in the least degree. One remarkable feature I must not fail to mention—his hair; this, while thin and scant upon the top of his head, was long, and reached to his shoulders; his beard was of unusual length, descending almost to his waist; his hair, eyebrows, and beard were all of singular whiteness and purity, almost transparent, a silvery whiteness that seemed an areolar sheen in the glare of the gaslight. What struck me as particularly remarkable was that his skin looked as soft and smooth as that of a child; there was not a blemish in it. His age was a puzzle none could guess; stripped of his hair, or the color of it changed, he might be twenty-five—given a few wrinkles, he might be ninety. Taken altogether, I had never seen his like, nor anything approaching his like, and for an instant there was a faint suggestion to my mind that he was not of this earth, but belonged to some other planet.

I now fancy he must have read my impressions of him as these ideas shaped themselves in my brain, and that he was quietly waiting for me to regain a degree of self-possession that would allow him to disclose the purpose of his visit.

He was first to break the silence: "I see that you are not disposed to pay your wager any more than I am to collect it, so we will not discuss that. I admit that my introduction to-night was abrupt, but you cannot deny that you challenged me to appear." I was not clear upon the point, and said so. "Your memory is at fault," he continued, "if you cannot recall your experiences of the day just past. Did you not attempt to interest yourself in modern book lore, to fix your mind in turn upon history, chemistry, botany, poetry, and general literature? And all these failing, did you not deliberately challenge Cicero to a practical demonstration of an old apothegm of his that has survived for centuries, and of your own free will did not you make a wager that, as an admirer of Cicero's, I am free to accept?" To all this I could but silently assent. "Very good, then; we will not pursue this subject further, as it is not relevant to my purpose, which is to acquaint you with a narrative of unusual interest, upon certain conditions, with which if you comply, you will not only serve yourself, but me as well."

"Please name the conditions," I said.

"They are simple enough," he answered. "The narrative I speak of is in manuscript. I will produce it in the near future, and my design is to read it aloud to you, or to allow you to read it to me, as you may select. Further, my wish is that during the reading you shall interpose any objection or question that you deem proper. This reading will occupy many evenings, and I shall of necessity be with you often. When the reading is concluded, we will seal the package securely, and I shall leave you forever. You will then deposit the manuscript in some safe place, and let it remain for thirty years. When this period has elapsed, I wish you to publish this history to the world."

"Your conditions seem easy," I said, after a few seconds' pause.

"They are certainly very simple; do you accept?"

I hesitated, for the prospect of giving myself up to a succession of interviews with this extraordinary and mysterious personage seemed to require consideration. He evidently divined my thoughts, for, rising from his chair, he said abruptly: "Let me have your answer now."

I debated the matter no further, but answered:

"I accept, conditionally."

"Name your conditions," the guest replied.

"I will either publish the work or induce some other man to do so."

"Good," he said; "I will see you again," with a polite bow; and turning to the door which I had previously locked, he opened it softly, and with a quiet "Good night" disappeared in the hall-way.

I looked after him with bewildered senses; but a sudden impulse caused me to glance toward the table, when I saw that he had forgotten his knife. With the view of returning this, I reached to pick it up, but my fingertips no sooner touched the handle than a sudden chill shivered along my nerves. Not as an electric shock, but rather as a sensation of extreme cold was the current that ran through me in an instant. Rushing into the hall-way to the landing of the stairs, I called after the mysterious being, "You have forgotten your knife," but beyond the faint echo of my voice, I heard no sound. The phantom was gone. A moment later I was at the foot of the stairs, and had thrown open the door. A street lamp shed an uncertain light in front of the house. I stepped out and listened intently for a moment, but not a sound was audible, if indeed I except the beating of my own heart, which throbbed so wildly that I fancied I heard it. No footfall echoed from the deserted streets; all was silent as a churchyard, and I closed and locked the door softly, tiptoed my way back to my room, and sank collapsed into an easy chair. I was more than exhausted; I quivered from head to foot, not with cold, but with a strange nervous chill that found intensest expression in my spinal column, and seemed to flash up and down my back vibrating like a feverous pulse. This active pain was succeeded by a feeling of frozen numbness, and I sat I know not how long, trying to tranquilize myself and think temperately of the night's occurrence.

"LET ME HAVE YOUR ANSWER NOW."

By degrees I recovered my normal sensations, and directing my will in the channel of sober reasoning, I said to myself: "There can be no mistake about his visit, for his knife is here as a witness to the fact. So much is sure, and I will secure that testimony at all events." With this reflection I turned to the table, but to my astonishment I discovered that the knife had disappeared. It needed but this miracle to start the perspiration in great cold beads from every pore. My brain was in a whirl, and reeling into a chair, I covered my face with my hands. How long I sat in this posture I do not remember. I only know that I began to doubt my own sanity, and wondered if this were not the way people became deranged. Had not my peculiar habits of isolation, irregular and intense study, erratic living, all conspired to unseat reason? Surely here was every ground to believe so; and yet I was able still to think consistently and hold steadily to a single line of thought. Insane people cannot do that, I reflected, and gradually the tremor and excitement wore away. When I had become calmer and more collected, and my sober judgment said, "Go to bed; sleep just as long as you can; hold your eyelids down, and when you awake refreshed, as you will, think out the whole subject at your leisure," I arose, threw open the shutters, and found that day was breaking. Hastily undressing I went to bed, and closed my eyes, vaguely conscious of some soothing guardianship. Perhaps because I was physically exhausted, I soon lost myself in the oblivion of sleep.

I did not dream—at least I could not afterwards remember my dream if I had one, but I recollect thinking that somebody struck ten distinct blows on my door, which seemed to me to be of metal and very sonorous. These ten blows in my semi-conscious state I counted. I lay very quiet for a time collecting my thoughts and noting various objects about the room, until my eye caught the dial of a French clock upon the mantel. It was a few minutes past ten, and the blows I had heard were the strokes of the hammer upon the gong in the clock. The sun was shining into the room, which was quite cold, for the fire had gone out. I arose, dressed myself quickly, and after thoroughly laving my face and hands in ice-cold water, felt considerably refreshed.

Before going out to breakfast, while looking around the room for a few things which I wanted to take with me, I espied upon the table a long white hair. This was indeed a surprise, for I had about concluded that my adventure of the previous night was a species of waking nightmare, the result of overworked brain and weakened body. But here was tangible evidence to the contrary, an assurance that my mysterious visitor was not a fancy or a dream, and his parting words, "I will see you again," recurred to me with singular effect. "He will see me again; very well; I will preserve this evidence of his visit for future use." I wound the delicate filament into a little coil, folded it carefully in a bit of paper, and consigned it to a corner in my pocket-book, though not without some misgiving that it too might disappear as did the knife.

The strange experience of that night had a good effect on me; I became more regular in all my habits, took abundant sleep and exercise, was more methodical in my modes of study and reasoning, and in a short time found myself vastly improved in every way, mentally and physically.

The days went fleeting into weeks, the weeks into months, and while the form and figure of the white-haired stranger were seldom absent from my mind, he came no more.

"I ESPIED UPON THE TABLE A LONG WHITE HAIR"

CHAPTER II.

A FRIENDLY CONFERENCE.

It is rare, in our present civilization, to find a man who lives alone. This remark does not apply to hermits or persons of abnormal or perverted mental tendencies, but to the majority of mankind living and moving actively among their fellows, and engaged in the ordinary occupations of humanity. Every man must have at least one confidant, either of his own household, or within the circle of his intimate friends. There may possibly be rare exceptions among persons of genius in statecraft, war, or commerce, but. it is doubtful even in such instances if any keep all their thoughts to themselves, hermetically sealed from their fellows. As a prevailing rule, either a loving wife or very near friend shares the inner thought of the most secretive individual, even when secrecy seems an indispensable element to success. The tendency to a free interchange of ideas and experiences is almost universal, instinct prompting the natural man to unburden his most sacred thought, when the proper confidant and the proper time come for the disclosure.

For months I kept to myself the events narrated in the preceding chapter. And this for several reasons: first, the dread of ridicule that would follow the relation of the fantastic occurrences, and the possible suspicion of my sanity, that might result from the recital; second, very grave doubts as to the reality of my experiences. But by degrees self-confidence was restored, as I reasoned the matter over and reassured myself by occasional contemplation of the silvery hair I had coiled in my pocket-book, and which at first, I had expected would vanish as did the stranger's knife. There came upon me a feeling that I should see my weird visitor again, and at an early day. I resisted this impression, for it was a feeling of the idea, rather than a thought, but the vague expectation grew upon me in spite of myself, until at length it became a conviction which no argument or logic could shake. Curiously enough, as the original incident receded into the past, this new idea thrust itself into the foreground, and I began in my own mind to court another interview. At times, sitting alone after night, I felt that I was watched by unseen eyes; these eyes haunted me in my solitude, and I was morally sure of the presence of another than myself in the room. The sensation was at first unpleasant, and I tried to throw it off; with partial success. But only for a little while could I banish the intrusive idea, and as the thought took form, and the invisible presence became more actual to consciousness, I hoped that the stranger would make good his parting promise, "I will see you again."

On one thing I was resolved; I would at least be better informed on the subject of hallucinations and apparitions, and not be taken unawares as I had been. To this end I decided to confer with my friend, Professor Chickering, a quiet, thoughtful man, of varied accomplishments, and thoroughly read upon a great number of topics, especially in the literature of the marvelous.

So, to the Professor I went, after due appointment, and confided to him full particulars of my adventure. He listened patiently throughout, and when I had finished, assured me in a matter-of-fact way that such hallucinations were by no means rare. His remark was provoking, for I did not expect from the patient interest he had shown while I was telling my story, that the whole matter would be dismissed thus summarily. I said with some warmth:

"But this was not a hallucination. I tried at first to persuade myself that it was illusory, but the more I have thought the experience over, the more real it becomes to me."

"Perhaps you were dreaming," suggested the Professor.

"No," I answered; "I have tried that hypothesis, and it will not do. Many things make that view untenable."

"Do not be too sure of that," he said; "you were, by your own account, in a highly nervous condition, and physically tired. It is possible, perhaps probable, that in this state, as you sat in your chair, you dozed off for a short interval, during which the illusion flashed through your mind."

"How do you explain the fact that incidents occupying a large portion of the night, occurred in an interval which you describe as a flash?"

"Easily enough; in dreams time may not exist: periods embracing weeks or mouths may be reduced to an instant. Long journeys, hours of conversation, or a multitude of transactions, may be compressed into a term measured by the opening or closing of a door, or the striking of a clock. In dreams, ordinary standards of reason find no place, while ideas or events chase through the mind more rapidly than thought."

"Conceding all this, why did I, considering the unusual character of the incidents, accept them as real, as substantial, as natural as the most commonplace events?"

"There is nothing extraordinary in that," he replied. "In dreams all sorts of absurdities, impossibilities, discordances, and violation of natural law appear realities, without exciting the least surprise or suspicion. Imagination runs riot and is supreme, and reason for the time is dormant. We see ghosts, spirits, the forms of persons dead or living, —we suffer pain, pleasure, hunger, — and all sensations and emotions, without a moment's question of their reality."

"Do any of the subjects of our dreams or visions leave tangible evidences of their presence?"

"Assuredly not," he answered, with an incredulous, half-impatient gesture; "the idea is absurd."

"Then I was not dreaming," I mused.

Without looking at me, the Professor went on: "These false presentiments may have their origin in other ways, as from mental disorders caused by indigestion. Nicolai, a noted bookseller of Berlin, was thus afflicted. His experiences are interesting and possibly suggestive. Let me read some of them to you."

The Professor hereupon glanced over his bookshelf, selected a volume, and proceeded to read: *

*(*This work I have found to be Vol. IV. of Chambers' Miscellany, published by Gould and Lincoln, Boston—J. U. L.)*

"I generally saw human forms of both sexes; but they usually seemed not to take the smallest notice of each other, moving as in a market place, where all are eager to press through the crowd; at times, however, they seemed to be transacting business with each other. I also saw several times, people on horseback, dogs, and birds.

"All these phantasms appeared to me in their natural size, and as distinct as if alive, exhibiting different shades of carnation in the uncovered parts, as well as different colors and fashions in their dresses, though the colors seemed somewhat paler than in real nature. None of the figures appeared particularly terrible, comical, or disgusting, most of them being of indifferent shape, and some presenting a pleasant aspect. The longer these phantasms continued to visit me, the more frequently did they return, while at the same time they increased in number about four weeks after they had first appeared. I also began to hear them talk: these phantoms conversed among themselves, but more frequently addressed their discourse to me; their speeches were uncommonly short, and never of an unpleasant turn. At different times there appeared to me both dear and sensible friends of both sexes, whose addresses tended to appease my grief, which had not yet wholly subsided: their consolatory speeches were in general addressed to me when I was alone. Sometimes, however, I was accosted by these consoling friends while I was engaged in company, and not unfrequently while real persons were speaking to ale. These consolatory addresses consisted sometimes of abrupt phrases, and at other times they were regularly executed."

Here I interrupted: "I note, Professor, that Mr. Nicolai knew these forms to be illusions."

Without answering my remark, he continued to read:

"There is in imagination a potency far exceeding the fabled power of Aladdin's lamp. How often does one sit in wintry evening musings, and trace in the glowing embers the features of an absent friend? Imagination, with its magic wand, will there build a city with its countless spires, or marshal contending armies, or drive the tempest-shattered ship upon the ocean. The following story, related by Scott, affords a good illustration of this principle:

"'Not long after the death of an illustrious poet, who had filled, while living, a great station in the eyes of the public, a literary friend, to whom the deceased had been well known, was engaged during the darkening twilight of an autumn evening, in perusing one of the publications which professed to detail the habits and opinions of the distinguished individual who was now no more. As the reader had enjoyed the intimacy of the deceased to a considerable degree, he was deeply interested in the publication, which contained some particulars relating to himself and other friends. A visitor was sitting in the apartment, who was also engaged in reading. Their sitting-room opened into an entrance hall, rather fantastically fitted up with articles of armor, skins of wild animals, and the like. It was when laying down his book, and passing into this hall, through which the moon was beginning to shine, that the individual of whom I speak saw right before him, in a standing posture, the exact representation of his departed friend, whose recollection had been so strongly brought to his imagination. He stopped for a single moment, so as to notice the wonderful accuracy with which fancy had impressed upon the bodily eye the peculiarities of dress and position of the illustrious poet. Sensible, however, of the delusion, he felt no sentiment save that of wonder at the extraordinary accuracy of the resemblance, and stepped onward to the figure, which resolved itself as he approached into the various materials of which it was composed. These were merely a screen occupied by great coats, shawls, plaids, and such, other articles as are usually found in a country entrance hall. The spectator returned to the spot from which he had seen the illusion, and endeavored with all his power to recall the image which had been so singularly vivid. But this he was unable to do... And the person who had witnessed the apparition, or, more properly, whose excited state had been the means of raising it, had only to return to the apartment, and tell his young friend under what a striking hallucination he had for a moment labored.'"

Here I was constrained to call the Professor to a halt. "Your stories are very interesting," I said, "but I fail to perceive any analogy in either the conditions or the incidents, to my experience. I was fully awake and conscious at the time, and the man I saw appeared and moved about in the full glare of the gaslight,"—"Perhaps not," he answered; "I am simply giving you some general illustrations of the subject. But here is a case more to the point."

Again, he read:

"A lady was once passing through a wood, in the darkening twilight of a stormy evening, to visit a friend who was watching over a dying child. The clouds were thick—the rain beginning to fall; darkness was increasing; the wind was moaning mournfully through the trees. The lady's heart almost failed her as she saw that she had a mile to walk through the woods in the gathering gloom. But the reflection of the situation of her friend forbade her turning back. Excited and trembling, she called to her aid a nervous resolution, and pressed onward. She had not proceeded far when she beheld in the path before her the movement of some very indistinct object. It appeared to keep a little distance ahead of her, and as she made efforts to get nearer to see what it was, it seemed proportionally to recede. The lady began to feel rather unpleasantly. There was some pale white object certainly discernible before her, and it appeared mysteriously to float along, at a regular distance, without any effort at motion. Notwithstanding the lady's good sense and unusual resolution, a cold chill began to come over her. She made every effort to resist leer fears, and soon succeeded in drawing nearer the mysterious object, when she was appalled at beholding the features of her friend's child, cold in death, wrapt in its shroud. She gazed earnestly, and there it remained distinct and clear before her eyes. She considered it a premonition that her friend's child was dead, and that she must hasten to her aid. But there was the apparition directly in her path. She must pass it. Taking up a little stick, she forced herself along to the object, and behold, some little animal scampered away. It was this that her excited imagination had transformed into the corpse of an infant in its winding sheet."

I was a little irritated, and once more interrupted the reader warmly: "This is exasperating. Now what resemblance is there between the vagaries of a hysterical, weak-minded woman, and my case?"

He smiled, and again read:

"The numerous stories told of ghosts, or the spirits of persons who are dead, will in most instances be found to have originated in diseased imagination, aggravated by some abnormal defect of mind. We may mention a remarkable case in point, and one which is not mentioned in English works on this subject; it is told by a compiler of Les Causes Célèbres. Two young noblemen, the Marquises De Rambouillet and De Precy, belonging to two of the first families of France, made an agreement, in the warmth of their friendship, that the one who died first should return to the other with tidings of the world to come. Soon afterwards De Rambouillet went to the wars in Flanders, while De Precy remained at Paris, stricken by a fever. Lying alone in bed, and severely ill, De Precy one day heard a rustling of his bed curtains, and turning round, saw his friend De Rambouillet, in full military attire. The sick man sprung over the bed to welcome his friend, but the other receded, and said that he had come to fulfill his promise, having been killed on that very day. He further said that it behooved De Precy to think more of the after world, as all that was said of it was true, and as he himself would die in his first battle. De Precy was then left by the phantom; and it was afterward found that De Rambouillet had fallen on that day."

"Ah," I said, "and so the phantom predicted an event that followed as indicated."

"Spiritual illusions," explained the Professor, "are not unusual, and well authenticated cases are not wanting in which they have been induced in persons of intelligence by functional or organic disorders. In the last case cited, the prediction was followed by a fulfillment, but this was chance or mere coincidence. It would be strange indeed if in the multitude of dreams that come to humanity, some few should not be followed by events so similar as to warrant the belief that they were prefigured. But here is an illustration that fits your case: let me read it:

"In some instances, it may be difficult to decide whether spectral appearances and spectral noises proceed from physical derangement or from an overwrought state of mind. Want of exercise and amusement may also be a prevailing cause. A friend mentions to us the following case: An acquaintance of his, a merchant, in London, who had for years paid very close attention to business, was one day, while alone in his counting house, very much surprised to hear, as he imagined, persons outside the door talking freely about him. Thinking it was some acquaintances who were playing off a trick, he opened the door to request them to come in, when to his amazement, he found that nobody was there. He again sat down to his desk, and in a few minutes the same dialogue recommenced. The language was very alarming. One voice seemed to say: 'We have the scoundrel in his own counting house; let us go in and seize him.' 'Certainly,' replied the other voice, 'it is right to take him; he has been guilty of a great crime, and ought to be brought to condign punishment.' Alarmed at these threats, the bewildered merchant rushed to the door; and there again no person was to be seen. He now locked his door and went home; but the voices, as he thought, followed him through the crowd, and he arrived at his house in a most unenviable state of mind. Inclined to ascribe the voices to derangement in mind, he sent for a medical attendant, and told his case, and a certain kind of treatment was prescribed. This, however, failed; the voices menacing him with punishment for purely imaginary crimes continued, and he was reduced to the brink of despair. At length a friend prescribed entire relaxation from business, and a daily game of cricket, which, to his great relief, proved an effectual remedy. The exercise banished the phantom voices, and they were no more heard."

"So, you think that I am in need of out-door exercise?"

"Exactly."

"And that my experience was illusory, the result of vertigo, or some temporary calenture of the brain?"

"To be plain with you, yes."

"But I asked you a while ago if specters or phantoms ever leave tangible evidence of their presence." The Professor's eyes dilated in interrogation. I continued: "Well, this one did. After I had followed him out, I found on the table a long, white hair, which I still have," and producing the little coil from my pocket-book, I handed it to him. He examined it curiously, eyed me furtively, and handed it back with the cautious remark:

"I think you had better commence your exercise at once."

CHAPTER III.

A SECOND INTERVIEW WITH THE MYSTERIOUS VISITOR.

It is not pleasant to have one's mental responsibility brought in question, and the result of my interview with Professor Chickering was, to put it mildly, unsatisfactory. Not that he had exactly questioned my sanity, but it was all too evident that he was disposed to accept my statement of a plain matter-of-fact occurrence with a too liberal modicum of salt. I say "matter-of-fact occurrence" in full knowledge of the truth that I myself had at first regarded the whole transaction as a fantasia or flight of mind, the result of extreme nervous tension; but in the interval succeeding I had abundant opportunity to correlate my thoughts, and to bring some sort of order out of the mental and physical chaos of that strange, eventful night. True, the preliminary events leading up to it were extraordinary; the dismal weather, the depression of body and spirit under which I labored, the wild whirl of thought keeping pace with the elements—in short, a general concatenation of events that seemed to be ordered especially for the introduction of some abnormal visitor—the night would indeed have been incomplete without a ghost! But was it a ghost? There was nothing ghostly about my visitor, except the manner of his entrance and exit. In other respects, he seemed substantial enough. He was, in his manners, courteous and polished as a Chesterfield; learned as a savant in his conversation; human in his thoughtful regard of my fears and misgivings; but that tremendous forehead, with its crown of silver hair, the long, translucent beard of pearly whiteness, and above all the astounding facility with which he read my hidden thoughts—these were not natural. The Professor had been patient with me—I had a right to expect that; he was entertaining to the extent of reading such excerpts as he had with him on the subject of hallucinations and their supposed causes, but had he not spoiled all by assigning me at last to a place with the questionable, unbalanced characters he had cited? I thought so, and the reflection provoked me; and this thought grew upon me until I came to regard his stories and attendant theories as so much literary trash.

My own reflections had been sober and deliberate, and had led me to seek a rational explanation of the unusual phenomena. I had gone to Professor Chickering for a certain measure of sympathy, and what was more to the point, to secure his suggestions and assistance in the further unraveling of a profound mystery that might contain a secret of untold use to humanity. Repulsed by the mode in which my confidence had been received, I decided to do what I should have done from the outset—to keep my own counsel, and to follow alone the investigation to the end, no matter what the result might be. I could not forget or ignore the silver hair I had so religiously preserved. That was genuine; it was as tangible, as real, as convincing a witness as would have been the entire head of my singular visitant, whatever might be his nature.

I began to feel at ease the moment my course was decided, and the feeling was at once renewed within me that the gray head would come again, and by degrees that expectation ripened into a desire, only intensified as the days sped by. The weeks passed into months; summer came and went; autumn was fast fading, but the mysterious unknown did not appear. A curious fancy led me now to regard him as my friend, for the mixed and indefinite feelings I felt at first towards him had almost unaccountably been changed to those of sincere regard. He was not always in my thoughts, for I had abundant occupation at all times to keep both brain and hands busy, but there were few evenings in which I did not, just before retiring, give myself up for a brief period to quiet communion with my own thoughts, and I must confess at such times the unknown occupied the larger share of attention. The constant contemplation of any theme begets a feeling of familiarity or acquaintance with the same, and if that subject be an individual, as in the present instance, such contemplation lessens the liability to surprise from any unexpected development. In fact, I not only anticipated a visit, but courted it. The old Latin maxim that I had played with, "Never less alone than when alone" had domiciled itself within my brain as a permanent lodger—a conviction; a feeling rather than a thought defined, and I had but little difficulty in associating an easy-chair which I had come to place in a certain position for my expected visitor, with his presence.

Indian summer had passed, and the fall was nearly gone when for some inexplicable reason the number seven began to haunt me. What had I to do with seven, or seven with me? When I sat down at night this persistent number mixed itself in my thoughts, to my intense annoyance. Bother take the mystic numeral! What was I to do with seven? I found myself asking this question audibly one evening, when it suddenly occurred to me that I would refer to the date of my friend's visit. I kept no journal, but reference to a record of some business transactions that I had associated with that event showed that it took place on November seventh. That settled the importunate seven! I should look for whomever he was on the first anniversary of his visit, which was the seventh, now close at hand. The instant I had reached this conclusion the number left me, and troubled' me no more.

November third had passed, the fourth, and the fifth had come, when a stubborn, protesting notion entered my mind that I was yielding to a superstitious idea, and that it was time to control my vacillating will. Accordingly, on this day I sent word to a friend that, if agreeable to him, I would call on him on the evening of the seventh for a short social chat, but as I expected to be engaged until later than usual, would he excuse me if I did not reach his apartments until ten? The request was singular, but as I was now accounted somewhat odd, it excited no comment, and the answer was returned, requesting me to come. The seventh of November came at last. I was nervous during the day, which seemed to drag tediously, and several times it was remarked of me that I seemed abstracted and ill at ease, but I held my peace. Night came cold and clear, and the stars shone brighter than usual, I thought. It was a sharp contrast to the night of a year ago. I took an early supper, for which I had no appetite, after which I strolled aimlessly about the streets, revolving how I should put in the time till ten o'clock, when I was to call upon my friend. I decided to go to the theater, and to the theater I went. The play was spectacular, "Aladdin; or, The Wonderful Lamp." The entertainment, to me, was a flat failure, for I was busy with my thoughts, and it was not long until my thoughts were busy with me, and I found myself attempting to answer a series of questions that finally became embarrassing. " Why did you make an appointment for ten o'clock instead of eight, if you wished to keep away from your apartments?" I had n't thought of that before; it was stupid to a degree, if not ill-mannered, and I frankly admitted as much. "Why did you make an appointment at all, in the face of the fact that you not only expected a visitor, but were anxious to meet him?" This was easily answered: because I did not wish to yield to what struck me as superstition. "But do you expect to extend your call until morning?" Well, no, I hadn't thought or arranged to do so. "Well, then, what is to prevent your expected guest from awaiting your return? Or, what assurance have you that he will not encounter you in the street, under circumstances that will provoke or, at the least, embarrass you?" None whatever. "Then what have you gained by your stupid perversity?" Nothing, beyond the assertion of my own individuality. "Why not go home and receive your guest in becoming style?" No; I would not do that. I had started on this course, and I would persevere in it. I would be consistent. And so, I persisted, at least until nine o'clock, when I quit the theater in sullen dejection, and went home to make some slight preparation for my evening call.

With my latch-key I let myself into the front door of the apartment house wherein I lodged, walked through the hall, up the staircase, and paused on the threshold of my room, wondering what I would find inside. Opening the door, I entered, leaving it open behind me so that the light from the hallway would shine into the room, which was dark, and there was no transom above the door. The grate fire had caked into a solid mass of charred bituminous coal, which shed no illumination beyond a faint red glow at the bottom, showing that it was barely alive, and no more. I struck a match on the underside of the mantel shelf, and as I lit the gas I heard the click of the door latch. I turned instantly; the door had been gently closed by some unknown force if not by unseen hands, for there was no breath of air stirring. This preternatural interference was not pleasant, for I had hoped in the event of another visit from my friend, if friend he was, that he would bring no uncanny or ghostly manifestation to disturb me. I looked at the clock; the index pointed to half past nine. I glanced about the room; it was orderly, everything in proper position, even to the arm-chair that I had been wont to place for my nondescript visitor. It was time to be going, so I turned to the dressing case, brushed my hair, put on a clean scarf, and moved towards the wash-stand, which stood in a little alcove on the opposite side of the room. My self-command well-nigh deserted me as I did so, for there, in the arm-chair that a moment before was empty, sat my guest of a year ago, facing me with placid features! The room began to revolve, a faint, sick feeling came over me, and I reeled into the first convenient chair, and covered my face with my hands. This depression lasted but an instant, however, and as I recovered self-possession, I felt or fancied I felt a pair of penetrating eyes fixed upon me with the same mild, searching gaze I remembered so well. I ventured to look up; sure enough, there they were, the beaming eyes, and there was he! Rising from his chair, he towered up to his full height, smiled pleasantly, and with a slight inclination of the head, murmured: "Permit me to wish you good evening; I am profoundly glad to meet you again."

It was full a minute before I could muster courage to answer: "I wish I could say as much for myself."

"And why shouldn't you?" he said, gently and courteously; "you have realized, for the past six months, that I would return; more than that—you have known for some time the very day and almost the exact hour of my coming, have even wished for it, and, in the face of all this, I find you preparing to evade the requirements of common hospitality— are you doing either me or yourself justice?"

I was nettled at the knowledge he displayed of my movements, and of my very thoughts; my old stubbornness asserted itself, and I was rude enough to say: "Perhaps it is as you say; at all events, I am obligated to keep an engagement, and with your permission will now retire."

It was curious to mark the effect of this speech upon the intruder. He immediately became grave, reached quietly into an inner pocket of his coat, drew thence the same glittering, horrible, mysterious knife that had so terrified and bewildered me a year before, and looking me steadily in the eye, said coldly, yet with a certain tone of sadness: "Well, I will not grant permission. It is unpleasant to resort to this style of argument, but I do it to save time and controversy."

I stepped back in terror, and reached for the old-fashioned bell-cord, with the heavy tassel at the end, that depended from the ceiling, and was on the point of grasping and giving it a vigorous pull.

"Not so fast, if you please," he said, sternly, as he stepped forward, and gave the knife a rapid swish through the air above my head, causing the cord to fall in a tangle about my hand, cut cleanly, high above my reach!

I gazed in dumb stupor at the rope about my hand, and raised my eyes to the remnant above. That was motionless; there was not the slightest perceptible vibration, such as would naturally be expected. I turned to look at my guest; he had resumed his seat, and had also regained his pleasant expression, but he still held the knife in his hand with his arm extended, at rest, upon the table, which stood upon his right.

"Let us have an end to this folly," he said; "think a moment, and you will see that you are in fault. Your error we will rectify easily, and then to business. I will first show you the futility of trying to escape this interview, and then we will proceed to work, for time presses, and there is much to do." Having delivered this remark, he detached a single silvery hair from his head, blew it from his fingers, and let it float gently upon the upturned edge of the knife, which was still resting on the table. The hair was divided

“THE SAME GLITTERING, MYSTERIOUS KNIFE.”

as readily as had been the bell-cord. I was transfixed with astonishment, for he had evidently aimed to exhibit the quality of the blade, though he made no allusion to the feat, but smilingly went on with his discourse: "It is just a year ago to-night since we first met. Upon that occasion you made an agreement with me which you are in honor bound to keep, and"—here he paused as if to note the effect of his words upon me, then added significantly— "will keep. I have been at some pains to impress upon your mind the fact that I would be here to-night. You responded, and knew that I was coming, and yet in obedience to a silly whim, deliberately made a meaningless engagement with no other purpose than to violate a solemn obligation. I now insist that you keep your prior engagement with me, but I do not wish that you should be rude to your friend, so you had better write him a polite note excusing yourself, and dispatch it at once."

I saw that he was right, and that there was no shadow of justification for my conduct, or at least I was subdued by his presence, so I wrote the note without delay, and was casting about for some way to send it, when he said: "Fold it, seal it, and address it; you seem to forget what is proper." I did as he directed, mechanically, and, without thinking what I was doing, handed it to him. He took it naturally, glanced at the superscription, went to the door which he opened slightly, and handed the billet as if to some messenger who seemed to be in waiting outside—then closed and locked the door. Turning toward me with the apparent object of seeing if I was looking, he deftly drew his knife twice across the front of the door-knob, making a deep cross, and then deposited the knife in his pocket, and resumed his seat. (I noted afterward that the door-knob, which was of solid metal, was cut deeply, as though made of putty.)

As soon as he was comfortably seated, he again began the conversation: "Now that we have settled the preliminaries, I will ask if you remember what I required of you a year ago?" I thought that I did. "Please repeat it; I wish to make sure that you do, then we will start fair."

"In the first place, you were to present me with a manuscript"

"Hardly correct," he interrupted; "I was to acquaint you with a narrative which is already in manuscript, acquaint you with it, read it to you, if you preferred not to read it to me"

"I beg your pardon," I answered; "that is correct. You were to read the manuscript to me, and during the reading I was to interpose such comments, remarks, or objections, as seemed proper; to embody as interludes, in the manuscript, as my own interpolations, however, and not as part of the original."

"Very good," he replied, "you have the idea exactly; proceed."

"I agreed that when the reading had been completed, I would seal the complete manuscript securely, deposit it in some safe place, there to remain for thirty years, when it must be published."

"DREW HIS KNIFE TWICE ACROSS THE FRONT OF THE DOOR-KNOB."

"Just so," he answered; "we understand each other as we should. Before we proceed further, however, can you think of any point on which you need enlightenment? If so, ask such questions as you choose, and I will answer them."

I thought for a moment, but no query occurred to me; after a pause he said: "Well, if you think of nothing now, perhaps hereafter questions will occur to you which you can ask; but as it is late, and you are tired, we will not commence now. I will see you just one week from to-night, when we will begin. From that time on, we will follow the subject as rapidly as you choose, but see to it that you make no engagements that will interfere with our work, for I shall be more exacting in the future." I promised, and he rose to go. A sudden impulse seized me, and I said:

"May I ask one question?"

"Certainly."

"What shall I call you?"

"Why call me aught? It is not necessary in addressing each other that any name be used."

"But what are you?" I persisted.

A pained expression for an instant rested upon his face, and he said, sadly, pausing between the words: "I—Am—The—Man Who—Did—It."

"Did what?"

"Ask not; the manuscript will tell you. Be content, Llewellyn, and remember this, that I—Am—The—Man."

So, saying he bade me good night, opened the door, and disappeared down the broad stair-case.

One week thereafter he appeared promptly, seated himself, and producing a roll of manuscript, handed it to me, saying, "I am listening; you may begin to read."

On examination I found each page to be somewhat larger than a sheet of letter paper, with the written matter occupying a much smaller space, so as to leave a wide white border. One hundred pages were in the package. The last sentence ending abruptly indicated that my guest did not expect to complete his task in one evening, and, I may anticipate by saying that with each successive interview he drew about the same amount of writing from his bosom. Upon attempting to read the manuscript I at first found myself puzzled by a style of chirography very peculiar and characteristic, but execrably bad. Vainly did I attempt to read it; even the opening sentence was not deciphered without long inspection and great difficulty.

The old man, whom I had promised that I would fulfill the task, observing my discomfiture, relieved me of the charge, and without a word of introduction, read fluently as follows:

THE MANUSCRIPT OF I—AM—THE—MAN.

CHAPTER IV.

A SEARCH FOR KNOWLEDGE — THE ALCHEMISTIC LETTER.

I am the man who, unfortunately for my future happiness, was dissatisfied with such knowledge as could be derived from ordinary books concerning semi-scientific subjects in which I had long been absorbed. I studied the current works of my day on philosophy and chemistry, hoping therein to find something tangible regarding the relationship that exists between matter and spirit, but studied in vain. Astronomy, history, philosophy and the mysterious, incoherent works of alchemy and occultism were finally appealed to, but likewise failed to satisfy me. These studies were pursued in secret, though I am not aware that any' necessity existed for concealment. Be that as it may, at every opportunity I covertly acquainted myself with such alchemical lore as could be obtained either by purchase or by correspondence with others whom I found to be pursuing investigations in the same direction. A translation of Geber's "De Claritate Alchemiæ," by chance came into my possession, and afterwards an original version from the Latin of Bœrhaave's "Elementa Chemiæ," published and translated in 1753 by Peter Shaw. This magnificent production threw a flood of light upon the early history of chemistry, being far more elaborate than any modern work. It inspired me with the deepest regard for its talented author, and ultimately introduced me to a brotherhood of adepts, for in this publication, although its author disclaims occultism, is to be found a talisman that will enable any earnest searcher after light to become a member of the society of secret "Chemical Improvers of Natural Philosophy," with which I affiliated as soon as the key was discovered. Then followed a systematic investigation of authorities of the Alchemical School, including Geber, Morienus, Roger Bacon, George Ripley, Raymond Lully, Bernard, Count of Trevise, Isaac Hollandus, Arnoldus de la Villanova, Paracelsus, and others, not omitting the learned researches of the distinguished scientist, Llewellyn.

I discovered that many talented men are still firm believers in the lost art of alchemy, and that among the followers of the "thrice-famed Hermes" are to be found statesmen, clergymen, lawyers, and scientific men who, for various reasons, invariably conceal with great tact their connection with the fraternity of adepts. Some of these men had written scientific treatises of a very different character from those circulating among the members of our brotherhood, and to their materialistic readers it would seem scarcely possible that the authors could be tainted with hallucinations of any description, while others, conspicuous leaders in the church, were seemingly beyond occult temptation.

The larger number, it was evident, hoped by studies of the works of the alchemists, to find the key to the alkahest of Van Helmont, that is, to discover the Philosopher's Stone, or the Elixir of Life, and from their writings it is plain that the inner consciousness of thoughtful and scientific men rebelled against confinement to the narrow bounds of materialistic science, within which they were forced to appear as dogmatic pessimists. To them scientific orthodoxy, acting as a weight, prohibited intellectual speculation, as rank heresy. A few of my co-laborers were expert manipulators, and worked experimentally, following in their laboratories the suggestions of those gifted students who had pored over precious old manuscripts, and had attempted to solve the enigmatical formulas recorded therein, puzzles familiar to students of Hermetic lore. It was thus demonstrated—for what I have related is history—that in this nineteenth century there exists a fraternity, the members of which are as earnest in their belief in the truth of Esoteric philosophy, as were the followers of Hermes himself; savants who, in secret, circulate among themselves a literature that the materialism of this selfsame nineteenth century has relegated to the deluded and murky periods that produced it.

One day a postal package came to my address, this being the manner in which some of our literature circulated, which, on examination, I found to be a letter of instruction and advice from some unknown member of our circle. I was already becoming disheartened over the mental confusion into which my studies were leading me, and the contents of the letter, in which I was greatly interested, made a lasting impression upon me. It seemed to have been circulating a long time among our members in Europe and America, for it bore numerous marginal notes of various dates, but each and every one of its readers had for one reason or another declined the task therein suggested. From the substance of the paper, which, written exquisitely, yet partook of the ambiguous alchemistic style, it was evident that the author was well versed in alchemy, and, in order that my position

"Lead on my friend I cried" lead on to these undescribed scenes, the occult wonderland that —" He interrupted me dramatically, and in a curious manner said, "Have you not learned that wonder is an exemplification of ignorance? The child wonders at a goblin story, the savage at a trinket, the man of science at an unexplained manifestation of a phenomenon of unperceived natural law; each wonders in ignorance and because of ignorance. Accept my, that all you have seen, from the day of your birth on the surface of the earth, to the present, and all that you will meet here are wonderful only because the finite mind of man is confronted with evidence that from whatever direction we meet them spring from an unsearchable infinity.

FAC-SIMILE OF PAGE OF MANUSCRIPT.

may be clearly understood at this turning point in a life of remarkable adventure, the letter is appended in full:

THE ALCHEMISTIC LETTER.
TO THE BROTHER ADEPT WHO DARES TRY TO DISCOVER ZOROASTER'S CAVE, OR THE PHILOSOPHERS' INTELLECTUAL ECHOES, BY MEANS OF WHICH THEY COMMUNICATE TO ONE ANOTHER FROM THEIR CAVES.

Know thou, that Hermes Trismegistus did not originate, but he gave to our philosophy his name—the Hermetic Art. Evolved in a dim, mystic age, before antiquity began, it endured through the slowly rolling cycles to be bandied about by the ever-ready flippancy of nineteenth century students. It has lived, because it is endowed with that quality which never dies—truth. Modern philosophy, of which chemistry is but a fragment, draws its sustenance from the prime facts which were revealed in ancient Egypt through Hermetic thought, and fixed by the Hermetic stylus.

"The Hermetic allegories," so various in interpretable susceptibility, led subsequent thinkers into speculations and experimentations, which have resulted profitably to the world. It is not strange that some of the followers of Hermes, especially the more mercurial and imaginative, should have evolved nebulous theories, no longer explainable, and involving recondite spiritual considerations. Know thou that the ultimate on psycho-chemical investigation is the proximate of the infinite. Accordingly, a class came to believe that a projection of natural mental faculties into an advanced state of consciousness called the "wisdom faculty" constitutes the final possibility of Alchemy. The attainment of this exalted condition is still believed practicable by many earnest savants. Once on this lofty plane, the individual would not be trammeled by material obstacles, but would abide in that spiritual placidity which is the exquisite realization of mortal perfection. So exalted, he would be in naked parallelism with Omniscience, and through his illuminated understanding, could feast his soul on those exalted pleasures which are only less than deific.

Notwithstanding the exploiting of a number of these philosophers, in which, by reason of our inability to comprehend, sense seemed lost in a passage of incohesive dreamery and resonance of terminology, some of the purest spiritual researches the world has ever known, were made in the dawn of history. The much-abused alchemical philosophers existed upon a plane, in some respects above the level of the science of to-day. Many of them lived for the good of the world only, in an atmosphere above the materialistic hordes that people the world, and toiling over their crucibles and alembics, died in their cells "uttering no voice." Take, for example, Eirenæus Philalethes, who, born in 1623, lived contemporaneously with Robert Boyle. A fragment from his writings will illustrate the purpose which impelled the searcher for the true light of alchemy to record his discoveries in allegories, and we have no right to question the honesty of his utterances:

"The Searcher of all hearts knows that I write the truth; nor is there any cause to accuse me of envy. I write with an unterrified quill in an unheard-of style, to the honor of God, to the profit of my neighbors, with contempt of the world and its riches, because Elias, the artist, is already born, and now glorious things are declared of the city of God. I dare affirm that I do possess more riches than the whole known world is worth, but I cannot make use of it because of the snares of knaves. I disdain, loathe, and detest the idolizing of silver and gold, by which the pomps and vanities of the world are celebrated. Ah! filthy evil! Ah! vain nothingness! Believe ye that I conceal the art out of envy? No, verily, I protest to you; I grieve from the very bottom of my soul that we (alchemists) are driven like vagabonds from the face of the Lord throughout the earth. But what need of many words? The thing that we have seen, taught, and made, which we have, possess, and know, that we do declare; being moved with compassion for the studious, and with indignation of gold, silver, and precious stones. Believe me, the time is at the door, I feel it in spirit, when we, adeptis, shall return from the four corners of the earth, nor shall we fear any snares that are laid against our lives, but we shall give thanks to the Lord our God. I would to God that every ingenious man in the whole earth understood this science; then it would be valued only for its wisdom, and virtue only would be had in honor."

Of course, there was a worldlier class, and a large contingent of mercenary impostors (as science is always encumbered), parasites, whose animus was shamefully unlike the purity of true esoteric psychologists. These men devoted their lives to experimentation for selfish advancement. They constructed alchemical outfits, and carried on a ceaseless inquiry into the nature of solvents, and studied their influences on earthly bodies, their ultimate object being the discovery of the Philosopher's Stone, and the alkahest which Bœrhaave asserts was never discovered. Their records were often a verbose mélange, purposely so written, no doubt, to cover their tracks, and to make themselves conspicuous. Other Hermetic believers occupied a more elevated position, and connected the intellectual with the material, hoping to gain by their philosophy and science not only gold and silver, which were secondary considerations, but the highest literary achievement, the Magnum Opus. Others still sought to draw from Astrology and Magic the secrets that would lead them to their ambitious goal. Thus, there were degrees of fineness in a fraternity, which the science of to-day must recognize and admit.

Bœrhaave, the illustrious, respected Geber, of the alchemistic school, and none need feel compromised in admiring the talented alchemists who, like Geber, wrought in the twilight of morn for the coming world's good. We are now enjoying a fragment of the ultimate results of their genius and industry in the materialistic outcomes of present-day chemistry, to be followed by others more valuable; and at last, when mankind is ripe in the wisdom faculty, by spiritual contentment in the complacent furthering beyond. Allow me briefly to refer to a few men of the alchemistic type whose records may be considered with advantage.

Rhasis, a conspicuous alchemist, born in 850, first mentioned orpiment, borax, compounds of iron, copper, arsenic, and other similar substances. It is said, too, that he discovered the art of making brandy. About a century later, Alfarabe (killed in 950), a great alchemist, astonished the King of Syria with his profound learning, and excited the admiration of the wise men of the East by his varied accomplishments. Later, Albertus Magnus (born 1205), noted for his talent and skill, believed firmly in the doctrine of transmutation. His beloved pupil, Thomas Aquinas, gave us the word amalgam, and it still serves us. Contemporaneously with these lived Roger Bacon (born 1214), who was a man of most extraordinary ability. There has never been a greater English intellect (not excepting his illustrious namesake, Lord Bacon), and his penetrating mind delved deeper into nature's laws than that of any successor. He told us of facts concerning the sciences, that scientific men cannot fully comprehend to-day; he told us of other things that lie beyond the science proving's of to-day, that modern philosophers cannot grasp. He was an enthusiastic believer in the Hermetic philosophy, and such were his erudition and advanced views, that his brother friars, through jealousy and superstition, had him thrown into prison—a common fate to men who in those days dared to think ahead of their age. Despite (as some would say) of his mighty reasoning power and splendid attainments, he believed the Philosopher's Stone to be a reality; he believed the secret of indefinite prolongation of life abode in alchemy; that the future could be predicted by means of a mirror which he called Almuchese, and that by alchemy an adept could produce pure gold. He asserted that by means of Aristotle's "Secret of Secrets," pure gold can be made; gold even purer and finer than what men now known as gold. In connection with other predictions he made an assertion that may with other seemingly unreasonable predictions be verified in time to come. He said: "It is equally possible to construct cars which may be set in motion with marvelous rapidity, independently of horses or other animals." He declared that the ancients had done this, and he believed the art might be revived.

Following came various enthusiasts, such as Raymond, the ephemeral (died 1315), who flared like a meteor into his brief, brilliant career; Arnold de Villanova (1240), a celebrated adept, whose books were burned by the Inquisition on account of the heresy they taught; Nicholas Flame, of France (1350), loved by the people for his charities, the wonder of his age (our age will not admit the facts) on account of the vast fortune he amassed without visible means or income, outside of alchemical lore; Johannes de Rupecissus, a man of such remarkable daring that he even (1357) reprimanded Pope Innocent VI., for which he was promptly imprisoned; Basil Valentine (1410), the author of many works, and the man who introduced antimony (antimonaches) into medicine; Isaac of Holland who, with his son, skillfully made artificial gems that could not be distinguished from the natural; Bernard Trevison (born 1406), who spent $30,000 in the study of alchemy, out of much of which he was cheated by cruel alchemic pretenders, for even in that day there were plenty of rogues to counterfeit a good thing. Under stress of his strong alchemic convictions, Thomas Dalton placed his head on the block by order of the virtuous (?) and conservative Thomas Herbert, 'squire to King Edward; Jacob Bohme (born 1575), the sweet, pure spirit of Christian mysticism, "The Voice of Heaven," than whom none stood higher in true alchemy, was a Christian, alchemist, theosophist; Robert Boyle, a conspicuous alchemical philosopher, in 1662 published his "Defense of the Doctrine touching the Spring and Weight of the Air," and illustrated his arguments by a series of ingenious and beautiful experiments, that stand to-day so high in the estimation of scientific men, that his remarks are copied verbatim by our highest authorities, and his apparatus is the best yet devised for the purpose. Boyle's "Law" was evolved and carefully defined fourteen years before Mariotte's "Discours de la Nature de l' Air" appeared, which did not, however, prevent French and German scientific men from giving the credit to Mariotte, and they still follow the false teacher who boldly pirated not only Boyle's ideas, but stole his apparatus.

Then appeared such men as Paracelsus (born 1493), the celebrated physician, who taught that occultism (esoteric philosophy) was superior to experimental chemistry in enlightening us concerning the transmutation of baser metals into gold and silver; and Gueppo Francisco (born 1627), who wrote a beautiful treatise on "Elementary Spirits," which was copied without credit by Compte de Gabalis. It seems incredible that the man (Gueppo Francisco), whose sweet spirit-thoughts are revivified and breathe anew in "Undine" and "The Rape of the Lock," should have been thrown into a prison to perish as a Hermetic follower; and this should teach us not to question the earnestness of those who left us as a legacy the beauty and truth so abundantly found in pure alchemy.

These and many others, cotemporaries, some conspicuous, and others whose names do not shine in written history, contributed incalculably to the grand aggregate of knowledge concerning the divine secret which enriched the world. Compare the benefits of Hermetic philosophy with the result of bloody wars ambitiously waged by self-exacting tyrants—tyrants whom history applauds as heroes, but whom we consider as butchers. Among the workers in alchemy are enumerated nobles, kings, and even popes. Pope John XXII. was an alchemist, which accounts for his bull against impostors, promulgated in order that true students might not be discredited; and King Frederick of Naples sanctioned the art, and protected its devotees.

At last, Count Cagliostro, the chequered "Joseph Balsamo" (born 1743), who combined alchemy, magic, astrology, sleight of hand, mesmerism, Free Masonry, and remarkable personal accomplishments, that altogether have never since been equaled, burst upon the world. Focusing the gaze of the church, kings, and the commons upon himself, in many respects the most audacious pretender that history records, he raised the Hermetic art to a dazzling height, and finally buried it in a blaze of splendor as he passed from existence beneath a mantle of shame. As a meteor streams into view from out the star mists of space, and in coruscating glory sinks into the sea, Cagliostro blazed into the sky of the eighteenth century, from the nebulae of alchemistic speculation, and extinguished both himself and his science in the light of the rising sun of materialism. Cagliostro the visionary, the poet, the inspired, the erratic comet in the universe of intellect, perished in prison as a mountebank, and then the plodding chemist of to-day, with his tedious mechanical methods, and cold, unresponsive, materialistic dogmas, arose from the ashes, and sprang into prominence.

Read the story backward, and you shall see that in alchemy we behold the beginning of all the sciences of to-day; alchemy is the cradle that rocked them. Fostered with necromancy, astrology, occultism, and all the progeny of mystic dreamery, the infant sciences struggled for existence through the dark ages, in care of the once persecuted and now traduced alchemist. The world owes a monument to-day more to Hermetic heroes, than to all other influences and instrumentalities, religion excepted, combined, for our present civilization is largely a legacy from the alchemist. Begin with Hermes Trismegistus, and close with Joseph Balsamo, and if you are inclined towards science, do not criticize too severely their verbal logorrhea, and their romanticism, for your science is treading backward; it will encroach upon their field again, and you may have to unsay your words of hasty censure. These men fulfilled their mission, and did it well. If they told more than men now think they knew, they also knew more than they told, and more than modern philosophy embraces. They could not live to see all the future they eagerly hoped for, but they started a future for mankind that will far exceed in sweetness and light the most entrancing visions of their most imaginative dreamers. They spoke of the existence of a "red elixir," and while they wrote, the barbarous world about them ran red with blood—blood of the pure in heart, blood of the saints, blood of a Saviour; and their allegory and wisdom formulae were recorded in blood of their own sacrifices. They dreamed of a "white elixir" that is yet to bless mankind, and a brighter day for man, a period of peace, happiness, long life, contentment, good will and brotherly love, and in the name of this "white elixir" they directed the world towards a vision of divine light. Even pure gold, as they told the materialistic world who worship gold, was penetrated and whelmed by this subtle, superlatively refined spirit of matter. Is not the day of the allegorical "white elixir" nearly at hand? Would that it was!

I say to you now, brothers of the eighteenth century, as one speaking by authority to you, cease (some of you) to study this entrancing past, look to the future by grasping the present, cast aside (some of you) the alchemical lore of other days, give up your loved allegories; it is a duty, you must relinquish them. There is a richer field. Do not delay. Unlock this mystic door that stands hinged and ready, waiting the touch of men who can interpret the talisman; place before mankind the knowledge that lies behind its rivets. In the secret lodges that have preserved the wisdom of the days of Enoch and Elias of Egypt, who propagated the Egyptian Order, a branch of your ancient brotherhood, is to be found concealed much knowledge that should now be spread before the world, and added to the treasures of our circle of adepts. This cabalistic wisdom is not recorded in books nor in manuscript, but has been purposely preserved from the uninitiated, in the unreadable brains of unresponsive men. Those who are selected to act as carriers thereof, are, as a rule, like dumb water hearers, or the dead sheet of paper that mechanically preserves an inspiration derived from minds unseen: they serve a purpose as a child mechanically commits to memory a blank verse to repeat to others, who in turn commit to repeat again—neither of them speaking understandingly. Search ye these hidden paths, for the day of mental liberation approaches, and publish to the world all that is locked within the doors of that antiquated organization. The world is nearly ripe for the wisdom faculty, and men are ready to unravel the golden threads that mystic wisdom has in-woven in her web of secret knowledge. Look for knowledge where I have indicated, and to gain it do not hesitate to swear allegiance to this sacred order, for so you must do to gain entrance to the brotherhood, and then you must act what men will call the traitor. You will, however, be doing a sacred duty, for the world will profit, humanity will be the gainer, "Peace on Earth, Good Will to Man," will be closer to mankind, and at last, when the sign appears, the "white elixir" will no longer be allegorical; it will become a reality. In the name of the Great Mystic Vase-Man, go thou into these lodges, learn of their secrets, and spread their treasures before those who can interpret them.

Here this letter ended. It was evident that the writer referred to a secret society into which I could probably enter; and taking the advice, I did not hesitate, but applied at once for membership. I determined, regardless of consequence, to follow the suggestion of the unknown writer, and by so doing, for I accepted their pledges, I invited my destiny.

My guest of the massive forehead paused for a moment, stroked his long, white beard, and then, after casting an inquiring glance on me, asked, "Shall I read on?"

"Yes," I replied, and The—Man—Who—Did—It, proceeded as follows:

CHAPTER V.

THE WRITING OF MY CONFESSION.

Having become a member of the Secret Society as directed by the writer of the letter I have just read, and having obtained the secrets hinted at in the mystic directions, my next desire was to find a secluded spot where, without interruption, I could prepare for publication what I had gathered surreptitiously in the lodges of the fraternity I designed to betray. This I entitled "My Confession." Alas! why did my evil genius prompt me to write it? Why did not some kind angel withhold my hand from the rash and wicked deed? All I can urge in defense or palliation is that I was infatuated by the fatal words of the letter, "You must act what men will call the traitor, but humanity will be the gainer."

In a section of the state in which I resided, a certain creek forms the boundary line between two townships, and also between two counties. Crossing this creek, a much-traveled road stretches east and west, uniting the extremes of the great state. Two villages on this road, about four miles apart, situated on opposite sides of the creek, also present themselves to my memory, and midway between them, on the north side of the road, was a substantial farm house. In going west from the easternmost of these villages, the traveler begins to descend from the very center of the town. In no place is the grade steep, as the road lies between the spurs of the hill abutting upon the valley that feeds the creek I have mentioned. Having reached the valley, the road winds a short distance to the right, then turning to the left, crosses the stream, and immediately begins to climb the western hill; here the ascent is more difficult, for the road lies diagonally over the edge of the hill. A mile of travel, as I recall the scene, sometimes up a steep, and again among rich, level farm lands, and then on the very height, close to the road, within a few feet of it, appears the square structure which was, at the time I mention, known as the Stone Tavern. On the opposite side of the road were located extensive stables, and a grain barn. In the northeast chamber of that stone building, during a summer in the twenties, I wrote for publication the description of the mystic work that my oath should have made forever a secret, a sacred trust. I am the man who wantonly committed the deplorable act. Under the infatuation of that alchemical manuscript, I strove to show the world that I could and would do that which might never benefit me in the least, but might serve humanity. It was fate. I was not a bad man, neither malignity, avarice, nor ambition forming a part of my nature. I was a close student, of a rather retiring disposition, a stone-mason by trade, careless and indifferent to public honors, and so thriftless that many trifling neighborhood debts had accumulated against me.

What I have reluctantly told, for I am forbidden to give the names of the localities, comprises an abstract of part of the record of my early life, and will introduce the extraordinary narrative which follows. That I have spoken the truth, and in no manner overdrawn, will be silently evidenced by hundreds of brethren, both of the occult society and the fraternal brotherhood, with which I united, who can (if they will) testify to the accuracy of the narrative. They know the story of my crime and disgrace; only myself and God know the full retribution that followed.

CHAPTER VI.

KIDNAPPED.

The events just narrated occurred in the prime of my life, and are partly matters of publicity. My attempted breach of faith in the way of disclosing their secrets was naturally infamous in the eyes of my society brethren, who endeavored to prevail upon me to relent of my design which, after writing my "Confession," I made no endeavor to conceal. Their importunities and threatening had generally been resisted, however, and with an obliquity that cannot be easily explained, I persisted in my unreasonable design. I was blessed as a husband and father, but neither the thought of home, wife, nor child, checked me in my inexplicable course. I was certainly irresponsible, perhaps a monomaniac, and yet on the subject in which I was absorbed, I preserved my mental equipoise, and knowingly followed a course that finally brought me into the deepest slough of trouble, and lost to me forever all that man loves most dearly. An overruling spirit, perhaps the shade of one of the old alchemists, possessed me, and in the face of obstacles that would have caused most men to reflect, and retrace their steps, I madly rushed onward. The influence that impelled me, whatever it may have been, was irresistible. I apparently acted the part of agent, subject to an ever-present master essence, and under this dominating spirit or demon my mind was powerless in its subjection. My soul was driven imperiously by that impelling and indescribable something, and was as passive and irresponsible as lycopodium that is borne onward in a steady current of air. Methods were vainly sought by those who loved me, brethren of the lodge, and others who endeavored to induce me to change my headstrong purpose, but I could neither accept their counsels nor heed their forebodings. Summons by law were served on me in order to disconcert me, and my numerous small debts became the pretext for legal warrants, until at last all my papers (excepting my "Confession"), and my person also, were seized, upon an execution served by a constable. Minor claims were quickly satisfied, but when I regained my liberty, the aggression continued. Even arson was resorted to, and the printing office that held my manuscript was fired one night, that the obnoxious revelation which I persisted in putting into print, might be destroyed. Finally, I found myself separated by process of law from home and friends, an inmate of a jail. My opponents, as I now came to consider them, had confined me in prison for a debt of only two dollars, a sufficient amount at that time, in that state, for my incarceration. Smarting under the humiliation, my spirit became still more rebellious, and I now, perhaps justly, came to view myself as a martyr. It had been at first asserted that I had stolen a shirt, but I was not afraid of any penalty that could be laid on me for this trumped-up charge, believing that the imputation and the arrest would be shown to be designed as willful oppression. Therefore, it was, that when this contemptible arraignment had been swept aside, and I was freed before a Justice of the Peace, I experienced more than a little surprise at the rearrest, and at finding myself again thrown into jail. I knew that it had been decreed by my brethren that I must retract and destroy my "Confession," and this fact made me the more determined to prevent its destruction, and I persisted sullenly in pursuing my course. On the evening of August 12th, 1826, my jailer's wife informed me that the debt for which I had been incarcerated had been paid by unknown "friends," and that I could depart; and I accepted the statement without question. Upon my stepping from the door of the jail, however, my arms were firmly grasped by two persons, one on each side of me, and before I could realize he fact that I was being kidnapped, I was thrust into a closed coach, which immediately rolled away, but not until I made an outcry which, if heard by anyone, was unheeded.

"For your own sake, be quiet," said one of my companions in confinement, for the carriage was draped to exclude the light, and was as dark as a dungeon. My spirit rebelled; I felt that I was on the brink of a remarkable, perhaps perilous experience, and I indignantly replied by asking:

"What have I done that you should presume forcibly to imprison me? Am I not a freeman of America?"

"What have you done?" he answered. "Have you not bound yourself by a series of vows that are sacred and should be inviolable, and have you not broken them as no other man has done before you? Have you not betrayed your trust, and merited a severe judgment? Did you not voluntarily ask admission into our ancient brotherhood, and in good faith were you not initiated into our sacred mysteries? Did you not obligate yourself before man, and on your sacred honor promise to preserve our secrets?"

"I did," I replied; "but previously I had sworn before a higher tribunal to scatter this precious wisdom to the world."

"Yes," he said, "and you know full well the depth of the self-sought solemn oath that you took with us—more solemn than that prescribed by any open court on earth."

"This I do not deny," I said, "and yet I am glad that I accomplished my object, even though you have now, as is evident, the power to pronounce my sentence."

"MY ARMS WERE FIRMLY GRASPED BY TWO PERSONS."

"You should look for the death sentence," was the reply, "but it has been ordained instead that you are to be given a lengthened life. You should expect bodily destruction; but on the contrary, you will pass on in consciousness of earth and earthly concerns when we are gone. Your name will be known to all lands, and yet from this time you will be unknown. For the welfare of future humanity, you will be thrust to a height in our order that will annihilate you as a mortal being, and yet you will exist, suspended between life and death, and in that intermediate state will know that you exist. You have, as you confess, merited a severe punishment, but we can only punish in accordance with an unwritten law, that instructs the person punished, and elevates the human race in consequence. You stand alone among mortals in that you have openly attempted to give broadly to those who have not earned it, our most sacred property, a property that did not belong to you, property that you have only been permitted to handle, that has been handed from man to man from before the time of Solomon, and which belongs to no one man, and will continue to pass in this way from one to another, as a hallowed trust, until there are no men, as men now exist, to receive it. You will soon go into the shadows of darkness, and will learn many of the mysteries of life, the undeveloped mysteries that are withheld from your fellows, but which you, who have been so presumptuous and anxious for knowledge, are destined to possess and solve. You will find secrets that man, as man is now constituted, cannot yet discover, and yet which the future man must gain and be instructed in. As you have sowed, so shall you reap. You wished to become a distributor of knowledge; you shall now by bodily trial and mental suffering obtain unsought knowledge to distribute, and in time to come you will be commanded to make your discoveries known. As your pathway is surely laid out, so must you walk. It is ordained; to rebel is useless."

"Who has pronounced this sentence?" I asked.

"A judge, neither of heaven nor of earth."

"You speak in enigmas."

"No; I speak openly, and the truth. Our brotherhood is linked with the past, and clasps hands with the antediluvians; the flood scattered the races of earth, but did not disturb our secrets. The great love of wisdom has from generation to generation led selected members of our organization to depths of study that our open work does not touch upon, and behind our highest officers there stand, in the occult shades between the here and the hereafter, unknown and unseen agents who are initiated into secrets above and beyond those known to the ordinary craft. Those who are introduced into these inner recesses acquire superhuman conceptions, and do not give an open sign of fellowship; they need no talisman. They walk our streets possessed of powers unknown to men, they concern themselves as mortals in the affairs of men, and even their brethren of the initiated, open order are unaware of their exalted condition. The means by which they have been instructed, their several individualities as well, have been concealed, because publicity would destroy their value, and injure humanity's cause."

Silence followed these vague disclosures, and the carriage rolled on. I was mystified and alarmed, and yet I knew that, whatever plight be the end of this nocturnal ride, I had invited it—yes, merited it—and I steeled myself to hear the sentence of my judges, in whose hands I was powerless. The persons on the seat opposite me continued their conversation in low tones, audible only to themselves. An individual by my side neither moved nor spoke. There were four of us in the carriage, as I learned intuitively, although we were surrounded by utter darkness. At length I addressed the companion beside me, for the silence was unbearable. Friend or enemy though he might be, anything rather than this long silence. "How long shall we continue in this carriage?"

He made no reply.

After a time, I again spoke.

"Can you not tell me, comrade, how long our journey will last? When shall we reach our destination?"

Silence only.

Putting out my hand, I ventured to touch my mate, and found that he was tightly strapped—bound upright to the seat and the back of the carriage. Leather thongs held him firmly in position; and as I pondered over the mystery, I thought to myself, if I make a disturbance, they will not hesitate to manacle me as securely. My custodians seemed, however, not to exercise a guard over me, and yet I felt that they were certain of my inability to escape. If the man on the seat was a prisoner, why was he so reticent? why did he not answer my questions? I came to the conclusion that he must be gagged as well as bound. Then I determined to find out if this were so. I began to realize more forcibly that a terrible sentence must have been meted me, and I half hoped that I could get from my partner in captivity some information regarding our destination. Sliding my hand cautiously along his chest, and under his chin, I intended to remove the gag from his mouth, when I felt my flesh creep, for it came in contact with the cold, rigid flesh of a corpse. The man was dead, and stiff.

The shock unnerved me. I had begun to experience the results of a severe mental strain, partly induced by the recent imprisonment and extended previous persecution, and partly by the mysterious significance of the language in which I had recently been addressed. The sentence, "You will now go into the Valley of the Shadow of Death, and learn the mysteries of life," kept ringing through my head, and even then, I sat beside a corpse. After this discovery I remained for a time in a semi-stupor, in a state of profound dejection—how long I cannot say. Then I experienced an inexplicable change, such as I imagine comes over a condemned man without hope of reprieve, and I became unconcerned as a man might who had accepted his destiny, and stoically determined to await it. Perhaps moments passed, it may have been hours, and then indifference gave place to reviving curiosity. I realized that I could die only once, and I coolly and complacently revolved the matter, speculating over my possible fate. As I look back on the night in which I rode beside that dead man, facing the mysterious agents of an all-powerful judge, I marvel over a mental condition that permitted me finally to rest in peace, and slumber in unconcern. So, I did, however, and after a period, the length of which I am not able to estimate, I awoke, and soon thereafter the carriage stopped, and our horses were changed, after which our journey was resumed, to continue hour after hour, and at last I slept again, leaning back in the corner. Suddenly I was violently shaken from slumber, and commanded to alight. It was in the gray of morning, and before I could realize what was happening, I was transferred by my captors to another carriage, and the dead man also was rudely hustled along and thrust beside me, my companions speaking to him as though he were alive. Indeed, as I look back on these maneuvers, I perceive that, to all appearances, I was one of the abducting party, and our actions were really such as to induce an observer to believe that this dead man was an obstinate prisoner, and myself one of his official guards. The drivers of the carriages seemed to give us no attention, but they sat upright and unconcerned, and certainly neither of them interested himself in our transfer. The second carriage, like that other previously described, was securely closed, and our journey was continued. The darkness was as of a dungeon. It may have been days, I could not tell anything about the passage of time; on and oh we rode. Occasionally food and drink were handed in, but my captors held to their course, and at last I was taken from the vehicle, and transferred to a block-house.

I had been carried rapidly and in secret a hundred or more miles, perhaps into another state, and probably all traces of my journey were effectually lost to outsiders. I was in the hands of men who implicitly obeyed the orders of their superiors, masters whom they had never seen, and probably did not know. I needed no reminder of the fact that I had violated every sacred pledge voluntarily made to the craft, and now that they held me powerless, I well knew that, whatever the punishment assigned, I had invited it, and could not prevent its fulfillment. That it would be severe, I realized; that it would not be in accordance with ordinary human law, I accepted.

Had I not in secret, in my little room in that obscure Stone Tavern, engrossed on paper the mystic sentences that never before had been penned, and were unknown excepting to persons initiated into our sacred mysteries? Had I not previously, in the most solemn manner, before these words had been imparted to my keeping, sworn to keep them inviolate and secret? and had I not deliberately broken that sacred vow, and scattered the hoarded sentences broadcast? My part as a brother in this fraternal organization was that of the holder only of property that belonged to no man, that had been handed from one to another through the ages, sacredly cherished, and faithfully protected by men of many tongues, always considered a trust, a charge of honor, and never before betrayed. My crime was deep and dark. I shuddered. "Come what may," I mused, reflecting over my perfidy, "I am ready for the penalty, and my fate is deserved; it cannot but be a righteous one."

"I WAS TAKEN FROM THE VEHICLE, AND TRANSFERRED TO A BLOCK-HOUSE."

The words of the occupant of the carriage occurred to me again and again; that one sentence kept ringing in my brain; I could not dismiss it: "You have been tried, convicted, and we are of those appointed to carry out the sentence of the judges."

The black silence of my lonely cell beat against me; I could feel the absence of sound, I could feel the dismal weight of nothingness, and in my solitude and distraction I cried out in anguish to the invisible judge: "I am ready for my sentence, whether it be death or imprisonment for life"; and still the further words of the occupant of the carriage passed through my mind: "You will now go into the Valley of the Shadow of Death, and will learn the mysteries of Life."

Then I slept, to awake and sleep again. I kept no note of time; it may have been days or weeks, so far as my record could determine. An attendant came at intervals to minister to my wants, always masked completely, ever silent.

That I was not entirely separated from mankind, however, I felt assured, for occasionally sounds of voices came to me from without. Once I ventured to shout aloud, hoping to attract attention; but the persons whom I felt assured overheard me, paid no attention to my lonely cry. At last one night, my door opened abruptly, and three men entered.

"Do not fear," said their spokesman, "we aim to protect you; keep still, and soon you will be a free man."

I consented quietly to accompany them, for to refuse would have been in vain; and I was conducted to a boat, which I found contained a corpse—the one I had journeyed with, I suppose—and embarking, we were silently rowed to the middle of the river, our course being diagonally from the shore, and the dead man was thrown overboard. Then our boat returned to the desolate bank.

Thrusting me into a carriage, that, on our return to the river bank we found awaiting us, my captors gave a signal, and I was driven away in the darkness, as silently as before, and our journey was continued I believe for fully two days. I was again confined in another log cabin, with but one door, and destitute of windows. My attendants were masked, they neither spoke to me as they day after day supplied my wants, nor did they information on any subject, until at last I abandoned all hope of ever regaining my liberty.

"THE DEAD MAN WAS THROWN OVERBOARD."

CHAPTER VII.

A WILD NIGHT — I AM PREMATURELY AGED.

In the depths of night, I was awakened by a noise made by the opening of a door, and one by one seven masked figures silently stalked into my prison. Each bore a lighted torch, and they passed me as I lay on the floor in my clothes (for I had no bedding) and ranged themselves in a line. I arose, and seated myself as directed to do, upon the only stool in the room. Swinging into a semi-circle, the weird line wound about me, and from the one seat on which I rested in the center of the room, I gazed successively upon seven pairs of gleaming eyes, each pair directed at myself; and as I turned from one to another, the black cowl of each deepened into darkness, and grew more hideous.

"Men or devils," I cried, "do your worst! Make me, if such is your will, as that sunken corpse beside which I was once seated; but cease your persecutions. I have atoned for my indiscretions a thousand-fold, and this suspense is unbearable; I demand to know what is to be my doom, and I desire its fulfilment."

Then one stepped forward, facing me squarely—the others closed together around him and me. Raising his forefinger, he pointed it close to my face, and as his sharp eyes glittered from behind the black mask, piercing through me, he slowly said: "Why do you not say brothers?"

"Horrible," I rejoined; "stop this mockery. Have I not suffered enough from your persecutions to make me reject that word as applied to yourselves? You can but murder; do your duty to your unseen masters and end this prolonged torture!"

"Brother," said the spokesman, "you well know that the sacred rules of our order will not permit us to murder any human being. We exist to benefit humanity, to lead the wayward back across the burning desert into the pathways of the righteous; not to destroy or persecute a brother. Ours is an eleemosynary institution, instructing its members, helping them to seek happiness. You are now expiating the crime you have committed, and the good in your spirit rightfully revolts against the bad, for in divulging to the world our mystic signs and brotherly greetings, you have sinned against yourself more than against others. The sting of conscience, the biting of remorse punishes you."

"True," I cried, as the full significance of what he said burst upon me, "too true; but I bitterly repent my treachery. Others can never know how my soul is harrowed by the recollection of the enormity of that breach of confidence. In spite of my open, careless, or defiant bearing, my heart is humble, and my spirit cries out for mercy. By night and by day I have in secret cursed myself for heeding an unhallowed mandate, and I have long looked forward to the judgment that I should suffer for my perfidy, for I have appreciated that the day of reckoning would surely appear. I do not rebel, and I recall my wild language; I recant my 'Confession,' I renounce myself! I say to you in all sincerity, brothers, do your duty, only I beg of you to slay me at once, and end my suspense. I await my doom. What might it be?"

Grasping my hand, the leader said: "You are ready as a member of our order; we can now judge you as we have been commanded; had you persisted in calling us devils in your mistaken frenzy, we should have been forced to reason with you until you returned again to us, and became one of us. Our judgment is for you only; the world must not now know its nature, at least so far as we are concerned. Those you see here, are not your judges; we are agents sent to labor with you, to draw you back into our ranks, to bring you into a condition that will enable you to carry out the sentence that you have drawn upon yourself, for you must be your own doomsman. In the first place, we are directed to gain your voluntary consent to leave this locality. You can no longer take part in affairs that interested you before. To the people of this State, and to your home, and kindred, you must become a stranger for all time. Do you consent?"

"Yes," I answered, for I knew that I must acquiesce.

"In the next place, you must help us to remove all traces of your identity. You must, so far as the world is concerned, leave your body where you have apparently been drowned, for a world's benefit, a harmless mockery to deceive the people, and also to make an example for others that are weak. Are you ready?"

"Yes."

"Then remove your clothing, and replace it with this suit."

I obeyed, and changed my garments, receiving others in return. One of the party then, taking from beneath his gown a box containing several bottles of liquids, proceeded artfully to mix and compound them, and then to paint my face with the combination, which after being mixed, formed a clear solution.

"Do not fear to wash;" said the spokesman, "the effect of this lotion is permanent enough to stay until you are well out of this State."

I passed my hand over my face; it was drawn into wrinkles as a film of gelatin might have been shriveled under the influence of a strong tannin or astringent liquid; beneath my fingers it felt like the furrowed face of a very old man, but I experienced no pain. I vainly tried to smooth the wrinkles; immediately upon removing the pressure of my hand, the furrows reappeared.

Next, another applied a colorless liquid freely to my hair and beard; he rubbed it well, and afterward wiped it dry with a towel. A mirror was thrust beneath my gaze. I started back, the transformation was complete. My appearance had entirely changed. My face had become aged and wrinkled, my hair as white as snow.

"A MIRROR WAS THRUST BENEATH MY GAZE."

I cried aloud in amazement: "Am I sane, is this a dream?"

"It is not a dream; but, under methods that are in exact accordance with natural physiological laws, we have been enabled to transform your appearance from that of one in the prime of manhood into the semblance of an old man, and that, too, without impairment of your vitality." Another of the masked men opened a curious little casket that I perceived was surmounted by an alembic and other alchemical figures, and embossed with an Oriental design. He drew from it a lamp which he lighted with a taper; the flame that resulted, first pale blue, then yellow, next violet and finally red, seemed to become more weird and ghastly with each mutation, as I gazed spellbound upon its fantastic changes. Then, after these transformations, it burned steadily with the final strange blood-red hue, and he now held over the blaze a tiny cup, which, in a few moments, commenced to sputter and then smoked, exhaling a curious, epipolic, semi-luminous vapor. I was commanded to inhale the vapor.

I hesitated; the thought rushed upon me, "Now I am another person, so cleverly disguised that even my own friends would perhaps not know me, this vapor is designed to suffocate me, and my body, if found, will not now be known, and could not be identified when discovered."

"Do not fear," said the spokesman, as if divining my thought, "there is no danger," and at once I realized, by quick reasoning, that if my death were demanded, my body might long since have been easily destroyed, and all this ceremony would have been unnecessary.

I hesitated no longer, but drew into my lungs the vapor that arose from the mysterious cup, freely expanding my chest several times, and then asked, "Is not that enough?" Despair now overcame me. My voice, no longer the full, strong tone of a man in middle life and perfect strength, squeaked and quavered, as if impaired by palsy. I had seen my image in a mirror, an old man with wrinkled face and white hair; I now heard myself speak with the voice of an octogenarian.

"What have you done?" I cried.

"We have obeyed your orders; you told us you were ready to leave your own self here, and the work is complete. The man who entered has disappeared. If you should now stand in the streets of your village home, and cry to your former friends, 'It is I, for whom you seek,' they would smile, and call you a madman. Know," continued the voice, "that there is in Eastern metaphysical lore, more true philosophy than is embodied in the sciences of today, and that by means of the ramifications of our order it becomes possible, when necessary, for him who stands beyond the inner and upper Worshipful Master, to draw these treasures from the occult Wisdom possessions of Oriental sages who forget nothing and lose nothing. Have we not been permitted to do his bidding well?"

"Yes," I squeaked; "and I wish that you had done it better. I would that I were dead."

"When the time comes, if necessary, your dead body will be fished from the water," was the reply; "witnesses have seen the drowning tragedy, and will surely identify the corpse."

"And may I go? am I free now?" I asked.

"Ah," said he, "that is not for us to say; our part of the work is fulfilled, and we can return to our native lands, and resume again our several studies. So far as we are concerned, you are free, but we have been directed to pass you over to the keeping of others who will carry forward this judgment—there is another step."

"Tell me," I cried, once more desponding, "tell me the full extent of my sentence."

"That is not known to us, and probably is not known to any one man. So far as the members of our order are concerned, you have now vanished. When you leave our sight this night, we will also separate from one another, we shall know no more of you and your future than will those of our working order who live in this section of the country. We have no personal acquaintance with the guide that has been selected to conduct you farther, and who will appear in due season, and we make no surmise concerning the result of your journey, only we know that you will not be killed, for you have a work to perform, and will continue to exist long after others of your age are dead. Farewell, brother; we have discharged our duty, and by your consent, now we must return to our various pursuits. In a short time all evidence of your unfortunate mistake, the crime committed by you in printing our sacred charges, will have vanished. Even now, emissaries are ordained to collect and destroy the written record that tells of your weakness, and with the destruction of that testimony, for every copy will surely be annihilated, and with your disappearance from among men, for this also is to follow, our responsibility for you will cease."

Each of the seven men advanced, and grasped my hand, giving me the grip of brotherhood, and then, without a word, they severally and silently departed into' the outer darkness. As the last man disappeared, a figure entered the door, clad and masked exactly like those who had gone. He removed the long black gown in which he was enveloped, threw the mask from his face and stood before me, a slender, graceful, bright-looking young man. By the light of the candle I saw him distinctly, and was at once struck by his amiable, cheerful countenance, and my heart bounded with a sudden hope. I had temporarily forgotten the transformation that had been made in my person, which, altogether painless, had left no physical sensation, and thought of myself as I had formerly existed; my soul was still my own, I imagined; my blood seemed unchanged, and must flow as rapidly as before; my strength was unaltered; indeed I was in self-consciousness still in the prime of life.

"Excuse me, Father," said the stranger, "but my services have been sought as a guide for the first part of a journey that I am informed you intend to take."

His voice was mild and pleasant, his bearing respectful, but the peculiar manner in which he spoke convinced me that he knew that, as a guide, he must conduct me to some previously designated spot, and that he purposed to do so was evident, with or without my consent.

"Why do you call me Father?" I attempted to say, but as the first few words escaped my lips, the recollection of the events of the night rushed upon me, for instead of my own, I recognized the piping voice of the old man I had now become, and my tongue faltered; the sentence was unspoken.

"You would ask me why I called you Father, I perceive; well, because I am directed to be a son to you, to care for your wants, to make your journey as easy and pleasant as possible, to guide you quietly and carefully to the point that will next prove of interest to you."

I stood before him a free man, in the prime of life, full of energy, and this stripling alone interposed between myself and liberty. Should I permit the slender youth to carry me away as a prisoner? would it not be best to thrust him aside, if necessary, crush him to the earth? go forth in my freedom? Yet I hesitated, for he might have friends outside; probably he was not alone.

"There are no companions near us," said he, reading my mind, "and, as I do not seem formidable, it is natural you should weigh in your mind the probabilities of escape; but you cannot evade your destiny, and you must not attempt to deny yourself the pleasure of my company. You must leave this locality and leave without a regret. In order that you may acquiesce willingly I propose that together we return to your former home, which you will, however, find no longer to be a home. I will accompany you as a companion, as your son. You may speak, with one exception, to whomever you care to address; may call on any of your old associates, may assert openly who you are, or whatever and whoever you please to represent yourself, only I must also have the privilege of joining in the conversation."

"Agreed," I cried, and extended my hand; he grasped it, and then by the light of the candle, I saw a peculiar expression flit over his face, as he added:

"To one person only, as I have said, and you have promised, you must not speak—your wife."

I bowed my head, and a flood of sorrowful reflections swept over me. Of all the world the one whom I longed to meet, to clasp in my arms, to counsel in my distress, was the wife of my bosom, and I begged him to withdraw his cruel injunction.

"You should have thought of her before; now it is too late. To permit you to meet, and speak with her would be dangerous; she might pierce your disguise. Of all others there is no fear."

"Must I go with you into an unknown future without a farewell kiss from my little child or from my babe scarce three months old?"

"It has been so ordained."

I threw myself on the floor and moaned. "This is too hard, too hard for human heart to bear. Life has no charm to a man who is thrust from all he holds most dear, home, friends, family."

"The men who relinquish such pleasures and such comforts are those who do the greatest good to humanity," said the youth. "The multitude exist to propagate the race, as animal progenitors of the multitudes that are to follow, and the exceptional philanthropist is he who denies himself material bliss, and punishes himself in order to work out a problem such as it has been ordained that you are to solve. Do not argue further—the line is marked, and you must walk direct."

Into the blaze of the old fireplace of that log house, for, although it was autumn, the night was chilly, he then cast his black robe and false face, and, as they turned to ashes, the last evidences of the vivid acts through which I had passed, were destroyed. As I lay moaning in my utter misery, I tried to reason with myself that what I experienced was all a hallucination. I dozed, and awoke startled, half conscious only, as one in a nightmare; I said to myself, "A dream! a dream!" and slept again.

CHAPTER VIII.

A LESSON IN MIND STUDY.

The door of the cabin was open when I awoke, the sun shone brightly, and my friend, apparently happy and unconcerned, said: "Father, we must soon start on our journey; I have taken advantage of your refreshing sleep, and have engaged breakfast at yonder farm-house; our meal awaits us."

I arose, washed my wrinkled face, combed my white hair, and shuddered as I saw in a pocket mirror the reflection of my figure, an aged, apparently decrepit man.

"Do not be disturbed at your feeble condition," said my companion; "your infirmities are not real. Few men have ever been permitted to drink of the richness of the revelations that await you; and in view of these expectations the fact that you are prematurely aged in appearance should not unnerve you... Be of good heart, and when you say the word, we will start on our journey, which will begin as soon as you have said farewell to former friends and acquaintances."

I made no reply, but silently accompanied him, for my thoughts were in the past, and my reflections were far from pleasant.

We reached the farm-house, and as I observed the care and attention extended me by the pleasant-faced housewife, I realized that, in one respect at least, old age brought its compensation. After breakfast a man appeared from the farmer's barn, driving a team of horses attached to an open spring-wagon which, in obedience to the request of my guide, I entered, accompanied by my young friend, who directed that we be driven toward the village from which I had been abducted. He seemed to know my past life as I knew it; he asked me to select those of my friends to whom I first wished to bid farewell, even mentioning their names; he seemed all that a patient, faithful son could be, and I began to wonder at his audacity, even as much as I admired his self-confidence.

As we journeyed onward we engaged in familiar talk. We sat together on the back seat of the open spring-wagon, in full sight of passers, no attempt being made to conceal my person. Thus, we traveled for two days, and on our course we passed through a large city with which I was acquainted, a city that my abductors had previously carried me through and beyond. I found that my "son" possessed fine conversational power, and a rich mine of information, and he became increasingly interesting as he drew from his fund of knowledge, and poured into my listening ears an entrancing strain of historical and metaphysical information. Never at a loss for a word or an idea, he appeared to discern my cogitations, and as my mind wandered in this or that direction he fell into the channel of my fancies, and answered my unspoken thoughts, my mind-questions or meditations, as pertinently as though I had spoken them.

His accomplishments, for the methods of his perception were unaccompanied by any endeavor to draw me into word expression, made me aware at least, that, in him, I had to deal with a man unquestionably possessed of more than ordinary intellect and education, and as this conviction entered my mind he changed his subject and promptly answered the silent inquiry, speaking as follows:

"Have you not sometimes felt that in yourself there may exist undeveloped senses that await an awakening touch to open to yourself a new world, senses that may be fully developed, but which saturate each other and neutralize themselves; quiescent, closed circles which you cannot reach, satisfied circuits slumbering within your body and that defy your efforts to utilize them? In your dreams have you not seen sights that words are inadequate to describe, that your faculties can not retain in waking moments, and which dissolve into intangible nothingness, leaving only a vague, shadowy outline as the mind quickens, or rather when the senses that possess you in sleep relinquish the body to the returning vital functions and spirit? This unconscious conception of other planes, a beyond or betwixt, that is neither mental nor material, neither here nor located elsewhere, belongs to humanity in general, and is made evident from the insatiable desire of men to pry into phenomena latent or recondite that offer no apparent return to humanity. This desire has given men the knowledge they now possess of the sciences; sciences yet in their infancy. Study in this direction is, at present, altogether of the material plane, but in time to come, men will gain control of outlying senses which will enable them to step from the seen into the consideration of matter or force that is now subtle and evasive, which must be accomplished by means of the latent faculties that I have indicated. There will be an unconscious development of new mind-forces in the student of nature as the rudiments of these so-called sciences are elaborated. Step by step, as the ages pass, the faculties of men will, under progressive series of evolutions, imperceptibly pass into higher phases until that which is even now possible with some individuals of the purified esoteric school, but which would seem miraculous if practiced openly at this day, will prove feasible to humanity generally and be found in exact accord with natural laws. The conversational method of men, whereby communion between human beings is carried on by disturbing the air by means of vocal organs so as to produce mechanical pulsations of that medium, is crude in the extreme. Mind craves to meet mind, but cannot yet thrust matter aside, and in order to communicate one with another, the impression one mind wishes to convey to another must be first made on the brain matter that accompanies it, which in turn influences the organs of speech, inducing a disturbance of the air by the motions of the vocal organs, which, by undulations that reach to another being, act on his ear, and secondarily on the earthly matter of his brain, and finally by this roundabout course, impress the second being's mind. In this transmission of motions there is great waste of energy and loss of time, but such methods are a necessity of the present slow, much-obstructed method of communication. There is, in cultivated man, an innate craving for something more facile, and often a partly developed conception, spectral and vague, appears, and the being feels that there may be for mortals a richer, brighter life, a higher earthly existence that science does not now indicate. Such intimation of a deeper play of faculties is now most vivid with men during the perfect loss of mental self as experienced in dreams, which as yet man in the quick cannot grasp, and which fade as he awakens. As mental sciences are developed, investigators will find that the medium known as air is unnecessary as a means of conveying mind conceptions from one person to another; that material sounds and word pulsations are cumbersome; that thought force unexpressed may be used to accomplish more than speech can do, and that physical exertions as exemplified in motion of matter such as I have described will be unnecessary for mental communication. As door after door in these directions shall open before men, mystery after mystery will be disclosed, and vanish as mysteries to reappear as simple facts. Phenomena that are impossible and unrevealed to the scientist of to-day will be familiar to the coining multitude, and at last, as by degrees, clearer knowledge is evolved, the vocal language of men will disappear, and humanity, regardless of nationality, will, in silence and even in darkness, converse eloquently together in mind language. That which is now esoteric will become exoteric. Then mind will meet mind as my mind now impinges on your own, and, in reply to your unuttered question regarding my apparently unaccountable powers of perception, I say they are perfectly natural, but while I can read your thoughts, because of the fact that you cannot reciprocate in this direction, I must use my voice to impress your mind. You will know more of this, however, at a future day, for it has been ordained that you are to be educated with an object that is now concealed. At present you are interested mainly in the affairs of life as you know them, and cannot enter into these purer spheres. We are approaching one of your former friends, and it may be your pleasure to ask him some questions and to bid him farewell."

CHAPTER IX.

I CAN NOT ESTABLISH MY IDENTITY.

In surprise I perceived coming towards us a light spring wagon, in which rode one of my old acquaintances. Pleasure at the discovery led me to raise my hat, wave it around my head, and salute him even at the considerable distance that then separated us. I was annoyed at the look of curiosity that passed over his countenance, and not until the two vehicles had stopped side by side did it occur to me that I was unrecognized. I had been so engrossed in my companion's revelations, that I had forgotten my unfortunate physical condition.

I stretched out my hand, I leaned over almost into the other vehicle, and earnestly said:

"Do you not know me? Only a short time ago we sat and conversed side by side."

A look of bewilderment came over his features. "I have never seen you that I can recall," he answered.

My spirit sank within me. Could it be possible that I was really so changed? I begged him to try and recall my former self, giving my name. "I am that person," I added; but he, with an expression of countenance that told as plainly as words could speak that he considered me deranged, touched his horse, and drove on.

My companion broke the awkward silence. "Do you know that I perceived between you two men an unconscious display of mind-language, especially evident on your part? You wished with all the earnestness of your soul to bring yourself as you formerly appeared, before that man, and when it proved impossible, without a word from him, his mind exhibited itself to your more earnest intellect, and you realized that he said to himself, 'This person is a poor lunatic.' He told you his thoughts in mind-language, as plainly as words could have spoken, because the intense earnestness on your part quickened your perceptive faculties, but he could not see your mental state, and the pleading voice of the apparent stranger before him could not convince the unconcerned lethargic mind within him. I observed, however, in addition to what you noticed, that he is really looking for you. That is the object of his journey, and I learn that in every direction men are now spreading the news that you have been kidnapped and carried from your jail. However, we shall soon be in the village, and you will then hear more about yourself."

We rode in silence while I meditated on my remarkable situation. I could not resign myself without a struggle to my approaching fate, and I felt even yet a hope, although I seemed powerless in the hands of destiny. Could I not, by some method, convince my friends of my identity? I determined, forgetting the fact that my guide was even then reading my mind, that upon the next opportunity I would pursue a different course.

"It will not avail," my companion replied. "You must do one of two things: you will voluntarily go with me, or you will involuntarily go to an insane asylum. Neither you nor I could by any method convince others that the obviously decrepit old man beside me was but yesterday hale, hearty, young and strong. You will find that you cannot prove your identity, and as a friend, one of the great brotherhood to which you belong, a craft that deals charitably with all men and all problems, I advise you to accept the situation as soon as possible after it becomes evident to your mind that you are lost to former affiliations, and must henceforth be a stranger to the people whom you know. Take my advice, and cease to regret the past and cheerfully turn your thoughts to the future. On one side of you the lunatic asylum is open; on the other, a journey into an unknown region, beyond the confines of any known country. On the one hand, imprisonment and subjection, perhaps abuse and neglect; on the other, liberation of soul, evolution of faculty, and a grasping of superior knowledge that is denied most men—yes, withheld from all but a few persons of each generation, for only a few, unknown to the millions of this world's inhabitants, have passed over the road you are to travel. Just now you wished to meet your jailer of a few hours ago; it is a wise conclusion, and if he does not recognize you, I ask in sincerity, who will be likely to do so? We will drive straight to his home; but, here he comes."

Indeed, we were now in the village, where my miserable journey began, and perhaps by chance—it seems that it could not have been otherwise—my former jailer actually approached us.

"If you please," said my companion, "I will assist you to alight from the wagon, and you may privately converse with him."

Our wagon stopped, my guide opened a conversation with the jailer, saying that his friend wished to speak with him, and then assisted me to alight and retired a distance. I was vexed at my infirmities, which embarrassed me most exasperatingly, but which I knew were artificial; my body appeared unwilling although my spirit was anxious; but do what I could to control my actions, I involuntarily behaved like a decrepit old man. However, my mind was made up; this attempt to prove my personality should be the last; failure now would prove the turning point, and I would go willingly with my companion upon the unknown journey if I could not convince the jailer of my identity.

Straightening myself before the expectant jailer, who, with a look of inquisitiveness, regarded me as a stranger, I asked if he knew my former self, giving my name.

"That I do," he replied, "and if I could find him at this moment I would be relieved of a load of worry."

"Would you surely know him if you met him?" I asked.

"Assuredly," he replied; " and if you bring tidings of his whereabouts, as your bearing indicates, speak, that I may rid myself of suspicion and suspense."

Calling the jailer by name, I asked him if my countenance did not remind him of the man he wished to find.

"Not at all."

"Listen, does not my voice resemble that of your escaped prisoner?"

"Not in the least."

With a violent effort I drew my form as straight as possible, and stood upright before him, with every facial muscle strained to its utmost, in a vain endeavor to bring my wrinkled countenance to its former smoothness, and with the energy that a drowning man might exert to grasp a passing object, I tried to control my voice, and preserve my identity by so doing, vehemently imploring him, begging him to listen to my story.

"I am the man you seek; I am the prisoner who, a few days ago, stood in the prime of life before you. I have been spirited away from you by men who are leagued with occult forces, which extend forward among hidden mysteries, into forces which illuminate the present, and reach backward into the past unseen. These persons, by artful and damnable manipulations under the guidance of a power that has been evolved in the secrecy of past ages, and transmitted only to a favored few, have changed the strong man you knew into the one apparently feeble, who now confronts you. Only a short period has passed since I was your unwilling captive, charged with debt, a trifling sum; and then, as your sullen prisoner, I longed for freedom. Now I plead before you, with all my soul, I beg of you to take me back to my cell. Seal your doors, and hold me again, for your dungeon will now be to me a paradise."

"I AM THE MAN YOU SEEK."

I felt that I was becoming frantic, for with each word I realized that the jailer became more and more impatient and annoyed. I perceived that he believed me to be a lunatic. Pleadings and entreaties were of no avail, and my eagerness rapidly changed into despair until at last I cried: "If you will not believe my words, I will throw myself on the mercy of my young companion. I ask you to consider his testimony, and if he says that I am not what I assert myself to be, I will leave my home and country, and go with him quietly into the unknown future."

He turned to depart, but I threw myself before him, and beckoned the young man who, up to this time, had stood aloof in respectful silence. He came forward, and addressing the jailer, called him by name, and corroborated my story. Yes, strange as it sounded to me, he reiterated the substance of my narrative as I had repeated it. " Now, you will believe it," I cried in ecstasy;" now you need no longer question the facts that I have related."

Instead, however, of accepting the story of the witness, the jailer upbraided him.

"This is a preconcerted arrangement to get me into ridicule or further trouble. You two have made up an incredible story that on its face is fit only to be told to men as crazy or designing as yourselves. This young man did not even overhear your conversation with me, and yet he repeats his lesson without a question from me as to what I wish to learn of him."

"He can see our minds," I cried in despair.

"Crazier than I should have believed from your countenance," the jailer replied. "Of all the improbable stories imaginable, you have attempted to inveigle me into accepting that which is most unreasonable. If you are leagued together intent on some swindling scheme, I give you warning now that I am in no mood for trifling. Go your way, and trouble me no more with this foolish scheming, which villainy or lunacy of some description must underlie." He turned in anger and left us.

"It is as I predicted," said my companion; "you are lost to man. Those who know you best will turn from you soonest. I might become as wild as you are, in your interest, and only serve to make your story appear more extravagant. In human affairs men judge and act according to the limited knowledge at command of the multitude. Witnesses who tell the truth are often, in our courts of law, stunned, as you have been, by the decisions of a narrow-minded jury. Men sit on juries with little conception of the facts of the case that is brought before them; the men who manipulate them are mere tools in unseen hands that throw their several minds in antagonisms unexplainable to man. The judge is unconsciously often a tool of his own errors or those of others. One learned judge unties what another has fastened, each basing his views on the same testimony, each rendering his decision in accordance with law derived from the same authority. Your case is that condition of mind that men call lunacy. You can see much that is hidden from others because you have become acquainted with facts that their narrow education forbids them to accept, but, because the majority is against you, they consider you mentally unbalanced. The philosophy of men does not yet comprehend the conditions that have operated on your person, and as you stand alone, although in the right, all men will oppose you, and you must submit to the views of a misguided majority. In the eyes of a present generation you are crazy. A jury of your former peers could not do else than so adjudge you, for you are not on the same mental plane, and I ask, will you again attempt to accomplish that which is as impossible as it would be for you to drink the waters of Seneca Lake at one draught? Go to those men and propose to drain that lake at one gulp, and you will be listened to as seriously as when you beg your former comrades to believe that you are another person than what you seem. Only lengthened life is credited with the production of physical changes that under favorable conditions, are possible of accomplishment in a brief period, and such testimony as you could bring, in the present state of human knowledge, would only add to the proof of your lunacy."

"I see, I see," I said; "and I submit. Lead on, I am ready. Whatever my destined career may be, wherever it may be, it can only lead to the grave."

"Do not be so sure of that," was the reply.

I shuddered instinctively, for this answer seemed to imply that the stillness of the grave would be preferable to my destiny.

We got into the wagon again, and a deep silence followed as we rode along, gazing abstractedly on the quiet fields and lonely farm-houses. Finally, we reached a little village. Here my companion dismissed the farmer, our driver, paying him liberally, and secured lodgings in a private family (I believe we were expected), and after a hearty supper we retired. From the time we left the jailer I never again attempted to reveal my identity. I had lost my interest in the past, and found myself craving to know what the future had in store for me.

CHAPTER X.

MY JOURNEY TOWARDS THE END OF EARTH BEGINS. THE ADEPTS' BROTHERHOOD.

My companion did not attempt to watch over my motions or in any way to interfere with my freedom.

"I will for a time necessarily be absent," he said, "arranging for our journey, and while I am getting ready you must employ yourself as best you can. I ask you, however, now to swear that, as you have promised, you will not seek your wife and children."

To this I agreed.

"Hold up your hand," he said, and I repeated after him: "All this I most solemnly and sincerely promise and swear, with a firm and steadfast resolution to keep and perform my oath, without the least equivocation, mental reservation or self-evasion whatever."

"That will answer; see that you keep your oath this time," he said, and he departed. Several days were consumed before he returned, and during that time I was an inquisitive and silent listener to the various conjectures others were making regarding my abduction which event was becoming of general interest. Some of the theories advanced were quite near the truth, others wild and erratic. How preposterous it seemed to me that the actor himself could be in the very seat of the disturbance, willing, anxious to testify, ready to prove the truth concerning his position, and yet unable even to obtain a respectful hearing from those most interested in his recovery. Men gathered together discussing the "outrage"; women, children, even, talked of little else, and it was evident that the entire country was aroused. New political issues took their rise from the event, but the man who was the prime cause of the excitement was for a period a willing and unwilling listener, as he had been a willing and unwilling actor in the tragedy.

One morning my companion drove up in a light carriage, drawn by a span of fine, spirited, black horses.

"We are ready now," he said, and my unprecedented journey began.

Wherever we stopped, I heard my name mentioned. Men combined against men, brother was declaiming against brother, neighbor was against neighbor, everywhere suspicion was in the air.

"The passage of time alone can quiet these people," said I.

"The usual conception of the term Time—an indescribable something flowing at a constant rate—is erroneous," replied my comrade. "Time is humanity's best friend, and should be pictured as a ministering angel, instead of a skeleton with hour-glass and scythe. Time does not fly, but is permanent and quiescent, while restless, force-impelled matter rushes onward. Force and matter fly; Time reposes. At our birth we are wound up like a machine, to move for a certain number of years, grating against Time. We grind against that complacent spirit, and wear not Time but ourselves away. We hold within ourselves a certain amount of energy, which, an evanescent form of matter, is the opponent of Time. Time has no existence with inanimate objects. It is a conception of the human intellect. Time is rest, perfect rest, tranquility such as man never realizes unless he becomes a part of the sweet silences toward which human life and human mind are drifting. So much for Time. Now for Life. Disturbed energy in one of its forms, we call Life; and this Life is the great enemy of peace, the opponent of steadfast perfection. Pure energy, the soul of the universe, permeates all things with which man is now acquainted, but when at rest is imperceptible to man, while disturbed energy, according to its condition, is apparent either as matter or as force. A substance or material body is a manifestation resulting from a disturbance of energy. The agitating cause removed, the manifestations disappear, and thus a universe may be extinguished, without unbalancing the cosmos that remains. The worlds known to man are conditions of abnormal energy moving on separate planes through what men call space. They attract to themselves bodies of similar description, and thus influence one another—they have each a separate existence, and are swayed to and from under the influence of the various disturbances in energy common to their rank or order, which we call forms of forces. Unsettled energy also assumes numerous other expressions that are unknown to man, but which in all perceptible forms is characterized by motion. Pure energy cannot be appreciated by the minds of mortals. There are invisible worlds besides those perceived by us in our planetary system, unreachable centers of ethereal structure about us that stand in a higher plane of development than earthly matter which is a gross form of disturbed energy. There are also lower planes. Man's acquaintance with the forms of energy is the result of his power of perceiving the forms of matter of which he is a part. Heat, light, gravitation, electricity and magnetism are ever present in all perceivable substances, and, although purer than earth, they are still manifestations of absolute energy, and for this reason are sensible to men, but more evanescent than material bodies. Perhaps you can conceive that if these disturbances could be removed, matter or force would be resolved back into pure energy, and would vanish. Such a dissociation is an ethereal existence, and as pure energy the life spirit of all material things is neither cold nor hot, heavy nor light, solid, liquid nor gaseous—men cannot, as mortals now exist, see, feel, smell, taste, or even conceive of it. It moves through space as we do through it, a world of itself as transparent to matter as matter is to it, insensible but ever present, a reality to higher existences that rest in other planes, but not to us an essence subject to scientific test, nor an entity. Of these problems and their connection with others in the unseen depths beyond, you are not yet in a position properly to judge, but before many years a new sense will be given you or a development of latent senses by the removal of those more gross, and a partial insight into an unsuspected unseen, into a realm to you at present unknown.

"It has been ordained that a select few must from time to time pass over the threshold that divides a mortal's present life from the future, and your lot has been cast among the favored ones. It is or should be deemed a privilege to be permitted to pass farther than human philosophy has yet gone, into an investigation of the problems of life; this I say to encourage you. We have in our order a handful of persons who have received the accumulated fruits of the close attention others have given to these subjects which have been handed to them by the generations of men who have preceded. You are destined to become as they are. This study of semi-occult forces has enabled those selected for the work to master some of the concealed truths of being, and by the partial development of a new sense or new senses, partly to triumph over death. These facts are hidden from ordinary man, and from the earth-bound workers of our brotherhood, who cannot even interpret the words they learn. The methods by which they are elucidated have been locked from plan because the world is not prepared to receive them, selfishness being the ruling passion of debased mankind, and publicity, until the chain of evidence is more complete, would embarrass their further evolutions, for man as yet lives on the selfish plane."

"Do you mean that, among men, there are a few persons possessed of powers such as you have mentioned?"

"Yes; they move here and there through all orders of society, and their attainments are unknown, except to one another, or, at most, to but few persons. These adepts are scientific men, and may not even be recognized as members of our organization; indeed, it is often necessary, for obvious reasons, that they should not be known as such. These studies must constantly be prosecuted in various directions, and some monitors must teach others to perform certain duties that are necessary to the grand evolution. Hence, when a man has become one of our brotherhood, from the promptings that made you one of us, and has been as ready and determined to instruct outsiders in our work as you have been, it is proper that he should in turn be compelled to serve our people, and eventually, mankind."

"Am I to infer from this," I exclaimed, a sudden light breaking upon me, "that the alchemistic manuscript that led me to the fraternity to which you are related may have been artfully designed to serve the interest of that organization?" To this question I received no reply. After an interval, I again sought information concerning the order, and with more success.

"I understand that you propose that I shall go on a journey of investigation for the good of our order and also of humanity."

"True; it is necessary that our discoveries be kept alive, and it is essential that the men who do this work accept the trust of their own accord. He who will not consent to add to the common stock of knowledge and understanding, must be deemed a drone in the hive of nature—but few persons, however, are called upon to serve as you must serve. Men are scattered over the world with this object in view, and are unknown to their families or even to other members of the order; they hold in solemn trust our sacred revelations, and impart them to others as is ordained, and thus nothing perishes; eventually humanity will profit."

"Others, as you soon will be doing, are now exploring assigned sections of this illimitable field, accumulating further knowledge, and they will report results to those whose duty it is to retain and formulate the collected sum of facts and principles. So, it is that, unknown to the great body of our brotherhood, a chosen number, under our esoteric teachings, are gradually passing the dividing line that separates life from death, matter from spirit, for we have members who have mastered these problems. We ask, however, no aid of evil forces or of necromancy or black art, and your study of alchemy was of no avail, although to save the vital truths alchemy is a part of our work. We proceed in exact accordance with natural laws, which will yet be known to all men. Sorrow, suffering, pain of all descriptions, are enemies to the members of our order, as they are to mankind broadly, and we hope in the future so to control the now hidden secrets of Nature as to be able to govern the antagonistic disturbances in energy with which man now is everywhere thwarted, to subdue the physical enemies of the race, to affiliate religious and scientific thought, cultivating brotherly love, the foundation and capstone, the cement and union of this ancient fraternity."

"And am I really to take an important part in this scheme? Have I been set apart to explore a section of the unknown for a bit of hidden knowledge, and to return again?"

"This I will say," he answered, evading a direct reply, "you have been selected for a part that one in a thousand has been required to undertake. You are to pass into a field that will carry you beyond the present limits of human observation. This much I have been instructed to impart to you in order to nerve you for your duty. I seem to be a young man; really, I am aged. You seem to be infirm and old, but you are young.

Many years ago, cycles ago as men record time, I was promoted to do a certain work because of my zealous nature; like you, I also had to do penance for an error. I disappeared, as you are destined to do, from the sight of men. I regained my youth; yours has been lost forever, but you will regain more than your former strength. We shall both exist after this generation of men has passed away, and shall mingle with generations yet to be born, for we shall learn how to restore our youthful vigor, and will supply it time and again to earthly matter. Rest assured also that the object of our labors is of the most laudable nature, and we must be upheld under all difficulties by the fact that multitudes of men who are yet to come will be benefited thereby."

CHAPTER XI.

MY JOURNEY CONTINUES — INSTINCT.

It is unnecessary for me to give the details of the first part of my long journey. My companion was guided by a perceptive faculty that, like the compass, enabled him to keep in the proper course. He did not question those whom we met, and made no endeavor to maintain a given direction; and yet he was traveling in a part of the country that was new to himself. I marveled at the accuracy of his intuitive perception, for he seemed never to be at fault. When the road forked, he turned to the right or the left in a perfectly careless manner, but the continuity of his course was never interrupted. I began mentally to question whether he could be guiding us aright, forgetting that he was reading my thoughts, and he answered:

"There is nothing strange in this self-directive faculty. Is not man capable of following where animals lead? One of the objects of my special study has been to ascertain the nature of the instinct-power of animals, the sagacity of brutes. The carrier pigeon will fly to its cote across hundreds of miles of strange country. The young pig will often return to its pen by a route unknown to it; the sluggish tortoise will find its home without a guide, without seeing a familiar object; cats, horses and other animals possess this power, which is not an unexplainable instinct, but a natural sense better developed in some of the lower creatures than it is in man. The power lies dormant in man, but exists, nevertheless. If we develop one faculty we lose acuteness in some other power. Men have lost in mental development in this particular direction while seeking to gain in others. If there were no record of the fact that light brings objects to the recognition of the mind through the agency of the eye, the sense of sight in an animal would be considered by men devoid of it as adaptability to extraordinary circumstances, or instinct. So it is that animals often see clearly where to the sense of man there is only darkness; such sight is not irresponsive action without consciousness of a purpose. Man is not very magnanimous. Instead of giving credit to the lower animals for superior perception in many directions, he denies to them the conscious possession of powers imperfectly developed in mankind. We egotistically aim to raise ourselves, and do so in our own estimation by clothing the actions of the lower animals in a garment of irresponsibility. Because we cannot understand the inwardness of their power, we assert that they act by the influence of instinct. The term instinct, as I would define it, is an expression applied by men to a series of senses which man possesses, but has not developed. The word is used by man to characterize the mental superiority of other animals in certain directions where his own senses are defective. Instead of crediting animals with these, to them, invaluable faculties, man conceitedly says they are involuntary actions. Ignorant of their mental status, man is too arrogant to admit that lower animals are superior to him in any way. But we are not consistent. Is it not true that in the direction in which you question my power, some men by cultivation often become expert beyond their fellows? and such men have also given very little systematic study to subjects connected with these undeniable mental qualities. The hunter will hold his course in utter darkness, passing inequalities in the ground, and avoiding obstructions he cannot see. The fact of his superiority in this way, over others, is not questioned, although he cannot explain his methods nor understand how he operates. His quickened sense is often as much entitled to be called instinct as is the divining power of the carrier pigeon. If scholars would cease to devote their entire energies to the development of the material, artistic, or scientific part of modern civilization, and turn their attention to other forms of mental culture, many beauties and powers of Nature now unknown would be revealed. However, this cannot be, for under existing conditions, the strife for food and warmth is the most important struggle that engages mankind, and controls our actions. In a time that is surely to come, however, when the knowledge of all men is united into a comprehensive whole, the book of life, illuminated thereby, will contain many beautiful pages that may be easily read, but which are now not suspected to exist. The power of the magnet is not uniform—engineers know that the needle of the compass inexplicably deviates from time to time as a line is run over the earth's surface, but they also know that aberrations of the needle finally correct themselves. The temporary variations of a few degrees that occur in the running of a compass line are usually overcome after a time, and without a change of course, the disturbed needle swerves back, and again points to the calculated direction, as is shown by the vernier. Should I err in my course, it would be by a trifle only, and we could not go far astray before I would unconsciously discover the true path, I carry my magnet in my mind."

Many such dissertations or explanations concerning related questions were subsequently made in what I then considered a very impressive, though always unsatisfactory, manner. I recall those episodes now, after other more remarkable experiences which are yet to be related, and record them briefly with little wonderment, because I have gone through adventures which demonstrate that there is nothing improbable in the statements, and I will not consume time with further details of this part of my journey.

We leisurely traversed State after State, crossed rivers, mountains and seemingly interminable forests. The ultimate object of our travels, a location in Kentucky, I afterward learned, led my companion to guide me by a roundabout course to Wheeling, Virginia, by the usual mountain roads of that day, instead of going, as he might perhaps have much more easily done, via Buffalo and the Lake Shore to Northern Ohio, and then southerly across the country. He said in explanation, that the time lost at the beginning of our journey by this route, was more than recompensed by the ease of the subsequent Ohio River trip. Upon reaching Wheeling, he disposed of the team, and we embarked on a keel boat, and journeyed down the Ohio to Cincinnati. The river was falling when we started, and became very low before Cincinnati was reached, too low for steamers, and our trip in that flat-bottomed boat, on the sluggish current of the tortuous stream, proved tedious and slow. Arriving at Cincinnati, my guide decided to wait for a rise in the river, designing then to complete our journey on a steamboat. I spent several days in Cincinnati quite pleasantly, expecting to continue our course on the steamer "Tecumseh," then in port, and ready for departure. At the last moment my guide changed his mind, and instead of embarking on that boat, we took passage on the steamer "George Washington," leaving Shipping-Port Wednesday, December 13, 1826.

During that entire journey, from the commencement to our final destination, my guide paid all the bills, and did not want either for money or attention from the people with whom we came in contact. He seemed everywhere a stranger, and yet was possessed of a talisman that opened every door to which he applied, and which gave us unlimited accommodations wherever he asked them. When the boat landed at Smithland, Kentucky, a village on the bank of the Ohio, just above Paducah, we disembarked, and my guide then for the first time seemed mentally disturbed.

"Our journey together is nearly over," he said; "in a few days my responsibility for you will cease. Nerve yourself for the future, and bear its trials and its pleasures manfully. I play never see you again, but as you are even now conspicuous in our history, and will be closely connected with the development of the plan in which I am also interested, although I am destined to take a different part, I shall probably hear of you again."

CHAPTER XII.

A CAVERN DISCOVERED — BISWELL'S HILL.

We stopped that night at a tavern in Smithland. Leaving this place after dinner the next day, on foot, we struck through the country, into the bottom lands of the Cumberland River traveling leisurely, lingering for hours in the course of a circuitous tramp of only a few miles. Although it was the month of December, the climate was mild and balmy. In my former home, a similar time of year would have been marked with snow, sleet, and ice, and I could not but draw a contrast between the two localities.

How different also the scenery from that of my native State. Great timber trees, oak, poplar, hickory, were in majestic possession of large tracts of territory, in the solitude of which man, so far as evidences of his presence were concerned, had never before trodden. From time to time we passed little clearings that probably were to be enlarged to thrifty plantations in the future, and finally we crossed the Cumberland River. That night we rested with Mr. Joseph Watts, a wealthy and cultured land owner, who resided on the river's bank. After leaving his home the next morning, we journeyed slowly, very slowly, my guide seemingly passing with reluctance into the country. He had become a very pleasant companion, and his conversation was very entertaining. We struck the sharp point of a ridge the morning we left Mr. Watts' hospitable house. It was four or five miles distant, but on the opposite side of the Cumberland, from Smithland. Here a steep bluff broke through the bottom land to the river's edge, the base of the bisected point being washed by the Cumberland River, which had probably cut its way through the stony mineral of this ridge in ages long passed. We climbed to its top and sat upon the pinnacle, and from that point of commanding observation I drank in the beauties of the scene around me. The river at our feet wound gracefully before us, and disappeared in both directions, its extremes dissolving in a bed of forest. A great black bluff, far up the stream, rose like a mountain, upon the left side of the river; bottom lands were about us, and hills appeared across the river in the far distance—towards the Tennessee River. With regret I finally drew my eyes from the vision, and we resumed the journey. We followed the left bank of the river to the base of the black bluff, —"Biswell's Hill," a squatter called it, —and then skirted the side of that hill, passing along precipitous stone bluffs and among stunted cedars. Above us towered cliff over cliff, almost perpendicularly; below us rolled the river.

I was deeply impressed by the changing beauties of this strange Kentucky scenery, but marveled at the fact that while I became light-hearted and enthusiastic, my guide grew correspondingly despondent and gloomy. From time to time he lapsed into thoughtful silence, and once I caught his eye directed toward me in a manner that I inferred to imply either pity or envy. We passed Biswell's Bluff, and left the Cumberland River at its upper extremity, where another small creek empties into the river. Thence, after ascending the creek some distance, we struck across the country, finding it undulating and fertile, with here and there a small clearing. During this journey we either camped out at night, or stopped with a resident, when one was to be found in that sparsely settled country. Sometimes there were exasperating intervals between our meals; but we did not suffer, for we carried with us supplies of food, such as cheese and crackers, purchased in Smithland, for emergencies. We thus proceeded a considerable distance into Livingston County, Kentucky.

I observed remarkable sinks in the earth, sometimes cone-shaped, again precipitous. These cavities were occasionally of considerable size and depth, and they were more numerous in the uplands than in the bottoms. They were somewhat like the familiar "sink-holes" of New York State, but monstrous in comparison. The first that attracted my attention was near the Cumberland River, just before we reached Biswell's Hill. It was about forty feet deep and thirty in diameter, with precipitous stone sides, shrubbery growing therein in exceptional spots where loose earth had collected on shelves of stone that cropped out along its rugged sides. The bottom of the depression was flat and fertile, covered with a luxuriant mass of vegetation. On one side of the base of the gigantic bowl, a cavern struck down into the earth. I stood upon the edge of this funnel-like sink, and marveled at its peculiar appearance. A spirit of curiosity, such as often influences men when an unusual natural scene presents itself, possessed me. I clambered down, swinging from brush to brush, and stepping from shelving-rock to shelving-rock, until I reached the bottom of the hollow, and placing my hand above the black hole in its center, I perceived that a current of cold air was rushing therefrom, upward. I probed with a long stick, but the direction of the opening was tortuous, and would not admit of examination in that manner. I dropped a large pebble-stone into the orifice; the pebble rolled and clanked down, down, and at last, the sound died away in the distance.

"I wish that I could go into the cavity as that stone has done, and find the secrets of this cave," I reflected, the natural love of exploration possessing me as it probably does most men.

My companion above, seated on the brink of the stone wall, replied to my thoughts: "Your wish shall be granted. You have requested that which has already been laid out for you. You will explore where few men have passed before, and will have the privilege of following your destiny into a realm of natural wonders. A fertile field of investigation awaits you, such as will surpass your most vivid imaginings. Come and seat yourself beside me, for it is my duty now to tell you something about the land we are approaching, the cavern fields of Kentucky."

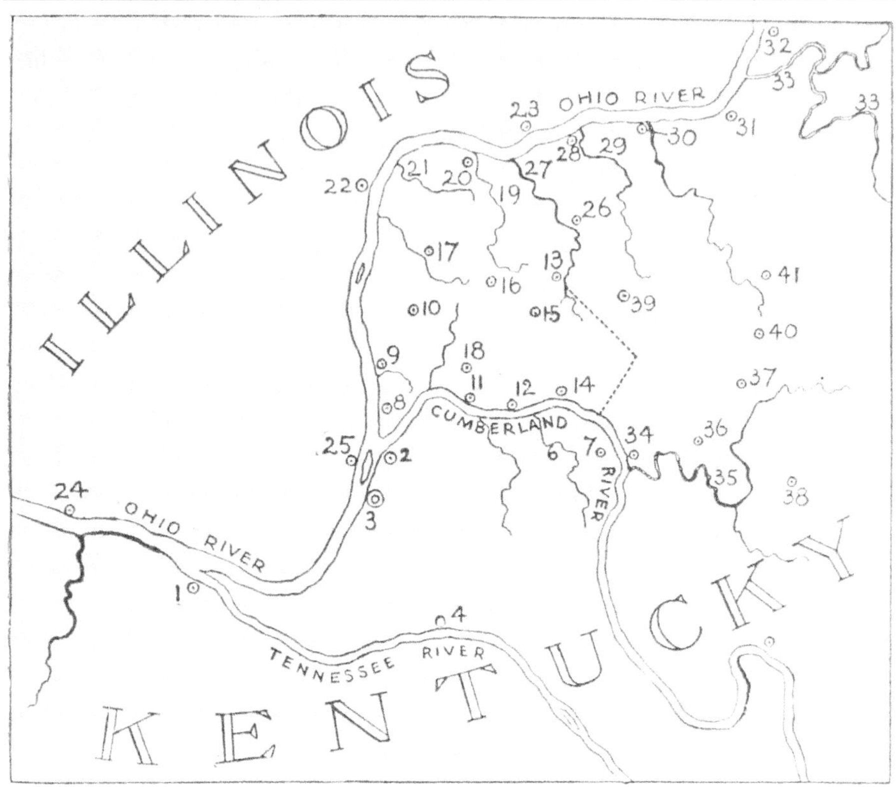

SECTION OF KENTUCKY, NEAR SMITHLAND, IN WHICH THE ENTRANCE TO THE KENTUCKY CAVERN IS SAID TO BE LOCATED.

1. Paducah.
2. Smithland.
3. Old Smithland.
4. Patterson.
5. Frenchtown.
6. Hickory Creek.
7. Underwood.
8. Birdsville.
9. Bayou Mills.
10. Oak Ridge.
11. Moxley's Landing.
12. Kildare.
13. Lola.
14. Pinckneyville.
15. Salem.
16. Hampton.
17. Faulkner.
18. Mullikin.
19. Back Creek.
20. Carrsville.
21. Given's Creek.
22. Golconda.
23. Elizabethtown.
24. Metropolis City.
25. Hamletsburgh.
26. Sheridan.
27. Deer Creek.
28. Hurricane.
29. Hurricane Creek.
30. Ford's Ferry.
31. Weston.
32. Caseyville.
33. Tradewater River.
34. Dycusburgh.
35. Livingstone Creek.
36. Francis.
37. Harrold. (View.)
38. Crider.
39. Levias.
40. Crayneville.
41. Marion.

CHAPTER XIII.

THE PUNCH-BOWLS AND CAVERNS OF KENTUCKY "INTO THE UNKNOWN COUNTRY."

"This part of Kentucky borders a field of caverns that reaches from near the State of Tennessee to the Ohio River, and from the mouth of the Cumberland, eastward to and beyond the center of the State. This great area is of irregular outline, and as yet has been little explored. Underneath the surface are layers of limestone and sandstone rock, the deposits ranging from ten to one hundred and fifty feet in thickness, and often great masses of conglomerate appear. This conglomerate sometimes caps the ridges, and varies in thickness from a few feet only, to sixty, or even a hundred, feet. It is of a diversified character, sometimes largely composed of pebbles cemented together by iron ore into compact beds, while again it passes abruptly into gritty sandstone, or a fine-grained compact rock destitute of pebbles. Sometimes the conglomerate rests directly on the limestone, but in the section about us, more often argillaceous shales or veins of coal intervene, and occasionally inferior and superior layers of conglomerate are separated by a bed of coal. In addition, lead-bearing veins now and then crop up, the crystals of galena being disseminated through masses of fluorspar, calc-spar, limestone and clay, which fill fissures between tilted walls of limestone and hard quartzose sandstone. Valleys, hills, and mountains, grow out of this remarkable crust. Rivers and creeks flow through and under it in crevices, either directly upon the bedstone or over deposits of clay which underlie it. In some places, beds of coal or slate alternate with layers of the lime rock; in others, the interspace is clay and sand. Sometimes the depth of the several limestone and conglomerate deposits is great, and they are often honeycombed by innumerable transverse and diagonal spaces. Water drips have here and there washed out the more friable earth and stone, forming grottoes which are as yet unknown to men, but which will be discovered to be wonderful and fantastic beyond anything of a like nature now familiar. In other places cavities exist between shelves of rock that lie one above the other—monstrous openings caused by the erosive action of rivers now lost, but that have flowed during unnumbered ages past; great parallel valleys and gigantic chambers, one over the other, remaining to tell the story of these former torrents. Occasionally the weight of a portion of the disintegrating rock above becomes too great for its tensile strength and the material crumbles and falls, producing caverns sometimes reaching so near to the earth's surface, as to cause sinks in its crust. These sinks, when first formed, as a rule, present clear rock fractures, and immediately after their formation there is usually a water-way beneath. In the course of time soil collects on their sides, they become cone-shaped hollows from the down-sliding of earth, and then vegetation appears on the living soil; trees grow within them, and in many places the sloping sides of great earth bowls of this nature are, after untold years, covered with the virgin forest; magnificent timber trees growing on soil that has been stratified over and upon decayed monarchs of the forest whose remains, imbedded in the earth, speak of the ages that have passed since the convulsions that made the depressions which, notwithstanding the accumulated debris, are still a hundred feet or more in depth. If the drain or exit at the vortex of one of these sinks becomes clogged, which often occurs, the entire cavity fills with water, and a pond results. Again, a slight orifice reaching far beneath the earth's surface may permit the soil to be gradually washed into a subterranean creek, and thus are formed great bowls, like funnels sunk in the earth—Kentucky punch-bowls.

"Take the country about us, especially towards the Mammoth Cave, and for miles beyond, the landscape in certain localities is pitted with this description of sinks, some recent, others very old. Many are small, but deep; others are large and shallow. Ponds often of great depth, curiously enough overflowing and giving rise to a creek, are to be found on a ridge, telling of underground supply springs, not outlets, beneath. Chains of such sinks, like a row of huge funnels, often appear; the soil between them is slowly washed through their exit into the river, flowing in the depths below, and as the earth that separates them is carried away by the subterranean streams, the bowls coalesce, and a ravine, closed at both ends, results. Along the bottom of such a ravine, a creek may flow, rushing from its natural tunnel at one end of the line, and disappearing in a gulf at the other. The stream begins in mystery, and ends in unfathomed darkness. Near Marion, Hurricane Creek thus disappears, and, so far as men know, is lost to sight forever. Near Cridersville, in this neighborhood, a valley such as I have described, takes in the surface floods of a large tract of country. The waters that run down its sides, during a storm form a torrent, and fence-rails, timbers, and other objects are gulped into the chasm where the creek plunges into the earth, and they never appear again. This part of Kentucky is the most remarkable portion of the known world, and although now neglected, in a time to come is surely destined to an extended distinction. I have referred only to the surface, the skin formation of this honeycombed labyrinth, the entrance to the future wonderland of the world. Portions of such a superficial cavern maze have been traversed by man in the ramifications known as the Mammoth Cave, but deeper than man has yet explored, the subcutaneous structure of that series of caverns is yet to be investigated. The Mammoth Cave as now traversed is simply a superficial series of grottoes and passages overlying the deeper cavern field that I have described. The explored chain of passages is of great interest to men, it is true, but of minor importance compared to others yet unknown, being in fact, the result of mere surface erosion. The river that bisects the cave, just beneath the surface of the earth, and known as Echo River, is a miniature stream: there are others more magnificent that flow majestically far, far beneath it. As we descend into the earth in that locality, caverns multiply in number and increase in size, retaining the general configuration of those I have described. The layers of rock are thicker, the intervening spaces broader; and the spaces stretch in increasingly expanded chambers for miles, while high above each series of caverns the solid ceilings of stone arch and inter-arch. Sheltered under these subterranean alcoves are streams, lakes, rivers and water-falls. Near the surface of the earth, such waters often teem with aquatic life, and some of the caves are inhabited by species of birds, reptiles and mammals as yet unknown to men, creatures possessed of senses and organs that are different from any we find with surface animals, and also apparently defective in particulars that would startle persons acquainted only with creatures that live in the sunshine. It is a world beneath a world, a world within a world—" My guide abruptly stopped.

I sat entranced, marveling at the young-old adept's knowledge, admiring his accomplishments. I gazed into the cavity that yawned beneath me, and imagined its possible but to me invisible secrets, enraptured with the thought of searching into them. Who would not feel elated at the prospect of an exploration, such as I foresaw might be pursued in my immediate future? I had often been charmed with narrative descriptions of discoveries, and book accounts of scientific investigations, but I had never pictured myself as a participant in such fascinating enterprises.

"Indeed, indeed," I cried exultingly; "lead me to this Wonderland, show me the entrance to this Subterranean World, and I promise willingly to do as you bid."

"Bravo!" he replied, "your heart is right, your courage sufficient; I have not disclosed a thousandth part of the wonders which I have knowledge of, and which await your research, and probably I have not gained even an insight into the mysteries that, if your courage permits, you will be privileged to comprehend. Your destiny lies beyond, far beyond that which I have pictured or experienced; and I, notwithstanding my opportunities, have no conception of its end, for at the critical moment my heart faltered—I can therefore only describe the beginning."

Thus, at the lower extremity of Biswell's Hill, I was made aware of the fact that, within a short time, I should be separated from my sympathetic guide, and that it was to be my duty to explore alone, or in other company, some portion of these Kentucky cavern deeps, and I longed for the beginning of my underground journey. Heavens! how different would have been my future life could I then have realized my position! Would that I could have seen the end. After a few days of uneventful travel, we rested, one afternoon, in a hilly country that before us appeared to be more rugged, even mountainous. We had wandered leisurely, and were now at a considerable distance from the Cumberland River, the aim of my guide being, as I surmised, to evade a direct approach to some object of interest which I must not locate exactly, and yet which I shall try to describe accurately enough for identification by a person familiar with the topography of that section. We stood on the side of a stony, sloping hill, back of which spread a wooded, undulating valley.

"I remember to have passed along a creek in that valley," I remarked, looking back over our pathway. "It appeared to rise from this direction, but the source ends abruptly in this chain of hills."

"The stream is beneath us," he answered. Advancing a few paces, he brought to my attention, on the hillside, an opening in the earth. This aperture was irregular in form, about the diameter of a well, and descended perpendicularly into the stony crust. I leaned far over the orifice, and heard the gurgle of rushing water beneath. The guide dropped a heavy stone into the gloomy shaft, and in some seconds a dull splash announced its plunge into underground water. Then he leaned over the stony edge, and—could I be mistaken? —seemed to signal to someone beneath; but it must be imagination on my part, I argued to myself, even against my very sense of sight. Rising, and taking me by the hand, my guardian spoke:

"Brother, we approach the spot where you and I must separate. I serve my masters and am destined to go where I shall next be commanded; you will descend into the earth, as you have recently desired to do. Here we part, most likely forever. This rocky fissure will admit the last ray of sunlight on your path."

My heart failed. How often are we courageous in daylight and timid by night? Men unflinchingly face in sunshine dangers at which they shudder in the darkness.

"How am I to descend into that abyss?" I gasped. "The sides are perpendicular; the depth is unknown!" Then I cried in alarm, the sense of distrust deepening: "Do you mean to drown me; is it for this you have led me away from my native State, from friends, home and kindred? You have enticed me into this wilderness. I have been decoyed, and, like a foolish child, have willingly accompanied my destroyer. You feared to murder me in my distant home; the earth could not have hidden me; Niagara even might have given up my body to dismay the murderers! In this underground river in the wilds of Kentucky, all trace of my existence will disappear forever."

I was growing furious. My frenzied eyes searched the ground for some missile of defense. By strange chance someone had left, on that solitary spot, a rude weapon, providentially dropped for my use, I thought. It was a small iron bolt or bar, somewhat rusted. I threw myself upon the earth, and, as I did so, picked this up quickly, and secreted it within my bosom. Then I arose and resumed my stormy denunciation:

"You have played your part well, you have led your unresisting victim to the sacrifice, but if I am compelled to plunge into this black grave, you shall go with me!" I shrieked in desperation, and suddenly threw my arms around the gentle adept, intending to hurl him into the chasm. At this point I felt my hands seized from behind in a cold, clammy, irresistible embrace, my fingers were loosed by a strong grasp, and I turned, to find myself confronted by a singular looking being, who quietly said:

"You are not to be destroyed; we wish only to do your bidding."

The speaker stood in a stooping position, with his face towards the earth as if to shelter it from the sunshine. He was less than five feet in height. His arms and legs were bare, and his skin, the color of light blue putty, glistened in the sunlight like the slimy hide of a water dog. He raised his head, and I shuddered in affright as I beheld that his face was not that of a human. His forehead extended in an unbroken plane from crown to cheek bone, and the chubby tip of an abortive nose without nostrils formed a short projection near the center of the level ridge which represented a countenance. There was no semblance of an eye, for there were no sockets. Yet his voice was singularly perfect. His face, if face it could be called, was wet, and water dripped from all parts of his slippery person. Yet, repulsive as he looked, I shuddered more at the remembrance of the touch of that cold, clammy hand than at the sight of his figure, for a dead man could not have chilled me as he had done, with his sappy skin, from which the moisture seemed to ooze as from the hide of a water lizard.

Turning to my guide, this freak of nature said, softly:

"I have come in obedience to the signal."

I realized at once that alone with these two I was powerless, and that to resist would be suicidal. Instantly my effervescing passion subsided, and I expressed no further surprise at this sudden and remarkable apparition, but mentally acquiesced. I was alone and helpless; rage gave place to inertia in the despondency that followed the realization of my hopeless condition. The grotesque newcomer who, though sightless, possessed a strange instinct, led us to the base of the hill a few hundred feet away, and there, gushing into the light from the rocky bluff, I saw a magnificent stream issuing many feet in width. This was the head-waters of the mysterious brook that I had previously noticed. It flowed from an archway in the solid stone, springing directly out of the rock-bound cliff; beautiful and picturesque in its surroundings. The limpid water, clear and sparkling, issued from the unknown source that was typical of darkness, but the brook of crystal leaped into a world of sunshine, light and freedom.

"Brother," said my companion, "this spring emerging from this prison of earth images to us what humanity will be when the prisoning walls of ignorance that now enthrall him are removed. Man has heretofore relied chiefly for his advancement, both mental and physical, on knowledge gained from so-called scientific explorations and researches with matter, from material studies rather than spiritual, all his investigations having been confined to the crude, coarse substance of the surface of the globe. Spiritualistic investigations, unfortunately, are considered by scientific men too often as reaching backward only. The religions of the world clasp hands with, and lean upon, the dead past, it is true, but point to a living future. Man must yet search by the agency of senses and spirit, the unfathomed

"CONFRONTED BY A SINGULAR LOOKING BEING."

mysteries that lie beneath his feet and over his head, and he who refuses to bow to the Creator and honor his handiwork discredits himself. When this work is accomplished, as it yet will be, the future man, able then to comprehend the problem of life in its broader significance, drawing from all directions the facts necessary to his mental advancement, will have reached a state in which he can enjoy bodily comfort and supreme spiritual perfection, while he is yet an earth-bound mortal. In hastening this consummation, it is necessary that an occasional human life should be lost to the world, but such sacrifices are noble—yes, sublime, because contributing to the future exaltation of our race. The secret workers in the sacred order of which you are still a member, have ever taken an important part in furthering such a system of evolution. This feature of our work is unknown to brethren of the ordinary fraternity, and the individual research of each secret messenger is unguessed, by the craft at large. Hence it is that the open workers of our order, those initiated by degrees only, who in lodge rooms carry on their beneficent labors among men, have had no hand other than as agents in your removal, and no knowledge of your present or future movements. Their function is to keep together our organization on earth, and from them only an occasional member is selected, as you have been, to perform special duties in certain adventurous studies. Are you willing to go on this journey of exploration? and are you brave enough to meet the trials you have invited?"

Again, my enthusiasm arose, and I felt the thrill experienced by an investigator who stands on the brink of an important discovery, and needs but courage to advance, and I answered,

"Yes."

"Then, farewell; this archway is the entrance that will admit you into your arcanum of usefulness. This mystic Brother, though a stranger to you, has long been apprised of our coming, and it was he who sped me on my journey to seek you, and who has since been waiting for us, and is to be your guide during the first stages of your subterranean progress. He is a Friend, and, if you trust him, will protect you from harm. You will find the necessaries of life supplied, for I have traversed part of your coming road; that part I therefore know, but, as I have said, you are to go deeper into the unexplored, —yes, into and beyond the Beyond, until finally you will come to the gateway that leads into the 'Unknown Country.'"

CHAPTER XIV.

FAREWELL TO GOD'S SUNSHINE. — THE ECHO OF THE CRY.

Thus speaking, my quiet leader, who had so long been as a shepherd to my wandering feet, on the upper earth, grasped my hands tightly, and placed them in those of my new companion, whose clammy fingers closed over them as with a grip of iron. The mysterious being, now my custodian, turned towards the creek, drawing me after him, and together we silently anti solemnly waded beneath the stone archway. As I passed under the shadow of that dismal, yawning cliff, I turned my head to take one last glimpse of the world I had known—that "warm precinct of the cheerful day,"—and tears sprang to my eyes. I thought of life, family, friends, —of all for which men live—and a melancholy vision arose, that of my lost, lost home. My dear companion of the journey that had just ended stood in the sunlight on the banks of the rippling stream, gazing at us intently, and waved an affectionate farewell. My uncouth new associate (guide or master, whichever he might be), of the journey to come, clasped me firmly by the arms, and waded slowly onward, thrusting me steadily against the cold current, and with irresistible force pressed me into the thickening darkness. The daylight disappeared, the pathway contracted, the water deepened and became chillier. We were constrained to bow our heads in order to avoid the overhanging vault of stone; the water reached to my chin, and now the down jutting proof touched the crown of my head; then I shuddered convulsively as the last ray of daylight disappeared.

Had it not been for my companion, I know that I should have sunk in despair, and drowned; but with a firm hand he held my head above the water, and steadily pushed me onward. I had reached the extreme of despondency: I neither feared nor cared for life nor death, and I realized that, powerless to control my own acts, my fate, the future, my existence depended on the strange being beside me. I was mysteriously sustained, however, by a sense of bodily security, such as comes over us as when in the hands of an experienced guide we journey through a wilderness, for I felt that my pilot of the underworld did not purpose to destroy me. We halted a moment, and then, as a faint light overspread us, my eyeless guide directed me to look upward.

"We now stand beneath the crevice which you were told by your former guide would admit the last ray of sunlight on your path. I also say to you; this struggling ray of sunlight is to be your last for years."

I gazed above me, feeling all the wretchedness of a dying man who, with faculties intact, might stand on the dark edge of the hillside of eternity, glancing back into the bright world; and that small opening far, far overhead, seemed as the gate to Paradise Lost. Many a person, assured of ascending at will, has stood at the bottom of a deep well or shaft to a mine, and even then, felt the indescribable sensation of dread, often terror, that is produced by such a situation. Awe, mystery, uncertainty of life and future superadded, may express my sensation. I trembled, shrinking in horror from my captor and struggled violently.

"Hold, hold," I begged, as one involuntarily prays a surgeon to delay the incision of the amputating knife, "just one moment." My companion, unheeding, moved on, the light vanished instantly, and we were surrounded by total darkness. God's sunshine was blotted out.

Then I again became unconcerned; I was not now responsible for my own existence, and the feeling that I experienced when a prisoner in the closed carriage returned. I grew careless as to my fate, and with stolid indifference struggled onward as we progressed slowly against the current of water. I began to interest myself in speculations regarding our surroundings, and the object or outcome of our journey. In places the water was shallow, scarce reaching to our ankles; again it was so deep that we could wade only with exertion, and at times the passage up which we toiled was so narrow, that it would scarcely admit us. After a long, laborious stemming of the unseen brook, my companion directed me to close my mouth, hold my nostrils with my fingers, and stoop; almost diving with me beneath the water, he drew me through the submerged crevice, and we ascended into an open chamber, and left the creek behind us. I fancied that we were in a large room, and as I shouted aloud to test my hypothesis, echo after echo answered, until at last the cry reverberated and died away in distant murmurs. We were evidently in a great pocket or cavern, through which my guide now walked rapidly; indeed, he passed along with unerring footsteps, as certain of his course as I might be on familiar ground in full daylight. I perceived that he systematically evaded inequalities that I could not anticipate nor see. He would tell me to step up or down, as the surroundings

"THIS STRUGGLING RAY OF SUNLIGHT IS TO BE YOUR LAST FOR YEARS."

required, and we ascended or descended -accordingly. Our path turned to the right or the left from time to time, but my eyeless guide passed through what were evidently the most tortuous windings without a mishap. I wondered much at this gift of knowledge, and at last overcame my reserve sufficiently to ask how we could thus unerringly proceed in utter darkness. The reply was:

"The path is plainly visible to me; I see as clearly in pitch darkness as you can in sunshine."

"Explain yourself further," I requested.

He replied, "Not yet;" and continued, "you are weary, we will rest."

He conducted me to a seat on a ledge, and left me for a time. Returning soon, he placed in my hands food which I ate with novel relish. The pabulum seemed to be of vegetable origin, though varieties of it had a peculiar flesh-like flavor. Several separate and distinct substances were contained in the queer viands, some portions savoring of wholesome flesh, while others possessed the delicate flavors of various fruits, such as the strawberry and the pineapple. The strange edibles were of a pulpy texture, homogeneous in consistence, parts being juicy and acid like grateful fruits. Some portions were in slices or films that I could hold in my hand like sections of a velvet melon. and yet were in many respects unlike any other food that I had ever tasted. There was neither rind nor seed; it seemed as though I were eating the gills of a fish, and in answer to my question the guide remarked:

"Yes; it is the gill, but not the gill of a fish. You will be instructed in due time." I will add that after this, whenever necessary, we were supplied with food, but both thirst and hunger disappeared altogether before our underground journey was finished.

After a while we again began our journey, which we continued in what was to me absolute darkness. My strength seemed to endure the fatigue to a wonderful degree, notwithstanding that we must have been walking hour after hour, and I expressed a curiosity about the fact. My guide replied that the atmosphere of the cavern possessed an intrinsic vitalizing power that neutralized fatigue, "or," he said, "there is here an inherent constitutional energy derived from an active gaseous substance that belongs to cavern air at this depth, and sustains the life force by contributing directly to its conservation, taking the place of food and drink."

"I do not understand," I said.

"No; and you do not comprehend how ordinary air supports mind and vitalizes muscle, and at the same time wears out both muscle and all other tissues. These are facts which are not satisfactorily explained by scientific statements concerning oxygenation of the blood. As we descend into the earth we find an increase in the life force of the cavern air."

This reference to surface earth recalled my former life, and led me to contrast my present situation with that I had forfeited. I was seized with an uncontrollable longing for home, and a painful craving for the past took possession of my heart, but with a strong effort I shook off the sensations. We traveled on and on in silence and in darkness, and I thought again of the strange remark of my former guide who had said: "You are destined to go deeper into the unknown; yes, into and beyond the Beyond."

CHAPTER XV.

A ZONE OF LIGHT DEEP WITHIN THE EARTH.

"Oh! for one glimpse of light, a ray of sunshine!"

In reply to this my mental ejaculation, my guide said: "Cannot you perceive that the darkness is becoming less intense?"

"No," I answered, "I cannot; night is absolute."

"Are you sure?" he asked. "Cover your eyes with your hands, then uncover and open them." I did so and fancied that by contrast a faint gray hue was apparent.

"This must be imagination."

"No; we now approach a zone of earth light; let us hasten on."

"A zone of light deep in the earth! Incomprehensible! Incredible!" I muttered, and yet as we went onward and time passed the darkness was less intense. The barely perceptible hue became gray and somber, and then of a pearly translucence, and although I could not distinguish the outline of objects, yet I unquestionably perceived light.

"I am amazed! What can be the cause of this phenomenon? What is the nature of this mysterious halo that surrounds us?" I held my open hand before my eyes, and perceived the darkness of my spread fingers.

"It is light, it is light," I shouted, "it is really light!" and from near and from far the echoes of that subterranean cavern answered back joyfully, "It is light, it is light!"

I wept in joy, and threw my arms about my guide, forgetting in the ecstasy his clammy cuticle, and danced in hysterical glee and alternately laughed and cried. How vividly I realized then that the imprisoned miner would give a world of gold, his former god, for a ray of light.

"Compose yourself; this emotional exhibition is an evidence of weakness; an investigator should neither become depressed over a reverse, nor unduly enthusiastic over a fortunate discovery."

"But we approach the earth's surface? Soon I will be back in the sunshine again."

"Upon the contrary, we have been continually descending into the earth, and we are now ten miles or more beneath the level of the ocean."

I shrank back, hesitated, and in despondency gazed at his hazy outline, then, as if palsied, sank upon the stony floor; but as I saw the light before me, I leaped up and shouted:

"What you say is not true; we approach daylight, I can see your form."

"WE APPROACH DAYLIGHT, I CAN SEE YOUR FORM."

"Listen to me," he said. "Cannot you understand that I have led you continually down a steep descent, and that for hours there has been no step upward? With but little exertion you have walked this distance without becoming wearied, and you could not, without great fatigue, have ascended for so long a period. You are entering a zone of inner earth light; we are in the surface, the upper edge of it. Let us hasten on, for when this cavern darkness is at an end—and I will say we have nearly passed that limit—your courage will return, and then we will rest."

"You surely do not speak the truth; science and philosophy, and I am somewhat versed in both, have never told me of such a light."

"Can philosophers more than speculate about that which they have not experienced if they have no data from which to calculate? Name the student in science who has reached this depth in earth, or has seen a man to tell him of these facts?"

"I cannot."

"Then why should you have expected any of them to describe our surroundings? Misguided men will torture science by refuting facts with theories; but a fact is no less a fact when science opposes."

I recognized the force of his arguments, and cordially grasped his hand in indication of submission. We continued our journey, and rapidly traveled downward and onward. The light gradually increased in intensity, until at length the cavern near about us seemed to be as bright as diffused daylight could have made it. There was apparently no central point of radiation; the light was such as to pervade and exist in the surrounding space, somewhat as the vapor of phosphorus spreads a self-luminous haze throughout the bubble into which it is blown. The visual agent surrounding us had a permanent, self-existing luminosity, and was a pervading, bright, unreachable essence that, without an obvious origin, diffused itself equally in all directions. It reminded me of the form of light that in previous years I had seen described as epipolic dispersion, and as I refer to the matter I am of the opinion that man will yet find that the same cause produces both phenomena. I was informed now by the sense of sight, that we were in a cavern room of considerable size. The apartment presented somewhat the appearance of the usual underground caverns that I had seen pictured in books, and yet was different. Stalactites, stalagmites, saline incrustations, occurring occasionally reminded me of travelers' stories, but these objects were not so abundant as might be supposed. Such accretions or deposits of saline substances as I noticed were also disappointing, in that, instead of having a dazzling brilliancy, like frosted snow crystals, they were of a uniform gray or brown hue. Indeed, my former imaginative mental creations regarding underground caverns were dispelled in this somber stone temple, for even the floor and the fragments of stone that, in considerable quantities, strewed the floor, were of the usual rock formations of upper earth. The glittering crystals of snowy white, or rainbow tints (fairy caverns) pictured by travelers, and described as inexpressibly grand and beautiful in other cavern labyrinths, were wanting here, and I saw only occasional small clusters of quartz crystals that were other than of a dull gray color. Finally, after hours or perhaps days of travel, interspersed with resting, conversations, and arguments, amid which I could form no idea of the flight of time, my companion seated himself on a natural bench of stone, and directed me to rest likewise. He broke the silence, and spoke as follows:

"SEATED HIMSELF ON A NATURAL BENCH OF STONE."

CHAPTER XVI.

VITALIZED DARKNESS. —THE NARROWS IN SCIENCE.

"In studying any branch of science men begin and end with an unknown. The chemist accepts as data such conditions of matter as he finds about him, and connects ponderable matter with the displays of energy that have impressed his senses, building therefrom a span of theoretical science, but he cannot formulate as yet an explanation regarding the origin or the end of either mind, matter, or energy. The piers supporting his fabric stand in a profound invisible gulf, into which even his imagination cannot look to form a theory concerning basic formations—corner-stones.

"The geologist, in a like manner, grasps feebly the lessons left in the superficial fragments of earth strata, impressions that remain to bear imperfect record of a few of the disturbances that have affected the earth's crust, and he endeavors to formulate a story of the world's life, but he is neither able to antedate the records shown by the meager testimony at his command, scraps of a leaf out of God's great book of history, nor to anticipate coming events. The birth, as well as the death, of this planet is beyond his page.

"The astronomer directs his telescope to the heavens, records the position of the planets, and hopes to discover the influences worlds exert upon one another. He explores space to obtain data to enable him to delineate a map of the visible solar universe, but the instruments he has at command are so imperfect, and mind is so feeble that, like mockery seems his attempt to study behind the facts connected with the motions and conditions of the nearest heavenly bodies, and he cannot offer an explanation of the beginning or cessation of their movements. He can neither account for their existence, nor foretell their end."

"Are you not mistaken?" I interrupted; "does not the astronomer foretell eclipses, and calculate the orbits of the planets, and has he not verified predictions concerning their several motions?"

"Yes; but this is simply a study of passing events. The astronomer is no more capable of grasping an idea that reaches into an explanation of the origin of motion, than the chemist or physicist, from exact scientific data, can account for the creation of matter. Give him any amount of material at rest, and he cannot conceive of any method by which motion can disturb any part of it, unless such motion be mass motion communicated from without, or molecular motion, already existing within. He accounts for the phases of present motion in heavenly bodies, not for the primal cause of the actual movements or intrinsic properties they possess. He can neither originate a theory that will permit of motion creating itself, and imparting itself to quiescent matter, nor imagine how an atom of quiescent matter can be moved, unless motion from without be communicated thereto. The astronomer, I assert, can neither from any data at his command postulate nor prove the beginning nor the end of the reverberating motion that exists in his solar system, which is itself the fragment of a system that is circulating and revolving in and about itself, and in which, since the birth of man, the universe he knows has not passed the first milestone in the road that universe is traveling in space immensity.

"The mathematician starts a line from an imaginary point that he informs us exists theoretically without occupying any space, which is a contradiction of terms according to his human acceptation of knowledge derived from scientific experiment, if science is based on verified facts. He assumes that straight lines exist, which is a necessity for his calculation; but such a line he has never made. Even the beam of sunshine, radiating through a clear atmosphere or a cloud bank, widens and contracts again as it progresses through the various mediums of air and vapor currents, and if it is ever spreading and deflecting can it be straight? He begins his study in the unknown, it ends with the unknowable.

"The biologist can conceive of no rational, scientific beginning to life of plant or animal, and men of science must admit the fact. Whenever we turn our attention to nature's laws and nature's substance, we find man surrounded by the infinity that obscures the origin and covers the end. But perseverance, study of nature's forces, and comparison of the past with the present, will yet clarify human knowledge and make plain much of this seemingly mysterious, but never will man reach the beginning or the end. The course of human education, to this day, has been mostly materialistic, although, together with the study of matter, there has been more or less attention given to its moving spirit. Newton was the dividing light in scientific thought; he stepped between the reasonings of the past and the provings of the present, and introduced problems that gave birth to a new scientific tendency, a change from tile study of matter from the material side to that of force and matter, but his thought has since been carried out in a mode too realistic by far. The study of material bodies has given way, it is true, in a few cases to the study of the spirit of matter, and evolution is beginning to teach men that matter is crude. As a result, thought will in its sequence yet show that modifications of energy expression are paramount. This work is not lost, however, for the consideration of the nature of sensible material, is preliminary and necessary to progression (as the life of the savage prepares the way for that of the cultivated student), and is a meager and primitive child's effort, compared with the richness of the study in unseen energy expressions that are linked with matter, of which men will yet learn."

"I comprehend some of this," I replied; "but I am neither prepared to assent to nor dissent from your conclusions, and my mind is not clear as to whether your logic is good or bad. I am readier to speak plainly about my own peculiar situation than to become absorbed in abstruse arguments in science, and I marvel more at the soft light that is here surrounding us than at the metaphysical reasoning in which you indulge."

"The child ignorant of letters wonders at the resources of those who can spell and read, and, in like manner, many obscure natural phenomena are marvelous to man only because of his ignorance. You do not comprehend the fact that sunlight is simply a matter-bred expression, an outburst of interrupted energy, and that the modification this energy undergoes makes it visible or sensible to man. What, think you, becomes of the flood of light energy that unceasingly flows from the sun? For ages, for an eternity, it has bathed this earth and seemingly streamed into space, and space it would seem must have long since have been filled with it, if, as men believe, space contains energy of any description. Man may say the earth casts the amount intercepted by it back into space, and yet does not your science teach that the great bulk of the earth is an absorber, and a poor radiator of light and heat? What think you, I repeat, becomes of the torrent of light and heat and other forces that radiate from the sun, the flood that strikes the earth? It disappears, and, in the economy of nature, is not replaced by any known force or any known motion of matter. Think you that earth substance really presents an obstacle to the passage of the sun's energy? Is it not probable that most of this light producing essence, as a subtle fluid, passes through the surface of the earth and into its interior, as light does through space, and returns thence to the sun Again, in a condition not discernible by man?" He grasped my arm and squeezed it as though to emphasize the words to follow. "You have used the term sunshine freely; tell me what is sunshine? Ah! you do not reply; well, what evidence have you to show that sunshine (heat and light) is not earth-bred, a condition that exists locally only, the result of contact between matter and some unknown force expression? What reason have you for accepting that, to other forms unknown and yet transparent to this energy, your sunshine may not be as intangible as the ether of space is to man? What reason have you to believe that a force torrent is not circulating to and from the sun and earth, inappreciable to man, excepting the mere trace of this force which, modified by contact action with matter appears as heat, light, and other force expressions? How can I, if this is true, in consideration of your ignorance, enter into details explanatory of the action that takes place between matter and a portion of this force, whereby in the earth, first at the surface, darkness is produced, and then deeper down an earth light that man can perceive by the sense of sight, as you now realize? I will only say that this luminous appearance about us is produced by a natural law, whereby the flood of energy, invisible to man, a something clothed now under the name of darkness, after streaming into the crust substance of the earth, is at this depth, revivified, and then is made apparent to mortal eye, to be modified again as it emerges from the opposite earth crust, but not annihilated. For my vision, however, this central light is not a necessity; my physical and mental development is such that the energy of darkness is communicable; I can respond to its touches on my nerves, and hence I can guide you in this dark cavern. I am all eye."

"Ah!" I exclaimed, "that reminds me of a remark made by my former guide who, referring to the instinct of animals, spoke of that as a natural power undeveloped in man. Is it true that by mental cultivation a new sense can be evolved whereby darkness may become as light?"

"Yes; that which you call light is a form of sensible energy to which the faculties of animals who live on the surface of the earth have become adapted, through their organs of sight. The sun's energy is modified when it strikes the surface of the earth; part is reflected, but most of it passes onward into the earth's substance, in an altered or disturbed condition. Animal organisms within the earth must possess a peculiar development to utilize it under its new form, but such a sense is really possessed in a degree by some creatures known to men. There is consciousness behind consciousness; there are grades and depths of consciousness. Earth worms, and some fishes and reptiles in underground streams (lower organizations, men call them) do not use the organ of sight, but recognize objects, seek their food, and flee from their enemies."

"They have no eyes," I exclaimed, forgetting that I spoke to an eyeless being; "how can they see?"

"You should reflect that man cannot offer a satisfactory explanation of the fact that he can see with his eyes. In one respect, these so-called lower creatures are higher in the scale of life than man is, for they see (appreciate) without eyes. The surfaces of their bodies really are sources of perception, and seats of consciousness. Man must yet learn to see with his skin, taste with his fingers, and hear with the surface of his body. The dissected nerve, or the pupil of man's eye, offers to the physiologist no explanation of its intrinsic power. Is not man unfortunate in having to risk so much on so frail an organ? The physiologist can not tell why or how the nerve of the tongue can distinguish between bitter and sweet, or convey any impression of taste, or why the nerve of the ear communicates sound, or the nerve of the eye communicates the impression of sight. There is an impassable barrier behind all forms of nerve impressions, that neither the microscope nor other methods of investigation can help the reasoning senses of man to remove. The void that separates the pulp of the material nerve from consciousness is broader than the solar universe, for even from the most distant known star we can imagine the never-ending flight of a ray of light, that has once started on its travels into space. Can any man outline the bridge that connects the intellect with nerve or brain, mind, or with any form of matter? The fact that the surface of the bodies of some animals is capable of performing the same functions for these animals that the eye of man performs for him, is not more mysterious than is the function of that eye itself. The term darkness is an expression used to denote the fact that to the brain which governs the eye of man, what man calls the absence of light, is unrecognizable. If men were more magnanimous and less egotistical, they would open their minds to the fact that some animals really possess certain senses that are better developed than they are in man. The teachers of men too often tell the little they know and neglect the great unseen. The cat tribe, some night birds, and many reptiles can see better in darkness than in daylight. Let man compare with the nerve expanse of his own eye that of the highly developed eye of any such creature, and he will understand that the difference is one of brain or intellect, and not altogether one of optical vision surface. When men are able to explain how light can affect the nerves of their own eyes and produce such an effect on distant brain tissues as to bring to his senses objects that he is not touching, he may be able to explain how the energy in darkness can affect the nerve of the eye in the owl and impress vision on the brain of that creature. Should not man's inferior sense of light lead him to question if, instead of deficient visual power, there be not a deficiency of the brain capacity of man? Instead of accepting that the eye of man is incapable of receiving the impression of night energy, and making no endeavor to improve himself in the direction of his imperfection, man should reflect whether or not his brain may, by proper cultivation or artificial stimulus, be yet developed so as to receive yet deeper nerve impressions, thereby changing darkness into daylight. Until man can explain the modus operandi of the senses he now possesses, he cannot consistently question the existence of a different sight power in other beings, and unquestioned existing conditions should lead him to hope for a yet higher development in himself."

"This dissertation is interesting, very," I said. "Although inclined toward agnosticism, my ideas of a possible future in consciousness that lies before mankind are broadened. I therefore accept your reasoning, perhaps because I cannot refute it, neither do I wish to do so. And now I ask again, cannot you explain to me how darkness, as deep as that of midnight, has been revivified so as to bring this great cavern to my view?"

"That may be made plain at a future time," he answered; "let us proceed with our journey."

We passed through a dry, well ventilated apartment. Stalactite formations still existed, indicative of former periods of water drippings, but as we journeyed onward I saw no evidence of present percolations, and the developing and erosive agencies that had worked in ages past must long ago have been suspended. The floor was of solid stone, entirely free from loose earth and fallen rocky fragments. It was smooth upon the surface, but generally disposed in gentle undulations. The peculiar, soft, radiant light to which my guide referred as "vitalized darkness" or "revivified sunshine," pervaded all the space about me, but I could not by its agency distinguish the sides of the vast cavern. The brightness was of a species that while it brought into distinctness objects that were near at hand, lost its unfolding power or vigor a short distance beyond. I would compare the effect to that of a bright light shining through a dense fog, were it not that the medium about us was transparent—not milky. The light shrunk into nothingness. It passed from existence behind and about me as if it were annihilated, without wasting away in the opalescent appearance once familiar as that of a spreading fog. Moreover, it seemed to detail such objects as were within the compass of a certain area close about me, but to lose in intensity beyond. The buttons on my coat appeared as distinct as they ever did when I stood in the sunlight, and fully one-half larger than I formerly knew them to be. The corrugations on the palms of my hands stood out in bold serpentine relief that I observed clearly when I held my hands near my eye, my fingers appeared clumsy, and all parts of my person were magnified in proportion. The region at the limits of my range of perception reminded me of nothingness, but not of darkness. A circle of obliteration defined the border of the luminous belt which advanced as we proceeded, and closed in behind us. This line, or rather zone of demarcation that separated the seen from the unseen, appeared to be about two hundred feet away, but it might have been more or less, as I had no method of measuring distances.

CHAPTER XVII.

THE FUNGUS FOREST. — ENCHANTMENT.

Along the chamber through which we now passed I saw by the mellow light great pillars, capped with umbrella-like covers, some of them reminding me of the common toadstool of upper earth, on a magnificent scale. Instead, however, of the gray or somber shades to which I had been accustomed, these objects were of various hues and combined the brilliancy of the primary prismatic colors, with the purity of clean snow. Now they would stand solitary, like gigantic sentinels; again, they would be arranged in rows, the alignment as true as if established by the hair of a transit, forming columnar avenues, and in other situations they were wedged together so as to produce masses, acres in extent, in which the stems became hexagonal by compression. The columnar stems, larger than my body, were often spiral; again, they were marked with diamond-shaped figures, or other regular geometrical forms in relief, beautifully exact, drawn as by a master's hand in rich and delicately blended colors, on pillars of pure alabaster. Not a few of the stems showed deep crimson, blue, or green, together with other rich colors combined; over which, as delicate as the rarest of lace, would be thrown, in white, an enamel-like intricate tracery, far surpassing in beauty of execution the most exquisite needle-work I had ever seen. There could be no doubt that I was in a forest of colossal fungi, the species of which are more numerous than those of upper earth cryptogamic vegetation. The expanded heads of these great thallogens were as varied as the stems I have described, and more so. Far above our path they spread like beautiful umbrellas, decorated as if by masters from whom the great painters of upper earth might humbly learn the art of mixing colors. Their under surfaces were of many different designs, and were of as many shapes as it is conceivable could be made of combinations of the circle and hyperbola. Stately and picturesque, silent and immovable as the sphinx, they studded the great cavern singly or in groups, reminding me of a grown child's wild imagination of fairy land. I stopped beside a group that was of unusual conspicuity and gazed in admiration on the huge and yet graceful, beautiful spectacle. I placed my hand on the stem of one plant, and found it soft and impressible; but instead of being moist, cold, and clammy as the repulsive toadstool of upper earth, I discovered, to my surprise, that it was pleasantly warm, and soft as velvet.

"Smell your hand," said my guide.

I did so, and breathed in an aroma like that of fresh strawberries. My guide observed (I had learned to judge of his emotions by his facial expressions) my surprised countenance with indifference.

"Try the next one," he said.

This being of a different species, when rubbed by my hand exhaled the odor of the pineapple.

"Extraordinary," I mused.

"Not at all. Should productions of surface earth have a monopoly of nature's methods, all the flavors, all the perfumes? You may with equal consistency express astonishment at the odors of the fruits of upper earth if you do so at the fragrance of these vegetables, for they are also created of odorless elements."

"But toadstools are foul structures of low organization. *

(The fungus Polyporus graveolens was neglected by the guide. This fungus exhales a delicate odor, and is used in Kentucky to perfume a room. Being quite large, it is employed to hold a door open, thus being useful as well as fragrant.—J. U. L.)*

They are neither animals nor true vegetables, but occupy a station below that of plants proper," I said.

"You are acquainted with this order of vegetation under the most unfavorable conditions; out of their native elements these plants degenerate and become then abnormal, often evolving into the poisonous earth fungi known to your woods and fields. Here they grow to perfection. This is their chosen habitat. They absorb from a pure atmosphere the combined foods of plants and animals, and during their existence meet no scorching sunrise. They flourish in a region of perfect tranquility, and without a tremor, without experiencing the change of a fraction of a degree in temperature, exist for ages. Many of these specimens are probably thousands of years old, and are still growing; why should they ever die? They have never been disturbed by a breath of moving air, and, balanced exactly on their succulent, pedestal-like stems, surrounded by an atmosphere of dead

“I WAS IN A FOREST OF COLOSSAL FUNGI.”

nitrogen, vapor, and other gases, with their roots imbedded in carbonates and minerals, they have food at command, nutrition inexhaustible."

"Still I do not see why they grow to such mammoth proportions."

"Plants adapt themselves to surrounding conditions," he remarked. "The oak tree in its proper latitude is tall and stately; trace it toward the Arctic circle, and it becomes knotted, gnarled, rheumatic, and dwindles to a shrub. The castor plant in the tropics is twenty or thirty feet in height, in the temperate zone it is an herbaceous plant, farther north it has no existence. Indian corn in Kentucky is luxuriant, tall, and graceful, and each stalk is supplied with roots to the second and third joint, while in the northland it scarcely reaches to the shoulder of a man, and, in order to escape the early northern frost, arrives at maturity before the more southern variety begins to tassel. The common jimson weed (datura stramonium) planted in early spring, in rich soil, grows luxuriantly, covers a broad expanse and bears an abundance of fruit; planted in midsummer it blossoms when but a few inches in height, and between two terminal leaves hastens to produce a single capsule on the apex of the short stem, in order to ripen its seed before the frost appears. These and other familiar examples might be cited concerning the difference some species of vegetation of your former lands undergo under climatic conditions less marked than between those that govern the growth of fungi here and on surface earth. Such specimens of fungi as grow in your former home have escaped from these underground regions, and are as much out of place as are the tropical plants transplanted to the edge of eternal snow. Indeed, more so, for on the earth the ordinary fungus, as a rule, germinates after sunset, and often dies when the sun rises, while here they may grow in peace eternally. These meandering caverns comprise thousands of miles of surface covered by these growths which shall yet fulfill a grand purpose in the economy of nature, for they are destined to feed tramping multitudes when the day appears in which the nations of men will desert the surface of the earth and pass as a single people through these caverns on their way to the immaculate existence to be found in the inner sphere."

"I cannot disprove your statement," I again repeated; "neither do I accept it. However, it still seems to me unnatural to find such delicious flavors and delicate odors connected with objects associated in memory with things insipid, or so disagreeable as toadstools and the rank forest fungi which I abhorred on earth."

CHAPTER XVIII.

THE FOOD OF MAN.

"This leads me to remark," answered the eyeless seer, "that you speak without due consideration of previous experience. You are, or should be, aware of other and as marked differences in food products of upper earth, induced by climate, soil and cultivation. The potato which, next to wheat, rice, or corn, you know supplies nations of men with starchy food, originated as a wild weed in South America and Mexico, where it yet exists as a small, watery, marble-like tuber, and its nearest kindred, botanically, is still poisonous. The luscious apple reached its present excellence by slow stages from knotty, wild, astringent fruit, to which it again returns when escaped from cultivation. The cucumber is a near cousin of the griping, medicinal cathartic bitter-apple, or colocynth, and occasionally partakes yet of the properties that result from that unfortunate alliance, as too often exemplified to persons who do not peel it deep enough to remove the bitter, cathartic principle that exists near the surface. Oranges, in their wild condition, are bitter, and are used principally as medicinal agents. Asparagus was once a weed, native to the salty edges of the sea, and as this weed has become a food, so it is possible for other wild weeds yet to do. Buckwheat is a weed proper, and not a cereal, and birds have learned that the seeds of many other weeds are even preferable to wheat. The wild parsnip is a poison, and the parsnip of cultivation relapses quickly into its natural condition if allowed to escape and roam again. The root of the tapioca plant contains a volatile poison, and is deadly; but when that same root is properly prepared, it becomes the wholesome food, tapioca. The nut of the African anacardium (cachew nut) contains a nourishing kernel that is eaten as food by the natives, and yet a drop of the juice of the oily shell placed on the skin will blister and produce terrible inflammations; only those experts in the removal of the kernel dare partake of the food. The berry of the berberis vulgaris is a pleasant acid fruit; the bough that bears it is intensely bitter. Such examples might be multiplied indefinitely, but I have cited enough to illustrate the fact that neither the difference in size and structure of the species in the mushroom forest through which we are passing, nor the conditions of these bodies, as compared with those you formerly knew, need excite your astonishment. Cultivate a potato in your former home so that the growing tuber is exposed to sunshine, and it becomes green and acrid, and strongly virulent. Cultivate the spores of the intra-earth fungi about us, on the face of the earth, and although now all parts of the plants are edible, the species will degenerate, and may even become poisonous. They lose their flavor under such unfavorable conditions, and although some species still retain vitality enough to resist poisonous degeneration, they dwindle in size, and adapt themselves to new and unnatural conditions. They have all degenerated. Here they live on water, pure nitrogen and its modifications, grasping with their roots the carbon of the disintegrated limestone, affiliating these substances, and evolving from these bodies rich and delicate flavors, far superior to the flavor of earth surface foods. On the surface of the earth, after they become abnormal, they live only on dead and devitalized organic matter, having lost the power of assimilating elementary matter. They then partake of the nature of animals, breathe oxygen and exhale carbonic acid, as animals do, being the reverse of other plant existences. Here they breathe oxygen, nitrogen, and the vapor of water; but exhale some of the carbon in combination with hydrogen, thus evolving these delicate ethereal essences instead of the poisonous gas, carbonic acid. Their substance is here made up of all the elements necessary for the support of animal life; nitrogen to make muscle, carbon and hydrogen for fat, lime for bone. This fungoid forest could feed a multitude. It is probable that in the time to come when man deserts the bleak earth surface, as he will someday be forced to do, as has been the case in frozen planets that are not now inhabited on the outer crust; nations will march through these spaces on their way from the dreary outside earth to the delights of the salubrious inner sphere. Here then, when that day of necessity appears, as it surely will come under inflexible climatic changes that will control the destiny of outer earth life, these constantly increasing stores adapted to nourish humanity, will be found accumulated and ready for food. You have already eaten of them, for the variety of food with which I supplied you has been selected from different portions of these nourishing products which, flavored and salted, ready for use as food, stand intermediate between animal and vegetable, supplying the place of both."

My instructor placed both hands on my shoulders, and in silence I stood gazing intently into his face. Then, in a smooth, captivating, entrancing manner, he continued:

"Can you not see that food is not matter? The material part of bread is carbon, water, gas, and earth; the material part of fat is charcoal and gas; the material part of flesh is water and gas; the material part of fruits is mostly water with a little charcoal and gas. *

(By the term gas, it is evident that hydrogen and nitrogen were designated, and yet, since the instructor insists that other gases form part of the atmosphere, so he may consistently imply that unknown gases are parts of food.—J. U. L.)*

The material constituents of all foods are plentiful, they abound everywhere, and yet amid the unlimited, unorganized materials that go to form foods man would starve.

"Give a healthy man a diet of charcoal, water, lime salts, and air; say to him, 'Bread contains no other substance, here is bread, the material food of man, live on this food,' and yet the man, if he eat of these, will die with his stomach distended. So, with all other foods; give man the unorganized materialistic constituents of food in unlimited amounts, and starvation results. No! matter is not food, but a carrier of food."

"What is food?"

"Sunshine. The grain of wheat is a food by virtue of the sunshine fixed within it. The flesh of animals, the food of living creatures, are simply carriers of sunshine energy. Break out the sunshine and you destroy the food, although the material remains. The growing plant locks the sunshine in its cells, and the living animal takes it out again. Hence it is that after the sunshine of any food is liberated during the metamorphosis of the tissues of an animal although the material part of the food remains, it is no longer a food, but becomes a poison, and then, if it is not promptly eliminated from the animal, it will destroy the life of the animal. This material becomes then injurious, but it is still material.

"The farmer plants a seed in the soil, the sunshine sprouts it, nourishes the growing plant, and during the season locks itself to and within its tissues, binding the otherwise dead materials of that tissue together into an organized structure. Animals eat these structures, break them from higher to lower compounds, and in doing so live on the stored up sunshine and then excrete the worthless material side of the food. The farmer spreads these excluded substances over the earth again to once more take up the sunshine in the coming plant organization, but not until it does once more lock in its cells the energy of sunshine can it be a food for that animal."

"Is manure a food?" he abruptly asked.

"No.

"Is not manure matter?"

"Yes."

"May it not become a food again, as the part of another plant, when another season passes?"

"Yes."

"In what else than energy (sunshine) does it differ from food?"

"Water is a necessity," I said.

"And locked in each molecule of water there is a mine of sunshine. Liberate suddenly the sun energy from the gases of the ocean held in subjection thereby, and the earth would disappear in an explosion that would reverberate throughout the universe. The water that you truly claim to be necessary to the life of man, is itself water by the grace of this same sun, for without its heat water would be ice, dry as dust. 'T is the sun that gives life and motion to creatures animate and substances inanimate; he who doubts distrusts his Creator. Food and drink are only carriers of bits of assimilable sunshine. When the fire worshipers kneeled to their god, the sun, they worshiped the great food reservoir of man. When they drew the quivering entrails from the body of a sacrificed victim they gave back to their God a spark of sunshine—it was due sooner or later. They built well in thus recognizing the source of all life, and yet they acted badly, for their God asked no premature sacrifice, the inevitable must soon occur, and as all organic life comes from that Sun-God, so back to that Creator the sun-spark must fly."

"But they are heathen; there is a God beyond their narrow conception of God."*

*(*It's sad to see how christians missunderstand their forebear's wisdom - Note from the Editor)*

"As there is also a God in the Beyond, past your idea of God. Perhaps to beings of higher mentalities, we may be heathen; but even if this is so, duty demands that we revere the God within our intellectual sphere. Let us not digress further; the subject now is food, not the Supreme Creator, and I say to you the food of man and the organic life of man is sunshine."

He ceased, and I reflected upon his words. All he had said seemed so consistent that I could not deny its plausibility, and yet it still appeared altogether unlikely as viewed in the light of my previous earth knowledge.

I did not quite comprehend all the semi-scientific expressions, but was at least certain that I could neither disprove nor verify his propositions. My thoughts wandered aimlessly, and I found myself questioning whether man could be prevailed upon to live contentedly in situations such as I was now passing through. In company with my learned and philosophical but fantastically created guardian and monitor, I moved on.

CHAPTER XIX.

THE CRY FROM A DISTANCE.
I REBEL AGAINST CONTINUING THE JOURNEY.

As we paced along, meditating, I became more sensibly impressed with the fact that our progress was down a rapid declination. The saline incrustations, fungi and stalagmites, rapidly changed in appearance, an endless variety of stony figures and vegetable cryptogams recurring successively before my eyes. They bore the shape of trees, shrubs, or animals, fixed and silent as statues: at least in my distorted condition of mind I could make out resemblances to many such familiar objects; the floor of the cavern became increasingly steeper, as was shown by the stalactites, which, hanging here and there from the invisible ceiling, made a decided angle with the floor, corresponding with a similar angle of the stalagmites below. Like an accompanying and encircling halo, the ever-present earth-light enveloped us, opening in front as we advanced, and vanishing in the rear. The sound of our footsteps gave back a peculiar, indescribable hollow echo, and our voices sounded ghost-like and unearthly, as if their origin was outside of our bodies, and at a distance. The peculiar resonance reminded me of noises reverberating in an empty cask or cistern. I was oppressed by an indescribable feeling of mystery and awe that grew deep and intense, until at last I could no longer bear the mental strain.

"Hold, hold," I shouted, or tried to shout, and stopped suddenly, for although I had cried aloud, no sound escaped my lips. Then from a distance—could I believe my senses? —from a distance as an echo, the cry came back in the tones of my own voice, "Hold, hold."

"Speak lower," said my guide, "speak very low, for now an effort such as you have made projects your voice far outside your body; the greater the exertion the farther away it appears."

I grasped him by the arm and said slowly, determinedly, and in a suppressed tone: "I have come far enough into the secret caverns of the earth, without knowing our destination; acquaint me now with the object of this mysterious journey, I demand, and at once relieve this sense of uncertainty; otherwise I shall go no farther."

"You are to proceed to the Sphere of Rest with me," he replied, "and in safety. Beyond that an Unknown Country lies, into which I have never ventured."

"AN ENDLESS VARIETY OF STONY FIGURES."

"You speak in enigmas; what is this Sphere of Rest? Where is it?"

"Your eyes have never seen anything similar; human philosophy has no conception of it, and I cannot describe it," he said. "It is located in the body of the earth, and we will meet it about one thousand miles beyond the North Pole."

"But I am in Kentucky," I replied; "do you think that I propose to walk to the North Pole, man—if man you be; that unreached goal is thousands of miles away."

"True," he answered, "as you measure distance on the surface of the earth, and you could not walk it in years of time; but you are now twenty-five miles below the surface, and you must be aware that instead of becoming wearier as we proceed, you are now and have for some time been gaining strength. I would also call to your attention that you neither hunger nor thirst."

"Proceed," I said, "it is useless to rebel; I am wholly in your power," and we resumed our journey, and rapidly went forward amid silences that were to me painful beyond description. We abruptly entered a cavern of crystal, every portion of which was of sparkling brilliancy, and as white as snow. The stalactites, stalagmites and fungi disappeared. I picked up a fragment of the bright material, tasted it, and found that it resembled pure salt. Monstrous, cubical crystals, a foot or more in diameter, stood out in bold relief, accumulations of them, as conglomerated masses, banked up here and there, making parts of great columnar cliffs, while in other formations the crystals were small, resembling in the aggregate masses of white sandstone.

"Is not this salt?" I asked.

"Yes; we are now in the dried bed of an underground lake."

"Dried bed?" I exclaimed; "a body of water sealed in the earth cannot evaporate."

"It has not evaporated; at some remote period, the water has been abstracted from the salt, and probably has escaped upon the surface of the earth as a fresh water spring."

"You contradict all laws of hydrostatics, as I understand that subject," I replied, "when you speak of abstracting water from a dissolved substance that is part of a liquid, and thus leaving the solids."

"Nevertheless, this is a constant act of nature," said he; "how else can you rationally account for the great salt beds and other deposits of saline materials that exist hermetically sealed beneath the earth's surface?"

"I will confess that I have not given the subject much thought; I simply accept the usual explanation to the effect that salty seas have lost their water by evaporation, and afterward the salt formations, by some convulsions of nature, have been covered with earth, perhaps sinking by earthquake convulsions bodily into the earth."

"These explanations are examples of some of the erroneous views of scientific writers," he replied; "they are true only to a limited extent. The great beds of salt, deep in the earth, are usually accumulations left there by water that is drawn from brine lakes, from which the liberated water often escaped as pure spring water at the surface of the earth. It does not escape by evaporation, at least not until it reaches the earth's surface."

“MONSTROUS CUBICAL CRYSTALS.”

INTERLUDE — THE STORY INTERRUPTED.

CHAPTER XX.

MY UNBIDDEN GUEST PROVES HIS STATEMENT AND REFUTES MY PHILOSOPHY.

Let the reader who has followed this strange story which I am directed to title "The End of Earth," and who, in imagination, has traversed the cavernous passages of the underworld and listened to the conversation of those two personages who journeyed towards the secrets of the Beyond, return now to upper earth, and once more enter my secluded lodgings, the home of Llewellen Drury, him who listened to the aged guest and who claims your present attention. Remember that I relate a story within a story. That importunate guest of mine, of the glittering knife and the silvery hair, like another Ancient Mariner, had constrained me to listen to his narrative, as he read it aloud to me from the manuscript. I patiently heard chapter after chapter, generally with pleasure, often with surprise, sometimes with incredulity, or downright dissent. Much of the narrative, I must say, —yes, most of it, appeared possible, if not probable, as taken in its connected sequence. The scientific sections were not uninteresting; the marvels of the fungus groves, the properties of the inner light, I was not disinclined to accept as true to natural laws; but when The—Man—Who—Did—It came to tell of the intra-earth salt deposits, and to explain the cause of the disappearance of lakes that formerly existed underground, and their simultaneous replacement by beds of salt, my credulity was overstrained.

"Permit me to interrupt your narrative," I remarked, and then in response to my request the venerable guest laid down his paper.

"Well?" he said, interrogatively.

"I do not believe that last statement concerning the salt lake, and, to speak plainly, I would not have accepted it as you did, even had I been in your situation."

"To what do you allude?" he asked.

"The physical abstraction of water from the salt of a solution of salt; I do not believe it possible unless by evaporation of the water."

"You seem to accept as conclusive the statements of men who have never investigated beneath the surface in these directions, and you question the evidence of a man who has seen the phenomenon. I presume you accept the prevailing notions about salt beds, as you do the assertion that liquids seek a common level, which your scientific authorities also teach as a law of nature?"

"Yes; I do believe that liquids seek a common level, and I am willing to credit your other improbable statements if you can demonstrate the principle of liquid equilibrium to be untrue."

"Then," said he, "to-morrow evening I will show you that fluids seek different levels, and also explain to you how liquids may leave the solids they hold in solution without evaporating from them."

He arose and abruptly departed. It was near morning, and yet I sat in my room alone pondering the story of my unique guest until I slept to dream of caverns and seances until daylight, when I was awakened by their vividness. The fire was out, the room was cold, and, shivering in nervous exhaustion, I crept into bed to sleep and dream again of horrible things I cannot describe, but which made me shudder in affright at their recollection. Late in the day. I awoke.

On the following evening my persevering teacher appeared punctually, and displayed a few glass tubes and some blotting or bibulous paper.

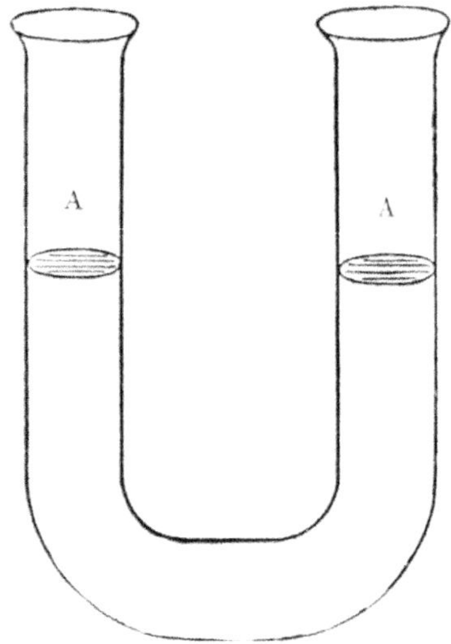

FIG. 11.—A A, water in tube seeks a level

"I will first show you that liquids may change their levels in opposition to the accepted laws of men, not contrary to nature's laws; however, let me lead to the experiments by a statement of facts, that, if you question, you can investigate at any time. If two vessels of water be connected by a channel from the bottom of each, the water surfaces will come to a common level."

He selected a curved glass tube, and poured water into it. The water assumed the position shown in Figure 11.

"You have not shown me anything new," I said; "my text-books taught me this."

"True, I have but exhibited that which is the foundation of your philosophy regarding the surface of liquids. Let me proceed:

"If we pour a solution of common salt into such a U tube, as I do now, you perceive that it also rises to the same level in both ends."

"Of course it does."

"Do not interrupt me. Into one arm of the tube containing the brine I now carefully pour pure water. You observe that the surfaces do not seek the same level." (Figure 12)

"Certainly not," I said; "the weight of the liquid in each arm is the same, however; the columns balance each other."

"Exactly; and on this assumption you base your assertion that connected liquids of the same gravity must always seek a common level, but you see from this test that if two liquids of different gravities be connected from beneath, the surface of the lighter one will assume a higher level than the surface of the heavier."

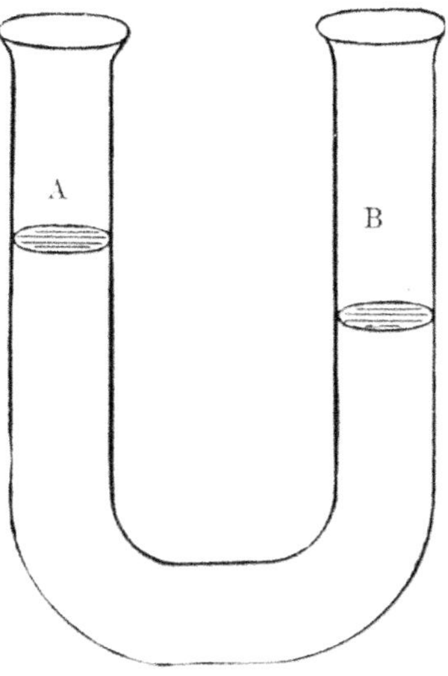

FIG. 12.—A, surface of water.
B, surface of brine.

"Agreed; however tortuous the channel that connects them, such must be the case."

"Is it not supposable," said he, "that there might be two pockets in the earth, one containing salt water, the other fresh water, which, if joined together, might be represented by such a figure as this, wherein the water surface would be raised above that of the brine?" And he drew upon the paper the accompanying diagram. (Figure 13)

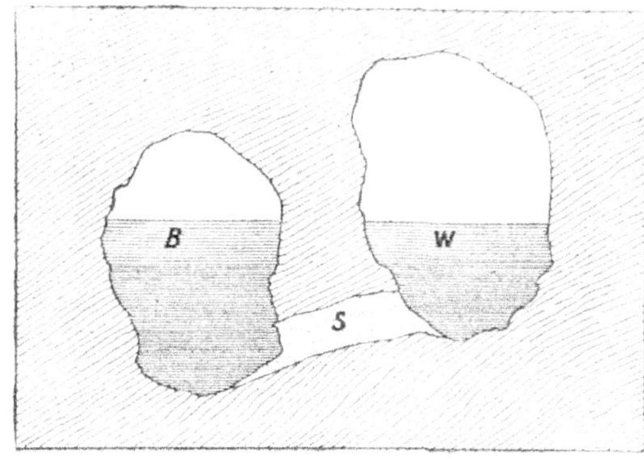

FIG. 13.—B, surface of brine.
W, surface of water.
S, sand strata connecting them.

"Yes," I admitted; "providing, of course, there was an equal pressure of air on the surface of each."

"Now I will draw a figure in which one pocket is above the other, and ask you to imagine that in the lower pocket we have pure water, in the upper pocket brine (Figure 14); can you bring any theory of your law to bear upon these liquids so that by connecting them together the water will rise and run into the brine?"

"No," I replied; "connect them, and then the brine will flow into the water."

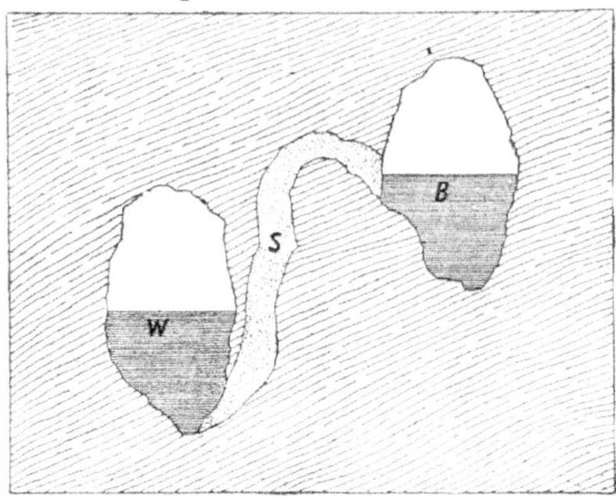

FIG. 14.—B, brine.
W, water.
S, sand stratum.
(The difference in altitude is somewhat exaggerated to make the phenomenon clear. A syphon may result under such circumstances.—L.)

"Upon the contrary," he said; "connect them, as innumerable cavities in the earth are joined, and the water will flow into the brine."

"The assertion is opposed to applied philosophy and common sense," I said.

"Where ignorance is bliss, 't is folly to be wise, you know to be a maxim with mortals," he replied; " but I must pardon you; your dogmatic education narrows your judgment. I now will prove you in error."

He took from his pocket two slender glass tubes, about an eighth of an inch in bore and four inches in length, each closed at one end, and stood them in a perforated cork that he placed upon the table.

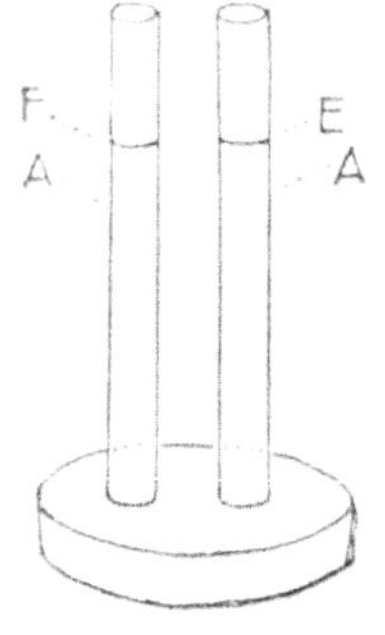

FIG. 15.
A A, glass tubes.
F, brine surface.
E, water surface.

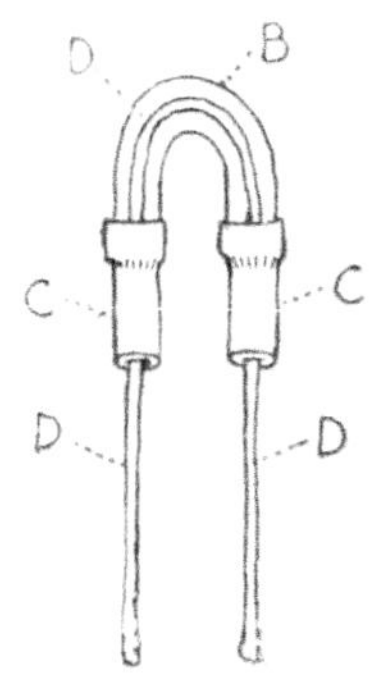

FIG. 16.
B. curved glass tube.
C C, rubber tubes.
D D D, bibulous paper.

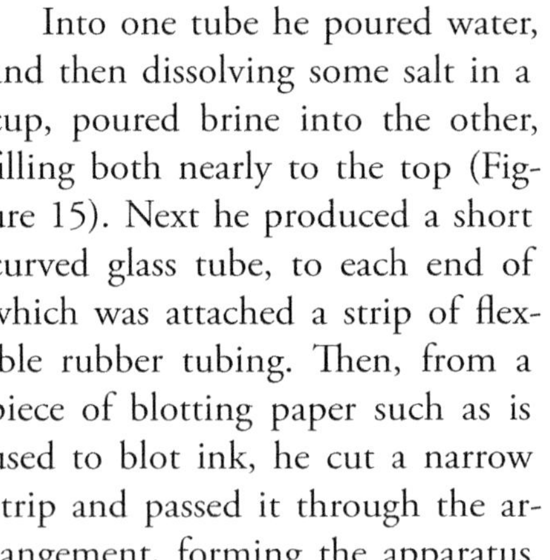

Into one tube he poured water, and then dissolving some salt in a cup, poured brine into the other, filling both nearly to the top (Figure 15). Next he produced a short curved glass tube, to each end of which was attached a strip of flexible rubber tubing. Then, from a piece of blotting paper such as is used to blot ink, he cut a narrow strip and passed it through the arrangement, forming the apparatus represented by. (Figure 16)

Then he inserted the two tubes into the rubber, the extremities of the paper being submerged in the liquids, producing a combination that rested upright in the cork as shown by. (Figure 17)

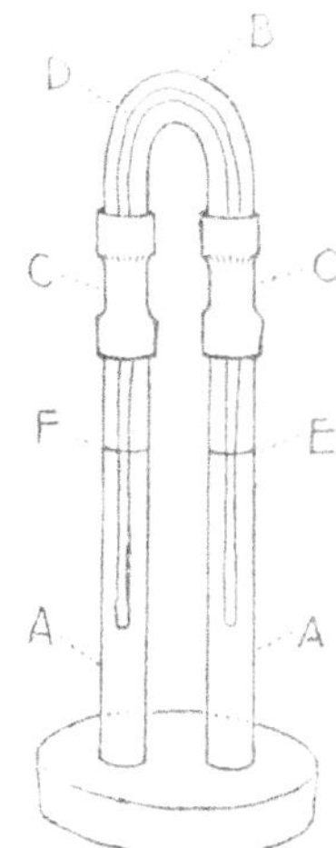

FIG. 17.
A A, glass tubes.
B, curved glass tube.
C rubber tubes.
E, water surface.
F, brine surface.

The surfaces of both liquids were at once lowered by reason of the suction of the bibulous paper, the water decreasing most rapidly, and soon the creeping liquids met by absorption in the paper, the point of contact, as the liquids met, being plainly discernible. Now the old man gently slid the tubes upon each other, raising one a little, so as to bring the surfaces of the two liquids exactly on a plane; he then marked the glass at the surface of each with a pen.

"Observe the result," he remarked as he replaced the tubes in the cork with their liquid surfaces on a line.

Together we sat and watched, and soon it became apparent that the surface of the water had decreased in height as compared with that of the brine. By fixing my gaze on the ink mark on the glass I also observed that the brine in the opposing tube was rising.

"I will call to-morrow evening," he said, "and we shall then discover which is true, man's theory or nature's practice."

Within a short time enough of the water in the glass tube had been transferred to the brine to raise its surface considerably above its former level, the surface of the water being lowered to a greater degree. (Figure 18) I was discomfited at the result, and upon his appearance next evening peevishly said to the experimenter:

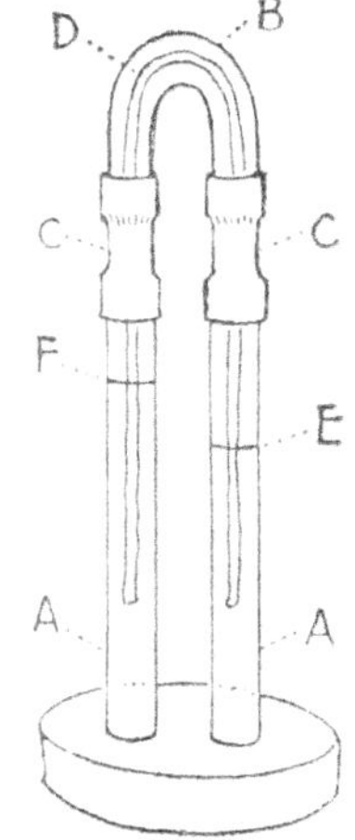

FIG. 18.
E, water surface.
F, brine surface.

"I do not know that this is fair."

"Have I not demonstrated that, by properly connecting the liquids, the lighter flows into the heavier, and raises itself above the former surface?"

"Yes; but there is no porous paper in the earth."

"True; I used this medium because it was convenient. There are, however, vast subterranean beds of porous materials, stone, sand, clay, various other earths, many of which will answer the same purpose. By perfectly natural laws, on a large scale, such molecular transfer of liquids is constantly taking place within the earth, and in these phenomena the law of gravitation seems ignored, and the rule which man believes from narrow experience, governs the flow of liquids, is reversed. The arched porous medium always transfers the lighter liquid into the heavier one until its surface is raised considerably above that of the light one. In the same way you can demonstrate that alcohol passes into water, sulphuric ether into alcohol, and other miscible light liquids into those heavier."

"I have seen you exemplify the statement on a small scale, with water and brine, and cannot question but that it is true on a large one," I replied.

"So, you admit that the assertion governing the surfaces of liquids is true only when the liquids are connected from beneath. In other words, your thought is one-sided, as science thought often is."

"Yes."

"Now as to the beds of salt deep within the earth. You are also mistaken concerning their origin. The water of the ocean that runs through an open channel from the one side may flow into an underground lake, that by means of the contact action (suction) of the overlying and surrounding strata is being continually emptied of its water, but not its salt. Thus, by absorption of water the brine of the lake becomes in time saturated, starting crystallization regularly over the floor and sides of the basin. Eventually the entire cavity is filled with salt, and a solid mass of rock salt remains. If, however, before the lake becomes solid, the brine supply is shut off by some natural cause as by salt closing the passage thereto, the underground lake is at last drained of its water, the salt crystallizing over the bottom, and upon the cliffs, leaving great crevices through the saline deposits, as chances to have been the case with the salt formations through which I passed with my guide, and have recently described to you."

"Even now I have my doubts as to the correctness of your explanations, especially concerning the liquid surfaces."

"They are facts, however; liquids capable of being mixed, if connected by porous arches (bibulous paper is convenient for illustrating by experiment) reverse the rule men have accepted to explain the phenomena of liquid equilibrium, for I repeat, the lighter one rushes into that which is heavier, and the surface of the heavier liquid rises. You can try the experiment with alcohol and water, taking precautions to prevent evaporation, or you can vary the experiment with solutions of various salts of different densities; the greater the difference in gravity between the two liquids, the more rapid will be the flow of the lighter one into the heavier, and after equilibrium, the greater will be the contrast in the final height of the resultant liquid surfaces."

"Men will yet explain this effect by natural laws," I said.

"Yes," he answered; "when they learn the facts; and they will then be able to solve certain phenomena connected with diffusion processes that they cannot now understand. Did I not tell you that after the fact had been made plain it was easy to see how Columbus stood the egg on its end? What I have demonstrated by experiment is perhaps no new principle in hydrostatics. But I have applied it in a natural manner to the explanation of obscure natural phenomena, that men now seek unreasonable methods to explain."

"You may proceed with your narrative. I accept that when certain liquids are connected, as you have shown, by means of porous substances, one will pass into the other, and the surface of the lighter liquid in this case will assume a position below that of the heavier."

"You must also accept," said he, "that when solutions of salt are subjected to earth attraction, under proper conditions, the solids may by capillary attraction be left behind, and pure water finally pass through the porous medium. Were it not for this law, the only natural surface spring water on earth would be brine, for the superficial crust of the earth is filled with saline solutions. All the spring-fed rivers and lakes would also be salty and fetid with sulphur compounds, for at great depths brine and foul water are always present. Even in countries where all the water below the immediate surface of the earth is briny, the running springs, if of capillary origin, are pure and fresh. You may imagine how different this would be were it not for the law I have cited, for the whole earth's crust is permeated by brine and saline waters. Did your 'philosophy' never lead you to think of this?"

Continuing, my guest argued as follows: "Do not lakes exist on the earth's surface into which rivers and streams flow, but which have no visible outlet? Are not such lakes saline, even though the source of supply is comparatively fresh? Has it never occurred to you to question whether capillarity assisted by surface evaporation (not evaporation only as men assert) is not separating the water of these lakes from the saline substances carried into them by the streams, thus producing brine lakes? Will not this action after a great length of time result in crystalline deposits over portions of the bottoms of such lakes, and ultimately produce a salt bed?"

"It is possible," I replied.

"Not only possible, but probable. Not only probable, but true. Across the intervening brine strata above the salt crystals the surface rivers may flow, indeed, owing to differences in specific gravity the surface of the lake may be comparatively fresh, while in the quiet depths below, beds of salt crystals are forming, and between these extremes may rest strata after strata of saline solutions, decreasing in gravity towards the top."

Then he took his manuscript, and continued to read in a clear, musical voice, while I sat a more contented listener than I had been previously. I was not only confuted, but convinced. And I recalled the saying of Socrates, that no better fortune can happen a man than to be confuted in an error.

MY UNBIDDEN GUEST CONTINUES READING HIS MANUSCRIPT.

CHAPTER XXI.

MY WEIGHT DISAPPEARING.

We halted suddenly, for we came unexpectedly to the edge of a precipice, twenty feet at least in depth.

"Let us jump down," said my guide.

"That would be dangerous," I answered; "cannot we descend at some point where it is not so deep?"

"No; the chasm stretches for miles across our path, and at this point we will meet with the least difficulty; besides, there is no danger. The specific gravity of our bodies is now so little that we could jump twice that distance with impunity."

"I cannot comprehend you; we are in the flesh, our bodies are possessed of weight, the concussion will be violent."

"You reason again from the condition of your former life, and, as usual, are mistaken; there will be little shock, for, as I have said, our bodies are comparatively light now. Have you forgotten that your motion is continuously accelerated, and that without perceptible exertion you move rapidly? This is partly because of the loss of weight. Your weight would now be only about fifty pounds if tested by a spring balance."

I stood incredulous.

"You trifle with me; I weigh over one hundred and fifty pounds; how have I lost weight? It is true that I have noticed the ease with which we have recently progressed on our journey, especially the latter part of it, but I attribute this, in part, to the fact that our course is down an incline, and also to the vitalizing power of this cavern air."

"This explains part of the matter," he said; " it answered at the time, and I stated a fact; but were it not that you are really consuming a comparatively small amount of energy, you would long before this have been completely exhausted. You have been gaining strength for some hours; have really been growing younger. Your wrinkled face has become smoother, and your voice is again natural. You were prematurely aged by your brothers on the surface of the earth, in order that when you pass the line of gravity, you might be vigorous and enjoying manhood again. Had this aging process not been accomplished you would now have become as a child in many respects."

"I BOUNDED UPWARD FULLY SIX FEET."

He halted before me. "Jump up," he said. I promptly obeyed the unexpected command, and sprung upward with sufficient force to carry me, as I supposed, six inches from the earth; however, I bounded upward fully six feet. My look of surprise as I gently alighted, for there was no concussion on my return, seemed lost on my guide, and he quietly said:

"If you can leap six feet upward without excessive exertion, or return shock, cannot you jump twenty feet down? Look!"

And he leaped lightly over the precipice and stood unharmed on the stony floor below.

Even then I hesitated, observing which, he cried:

"Hang by your hands from the edge then, and drop."

I did so, and the fourteen feet of fall seemed to affect me as though I had become as light as cork. I fluttered to the earth as a leaf would fall, and leaned against the precipice in surprised, meditation.

"Others have been through your experience," he remarked, "and I therefore can overlook your incredulity; but experiences such as you now meet, remove distrust. Doing is believing." He smiled benignantly.

I pondered, revolving in my mind the fact that persons had in mental abstraction, passed through unusual experiences in ignorance of conditions about them, until their attention had been called to the seen and yet unnoticed surroundings, and they had then beheld the facts plainly. The puzzle picture stares the eye and impresses the retina, but is devoid of character until the hidden form is developed in the mind, and then that form is always prominent to the eye. My remarkably light step, now that my attention had been directed thereto, was constantly in my mind, and I found myself suddenly possessed of the strength of a man, but with weight of an infant. I raised my feet without an effort; they seemed destitute of

"I FLUTTERED TO THE EARTH AS A LEAF WOULD FALL."

weight; I leaped about, tumbled, and rolled over and over on the smooth stone floor without injury. It appeared that I had become the airy similitude of my former self, my material substance having wasted away without a corresponding impairment of strength. I pinched my flesh to be assured that all was not a dream, and then endeavored to convince myself that I was the victim of delirium; but in vain. Too sternly my self-existence confronted me as a reality, a cruel reality. A species of intoxication possessed me once more, and I now hoped for the end, whatever it might be. We resumed our journey, and rushed on with increasing rapidity, galloping hand in hand, down, down, ever downward into the illuminated crevice of the earth. The spectral light by which we were aureoled increased in intensity, as by arithmetical progression, and I could now distinguish objects at a considerable distance before us. My spirits rose as if I were under the influence of a potent stimulant; a liveliness that was the opposite of my recent despondency had gained control, and I was again possessed of a delicious mental sensation, to which I can only refer as a most rapturous exhilaration. My guide grasped my hand firmly, and his touch, instead of revolting me as formerly it had done, gave pleasure. We together leaped over great inequalities in the floor, performing these aerial feats almost as easily as a bird flies. Indeed, I felt that I possessed the power of flight, for we bounded fearlessly down great declivities and over abysses that were often perpendicular, and many times our height. A very slight muscular exertion was sufficient to carry us rods of distance, and almost tiptoeing we skimmed with ever-increasing speed down the steps of that unknown declivity. At length my guide held back; we gradually lessened our velocity, and, after a time, rested beside a horizontal substance that lay before us, apparently a sheet of glass, rigid, immovable, immeasurably great, that stretched as a level surface before us, vividly distinct in the brightness of an earth light, that now proved to be superior to sunshine. Far as the eye could reach, the glassy barrier to our further progress spread as a crystal mirror in front, and vanishing in the distance, shut off the beyond.

"WE LEAPED OVER GREAT INEQUALITIES."

"FAR AS THE EYE COULD REACH THE GLASSY BARRIER SPREAD AS A CRYSTAL MIRROR."

INTERLUDE. — THE STORY AGAIN INTERRUPTED.

CHAPTER XXII.

MY UNBIDDEN GUEST DEPARTS.

Once more I must presume to interrupt this narrative, and call back the reader's thoughts from those mysterious caverns through which we have been tracing the rapid footsteps of the man who was abducted, and his uncouth pilot of the lower realms. Let us now see and hear what took place in my room, in Cincinnati, just after my visitor, known to us as The-Man-Who-Did-It, had finished reading to me, Lewellyn Drury, the custodian of this manuscript, the curious chapter relating how the underground explorers lost weight as they descended in the hollows of the earth. My French clock struck twelve of its clear silvery notes before the gray-bearded reader finished his stint for the occasion, and folded his manuscript preparatory to placing it within his bosom.

"It is past midnight," he said, "and it is time for me to depart; but I will come to you again within a year.

"Meanwhile, during my absence, search the records, question authorities, and note such objections as rise therefrom concerning the statements I have made. Establish or disprove historically, or scientifically, any portion of the life history that I have given, and when I return I will hear what you have to say, and meet your argument. If there is a doubt concerning the authenticity of any part of the history, investigate; but make no mention to others of the details of our meetings."

I sat some time in thought, then said: "I decline to concern myself in verifying the historical part of your narrative. The localities you mention may be true to name, and it is possible that you have related a personal history; but I cannot perceive that I am interested in either proving or disproving it. I will say, however, that it does not seem probable that at any time a man can disappear from a community, as you claim to have done, and have been the means of creating a commotion in his neighborhood that affected political parties, or even led to an unusual local excitement, outside his immediate circle of acquaintances, for a man is not of sufficient importance unless he is very conspicuous. By your own admission, you were simply a studious mechanic, a credulous believer in alchemistic vagaries, and as I revolve the matter over, I am afraid that you are now trying to impose on my credulity. The story of a forcible abduction, in the manner you related, seems to me incredible, and not worthy of investigation, even had I the inclination to concern myself in your personal affairs. The statements, however, that you make regarding the nature of the crust of the earth, gravitation, light, instinct, and human senses are highly interesting, and even plausible as you artfully present the subjects, I candidly admit, and I shall take some pains to make inquiries concerning the recorded researches of experts who have investigated in that direction."

"Collect your evidence," said he, "and I shall listen to your views when I return."

He opened the door, glided away, and I was alone again.

CHAPTER XXIII.

I QUESTION SCIENTIFIC MEN. — ARISTOTLE'S ETHER.

Days and weeks passed. When the opportunity presented, I consulted Dr. W. B. Chapman, the druggist and student of science, regarding the nature of light and earth, who in turn referred me to Prof. Daniel Vaughn. This learned man, in reply to my question concerning gravitation, declared that there was much that men wished to understand in regard to this mighty force, that might yet be explained, but which may never become known to mortal man.

"The correlation of forces," said he, "was prominently introduced and considered by a painstaking scientific writer named Joule, in several papers that appeared between 1843 and 1850, and he was followed by others, who engaged themselves in experimenting and theorizing, and I may add that Joule was indeed preceded in such thought by Mayer. This department of scientific study just now appears of unusual interest to scientists, and your questions embrace problems connected with some phases of its phenomena. We believe that light, heat, and electricity are mutually convertible, in fact, the evidences recently opened up to us show—that such must be the case. These agencies or manifestations are now known to be so related that whenever one) disappears others spring into existence. Study the beautiful experiments and remarkable investigations of Sir William Thomson in these directions."

"And what of gravitation?" I asked, observing that Prof. Vaughn neglected to include gravitation among his numerous enumerated forces, and recollecting that the force gravitation was more closely connected with my visitor's story than perhaps were any of the others, excepting the mysterious mid-earth illumination.

"Of that force we are in greater ignorance than of the others," he replied. "It affects bodies terrestrial and celestial, drawing a material substance, or pressing to the earth; also holds, we believe, the earth and all other bodies in position in the heavens, thus maintaining the equilibrium of the planets. Seemingly gravitation is not derived from, or sustained by, an external force, or supply reservoir, but is an intrinsic entity, a characteristic of matter that decreases in intensity at the rate of the square of the increasing distance, as bodies recede from each other, or from the surface of the earth. However, gravitation neither escapes by radiation from bodies nor needs to be replenished, so far as we know, from without. It may be compared to an elastic band, but there is no intermediate tangible substance to influence bodies that are affected by it, and it remains in undying tension, unlike all elastic material substances known, neither losing nor acquiring energy as time passes. Unlike cohesion, or chemical attraction, it exerts its influence upon bodies that are out of contact, and have no material connection, and this necessitates a purely fanciful explanation concerning the medium that conducts such influences, bringing into existence the illogical, hypothetical, fifth ether, made conspicuous by Aristotle."

"What of this ether?" I queried.

"It is a necessity in science, but intangible, undemonstrated, unknown, and wholly theoretical. It is accepted as an existing fluid by scientists, because human theory cannot conceive of a substance capable of, or explain how a substance can be capable of affecting a separate body unless there is an intermediate medium to convey force impressions. Hence to material substances Aristotle added (or at least made conspicuous) a speculative ether that, he assumed, pervades all space, and all material bodies as well, in order to account for the passage of heat and light to and from the sun, stars, and planets."

"Explain further," I requested.

"To conceive of such an entity, we must imagine a material that is more evanescent than any known gas, even in its most diffused condition. It must combine the solidity of the most perfect conductor of heat (exceeding any known body in this respect to an infinite degree), with the transparency of an absolute vacuum. It must neither create friction by contact with any substance, nor possess attraction for matter; must neither possess weight (and yet carry the force that produces weight), nor respond to the influence of any chemical agent, or exhibit itself to any optical instrument. It must be invisible, and yet carry the force that produces the sensation of sight. It must be of such a nature that it cannot, according to our philosophy, affect the corpuscles of earthly substances while permeating them without contact or friction, and yet, as a scientific incongruity, it must act so readily on physical bodies as to convey to the material eye the sensation of sight, and from the sun to creatures on distant planets it must carry the heat force, thus giving rise to the sensation of warmth. Through this medium, yet without sensible contact with it, worlds must move, and planetary systems revolve, cutting and piercing it in every direction, without loss of momentum. And yet, as I have said, this ether must be in such close contact as to convey to them the essence that warms the universe, lights the universe, and must supply the attractive bonds that hold the stellar worlds in position. A nothing in itself, so far as man's senses indicate, the ether of space must be denser than iridium, more mobile than any known liquid, and stronger than the finest steel."

"I cannot conceive of such an entity," I replied.

"No; neither can any man, for the theory is irrational, and cannot be supported by comparison with laws known to man, but the conception is nevertheless a primary necessity in scientific study. Can man, by any rational theory, combine a vacuum and a substance, and create a result that is neither material nor vacuity, neither something nor nothing, and yet an intensified all; being more attenuated than the most perfect of known vacuums, and a conductor better than the densest metal? This we do when we attempt to describe the scientists' all-pervading ether of space, and to account for its influence on matter. This hypothetical ether is, for want of a better theory of causes, as supreme in philosophy to-day as the alkahest of the talented old alchemist Van Helmont was in former times, a universal spirit that exists in conception; and yet does not exist in perception, and of which modern science knows as little as its speculative promulgator, Aristotle, did. We who pride ourselves on our exact science, smile at some of Aristotle's statements in other directions, for science has disproved them, and yet necessity forces us to accept this illogical ether speculation, which is, perhaps, the most unreasonable of all theories. Did not this Greek philosopher also gravely assert that the lion has but one vertebra in his neck; that the breath of man enters the heart; that the back of the head is empty, and that man has but eight ribs?"

"Aristotle must have been a careless observer," I said.

"Yes," he answered; "it would seem so, and science, to-day, bases its teachings concerning the passage of all forces from planet to planet, and sun to sun, on dicta such as I have cited, and no more reasonable in applied experiment."

"And I have been referred to you as a conscientious scientific teacher," I said; "why do you speak so facetiously?"

"I am well enough versed in what we call science, to have no fear of injuring the cause by telling the truth, and you asked a direct question. If your questions carry you farther in the direction of force studies, accept at once, that, of the intrinsic constitution of force itself, nothing is known. Heat, light, magnetism, electricity, galvanism (until recently known as imponderable bodies) are now considered as modifications of force; but, in my opinion, the time will come when they will be known as disturbances."

"Disturbances of what?"

"I do not know precisely; but of something that lies behind them all, perhaps creates them all, but yet is in essence unknown to men."

"Give me a clearer idea of your meaning."

"It seems impossible," he replied; "I cannot find words in which to express myself; I do not believe that forces, as we know them (imponderable bodies), are as modern physics defines them. I am tempted to say that, in my opinion, forces are disturbance expressions of a something with which we are not acquainted, and yet in which we are submerged and permeated. Aristotle's ether perhaps. It seems to me, that, behind all material substances, including forces, there is an unknown spirit, which, by certain influences, may be ruffled into the exhibition of an expression, which exhibition of temper we call a force. From this spirit these force expressions (wavelets or disturbances) arise, and yet they may become again quiescent, and again rest in its absorbing unity. The water from the outlet of a calm lake flows over a gentle decline in ripples, or quiet undulations, over the rapids in musical laughings, over a precipice in thunder tones, —always water, each a different phase, however, to become quiet in another lake (as ripples in this universe may awaken to our perception, to repose again), and still be water."

He hesitated.

"Go on," I said.

"So, I sometimes have dared to dream that gravitation may be the reservoir that conserves the energy for all mundane forces, and that what we call modifications of force are intermediate conditions, ripples, rapids, or cascades, in gravitation."

"Continue," I said, eagerly, as he hesitated.

He shook his head.

CHAPTER XXIV.

THE SOLILOQUY OF PROF. DANIEL VAUGHN. "GRAVITATION IS THE BEGINNING AND GRAVITATION IS THE END: ALL EARTHLY BODIES KNEEL TO GRAVITATION."

"Please continue, I am intensely interested; I wish that I could give you my reasons for the desire; I cannot do so, but I beg you to continue."

"I should add," continued Vaughn, ignoring my remarks, "that we have established rules to measure the force of gravitation, and have estimated the decrease of attraction as we leave the surfaces of the planets. We have made comparative estimates of the weight of the earth and planets, and have reason to believe that the force expression of gravitation attains a maximum at about one-sixth the distance toward the center of the earth, then decreases, until at the very center of our planet, matter has no weight. This, together with the rule I repeated a few moments ago, is about all we know, or think we know, of gravitation. Gravitation is the beginning and gravitation is the end; all earthly bodies kneel to gravitation. I cannot imagine a Beyond, and yet gravitation," mused the rapt philosopher, "may also be an expression of"—he hesitated again, forgetting me completely, and leaned his shaggy head upon his hands. I realized that his mind was lost in conjecture, and that he was absorbed in the mysteries of the scientific immensity. Would he speak again? I could not think of disturbing his reverie, and minutes passed in silence. Then he slowly, softly, reverently murmured: "Gravitation, Gravitation, thou art seemingly the one permanent, ever present earth-bound expression of Omnipotence. Heat and light come and go, as vapors of water condense into rain and dissolve into vapor to return again to the atmosphere. Electricity and magnetism appear and disappear; like summer storms they move in diversified channels, or even turn and fly from contact with some bodies, seemingly forbidden to appear, but thou, Gravitation, art omnipresent and omnipotent. Thou createst motion, and yet maintainest the equilibrium of all things mundane and celestial. An attempt to imagine a body destitute of thy potency, would be to bankrupt and deaden the material universe. O! Gravitation, art thou a voice out of the Beyond, and are other forces but echoes—tremulous reverberations that start into life to vibrate for a spell and die in the space caverns of the universe while thou continuest supreme?"

His bowed head and rounded shoulders stooped yet lower; he unconsciously brushed his shaggy locks with his hand, and seemed to confer with a familiar Being whom others could not see.

"A voice from without," he repeated; " from beyond our realm! Shall the subtle ears of future scientists catch yet lighter echoes? Will the brighter thoughts of more gifted men, under such furtherings as the future may bring, perchance commune with beings who people immensity, distance disappearing before thy ever-reaching spirit? For with thee, who holdest the universe together, space is not space, and there is no word expressing time. Art thou a voice that carriest the history of the past from the past unto and into the present, and for which there is no future, all conditions of time being as one to thee, thy self-covering all and connecting all together? Art thou, Gravitation, a voice? If so, there must be a something farther out in those fathomless caverns, beyond mind imaginings, from which thou comest, for how could nothingness have formulated itself into a voice? The suns and universe of suns about us, may be only vacant points in the depths of an all-pervading entity in which even thyself dost exist as a momentary echo, linked to substances ponderous, destined to fade away in the interstellar expanse outside, where disturbances disappear, and matter and gravitation together die; where all is pure, quiescent, peaceful and dark. Gravitation, Gravitation, imperishable Gravitation; thou seemingly art the ever-pervading, unalterable, but yet moving spirit of a cosmos of solemn mysteries. Art thou now, in unperceived force expressions, speaking to dumb humanity of other universes; of suns and vortices of suns; bringing tidings from the solar planets, or even infinitely distant star mists, the silent unresolved nebulae, and spreading before earth-bound mortal minds, each instant, fresh tidings from without, that, in ignorance, we cannot read? May not beings, perhaps like ourselves but higher in the scale of intelligence, those who people some of the planets about us, even now beckon and try to converse with us through thy subtle, ever-present self? And may not their efforts at communication fail because of our ignorance of a language they can read? Are not light and heat, electricity and magnetism plodding, vacillating agents compared with thy steady existence, and is it even further possible?"—

His voice had gradually lowered, and now it became inaudible; he was oblivious to my presence, and had gone forth from his own self; he was lost in matters celestial, and abstractedly continued unintelligibly to mutter to himself as, brushing his hair from his forehead, he picked up his well-worn felt hat, and placed it awkwardly on his shaggy head, and then shuffled away without bidding me farewell. The bent form, prematurely shattered by privation; uncouth, unkempt, typical of suffering and neglect, impressed me with the fact that in him man's life essence, the immortal mind, had forgotten the material part of man. The physical half of man, even of his own being, in Daniel Vaughn's estimation, was an encumbrance unworthy of serious attention, his spirit communed with the pure in nature, and to him science was a study of the great Beyond.

(Mr. Drury cannot claim to have recorded verbatim Prof. Vaughn's remarks, but has endeavored to give the substance. His language was faultless, his word selections beautiful, his soliloquy impressive beyond description. Perhaps Drury even misstated an idea, or more than one, evolved then by the great mind of that patient man. Prof. Daniel Vaughn was fitted for a scientific throne, a position of the highest honor; but, neglected by man, proud as a king, he bore uncomplainingly privations most bitter, and suffered alone until finally he died from starvation and neglect in the city of his adoption. Some persons are ready to cry, "Shame! Shame!" at wealthy Cincinnati; others assert that men could not give to Daniel Vaughn, and since the first edition of Etidorhpa appeared, the undersigned has learned of one vain attempt to serve the interests of this peculiar man. He would not beg, and knowing his capacities, if he could not procure a position in which to earn a living, he preferred to starve. The only bitterness of his nature, it is said, went out against those who, in his opinion, kept from him such employment as returns a livelihood to scientific men; for he well knew his intellect earned for him such a right in Cincinnati. will the spirit of that great man, talented Daniel Vaughn, bear malice against the people of the city in which none who knew him will deny that he perished from cold and privation? Commemorated is he not by a bust of bronze that distorts the facts in that the garments are not seedy and unkempt, the figure stooping, the cheek hollow and the eye pitifully expressive of an empty stomach? That bust modestly rests in the public library he loved so well, in which he suffered so uncomplainingly, and starved so patiently. J. U. L.)

I embraced the first opportunity that presented itself to read the works that Prof. Vaughn suggested, and sought him more than once to question further. However, he would not commit himself in regard to the possible existence of other forces than those with which we are acquainted, and when I interrogated him as to possibilities in the study of obscure force expressions, he declined to express an opinion concerning the subject. Indeed, I fancied that he believed it probable, or at least not impossible, that a closer acquaintance with conditions of matter and energy might be the heirloom of future scientific students. At last I gave up the subject, convinced that all the information I was able to obtain from other persons whom I questioned, and whose answers were prompt and positive, was evolved largely from ignorance and self-conceit, and such information was insufficient to satisfy my understanding, or to command my attention. After hearing Vaughn, all other voices sounded empty.

I therefore applied myself to my daily tasks, and awaited the promised return of the interesting, though inscrutable being whose subterranean so journeying was possibly fraught with so much potential value to science and to man.

SOLILOQUY OF PROF. DANIEL VAUGHN.
"GRAVITATION IS THE BEGINNING, AND GRAVITATION IS THE END; ALL EARTHLY BODIES KNEEL TO GRAVITATION."

THE UNBIDDEN GUEST RETURNS TO READ HIS MANUSCRIPT. — CONTINUING HIS NARRATIVE.

CHAPTER XXV.

THE MOTHER OF A VOLCANO.
"YOU CAN NOT DISPROVE, AND YOU DARE NOT ADMIT."

A year from the evening of the departure of the old man, found me in my room, expecting his presence; and I was not surprised when he opened the door, and seated himself in his accustomed chair.

"Are you ready to challenge my statements?" he said, taking up the subject as though our conversation had not been interrupted.

"No."

"Do you accept my history?"

"No."

"You cannot disprove, and you dare not admit. Is not that your predicament?" he asked. "You have failed in every endeavor to discredit the truth, and your would-be scientists, much as they would like to do so, cannot serve you. Now we will continue the narrative, and I shall await your next attempt to cast a shadow over the facts."

Then with his usual pleasant smile, he read from his manuscript a continuation of the intra-earth journey as follows:

"Be seated," said my eyeless guide, "and I will explain some facts that may prove of interest in connection with the nature of the superficial crust of the earth. This crystal liquid spreading before us is a placid sheet of water, and is the feeder of the volcano, Mount Epomeo."

"Can that be a surface of water?" I interrogated. " I find it hard to realize that water can be so immovable. I supposed the substance before us to be a rigid material, like glass, perhaps."

"There is no wind to ruffle this aqueous surface, —why should it not be quiescent? This is the only perfectly smooth sheet of water that you have ever seen. It is in absolute rest, and thus appears a rigid level plane."

"Grant that your explanation is correct," I said, "yet I cannot understand how a quiet lake of water can give rise to a convulsion such as the eruption of a volcano."

"Not only is this possible," he responded, "but water usually causes the exhibition of phenomena known as volcanic action. The Island of Ischia, in which the volcanic crater Epomeo is situated, is connected by a tortuous crevice with the peaceful pool by which we now stand, and at periods, separated by great intervals of time, the lake is partly emptied by a simple natural process, and a part of its water is expelled above the earth's surface in the form of superheated steam, which escapes through that distant crater."

"But I see no evidence of heat or even motion of any kind."

"Not here," he replied; "in this place there is none. The energy is developed thousands of miles away, but since the phenomena of volcanic action are to be partially explained to you at a future clay, I will leave that matter for the present. We shall cross this lake."

I observed as we walked along its edge that the shore of the lake was precipitous in places, again formed a gradually descending beach, and the dead silence of the space about us, in connection with the death-like stillness of that rigid mass of water and its surroundings, became increasingly impressive and awe-inspiring. Never before had I seen such a perfectly quiet glass-like surface. Not a vibration or undulation appeared in any direction. The solidity of steel was exemplified in its steady, apparently inflexible contour, and yet the pure element was so transparent that the bottom of the pool was as clearly defined as the top of the cavern above me. The lights and shades of the familiar lakes of Western New York were wanting here, and it suddenly came to my mind that there were surface reflections, but no shadows, and musing on this extraordinary fact, I stood motionless on a jutting cliff absorbed in meditation, abstractedly gazing down into that transparent depth. Without sun or moon, without apparent source of light, and yet perfectly illuminated, the lofty caverns seemed cut by that aqueous plane into two sections, one above and one below a transparent, rigid surface line. The dividing line, or horizontal plane, appeared as much a surface of air as a surface of water, and the material above that plane seemed no more nor less a gas, or liquid, than that beneath it. If two limpid, transparent liquids, immiscible, but of different gravities, be poured into the same vessel, the line of demarcation will be as a brilliant mirror, such as I now beheld parting and yet uniting the surfaces of air and water.

Lost in contemplation, I unconsciously asked the mental question: "Where are the shadows?"

My guide replied:

"You have been accustomed to lakes on the surface of the earth; water that is illuminated from above; now you see by a light that is developed from within and below, as well as from above. There is no outside point of illumination, for the light of this cavern, as you know, is neither transmitted through an overlying atmosphere nor radiated from a luminous center. It is an inherent quality, and as objects above us and within the lake are illuminated alike from all sides, there can be no shadows."

Musingly, I said:

"That which has occurred before in this journey to the unknown country of which I have been advised, seemed mysterious; but each succeeding step discovers to me another novelty that is more mysterious, with unlooked-for phenomena that are more obscure."

"This phenomenon is not more of a mystery than is the fact that light radiates from the sun. Man cannot explain that, and I shall not now attempt to explain this. Both conditions are attributes of force, but with this distinction—the crude light and heat of the sun, such as men experience on the surface of the earth, is here refined and softened, and the characteristic glare and harshness of the light that is known to those who live on the earth's surface is absent here. The solar ray, after penetrating the earth's crust, is tempered and refined by agencies which man will yet investigate understandingly, but which he can not now comprehend."

"Am I destined to deal with these problems?"

"Only in part."

"Are still greater wonders before us?"

"If your courage is sufficient to carry you onward, you have yet to enter the portal of the expanse we approach."

"Lead on, my friend," I cried; "lead on to these undescribed scenes, the occult wonderland that"—

He interrupted me almost rudely, and in a serious manner said:

"Have you not learned that wonder is an exemplification of ignorance? The child wonders at a goblin story, the savage at a trinket, the man of science at an unexplained manifestation of a previously unperceived natural law; each wonder in ignorance, because of ignorance. Accept now that all you have seen from the day of your birth on the surface of the earth, to the present, and all that you will meet here are wonderful only because the finite mind of man is confused with fragments of evidence, that, from whatever direction we meet them, spring from an unreachable infinity. We will continue our journey."

Proceeding farther along the edge of the lake we came to a metallic boat. This my guide picked up as easily as though it were of paper, for be it remembered that gravitation had slackened its hold here. Placing it upon the water, he stepped into it, and as directed I seated myself near the stern, my face to the bow, my back to the shore. The guide, directly in front of me, gently and very slowly moved a small lever that rested on a projection before him, and I gazed intently upon him as we sat together in silence. At last I became impatient, and asked him if we would not soon begin our journey.

"We have been on our way since we have been seated," he answered.

I gazed behind with incredulity: the shore had disappeared, and the diverging wake of the ripples showed that we were rapidly skimming the water.

"This is marvelous," I said; "incomprehensible, for without sail or oar, wind or steam, we are fleeing over a lake that has no current."

"True, but not marvelous. Motion of matter is a result of disturbance of energy connected therewith. Is it not scientifically demonstrated, at least in theory, that if the motion of the spirit that causes the magnetic needle to assume its familiar position were really arrested in the substance of the needle, either the metal would fuse and vaporize or (if the forces did not appear in some other form such as heat, electricity, magnetism, or other force) the needle would be hurled onward with great speed?"

“WE CAME TO A METAL BOAT.”

CHAPTER XXVI.

MOTION FROM INHERENT ENERGY. "LEAD ME DEEPER INTO THIS EXPANDING STUDY."

"I partly comprehend that such would be the case," I said.

"If a series of knife blades on pivot ends be set in a frame, and turned edgewise to a rapid current of water, the swiftly moving stream flows through this sieve of metallic edges about as easily as if there were no obstructions. Slowly turn the blades so as to present their oblique sides to the current, and an immediate pressure is apparent upon the frame that holds them; turn the blades so as to shut up the space, and they will be torn from their sockets, or the entire frame will be shattered into pieces."

"I understand; go on."

"The ethereal current that generates the magnetic force passes through material bodies with inconceivable rapidity, and the molecules of a few substances only, present to it the least obstruction. Material molecules are edgewise in it, and meet no retardation in the subtle flood. This force is a disturbance of space energy that is rushing into the earth in one form, and out of it in another. But your mind is not yet in a condition to grasp the subject, for at best there is no method of explaining to men that which their experimental education has failed to prepare them to receive, and for which first absolutely new ideas, and next words with new meaning, must be formed. Now we, (by we I mean those with whom I am connected) have learned to disturb the molecules in matter so as to turn them partly, or entirely, across the path of this magnetic current, and thus interrupt the motion of this ever-present energy. We can retard its velocity without, however, producing either magnetism (as is the case in a bar of steel), electricity, or heat, but motion instead, and thus a portion of this retarded energy springs into its new existence as motion of my boat. It is force changed into movement of matter, for the molecules of the boat, as a mass, must move onward as the force disappears as a current. Perhaps you can accept now that instead of light, heat, electricity, magnetism, and gravitation being really modifications of force they are disturbances."

"Disturbances of what?"

"Disturbances of motion."

"Motion of what?"

"Motion of itself, pure and simple."

"I cannot comprehend, I cannot conceive of motion pure and simple."

"I will explain at a future time so that you can comprehend more clearly. Other lessons must come first, but never will you see the end. Truth is infinite."

Continuing, he said:

"Let me ask if there is anything marvelous in this statement. On the earth's surface men arrest the fitful wind; and by so doing divert the energy of its motion into movement of machinery; they induce it to turn mills and propel vessels. This motion of air is a disturbance, mass motion transmitted to the air by heat, heat in turn being a disturbance or interruption of pure motion. When men learn to interrupt this unperceived stream of energy so as to change directly into material motion the spirit that saturates tire universe, and that produces force expressions, as it is constantly rushing from earth into space, and from space back again, they will have at command wherever they may be an endless source of power, light, and heat; mass motion, light and heat being convertible. Motion lies behind heat, light, and electricity, and produces them, and so long as the earth revolves on its axis, and circles in its orbit, man needs no light and heat from such indirect sources as combustion. Men will, however, yet obtain motion of molecules (heat), and material mass motion as well, from earth motion, without the other dangerous intermediate force expressions now deemed necessary in their production."

"Do you wish me to understand that on all parts of the earth's surface there is a continual expenditure of energy, an ever-ready current, that is really distinct from the light and heat of the sun, and also that the imponderable bodies that we call heat, light, electricity, and magnetism are not substances at all?"

"Yes," he replied.

"And that this imperceptible something—fluid I will say, for want of a better term—now invisible and unknown to man, is as a medium in which the earth, submerged, floats as a speck of dust in a flood of space?"

"Certainly," he replied.

"Am I to infer from your remarks that, in the course of time, man will be able to economize this force, and adapt it to his wants?"

"Yes."

"Go on with your exposition, I again beg of you; lead me deeper into this expanding study."

"There is but little more that you can comprehend now, as I have said," he answered. "All materials known to man are of coarse texture, and the minds of men are not yet in a condition to comprehend finer exhibitions of force, or of motion modifications. Pure energy, in all its modifications, is absolutely unknown to man. What men call heat, gravitation, light, electricity, and magnetism are the grosser attributes attending alterations in an unknown, attenuated, highly developed force producer. They are results, not causes. The real force, an unreached energy, is now flooding all space, pervading all materials. Everywhere there exists an infinite sea of motion absolute. Since this primeval entity cannot now affect matter, as matter is known to man, man's sense can only be influenced by secondary attributes of this energy. Unconscious of its all-pervading presence, however, man is working towards the power that will someday, upon the development of latent senses, open to him this new world. Then at last he will move without muscular exertion, or the use of heat as an agent of motion, and will, as I am now doing, bridle the motion of space. Wherever he may be situated, there will then be warmth to any degree that he wishes, for he will be able to temper the seasons, and mass motion illimitable, also, for this energy, I reiterate, is omnipresent. However, as you will know more of this before long, we will pass the subject for the present."

My guide slowly moved the lever. I sat in deep reflection, beginning to comprehend somewhat of his reasoning, and yet my mind was more than clouded. The several ambiguous repetitions he had made since our journey commenced, each time suggesting the same idea, clothing it in different forms of expression, impressed me vaguely with the conception of a certain something for which I was gradually being prepared, and that I might eventually be educated to grasp, but which he believed my mind was not yet ready to receive. I gathered from what he said that he could have given clearer explanations than he was now doing, and that he clothed his language intentionally in mysticism, and that, for some reason, he preferred to leave my mind in a condition of uncertainty. The velocity of the boat increased as he again and again cautiously touched the lever, and at last the responsive craft rose nearly out of the water, and skimmed like a bird over its surface. There was no object in that lake of pure crystal to govern me in calculating as to the rapidity of our motion, and I studied to evolve a method by which I could time our movements. With this object in view I tore a scrap from my clothing and tossed it into the air. It fell at my feet as if in a calm. There was no breeze. I picked the fragment up, in bewilderment, for I had expected it to fall behind us. Then it occurred to me, as by a flash, that notwithstanding our apparently rapid motion, there was an entire absence of atmospheric resistance. What could explain the paradox? I turned to my guide and again tossed the fragment of cloth upward, and again it settled at my feet. He smiled, and answered my silent inquiry.

"There is a protecting sheet before us, radiating, fan-like, from the bow of our boat as if a large pane of glass were resting on edge, thus shedding the force of the wind. This diaphragm catches the attenuated atmosphere and protects us from its friction."

"But I see no such protecting object," I answered.

"No; it is invisible. You cannot see the obstructing power, for it is really a gyrating section of force, and is colorless. That spray of metal on the brow of our boat is the developer of this protecting medium. Imagine a transverse section of an eddy of water on edge before us, and you can form a comparison. Throw the bit of garment as far as you can beyond the side of the boat."

I did so, and saw it flutter slowly away to a considerable distance parallel with our position in the boat as though in a perfect calm, and then it disappeared. It seemed to have been dissolved. I gazed at my guide in amazement.

"Try again," said he.

I tore another and a larger fragment from my coat sleeve. I fixed my eyes closely upon it, and cast it from me. The bit of garment fluttered listlessly away to the same distance, and then—vacancy. Wonders of wonderland, mysteries of the mysterious! What would be the end of this marvelous journey? Suspicion again possessed me, and distrust arose. Could not my self-existence be blotted out in like manner? I thought again of my New York home, and the recollection of upper earth, and those broken family ties brought to my heart a flood of bitter emotions. I inwardly cursed the writer of that alchemistic letter, and cursed myself for heeding the contents. The tears gushed from my eyes and trickled through my fingers as I covered my face with my hands and groaned aloud. Then, with a gentle touch, my guide's hand rested on my shoulder.

"Calm yourself," he said; "this phenomenon is a natural sequence to a deeper study of nature than man has reached. It is simply the result of an exhibition of rapid motion. You are upon a great underground lake, that, on a shelf of earth substance one hundred and fifty miles below the earth's surface, covers an area of many thousand square miles, and which has an average depth of five miles. We are now crossing it diagonally at a rapid rate by the aid of the force that man will yet use in a perfectly natural manner on the rough upper ocean and bleak lands of the earth's coarse surface. The fragments of cloth disappeared from sight when thrown beyond the influence of our protecting diaphragm, because when they struck the outer motionless atmosphere they were instantly left behind; the eye could

"THE BIT OF GARMENT FLUTTERED LISTLESSLY AWAY TO THE SAME DISTANCE, AND THEN—VACANCY."

not catch their sudden change in motion. A period of time is necessary to convey from eye to mind the sensation of sight. The bullet shot from a gun is invisible by reason of the fact that the eye cannot discern the momentary interruption to the light. A cannon ball will compass the field of vision of the eye, moving across it without making itself known, and yet the fact does not excite surprise. We are traveling so fast that small, stationary objects outside our track are invisible."

Then in a kind, pathetic tone of voice, he said:

"An important lesson you should learn, I have mentioned it before. Whatever seems to be mysterious, or marvelous, is only so because of the lack of knowledge of associated natural phenomena and connected conditions. All that you have experienced, all that you have yet to meet in your future journey, is as I have endeavored to teach you, in exact accordance with the laws that govern the universe, of which the earth constitutes so small a portion that, were the conditions favorable, it could be blotted from its present existence as quickly as that bit of garment disappeared, and with as little disturbance of the mechanism of the moving universe."

I leaned over, resting my face upon my elbow; my thoughts were immethodically wandering in the midst of multiplying perplexities; I closed my eyes as a weary child, and slept.

CHAPTER XXVII.

SLEEP, DREAMS, NIGHTMARE.
"STRANGLE THE LIFE FROM MY BODY."

I KNOW not how long I sat wrapped in slumber. Even if my body had not been wearing away as formerly, my mind had become excessively wearied. I had existed in a state of abnormal mental intoxication far beyond the period of accustomed wakefulness, and had taxed my mental organization beyond endurance. In the midst of events of the most startling description, I had abruptly passed into what was at its commencement the sweetest sleep of my recollection, but which came to a horrible termination.

In my dream I was transported once more to my native land, and roamed in freedom throughout the streets of my lost home. I lived over again my early life in Virginia, and I seemed to have lost all recollection of the weird journey which I had lately taken. My subsequent connection with the brother. hood of alchemists, and the unfortunate letter that led to my present condition, were forgotten. There came no thought suggestive of the train of events that are here chronicled, and as a child I tasted again the pleasures of innocence, the joys of boyhood.

Then my dream of childhood vanished, and the scenes of later days spread themselves before me. I saw, after a time, the scenes of my later life, as though I viewed them from a distance, and was impressed with the idea that they were not real, but only the fragments of a dream. I shuddered in my childish dreamland, and trembled as a child would at confronting events of the real life that I had passed through on earth, and that gradually assuming the shape of man approached and stood before me, a hideous specter seemingly ready to absorb me. The peaceful child in which I existed shrunk back, and recoiled from the approaching living man.

"Away, away," I cried, "you shall not grasp me, I do not wish to become a man; this cannot, must not be the horrible end to a sweet existence."

Gradually the Man Life approached, seized and enveloped me, closing around me as a jelly fish surrounds its living victim, while the horrors of a nightmare came over my soul.

"Man's life is a fearful dream," I shouted, as I writhed in agony; "I am still a child, and will remain one; keep off! Life of man, away! let me live and die a child."

The Specter of Man's Life seized me more firmly as I struggled to escape, and holding me in its irresistible clutch absorbed my substance as a vampire might suck the blood of an infant, and while the childish dream disappeared in that hideous embrace, the miserable man awoke.

I found myself on land. The guide, seated at my side, remarked:

"You have slept."

"I have lived again," I said in bitterness.

"You have not lived at all as yet," he replied; "life is a dream, usually it is an unsatisfied nightmare."

"Then let me dream again as at the beginning of this slumber," I said; "and while I dream as a child, do you strangle the life from my body, — spare me the nightmare, I would not live to reach the Life of Man."

"This is sarcasm," he replied; "you are as changeable as the winds of the earth's surface. Now as you are about to approach a part of our journey where fortitude is necessary, behold, you waver as a little child might. Nerve yourself; the trials of the present require a steady mind, let the future care for itself; you cannot recall the past."

I became attentive again; the depressing effects of that repulsive dream rapidly lifted, and wasted away, as I realized that I was a man, and was destined to see more than can be seen in the future of other mortals. This elevation of my spirit was evidently understood by my guide. He turned to the lake, and pointing to its quiet bosom, remarked:

"For five hours we have journeyed over this sheet of water at the average rate of nine hundred miles an hour. At the time you threw the fragments of cloth overboard, we were traveling at a speed of not less than twenty miles per minute. You remember that some hours ago you criticized my assertion when I said that we would soon be near the axis of the earth beneath the North Pole, and now we are beyond that point, and are about six thousand miles from where we stood at that time."

"You must have your way," I replied; "I cannot disprove your assertion, but were it not that I have passed through so many marvelous experiences since first we met, I would question the reliability of your information."

My guide continued:

"The surface of this lake lies as a mirror beneath both the ocean and the land. The force effect that preserves the configuration of the ocean preserves the form of this also, but influences it to a less extent, and the two surfaces lie nearly parallel with each other, this one being one hundred and fifty miles beneath the surface of the earth. The shell of the earth above us is honeycombed by caverns in some places, in others it is compact, and yet, in most places, is impervious to water. At the farther extremity of the lake, a stratum of porous material extends through the space intervening between the bottom of the ocean and this lake. By capillary attraction, assisted by gravitation, part of the water of the ocean is being transferred through this stratum to the underground cavity. The lake is slowly rising."

At this remark I interrupted him: "You say the water in the ocean is being slowly transferred down to this underground lake less by gravity than by capillarity."

"Yes."

"I believe that I have reason to question that statement, if you do not include the salt," I replied.

"Pray state your objections."

I answered: "Whether a tube be long or short, if it penetrates the bottom of a vessel of brine, and extend downward, the brine will flow into and out of it by reason of its weight."

"You mistake," he asserted; "the attraction of the sides of the capillary tube, if the tube is long enough, will eventually separate the water from the salt, and at length a downward flow of water only will result."

I again expressed my incredulity.

"More than this, by perfectly natural laws the water that is freed from the tubes might again force itself upward perfectly fresh, to the surface of the earth—yes, under proper conditions, above the surface of the ocean."

"Do you take me for a fool?" I said. "Is it not self-evident that a fountain cannot rise above its source?"

"It often does," he answered.

"You trifle with me," I said, acrimoniously.

"No," he replied; "I am telling you the truth. Have you never heard of what men call artesian wells?"

"Yes, and" (here I attempted in turn to become sarcastic) "have you never learned that they are caused by water flowing into crevices in uplands where layers of stone or of clay strata separated by sand or gravel slant upward. The water conducted thence by these channels afterwards springs up in the valleys to which it has been carried by means of the crevices in these strata, but it never rises above its source."

To my surprise he answered:

"This is another of man's scientific speculations, based on some facts, it is true, and now and then correct, but not invariably. The water of an artesian well on an elevated plane may flow into the earth from a creek, pond, or river, that is lower than the mouth of the well it feeds, and still it may spout into the air from either a near or distant elevation that is higher than its source."

"I cannot admit the truth of this," I said; "I am willing to listen to reason, but such statements as these seem altogether absurd."

"As you please," he replied; "we will continue our journey."

INTERLUDE. — THE STORY INTERRUPTED.

CHAPTER XXVIII.

A CHALLENGE. — MY UNBIDDEN GUEST ACCEPTS IT.

THE white-haired reader, in whom I had now become deeply interested, no longer an unwelcome stranger, suspended his reading, laid down his manuscript, and looking me in the face, asked:

"Are you a believer?"

"No," I promptly answered.

"What part of the narrative do you question?"

"All of it."

"Have you not already investigated some of the statements I previously made?" he queried.

"Yes," I said; "but you had not then given utterance to. such preposterous expressions."

"Is not the truth, the truth?" he answered.

"You ask me to believe impossibilities," I replied. "Name one."

"You yourself admit," I said warmly, "that you were incredulous, and shook your head when your guide asserted that the bottom of the ocean might be as porous as a sieve, and still hold water. A fountain cannot rise above its source."

"It often does, however," he replied.

"I do not believe you," I said boldly. "And, furthermore, I assert that you might as reasonably ask me to believe that I can see my own brain, as to accept your fiction regarding the production of light, miles below the surface of the earth."

"I can make your brain visible to you, and if you dare to accompany me, I will carry you beneath the surface of the earth and prove my other statement," he said. "Come!" He arose and grasped my arm.

I hesitated.

"You confess that you fear the journey."

I made no reply.

"Well, since you fear that method, I am ready to convince you of the facts by any rational course you may select, and if you wish to stake your entire argument on the general statement that a stream of water cannot rise above its head, I will accept the challenge; but I insist that you do not divulge the nature of the experiment until, as you are directed, you make public my story."

"Of course, a fluid can be pumped up," I sarcastically observed. "However, I promise the secrecy you ask."

"I am speaking seriously," he said, "and I have accepted your challenge; your own eyes shall view the facts, your own hands prepare the conditions necessary. Procure a few pints of sand, and a few pounds of salt; to-morrow evening I will be ready to make the experiment."

"Agreed; if you will induce a stream of water to run up hill, a fountain to rise above its head, I will believe any statement you may henceforth make."

"Be ready, then," he replied, "and procure the materials named." So saying he picked up his hat and abruptly departed.

These substances I purchased the next day, procuring the silver sand from Gordon's pharmacy, corner of Eighth and Western Row, and promptly at the specified time we met in my room.

He came, provided with a cylindrical glass jar about eighteen inches high .and two inches in diameter (such as I have since learned is called a hydrometer jar), and a long, slender drawn glass tube, the internal diameter of which was about one-sixteenth of an inch.

"You have deceived me," I said; "I know well enough that capillary attraction will draw a liquid above its surface. You demonstrated that quite recently to my entire satisfaction."

"True, and yet not true of this experiment," he said. "I propose to force water through and out of this tube; capillary attraction will not expel a liquid from a tube if its mouth be above the surface of the supply."

He dipped the tip of a capillary tube into a tumbler of water; the water rose inside the tube about an inch above the surface of the water in the tumbler.

"Capillary attraction can do no more," he said. "Break the tube one-eighth of an inch above the water (far below the present capillary surface), and it will not overflow. The exit of the tube must be lower than the surface of the liquid if circulation ensues."

He broke off a fragment, and the result was as predicted.

Then he poured water into the glass jar to the depth of about six inches, and selecting a piece of very thin muslin, about an inch square, turned it over the end of the glass tube, tied it in position, and dropped that end of the tube into the cylinder.

"The muslin simply prevents the tube from filling with sand," he explained. Then he poured sand into the cylinder until it reached the surface of the water.

"Your apparatus is simple enough," I remarked, I am afraid with some sarcasm.

"Nature works with exceeding simplicity," he replied; "there is no complex apparatus in her laboratory, and I copy after nature."

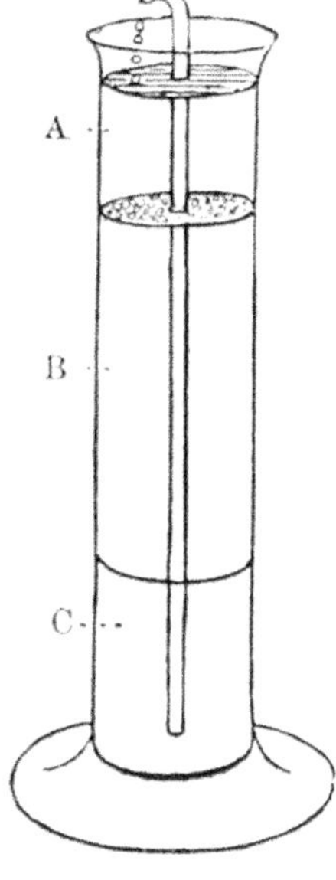

FIG. 23.
A, brine.
B, sand and brine mixed.
C, sand and water.

Then he dissolved the salt in a portion of water that he drew from the hydrant into my wash bowl, making a strong brine, and stirred sand into the brine to make a thick mush. This mixture of sand and brine he then poured into the cylinder, filling it nearly to the top. (See, B. The sand settling soon left a layer of brine above it, as shown by A.) I had previously noticed that the upper end of the glass tube was curved, and my surprise can be imagined when I saw that at once water began to flow through the tube, dropping quite rapidly into the cylinder. The lower end of the curve of the glass tube was fully half an inch above the surface of the liquid in the cylinder.

I here present a figure of the apparatus. (Figure 23)

The strange man, or man image, I do not know which, sat before me, and in silence we watched the steady flow of water, water rising above its surface and flowing into the reservoir from which it was being continually derived.

"Do you give up?" he asked.

"Let me think," I said.

"As you please," he replied.

"How long will this continue?" I inquired.

"Until strong salt water flows from the tube."

Then the old man continued:

"I would suggest that after I depart you repeat these experiments. The observations of those interested in science must be repeated time and again by separate individuals.

It is not sufficient that one person should observe a phenomenon;

repeated experiments are necessary in order to overcome error of manipulation, and to convince others of their correctness. Not only yourself, but many others, after this manuscript appears, should go through with similar investigations, varied in detail as mind expansion may suggest. This experiment is but the germ of a thought which will be enlarged upon by many minds under other conditions. An event meteorological may occur in the experience of one observer, and never repeat itself. This is possible. The results of such experiments as you are observing, however, must be followed by similar results in the hands of others, and in behalf of science it is necessary that others should be able to verify your experience. In the time to come it will be necessary to support your statements in order to demonstrate that your perceptive faculties are now in a normal condition. Are you sure that your conceptions of these results are justified by normal perception? May you not be in an exalted state of mind that hinders clear perception, and compels you to imagine and accept as fact that which does not exist? Do you see what you think you see? After I am gone, and the influences that my person and mind exert on your own mind have been removed, will these results, as shown by my experiments, follow similar experimental conditions? In the years that are to pass before this paper is to be made public, it will be your duty to verify your present sense faculty. This you must do as opportunities present, and with different devices, so that no question may arise as to what will follow when others repeat our experiments. Tomorrow evening I will call again, but remember, you must not tell others of this experiment, nor show the devices to them."

"I have promised," I answered.

He gathered his manuscript and departed, and I sat in meditation watching the mysterious fountain.

As he had predicted, finally, after a long time, the flow slackened, and by morning, when I arose from my bed, the water had ceased to drip, and then I found it salty to the taste.

The next evening, he appeared as usual, and prepared to resume his reading, making no mention of the previous test of my faith. I interrupted him, however, by saying that I had observed that the sand had settled in the cylinder, and that in my opinion his experiment was not true to appearances, but was a deception, since the sand by its greater weight displaced the water, which escaped through the tube, where there was least resistance.

"Ah," he said, "and so you refuse to believe your own eyesight, and are contriving to escape the deserved penalty; I will, however, acquiesce in your outspoken desire for further light, and repeat the experiment without using sand. But I tell you that mother earth, in the phenomena known as artesian wells, uses sand and clay, pools of mineral waters of different gravities, and running streams. The waters beneath the earth are under pressure, induced by such natural causes as I have presented you in miniature, the chief difference being that the supplies of both salt and fresh water are inexhaustible, and by natural combinations similar to what you have seen; the streams within the earth, if a pipe be thrust into them, may rise continuously, eternally, from a reservoir higher than the head. In addition, there are pressures of gases, and solutions of many salts, other than chloride of soda, that tend to favor the phenomenon.

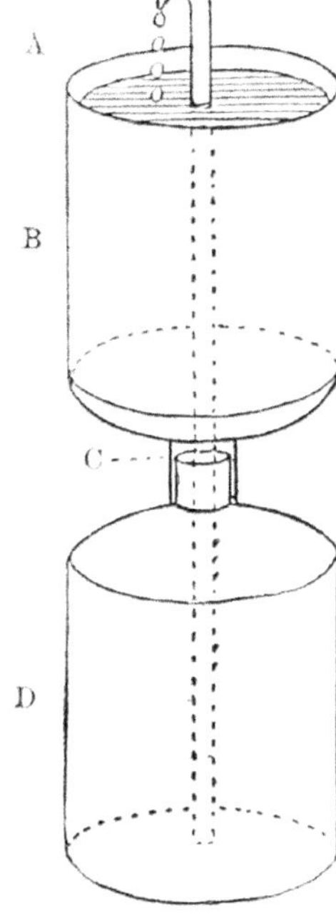

FIG. 24.
A, surface of brine.
B, upper can filled with brine.
C, necks of cans telescoped.
D, lower can full of water.

You are unduly incredulous, and you ask of me more than your right after staking your faith on an experiment of your own selection. You demand more of me even than nature often accomplishes in earth structure; but to-morrow night I will show you that this seemingly impossible feat is possible."

He then abruptly left the room. The following evening, he presented himself with a couple of one-gallon cans, one of them without a bottom I thought I could detect some impatience of manner as he filled the perfect can (D) with water from the hydrant, and having spread a strip of thin muslin over the mouth of the other can (B), pressed it firmly over the mouth (C) of the can of water, which it fitted tightly, thus connecting them together, the upper (bottomless) can being inverted. Then be made a narrow slit in the center of the muslin with his penknife, and through it thrust a glass tube like that of our former experiment. Next, he wrapped a string around the open top of the upper can, crossed it over the top, and tied the glass tube to the center of the cross string.

"Simply to hold this tube in position," he explained.

The remainder of the bag of salt left from the experiment of the preceding evening was then dissolved in water, and the brine poured into the upper can, filling it to the top. Then carefully thrusting the glass tube downward, he brought the tip of the curve to within about one-half inch of the surface of the brine, when immediately a rapid flow of liquid exhibited itself.

"It rises above its source without sand," he observed.

"I cannot deny the fact," I replied, "and furthermore I am determined that I shall not question any subsequent statement that you may make." We sat in silence for some time, and the water ran continuously through the tube. I was becoming alarmed, afraid of my occult guest, who accepted my self-selected challenges, and worked out his results so rapidly; he seemed to be more than human.

"I am a mortal, but a resident of a higher plane than you," he replied, divining my thoughts. "Is not this experiment a natural one?"

"Yes," I said.

"Did not Shakspeare write, 'There are more things in heaven and earth, Horatio, than are dreamt of in your philosophy'?"

"Yes," I said.

And my guest continued:

"He might have added, 'and always will be'."

"Scientific men will explain this phenomenon," I suggested.

"Yes, when they observe the facts," he replied, "it is very simple. They can now tell, as I have before remarked, how Columbus stood the egg on end; however, given the problem before Columbus expounded it, they would probably have wandered as far from the true solution as the mountain with its edgewise layers, of stone is from the disconnected artesian wells on, a distant sea coast where the underground fresh and salt water in overlying currents and layers clash together. The explanation, of course, is simple. The brine is of greater specific gravity than the pure water; the pressure of the heavier fluid forces the lighter up in the tube. This action continues until, as you will see by this experiment, in the gradual diffusion of brine and pure water the salt is disseminated equally throughout the vessels, and the specific gravity of the mixed liquid becomes the same throughout, when the flow will cease. However, in the earth, where supplies are inexhaustible, the fountain flows unceasingly."

CHAPTER XXIX.

BEWARE OF BIOLOGY, THE SCIENCE OF THE LIFE OF MAN.

(The old man relates a story as an object lesson.)

"But you have not lived up to the promise; you have evaded part of the bargain," I continued. "While you have certainly performed some curious experiments in physics which seem to be unique, yet, I am only an amateur in science, and your hydrostatic illustrations play be repetitions of investigations already recorded, that have escaped the attention of the scientific gentlemen to whom I have hitherto applied."

"Man's mind is a creature of doubts and questions," he observed. "Answer one query, and others rise. His inner self is never satisfied, and you are not to blame for wishing for a sign, as all self-conscious conditions of your former existence compel. Now that I have brushed aside the more prominent questionings, you insist upon those omitted, and appeal to me to"—he hesitated.

"To what?" I asked, curious to see if he had intuitively grasped my unspoken sentence.

"To exhibit to you your own brain," he replied.

"That is it exactly," I said; "you promised it, and you shall be held strictly to your bargain. You agreed to show me my own brain, and it seems evident that you have purposely evaded the promise."

"That I have made the promise and deferred its completion cannot be denied, but not by reason of an inability to fulfill the contract. I will admit that I purposely deferred the exhibition, hoping on your own account that you would forget the hasty promise. You would better release me from the promise; you do not know what you ask."

"I believe that I ask more than you can perform," I answered, "and that you know it."

(The reader is invited to skip this chapter of horrors.—J. U. L.)

"Let me give you a history," he said, "and then perhaps you will relent. Listen. A man once became involved in the study of anatomy. It led him to destruction. He commenced the study in order to learn a profession; he hoped to become a physician. Materia medica, pharmacy, chemistry, enticed him at first, but after a time presented no charms. He was a dull student in much that men usually consider essential to the practice of medicine. He was not fitted to be a physician. Gradually he became absorbed in two branches, physiology and anatomy. Within his mental self a latent something developed that neither himself nor his friends had suspected. This was an increasing desire for knowledge concerning the human body. The insatiable craving for anatomy grew upon him, and as it did so other sections of medicine were neglected. Gradually he lost sight of his professional object; he dropped chemistry, materia medica, pharmacy, and at last, morbidly lived only in the aforenamed two branches.

"His first visit to the dissecting room was disagreeable. The odor of putrid flesh, the sight of the mutilated bodies repulsed him. When first his hand, warm in life, touched the clammy flesh of a corpse, he shuddered. Then when his fingers came in contact with the viscera of a cadaver, that of a little child, he cried out in horror. The demonstrator of anatomy urged him on; he finally was induced to dissect part of the infant. The reflex action on his sensitive mind first stunned, and then warped his senses. His companions had to lead him from the room. 'Wash it off, wash it off,' he repeated, trying to throw his hand from his person. 'Horrid, horrible, unclean. The child is yet before me,' he insisted. Then he went into a fever and raved. 'Some mother will meet me on the street and curse me,' he cried. "That hand is red with the blood of my darling; it has desecrated the innocent dead, and mutilated that which is most precious to a mother." 'Take the hand away, wash it,' he shouted. 'The mother curses me; she demands retribution. Better that a man be dead than cursed by a mother whose child has been desecrated.' So the unfortunate being raved, dreaming all miner of horrid imaginings. But at last he recovered, a different man. He returned voluntarily to the dissecting-room, and wrapped himself in the uncouth work.

Nothing in connection with corpse-mutilation was now offensive or unclean. He threw aside his other studies, he became a slave possessed of one idea. He scarcely took time to dine respectably; indeed, he often ate his lunch in the dissecting-room. The blood of a child was again and again on his fingers; it mattered not, he did not take the trouble to wash it off. 'The liver of man is not more sacred than the liver of a hog,' he argued; the flesh of a man is the same as other forms of animal food. When a person dies the vital heat escapes, consciousness is dissipated, and the cold, rigid remains are only animal. Consciousness and life are all that is of man—one is force, the other matter; when man dies both perish and are dissipated.' His friends perceived, his fondness for dissection, and argued with him again, endeavoring now to overcome his infatuation; he repelled them. 'I learned in my vision,' he said, referring to his fever, that Pope was right in saying that the "proper study of mankind is man"; I care nothing for your priestly superstitions concerning the dead. These fables are the invention of designing churchmen who live on the superstitions of the ignorant. I am an infidel, and believe in no spirit intangible; that which can be seen, felt, and weighed is, all else is not. Life is simply a sensation. All beyond is chimerical, less than fantastic, believed in only by, dupes and weak-minded, credulous tools of knaves, or creatures of blind superstition.' He carried the finely articulated, bleached skull of a cadaver to his room, and placed it beside a marble statue that was a valued heirloom, the model of Venus of Milo. 'Both are lime compounds,' he cynically observed, 'neither is better than the other.' His friends protested. 'Your superstitious education is at fault,' he answered; you mentally clothe one of these objects in a quality it does not deserve, and the thought creates a pleasant emotion. The other, equally as pure, reminds you of the grave that you fear, and you shudder. These mental pulsations are artificial, both being either survivals of superstition, or creations of your own mind. The lime in the skull is now as inanimate as that of the statue; neither object is responsible for its form, neither is unclean. To me, the delicate configuration, the exact articulation, the perfect adaptation for the office it originally filled, makes each bone of this skull a thing of beauty, an object of admiration. As a whole, it gives me pleasure to think of this wonderful, exquisitely arranged piece of mechanism. The statue you admire is in every respect outrivaled by the skull, and I have placed the two together because it pleases me to demonstrate that man's most artistic creation is far inferior to material man. Throw aside your sentimental prejudices, and join with me in the admiration of this thing of beauty;' and he toyed with the skull as if it were a work of art. So, he argued, and arguing passed from bone to bone, and from organ to organ. He filled his room with abnormal fragments of the human body, and surrounded himself with jars of preserved anatomical specimens. His friends fled in disgust, and he smiled, glad to be alone with his ghastly subjects. He was infatuated in one of the alcoves of science."

The old man paused.

"Shall I proceed?" he asked.

"Yes," I said, but involuntarily moved my chair back, for I began again to be afraid of the speaker.

"At last this scientific man had mastered all that was known concerning physiology and anatomy. He learned by heart the wording of great volumes devoted to these subjects. The human frame became to him as an open book. He knew the articulation of every muscle, could name a bone from a mere fragment. The microscope ceased to be an object of interest, the secrets of pathology and physiology had been mastered. Then, unconsciously, he was infected by another tendency; a new thought was destined to dominate his brain. 'What is it that animates this frame? What lies inside to give it life?' He became enthused again: The dead body, to which I have given my time, is not the conscious part of man,' he said to himself; I must find this thing of life within; I have been only a butcher of the dead. My knowledge is superficial.'"

Again, the old man hesitated and looked at me inquiringly. "Shall I proceed?" he repeated.

I was possessed by horror, but yet fascinated, and answered determinedly: "Go on."

"Beware," he added, "beware of the Science of Life." Pleadingly he looked at me.

"Go on," I commanded.

He continued:

"With the cunning of a madman, this person of profound learning, led from the innocence of ignorance to the heartlessness of advanced biological science, secretly planned to seek the vital forces. 'I must begin with a child, for the life essence shows its first manifestations in children,' he reasoned. He moved to an unfrequented locality, discharged his servants, and notified his former friends that visitors were unwelcome. He had determined that no interruption to his work should occur. This course was unnecessary, however, for now he had neither friends nor visitors. He employed carpenters and artisans, and perfected a series of mechanical tables, beautiful examples of automatic mechanism. From the inner room of that house no cry could be heard by persons outside. . . .

[It will be seen, by referring to the epilogue, that Mr. Drury agreed to mutilate part of the book. This I have gladly done, excising the heart-rending passages that follow. To use the words of Prof. Venable, they do not "comport with the general delicacy of the book."—J. U. L.]

"Hold, old man, cease," I cried aghast; "I have had enough of this. You trifle with me, demon; I have not asked for nightmare stories, heart-curdling accounts of maniacal investigators, who madly pursue their revolting calling, and discredit the name of science."

"You asked to see your own brain," he replied.

"And have been given a terrible story instead," I retorted.

"So, men perverted, misconstruing the aim of science, answer the cry of humanity," he said. "One by one the cherished treasures of Christianity have been stolen from the faithful. What, to the mother, can replace the babe that has been lost?"

"The next world," I answered, "offers a comfort."

"Bah," he said; "does not another searcher in that same science field tell the mother that there is no personal hereafter, that she will never see her babe again? One man of science steals the body, another man of science takes away the soul, the third annihilates heaven; they go like pestilence and famine, hand in hand, subsisting on all that craving humanity considers sacred, and offering no tangible return beyond a materialistic present. This same science that seems to be doing so much for humanity will continue to elevate so-called material civilization until, as the yeast ferment is smothered in its own excretion, so will science-thought create conditions to blot itself from existence, and destroy the civilization it creates. Science is heartless, notwithstanding the personal purity of the majority of her helpless votaries. She is a thief, not of ordinary riches, but of treasures that cannot be replaced. Before science provings, the love of a mother perishes, the hope of immortality is annihilated. Beware of materialism, the end of the science of man. Beware of the beginning of biological inquiry, for he who commences, cannot foresee the termination. I say to you in candor, no man ever engaged in the part of science lore that questions the life essence, realizing the possible end of his investigations. The insidious servant becomes a tyrannical master; the housebreaker is innocent, the horse thief guiltless in comparison. Science thought begins in the brain of man; science provings end all things with the end of the material brain of man. Beware of your own brain."

"I have no fear," I replied, "that I will ever be led to disturb the creeds of the faithful, and I will not be diverted. I demand to see my brain."

"Your demand shall now be fulfilled; you have been warned of the return that may follow the commencement of this study; you force the issue; my responsibility ceases. No man of science realized the end when he began to investigate his throbbing brain, and the end of the fabric that science is weaving for man rests in the hidden future. The story I have related is a true one, as thousands of faithful men who unconsciously have been led into infidelity have experienced; and as the faithful followers of sacred teachings can also perceive, who recognize that their religion and the hope of heaven is slipping away beneath the steady inroad of the heartless materialistic investigator, who clothes himself in the garb of science."

Rising abruptly from his chair, he grasped my hand. "You shall see your brain, man; come."

"RISING ABRUPTLY, HE GRASPED MY HAND."

CHAPTER XXX.

LOOKING BACKWARD. — THE LIVING BRAIN.

The old man accompanied his word "come," as I have said, by rising from his chair, and then with a display of strength quite out of proportion to his age, he grasped my wrist and drew me toward the door. Realizing at once that he intended I should accompany him into the night, I protested, saying that I was quite unprepared.

"My hat, at least," I insisted, as he made no recognition of my first demur.

"Your hat is on your head," he replied.

This was true, although I am sure the hat had been previously hung on a rack in a distant part of the room, and I am equally certain that neither my companion nor myself had touched it. heaving me no time for reflection, he opened the door, and drew me through the hallway and into the gloom. As though perfectly familiar with the city, he guided me from my cozy home, on the retired side street in which I resided, eastwardly into the busy thoroughfare, Western Row. Our course led us down towards the river, past Ninth, Eighth, Seventh Streets. Now and then a pedestrian stopped to gaze in surprise at the unique spectacle, the old man leading the young one, but none made any attempt to molest us. We passed on in silence, out of the busy part of the thoroughfare and into the shady part of the city, into the darkness below Fifth Street. Here the residences were poorer, and tenement-houses and factories began to appear. We were now in a quarter of the city into which strangers seldom, if ever, penetrated after night, and in which I would not have cared to be found unprotected at any time after sunset, much less in such questionable company. I protested against the indiscretion; my leader made no reply, but drew me on past the flickering gas lights that now and then appeared at the intersection of Third, Pearl, Second, and Water Streets, until at last we stood, in darkness, on the bank of the Ohio River.

Strange, the ferry-boat at that time of night only made a trip every thirty minutes, and yet it was at the landing as though by appointment. Fear began to possess me, and as my thoughts recur to that evening, I cannot understand how it was that I allowed myself to be drawn without cry or resistance from my secure home to the Ohio River, in such companionship. I can account for the adventure only by the fact that I had deliberately challenged my companion to make the test he was fulfilling, and that an innate consciousness of pride and justice compelled me to permit him to employ his own methods. We crossed the river without speaking, and rapidly ascending the levee we took our course up Main Street into Covington. Still in the lead, my aged guide, without hesitation, went onward to the intersection of Main and Pike Streets; thence he turned to the right, and following the latter thoroughfare we passed the old tannery, that I recalled as a familiar landmark, and then started up the hill. Onward we strode, past a hotel named "Niemeyer's," and soon were in the open country on the Lexington Pike, treading through the mud, diagonally up the hill back of Covington. Then, at a sharp curve in the road where it rounded the point of the hill, we left the highway, and struck down the hillside into a ravine that bounded the lower side of the avenue. We had long since left the city lamps and sidewalks behind us, and now, when we left the roadway, were on the muddy pike at a considerable elevation upon the hillside and, looking backward, I beheld innumerable lights throughout the cities of Cincinnati, Covington, and the village of Newport, sparkling away in the distance behind and below us.

"Come," my companion said again, as I hesitated, repeating the only word he had uttered since telling his horrible story, "Come!"

Down the hill into the valley we plunged, and at last he opened the door of an isolated log cabin, which we entered. He lighted a candle that he drew from his pocket, and together we stood facing each other.

"Be seated," he said dryly.

And then I observed that the cold excuse for furniture in that desolate room consisted of a single rude, hand-made chair with corn-shuck bottom. However, I did not need a second invitation, but sank exhausted and disconsolate upon the welcome object.

My companion lost no time, but struck at once into the subject that concerned us, arguing as follows:

"One of the troubles with humanity is that of changing a thought from the old to a new channel; to grasp at one effort an entirely new idea is an impossibility. Men follow men in trains of thought expression, as in bodily form generations of men follow generations. A child born with three legs is a freak of nature, a monstrosity, yet it sometimes appears. A man, possessed of a new idea is an anomaly, a something that may not be impossible, but which has never appeared. It is almost. as difficult to conceive of a new idea as it is to create out of nothing a new material or an element. Neither thoughts nor things can be invented, both must be evolved out of a preexisting something which it necessarily resembles. Every advanced idea that appears in the brain of man is the result of a suggestion from without. Men have gone on and on ceaselessly, with their minds bent in one direction, ever looking outwardly, never inwardly. It has not occurred to them to question at all in the direction of backward sight. Mind has been enabled to read the impressions that are made in and on the substance of brain convolutions, but at the same time has been and is insensible to the existence of the convolutions themselves. It is as though we could read the letters of the manuscript that bears them without having conceived of a necessity for the existence of a printed surface, such as paper or anything outside the letters. Had anatomists never dissected a brain, the human family would to-day live in absolute ignorance of the nature of the substance that lies within the skull. Did you ever stop to think that the mind cannot now bring to the senses the configuration, or nature, of the substance in which mind exists? Its own house is unknown. This is in consequence of the fact that physical existence has always depended upon the study of external surroundings, and consequently the power of internal sight lies undeveloped. It has never been deemed necessary for man to attempt to view the internal construction of his body, and hence the sense of feeling only advises him of that which lies within his own self. This sense is abstract, not descriptive. Normal organs have no sensible existence. Thus, an abnormal condition of an organ creates the sensation of pain or pleasure, but discloses nothing concerning the appearance or construction of the organ affected. The perfect liver is as vacancy. The normal brain never throbs and aches. The quiescent arm presents no evidence to the mind concerning its shape, size, or color. Man cannot count his fingers unless some outside object touches them, or they press successively against each other, or he perceives them by sight. The brain of man, the seat of knowledge, in which mind centers, is not perceptible through the senses. Does it not seem irrational, however, to believe that mind itself is not aware, or could not be made cognizant, of the nature of its material surroundings?"

"I must confess that I have not given the subject a thought," I replied.

"As I predicted," he said. "It is a step toward a new idea, and simple as it seems, now that the subject has been suggested, you must agree that thousands of intelligent men have not been able to formulate the thought. The idea had never occurred to them. Even after our previous conversation concerning the possibility of showing you your own brain, you were powerless and could not conceive of the train of thought which I started, and along which I shall, now further direct your senses."

"The eye is so constituted that light produces an impression on a nervous film in the rear of that organ, this film is named the retina, the impression being carried backward therefrom through a magma of nerve fibers (the optic nerve) and reaching the brain; is recorded on that organ and thus affects the mind. Is it not rational to suppose it possible for this sequence to be reversed? In other words, if the order were reversed could not the same set of nerves carry an impression from behind to the retina, and picture thereon an image of the object which lies anterior thereto, to be again, by reflex action, carried back to the brain, thus bringing the brain substance itself to the view of the mind, and thus impress the senses? To recapitulate: If the nerve sensation, or force expression, should travel from the brain to the retina, instead of from an outward object, it will on the reverse of the retina produce the image of that which lies behind, and then if the optic nerve carries the image back to the brain, the mind will bring to the senses the appearance of the image depicted thereon."

"This is my first consideration of the subject," I replied.

"Exactly," he said; "you have passed through life looking at outside objects, and have been heedlessly ignorant of your own brain. You have never made an exclamation of surprise at the statement that you really see a star that exists in the depths of space millions of miles beyond our solar system, and yet you became incredulous and scornful when it was suggested that I could show you how you could see the configuration of your brain, an object with which the organ of sight is nearly in contact. How inconsistent."

"The chain of reasoning is certainly novel, and yet I cannot think of a mode by which I can reverse my method of sight and look backward," I now respectfully answered.

"It is very simple; all that is required is a counter excitation of the nerve, and we have with us to-night what any person who cares to consider the subject can employ at any time, and thus behold an outline of a part of his own brain. I will give you the lesson."

Placing himself before the sashless window of the cabin, which opening appeared as a black space pictured against the night, the sage took the candle in his right hand, holding it so that the flame was just below the tip of the nose, and about six inches from his face. Then facing the open window, he turned the pupils of his eyes upward, seeming to fix his gaze on the upper part of the open window space, and then he slowly moved the candle transversely, backward and forward, across, in front of his face, keeping it in such position that the flickering flame made a parallel line with his eyes, and as just remarked, about six inches from his face, and just below the tip of his nose. Speaking deliberately, he said:

"Now, were I you, this movement would produce a counter irritation of the retina; a rhythm of the optic nerve would follow, a reflex action of the brain accompanying, and now a figure of part of the brain that rests against the skull in the back of my head would be pictured on the retina. I would see it plainly, apparently pictured or thrown across the open space before me."

"Incredible!" I replied.

"Try for yourself," quietly said my guide.

Placing myself in the position designated, I repeated the maneuver, when slowly a shadowy something seemed to be evolved out of the blank space before me. It seemed to be as a gray veil, or like a corrugated sheet as thin as gauze, which as I gazed upon it and discovered its outline, became more apparent and real. Soon the convolutions assumed. a more decided form, the gray matter was visible, filled with venations, first gray and then red, and as I became familiar with the sight, suddenly the convolutions of a brain in all its exactness, with a network of red blood venations, burst into existence.

I beheld a brain, a brain, a living brain, my own brain, and as an uncanny sensation possessed me I shudderingly stopped the motion of the candle, and in an instant the shadowy figure disappeared.

"Have I won the wager?"

"Yes," I answered.

"Then," said my companion, "make no further investigations in this direction."

"But I wish to verify the experiment," I replied. "Although it is not a pleasant test, I cannot withstand the temptation to repeat it."

And again, I moved the candle backward and forward, when the figure of my brain sprung at once into existence.

"It is more vivid," I said; "I see it plainer, and more quickly than before."

"FACING THE OPEN WINDOW, HE TURNED THE PUPILS OF HIS EYES UPWARD."

"Beware of the science of man I repeat," he replied; "now, before you are deep in the toils, and cannot foresee the end, beware of the science of human biology. Remember the story recently related, that of the physician who was led to destruction by the alluring voice."

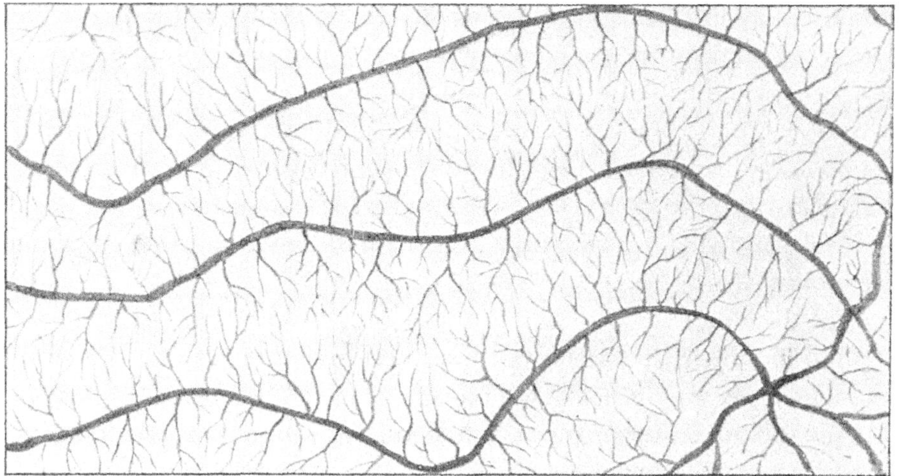

"A BRAIN, A LIVING BRAIN, MY OWN BRAIN."

(This experiment is not claimed as original. Gee Purkinje's Beitrage zur Kenntniss des Sehens in subjectiver Hinsicht (Prague, 1823 and 1825), whose conclusions to the effect that the shadow of the retina is seen, I-Am-The-Man ignores.—J. U. L.)

I made no reply, but stood with my face fixed, slowly moving the candle backward and forward, gazing intently into the depths of my own brain.

After a time, the old man removed the candle from my hand, and said: "Do you accept the fact? Have I demonstrated the truth of the assertion?"

"Yes," I replied; "but tell me further, now that you have excited my interest, have I seen and learned all that man can discover in this direction?"

"No; you have seen but a small portion of the brain convolutions, only those that lie directly back of the optic nerve. By systematic research, under proper conditions, every part of the living brain may become as plainly pictured as that which you have seen."

"And is that all that could be learned?" I asked.

"No," he continued. "Further development may enable men to picture the figures engraved on the convolutions, and at last to read the thoughts that are engraved within the brains of others, and thus through material investigation the observer will perceive the recorded thought of another person. An instrument capable of searching and illuminating the retina could be easily affixed to the eye of a criminal, after which, if the mind of the person operated upon were stimulated by the suggestion of an occurrence either remote or recent, the mind faculty would excite the brain, produce the record, and spread the circumstances as a picture before the observer. The brain would tell its own story, and the investigator could read the truth as recorded in the brain of the other man. A criminal subjected to such an examination could not tell an untruth or equivocate; his very brain would present itself to the observer."

"And you make this assertion, and then ask me to go no further into the subject?"

"Yes; decidedly yes."

"Tell me, then, could you not have performed this experiment in my room, or in the dark cellar of my house?"

"Anyone can repeat it with a candle in any room not otherwise lighted, by looking at a blackboard, a blank wall, or black space," he said.

I was indignant.

"Why have you treated me so inhumanly? Was there a necessity for this journey, these mysterious movements, this physical exertion? Look at the mud with which I am covered, and consider the return trip which yet lies before me, and which must prove even more exhausting?"

"Ah," he said, "you overdraw. The lesson has been easily acquired. Science is not an easy road to travel. Those who propose to profit thereby must work circuitously, soil their hands and person, meet discouragements, and must expect hardships, reverses, abuse, and discomfort. Do not complain, but thank me for giving you the lesson without other tribulations that might have accompanied it. Besides, there was another object in my journey, an object that I have quietly accomplished, and which you may never know. Come, we must return."

He extinguished the light of the candle, and we departed together, trudging back through the mud and the night.

Of that wearisome return trip, I have nothing to say beyond the fact that before reaching home my companion disappeared in the darkness of a side street, and that the Cathedral chimes were playing for three o'clock A. M., as I passed the corner of Eighth Street and Western Row.

The next evening my visitor appeared as usual, and realizing his complete victory, he made no reference to the occurrences of the previous night.

In his usual calm and deliberate manner, he produced the roll of manuscript saying benignantly, and in a gentle tone:

"Do you recollect where I left off reading?"

"You had reached that point in your narrative," I answered, "at which your guide had replaced the boat on the surface of the lake."

And the mysterious being resumed his reading.

THE MANUSCRIPT CONTINUED.

CHAPTER XXXI.

A LESSON ON VOLCANOES. — PRIMARY COLORS ARE CAPABLE OF FARTHER SUBDIVISION.

"Get into the boat," said my eyeless pilot, "and we will proceed to the farther edge of the lake, over the barrier of which at great intervals of time, the surface water flows, and induces the convulsion known as Mount Epomeo."

We accordingly embarked, and a gentle touch of the lever enabled us rapidly to skirt the shore of the underground sea. The soft, bright, pleasant earth-light continually enveloped us, and the absence of either excessive heat or cold, rendered existence delightful. The weird forms taken by the objects that successively presented themselves on the shore were a source of continual delight to my mind. The motion of our boat was constantly at the will of my guide. Now we would skim across a great bay, flashing from point to point; again, we wound slowly through tortuous channels and among partly submerged stones.

"What a blessing this mode of locomotion would be to humanity," I murmured.

"Humanity will yet attain it," he replied. "Step by step men have stumbled along towards the goal that the light of coining centuries is destined to illuminate. They have studied, and are still engaged in studying, the properties of grosser forces, such as heat and electricity, and they will be led by the thread they are following, to this and other achievements yet unthought of, but which lie back of those more conspicuous."

We finally reached a precipitous bluff, that sprung to my view as by magic, and which, with a glass-like surface, stretched upward to a height beyond the scope of my vision, rising straight from the surface of the lake. It was composed of a material seemingly black as jet, and yet when seen under varying spectacular conditions as we skirted its base it reflected, or emitted, most gorgeously the brilliant hues of the rainbow, and also other colors hitherto unknown to me.

"There is something unique in these shades; species of color appear that

I cannot identify; I seem to perceive colors utterly unlike any that I know as the result of deflected, or transmitted, sunlight rays, and they look unlike the combinations of primary colors with which I am familiar."

"Your observations are true; some of these colors are unknown on earth."

"But on the surface of the earth we have all possible combinations of the seven prismatic rays," I answered. "How can there be others here?"

"Because, first, your primary colors are capable of further subdivision.

"Second, other rays, invisible to men under usual conditions, also emanate from the sun, and under favorable circumstances may be brought to the sense of sight."

"Do you assert that the prism is capable of only partly analyzing the sunlight?"

"Yes; what reason have you to argue that, because a triangular bit of glass resolves a white ray into seven fractions that are, as men say, differently colored, you could not by proper methods subdivide each of these so-called primary shades into others? What reason have you to doubt that rays now invisible to man accompany those capable of impressing his senses, and might by proper methods become perceptible as new colors?"

"None," I answered; "only that I have no proof that such rays exist."

"But they do exist, and men will yet learn that the term 'primitive' ray, as applied to each of the seven colors of the rainbow, is incorrect. Each will yet be resolved, and as our faculties multiply and become more subtle, other colors will be developed, possessed of a delicacy and richness indescribable now, for as yet man cannot comprehend the possibilities of education beyond the limits of his present condition."

During this period of conversation, we skirted the richly colored bluff with a rapid motion, and at last shot beyond it, as with a flash, into seeming vacancy. I was sitting with my gaze directed toward the bluff, and when it instantly disappeared, I rubbed my eyes to convince myself of their truthfulness, and as I did so our boat came gradually to a stand on the edge of what appeared to be an unfathomable abyss. Beneath me on the side where had risen the bluff that disappeared so abruptly, as far as the eye could reach, was an absolute void. To our right, and before and behind us, stretched the surface of that great smooth lake on whose bosom we rested. To our left, our boat brushing its rim, a narrow ledge, a continuation of the black, glass-like material, reached only a foot above the water, and beyond this narrow brink the mass descended perpendicularly to seemingly infinite depths. Involuntarily I grasped the sides of the boat, and recoiled

"WE FINALLY REACHED A PRECIPITOUS BLUFF."

from the frightful chasm, over which I had been so suddenly suspended, and which exceeded anything of a similar description that I had ever seen. The immeasurable depth of the abyss, in connection with the apparently frail barrier that held the great lake in its bounds, caused me to shudder and shrink back, and my brain reeled in dizzy fright. An inexplicable attraction, however, notwithstanding my dread, held me spell-bound, and although I struggled to shut out that view, the endeavor failed. I seemed to be drawn by an irresistible power, and yet I shuddered at the awful majesty of that yawning gulf which threatened to end the world on which I then existed. Fascinated, entranced, I could not help gazing, I knew not how long, down, down into that fathomless, silent profundity. Composing myself, I turned a questioning glance on my guide.

He informed me that this hard, glass-like dam, confined the waters of the slowly rising lake that we were sailing over, and which finally would rise high enough to overflow the barrier.

"The cycle of the periodic overflow is measured by great intervals," he said; "centuries are required to raise the level of the lake a fraction of an inch, and thousands of years may elapse before its surface will again reach the top of the adamantine wall. Then, governed by the law that attracts a liquid to itself, and heaps the teaspoon with liquid, the water of the quiet lake piles upon this narrow wall, forming a ledge along its summit. Finally, the superimposed surface water gives way, and a skim of water pours over into the abyss."

He paused; I leaned over and meditated, for I had now accustomed myself to the situation.

"There is no bottom," I exclaimed.

"Upon the contrary," he answered, "the bottom is less than ten miles beneath us, and is a great funnel-shaped orifice, the neck of the funnel reaching first down and then upward from us diagonally toward the surface of the earth. Although the light by which we are enveloped is bright, yet it is deficient in penetrating power, and is not capable of giving the contour of objects even five miles away, hence the chasm seems bottomless, and the gulf measureless."

"Is it not natural to suppose that a mass of water like this great lake would overflow the barrier immediately, as soon as the surface reached the upper edge, for the pressure of the immense volume must be beyond calculation."

"THE WALL DESCENDED PERPENDICULARLY TO SEEMINGLY INFINITE DEPTHS."

"No, for it is height, not expanse, which, as hydrostatic engineers understand, governs the pressure of water. A liquid column, one foot in width, would press against the retaining dam with the force of a body of the same liquid, the same depth, one thousand miles in extent. Then the decrease of gravity here permits the molecular attraction of the water's molecules to exert itself more forcibly than would be the case on the surface of the earth, and this holds the liquid mass together more firmly."

"See," he observed, and dipping his finger into the water he held it before him with a drop of water attached thereto (Figure 27), the globule being of considerable size, and lengthened as though it consisted of some glutinous liquid.

FIG. 27.

"How can a thin stratum of water give rise to a volcanic eruption?" I next queried. "There seems to be no melted rock, no evidence of intense heat, either beneath or about us."

"I informed you some time ago that I would partially explain these facts. Know then, that the theories of man concerning volcanic eruptions, in connection with a molten interior of the earth, are such as are evolved in ignorance of even the subsurface of the globe. The earth's interior is to mankind a sealed chamber, and the wise men who elucidate the curious theories concerning natural phenomena occurring therein are forced to draw entirely upon their imagination. Few personae realize the paucity of data at the command of workers in science. Theories concerning the earth are formulated from so little real knowledge of that body, that our science may be said to be all theory, with scarcely a trace of actual evidence to support it. If a globe ten inches in diameter be covered with a sheet of paper, such as I hold in my hand, the thickness of that sheet will be greater in proportion to that of such a globe than the depth men have explored within the earth is compared with the thickness of the crust of the earth. The outer surface of a pencil line represents the surface of the earth; the inner surface of the line represents the depth of man's explorations; the highest mountain would be represented by a comma resting on the line. The geologist studies the substances that are thrust from the crater of an active volcano, and from this makes conjectures regarding the strata beneath, and the force that casts the excretions out. The results must with men, therefore, furnish evidence from which to explain the cause. It is as though an anatomist would form his idea of the anatomy of the liver by the secretion thrown out of that organ, or of the lung texture by the breath and sputum. In fact, volcanoes are of several descriptions, and usually are extremely superficial. This lake, the surface of which is but one hundred and fifty miles underground, is the mother of an exceptionally deep one. When the water pours over this ledge it strikes an element below us, the metallic base of salt, which lies in great masses in some portions of the earth's crust. Then an immediate chemical reaction ensues, the water is dissociated, intense heat results, part of the water combines with the metal, part is vaporized as steam, while part escapes as an inflammable gas. The sudden liberation of these gases causes an irregular pressure of vapor on the surface of the lake, the result being a throbbing and rebounding of the attenuated atmosphere above, which, in gigantic waves, like swelling tides, dashes great volumes of water over the ledge beside us, and into the depth below. This water in turn reacts on fresh portions of the metallic base, and the reflex action increases the vapor discharges, and as a consequence the chamber we are in becomes a gasholder, containing vapors of unequal gas pressures, and the resultant agitation of the lake from the turmoil continues, and the pulsations are repeated until the surface of the lake is lowered to such a degree as at last to prevent the water from overflowing the barrier. Finally, the lake quiets itself, the gases slowly disappear by earth absorption, and by escape from the volcanic exit, and for an unrecorded period of time thereafter the surface of the lake continues to rise slowly as it is doing now."

"But what has this phenomenon to do with the volcano?"

"It produces the eruption; the water that rushes down into the chasm, partly as steam, partly as gas, is forced onward and upward through a crevice that leads to the old crater of the presumed extinct but periodically active Mount Epomeo. These gases are intensely heated, and they move with fearful velocity. They tear off great masses of stone, which the resultant energy disturbances, pressure, gas, and friction, redden with heat. The mixture of gases from the decomposed water is in large amount, is burning and exploding, and in this fiery furnace amid such convulsions as have been described, the adjacent earth substance is fused, and even clay is melted, and carried on with the fiery blast. Finally, the current reaches the earth's surface through the funnel passage, the apex of which is a volcano—the blast described a volcanic eruption."

"One thing is still obscure in my mind," I said. "You assert that the reaction which follows the contact of the flowing water and metallic bases in the crevice below us liberates the explosive gases, and also volumes of vapor of water. These gases rush, you say, and produce a volcanic eruption in a distant part of the crust of the earth. I cannot understand why they do not rush backward as well, and produce another eruption in Kentucky. Surely the pressure of a gas in confinement is the same in all directions, is it not?"

"Yes," he replied, "but the conditions in the different directions are dissimilar. In the direction of the Kentucky cavern, the passage is tortuous, and often contracts to a narrow crevice. In one place near the cavern's mouth, as you will remember, we had to dive beneath the surface of a stream of water. That stratum of water as effectually closed the exit from the earth as the stopper prevents water escaping from a bottle. Between the point we now occupy and that water stopper, rest thousands of miles of quiescent air. The inertia of a thousand miles of air is great beyond your comprehension. To move that column of air by pushing against this end of it, and thus shoving it instantly out of the other end, would require greater force than would burst the one hundred and fifty miles of inelastic stone above us. Then, the friction of the sides is another thing that prevents its accomplishment. While a gradually applied pressure would in time overcome both the inertia of the air and the friction of the stone passages, it would take a supply of energy greater than you can imagine to start into motion the elastic mass that stands as solid and immovable as a sentinel of adamant, between the cavern you entered, and the spot we now occupy. Time and energy combined would be able to accomplish the result, but not under present conditions.

"In the other direction a broad open channel reaches directly to and connects with the volcanic shaft. Through this channel the air is in motion, moving towards the extinct crater, being supplied from another surface orifice. The gases liberated in the manner I have described, naturally follow the line of least resistance. They turn at once away from the inert mass of air that rests behind us, and move with increasing velocity towards the volcanic exit. Before the pressure that might be exerted towards the Kentucky cavern would have more than compressed the intervening column of air enough to raise the water of a well from its usual level to the surface of the earth, the velocity in the other direction would have augmented prodigiously, and with its increased rapidity a suction would follow more than sufficient to consume the increasingly abundant gases from behind."

"Volcanoes are therefore local, and the interior of the earth is not a molten mass as I have been taught;" I exclaimed.

He answered: "If men were far enough along in their thought journey (for the evolution of the mental side of man is a journey in the world of thought), they would avoid such theories as that which ascribes a molten interior to the earth. Volcanoes are superficial. They are as a rule, when in activity but little blisters or excoriations upon the surface of the earth, although their underground connections may be extensive. Some of them are in a continual fret with frequent eruptions, others, like the one under consideration, awaken only after great periods of time. The entire surface of this globe has been or will be subject to volcanic action. The phenomenon is one of the steps in the world-making, matter-leveling process. When the deposit of substances that I have indicated, and of which much of the earth's interior is composed, the bases of salt, potash, and lime and clay is exhausted, there will be no further volcanic action from this cause, and, in some places, this deposit has already disappeared, or is covered deeply by layers of earth that serve as a protection."

"Is water, then, the universal cause of volcanoes?"

"Water and air together cause most of them. The action of water and its vapor produces from metallic space dust, limestone, and clay soil, potash and soda salts. This perfectly rational and natural action must continue as long as there is water above, and free elementary bases in contact with the earth bubbles. Volcanoes, earthquakes, geysers, mud springs, and hot springs, are the natural result of that reaction. Mountains are thereby forming by upheavals from beneath, and the corresponding surface valleys are consequently filling up, either by the slow deposit of the matter from the saline water of hot springs, or by the sudden eruption of a new or presumably extinct volcano."

"What would happen if a crevice in the bottom of the ocean should conduct the waters of the ocean into a deposit of metallic bases?"

"That often occurs," was the reply; "a volcanic wave results, and a volcano may thus rise from the ocean's depths."

"Is there any danger to the earth itself? May it not be driven into fragments from such a convulsion?" I hesitatingly questioned.

"No; while the configuration of continents is continually being altered, each disturbance must be practically superficial, and of limited area."

"But," I persisted, "the rigid, solid earth may be blown to fragments; in such convulsions a result like that seems not impossible."

"You argue from an erroneous hypothesis. The earth is neither rigid nor solid."

"True," I answered. "If it were solid I could not be a hundred miles beneath its surface in conversation with another being; but there cannot be many such cavities as that which we are now traversing, and they cannot surely extend entirely through its mass; the great weight of the superincumbent material would crush together the strongest materials, if a globe as large as our earth were extensively honeycombed in this manner."

"Quite the contrary," he replied; "and here let me, for the first time, enlighten you as to the interior structure of the terrestrial globe. The earth-forming principle consists of an invisible sphere of energy that, spinning through space, supports the space dust which collects on it, as dust on a bubble. By gradual accumulation of substance on that sphere a hollow ball has resulted, on the outer surface of which you have hitherto dwelt. The crust of the earth is comparatively thin, not more than eight hundred miles in average thickness, and is held in position by the central sphere of energy that now exists at a distance about seven hundred miles beneath the ocean level. The force inherent to this sphere manifests itself upon the matter which it supports on both sides, rendering matter the lighter the nearer it lies to the center sphere. In other words, let me say to you: "The crust, or shell, which I have just described as being but about eight hundred miles in thickness, is firm and solid on both its convex and concave surface, but gradually loses in weight, whether we penetrate from the outer surface toward the center, or from any point of the inner surface towards the outside, until at the central sphere matter has no weight at all. Do you conceive my meaning?"

"Yes," I replied; "I understand you perfectly."

After a pause my pilot asked me abruptly:

"What do you most desire?"

The question caused my mind to revert instantly to my old home on the earth above me, and although I felt the hope of returning to it spring up in my heart, the force of habit caused me involuntarily to answer, "More light!"

"More light being your desire, you shall receive it."

Obedient to his touch, the bow of the boat turned from the gulf we had been considering towards the center of the lake; the responsive craft leaped forward, and in an instant the obsidian parapet disappeared behind us. On and over the trackless waste of glass-like water we sped, until the dead silence became painfully oppressive, and I asked:

"Whither are we bound?"

"Towards the east."

The well-timed answer raised my spirits; I thought again that in this man, despite his repulsive shape, I beheld a friend, a brother; suspicion vanished, and my courage rose. He touched the lever, and the craft, subject to his will, nearly rose from the water, and sped with amazing velocity, as was evident from the appearance of the luminous road behind us. So rapid was our flight that the wake of the boat seemed as if made of rigid parallel lines that disappeared in the distance, too quick for the eye to catch the tremor.

Continuing his conversation, my companion informed me that he had now directed the bark toward a point east of the spot where we struck the shore, after crossing the lake, in order that we might continue our journey downward, diagonally to the under surface of the earth crust.

"This recent digression from our journey proper," said he, "has been made to acquaint you with a subject, regarding which you have exhibited a curiosity, and about which you have heretofore been misinformed; now you understand more clearly part of the philosophy of volcanoes and earthquakes. You have yet much to learn in connection with allied phenomena, but this study of the crude exhibition of force-disturbed matter, the manipulation of which is familiar to man under the above names, is an introduction to the more wonderful study destined yet to be a part of your field, an investigation of quiescent matter, and pure motion."

"I cannot comprehend you," I replied, "as I stated once before when you referred to what you designated as pure motion."

CHAPTER XXXII.

MATTER IS RETARDED MOTION.

"It is possible—is it not? —for you to imagine a continuous volley of iron balls passing near you in one line, in a horizontal direction, with considerable velocity. Suppose that a pane of glass was to be gradually moved so that a corner of it would be struck by one of the balls; then the entire sheet of glass would be shivered by the concussion, even though the bullet struck but a single spot of glass, the point of contact covering only a small area. Imagine now that the velocity of the volley of bullets be increased a thousand-fold; then a plate of glass thrust into their track would be smoothly cut, as though with a file that would gnaw its way without producing a single radiating fracture. A person standing near the volley would now hear a deep purr or growling sound, caused by the friction between the bullets and the air. Increase gradually the rapidity of their motion, and this growl would become more acute, passing from a deep, low murmur, into one less grave, and as the velocity increased, the tone would become sharper, and at last piercingly shrill. Increase now the rapidity of the train of bullets again, and again the notes would decrease in turn, passing back again successively through the several keys that had preceded, and finally would reach the low growl which first struck the ear, and with a further increase of speed silence would ensue, silence evermore, regardless of increasing velocity. From these hundreds of miles in a second at which the volley is now passing, let the rapidity be augmented a thousand times, reaching in their flight into millions of miles each second, and to the eye, from the point where the sound disappeared, as the velocity increased, a dim redness would appear, a glow just perceptible, indicating to the sense of sight, by a continuous line, the track of the moving missiles. To all appearance, the line would be as uniform as an illuminated pencil mark, even though the several integral bullets of the trail might be separated one from another by miles of space. Let a pane of glass now be thrust across their track, and from the point of contact a shower of sparks would fly, and the edges of glass close to either side of the orifice would be shown, on withdrawing the glass, to have been fused. Conceive now that the velocity of the bullets be doubled and trebled, again and again, the line of red light becomes brighter, then brilliant, and finally as the velocity increases, at a certain point pure white results, and to man's sense the trail would now be a continuous something, as solid as a bar of metal if at a white heat, and (even if the bullets were a thousand miles apart) man could not bring proof of their separate existence to his senses. That portion of a pane of glass or other substance, even steel or adamant, which should cross its track now would simply melt away, the portion excised and carried out of that pathway neither showing itself as scintillations, nor as fragments of matter. The solid would instantly liquefy, and would spread itself as a thin film over the surface of each ball of that white, hot mass of fleeing metal, now to all essential conditions as uniform as a bar of iron. Madly increase the velocity to millions upon millions of miles per second, and the heat will disappear gradually as did the sound, while the bright light will pass backward successively through the primary shades of color that are now known to man, beginning with violet, and ending with red, and as the red fades away the train of bullets will disappear to the sense of man. Neither light nor sound now accompanies the volley, neither the human eye nor the human ear can perceive its presence. Drop a pane of glass or any other object edgewise through it, and it gives to the sense of man no evidence; the molecules of the glass separate from in front to close in from behind, and the moving train passes through it as freely as light, leaving the surface of the glass unaffected."

"Hold," I interrupted; "that would be as one quality of matter passing through another quality of matter without disturbance to either, and it is a law in physics that two substances cannot occupy the same space at the same time."

"That law holds good as man understands the subject, but bullets are no longer matter. Motion of mass was first changed into motion of molecules, and motion of molecule became finally augmented into motion of free force entities as the bullets disintegrated into molecular corpuscles, and then were dissociated, atoms resulting. At this last point the sense of vision, and of touch, ceased to be affected by that moving column (neither matter nor force), and at the next jump in velocity the atoms themselves disappeared, and free intangible motion resulted—nothing, vacancy.

"This result is the all-pervading spirit of space (the ether of mankind), as solid as adamant and as mobile as vacuity. If you can reverse the order of this phenomenon, and imagine an irregular retardation of the rapidity of such atomic motion, you can read the story of the formation of the material universe. Follow the chain backward, and with the decrease of velocity, motion becomes tangible matter again, and in accordance with conditions governing the change of motion into matter, from time to time the various elements successively appear. The planets may grow without and within, and ethereal space can generate elemental dirt. If you can conceive of an intermediate condition whereby pure space motion becomes partly tangible, and yet is not gross enough to be earthy matter, you can imagine how such forces as man is acquainted with, light, heat, electricity, magnetism, or gravity even are produced, for these are also disturbances in space motion. It should be easily understood that, according to the same simple principle, other elements and unknown forces as well, now imperceptible to man's limited faculties, could be and are formed outside and inside his field of perception."

"I fear that I cannot comprehend all this," I answered.

"So, I feared, and perhaps I have given you this lesson too soon, although some time ago you asked me to teach you concerning the assertion that electricity, light, heat, magnetism, and gravity are disturbances, and you said, 'Disturbances of what?' Think the lesson over, and you will perceive that it is easy. Let us hope that the time will come when we will be able to glance beneath the rough, material, earth surface knowledge that man has acquired, and experience the mind expansion that leads, to the blissful insight possessed by superior beings who do not have to contend with the rasping elements that encompass all who dwell upon the surface of the earth."

I pondered over these words, and a vague light, an undefined, inexpressible something that I could not put into words broke into my mind; I inferred that we were destined to meet with persons, or existences, possessed of new senses, of a mind development that man had not reached, and I was on the point of questioning my pilot when the motion of the boat was suspended, land appeared ahead, we drew up to it, and disembarked. Lifting the boat from the water my guide placed it on land at the edge of the motionless lake, and we resumed our journey. The scenery seemed but little changed from that of the latter part of our previous line of travel down the inclined plane of the opposite side of the lake that we had crossed. The direction was still downward after leaving the high ridge that bordered the edge of the lake, the floor of the cavern being usually smooth, although occasionally it was rough and covered with stony debris.

The mysterious light grew perceptibly brighter as we progressed, the fog-like halo previously mentioned became less dense, and the ring of obscurity widened rapidly. I could distinctly perceive objects at a great distance. I turned to my companion to ask why this was, and he replied:

"Because we are leaving one of the undiscovered conditions of the upper atmosphere that disturbs the sunlight."

"Do you say that the atmosphere is composed of substances unknown to man?"

"Yes; several of them are gases, and others are qualities of space condition, neither gas, liquid, nor solid. *

*(*This has since been partly supported by the discovery of the element Argon. However, the statement has been recorded many years. Miss Ella Burbige, stenographer, Newport, Ky., copied the original in 1887; Mr. S. D. Rouse, attorney, Covington, Ky., read it in 1889; Mr. Russell Errett, editor of the Christian Standard, in 1890, and Mr. H. C. Meader, President of the American Ticket Brokers' Association, in 1892. It seems proper to make this explanation in order to absolve the author from any charge of plagiarism, for each of these persons will recall distinctly this improbable [then] assertion.—J. U. L.)*

One particularly interferes with light in its passage. It is an entity that is not moved by the motion of the air, and is unequally distributed over the earth's surface. As we ascend above the earth it decreases, so it does as we descend into it. It is not vapor of water, is neither smoke, nor a true gas, and is as yet sensible to man only by its power of modifying the intensity of light. It has no color, is chemically inactive, and yet modifies the sun's rays so as to blot objects from view at a comparatively small distance from a person on the face of the earth. That this fact is known to man is evident from the knowledge he possesses of the difference in the power of his organs of vision at different parts of the earth. His sight is especially acute on the table lands of the Western Territories."

"I have been told," I answered, "that vapor of water causes this obscuration, or absorption, of light."

"Vapor of water, unless in strata of different densities, is absolutely transparent, and presents no obstacle to the passage of light," he said. "When vapor obstructs light, it is owing to impurities contained in it, to currents of varying densities, or wave motions, or to a mechanical mixture of condensed water and air, whereby multitudes of tiny globular water surfaces are produced. Pure vapor of water, free from motion, is passive to the sunlight."

"I can scarcely believe that a substance such as you describe, or that any constituent of the air, can have escaped the perception of the chemist," I replied.

In, as I thought, a facetious manner he repeated after me the word "chemist," and continued:

"Have chemists detected the ether of Aristotle, that you have mentioned, and I have defined, which scientists nevertheless accept pervades all space and every description of matter, and that I have told you is really matter itself changed into ultra-atomic motion? Have chemists explained why one object is transparent, and another of equal weight and solidity is opaque? Have chemists told you why vermilion is red and indigo is blue (the statement that they respectively reflect these rays of light is not an explanation of the cause for such action)? Have chemists told you why the prism disarranges or distorts sunlight to produce the abnormal hues that men assume compose elementary rays of light? Have chemists explained anything concerning the why or wherefore of the attributes of matter, or force, or even proven that the so-called primary forms of matter, or elements, are not compounds? Upon the contrary, does not the evolution that results in the recorded discoveries of the chemist foretell, or at least indicate, the possible future of the art, and promise that surrounding mysteries are yet to be developed and expanded into open truths, thus elaborating hidden forces; and that other forms of matter and unseen force expressions, are destined to spring into existence as the sciences progress? The chemist of to-day is groping in darkness; he is a novice as compared with the elaborated chemist of the near future; the imperfectly seen of the present, the silent and unsuspected, will become distinctly visible in a time that is to come, and a brightening of the intellect by these successively upward steps, upstairs of science, will, if science serves herself best, broaden the mind and give power to the imagination, resulting finally in"—

He hesitated.

"Go on," I said.

"The passage of mortal man, with the faculties of man intact, into communion with the spirit world."

CHAPTER XXXIII.

"A STUDY OF SCIENCE IS A STUDY OF GOD." COMMUNING WITH ANGELS.

"This is incredible," I exclaimed.

"You need not be astonished," he answered. "Is there any argument that can be offered to controvert the assertion that man is ignorant of many natural laws?"

"I can offer none."

"Is there any doubt that a force, distinct and separate from matter, influences matter and vivifies it into a living personality?"

"I do not deny that there is such force."

"What then should prevent this force from existing separate from the body if it be capable of existing in it?"

"I cannot argue against such a position."

"If, as is hoped and believed by the majority of mankind, even though some try to deny the fact, it is possible for man to exist as an association of earth matters, linked to a personal spirit force, the soul, and for the spirit force, after the death of the body, to exist independent of the grosser attributes of man, free from his mortal body, is it not reasonable to infer that the spirit, while it is still in man and linked to his body, may be educated and developed so as, under favorable conditions, to meet and communicate with other spirits that have been previously liberated front earthly bondage?"

"I submit," I answered; "but you shock my sensibilities when you thus imply that by cold, scientific investigation we can place ourselves in a position to meet the unseen spirit world"—

It was now my turn to hesitate.

"Go on," he said.

"To commune with the angels," I answered.

"A study of true science is a study of God," he continued. "Angels are organizations natural in accordance with God's laws. They appear superhuman, because of our ignorance concerning the higher natural forces. They exist in exact accordance with the laws that govern the universe; but as yet the attraction between clay and clay-bound spirit is so great as to prevent the enthralled soul of man from communicating with them. The faith of the religionist is an example of the unquenchable feeling that creates a belief as well as a hope that there is a self-existence separate from earthy substances. The scoffing scientific agnostic, working for other objects, will yet astonish himself by elaborating a method that will practically demonstrate these facts, and then empirical religion, as exemplified by the unquestioning faithful believer, and systematic science, as typified in the experimental materialist, will meet on common ground."

CHAPTER XXXIV.

I CEASE TO BREATHE, AND YET LIVE.

During this conversation we had been rapidly walking, or I should better say advancing, for we no longer walked as men do, but skipped down into the earth, down, ever downward. There were long periods of silence, in which I was engaged in meditating over the problems that successively demanded solution, and even had I desired to do so I could have kept no record of time; days, or even weeks, may have been consumed in this journey. Neither have I any method of judging of the rapidity of our motion. I was sensible of a marked decrease in the amount of muscular energy required to carry us onward, and I realized that my body was quite exempt from weariness. Motion became restful instead of exhausting, and it seemed to me that the ratio of the loss of weight, as shown by our free movements, in proportion to the distance we traversed, was greater than formerly. The slightest exhibition of propelling force cast us rapidly forward. Instead of the laborious, short step of upper earth, a single leap would carry us many yards. A slight spring, and with our bodies in space, we would skip several rods, alighting gently, to move again as easily. I marveled, for, although I had been led to anticipate something unusual, the practical evidence was wonderfully impressive, and I again questioned my guide.

"We are now nearing what physicists would call the center of gravity," he replied, "and our weight is rapidly diminishing. This is in exact accordance with the laws that govern the force called gravitation, which, at the earth's surface, is apparently uniform, though no instrument known to man can demonstrate its exact variation within the field man occupies. Men have not, as yet, been in a position to estimate this change, although it is known that mountains attract objects, and that a change in weight as we descend into the earth is perceptible; but to evolve the true law, observation, at a distance of at least ten miles beneath the surface of the ocean is necessary, and man, being a creature whose motions are confined to a thin, horizontal skin of earth, has never been one mile beneath its surface, and in consequence his opportunities for comparison are extremely limited."

"I have been taught," I replied, "that the force of gravitation decreases until the center of the earth is reached, at which point a body is without weight; and I can scarcely understand how such positive statements from scientific men can be far from the truth."

"WE WOULD SKIP SEVERAL RODS, ALIGHTING GENTLY."

"It is supposed by your surface men that the maximum of weight is to be found at one-sixth the distance beneath the surface of the earth, and therefrom decreases until at the center it is nothing at all," he replied. "This hypothesis, though, a stagger toward the right, is far from the truth, but as near as could be expected, when we consider the data upon which men base their calculations. Were it not for the purpose of controverting erroneous views, men would have little incentive to continue their investigations, and as has been the rule in science heretofore, the truth will, in time, appear in this case. One generation of students disproves the accepted theories of that which precedes, all working to eliminate error, all adding factors of error, and all together moving toward a common goal, a grand generalization, that as yet cannot be perceived. And still each series of workers is overlooking phenomena that, though obvious, are yet unperceived, but which will make evident to future scientists the mistakes of the present. As an example of the manner in which facts are thus overlooked, in your journey you have been impressed with certain surprising external conditions, or surroundings, and yet are oblivious to conditions more remarkable in your own body. So, it is with scientists. They overlook prominent facts that stare them boldly in the face, facts that are so conspicuous as to be invisible by reason of their very nearness."

"This statement I cannot disprove, and therefore must admit under protest. Where there is so much that appears mysterious I may have overlooked some things, but I can scarcely accept that, in ignorance, I have passed conditions in my own organization so marked as this decrease in gravity which has so strikingly been called to my attention."

"You have, and to convince you I need only say that you have nearly ceased to breathe, and are unconscious of the fact."

I stopped short, in momentary alarm, and now that my mind was directed to the fact, I became aware that I did not desire to breathe, and that my chest had ceased to heave with the alternate inhalation and exhalation of former times. I closed my lips firmly, and for a long period there was no desire for breath, then a slight involuntary inhalation followed, and an exhalation, scarcely noticeable, succeeded by a great interval of inaction. I impulsively turned my face toward the passage we had trod; a feeling of alarm possessed me, an uncontrollable, inexpressible desire to flee from the mysterious earth-being beside me, to return to men, and be an earth-surface man again, and I started backward through the chamber we had passed.

The guide seized me by the hand, "Hold, hold," he cried; "where would you go, fickle mortal?"

"To the surface," I shouted; "to daylight again. Unhand me, unearthly creature, abnormal being, man or devil; have you not inveigled me far enough into occult realms that should be forever sealed from mankind? Have you not taken from me all that men love or cherish, and undone every tie of kith or kin? Have you not led me into paths that the imagination of the novelist dare not conjure, and into experiences that pen in human hand would not venture to describe as possible, until I now stand with my feet on the boundary line that borders vacancy, and utter loss of weight; with a body nearly lost as a material substance, verging into nothing, and lastly with breath practically extinguished, I say, and repeat, is it not time that I should hesitate and pause in my reckless career?"

"It is not time," he answered.

"When will that hour come?" I asked in desperation, and I trembled as he replied:

"When the three Great Lights are closed."

"AN UNCONTROLLABLE, INEXPRESSIBLE DESIRE TO FLEE."

CHAPTER XXXV.

"A CERTAIN POINT WITHIN A SPHERE." MEN ARE AS PARASITES ON THE ROOF OF EARTH.

I realized again, as I had so many times before, that it was useless for me to rebel. "The self-imposed mystery of a sacrificed life lies before me," I murmured, "and there is no chance to retrace my footsteps. The 'Beyond' of the course that I have voluntarily selected, and sworn to follow, is hidden; I must nerve myself to pursue it to the bitter end, and so help me God, and keep me steadfast."

"Well said," he replied; "and since you have so wisely determined, I am free to inform you that these new obligations, like those you have heretofore taken, contain nothing which can conflict with your duty to God, your country, your neighbor, or yourself. In considering the phenomena presented by the suspension of the act of breathing, it should occur to you that where little labor is to be performed, little consumption of energy is required. Where there is such a trifling destruction of the vital force (not mind force) as at present is the case with us, it requires but slight respiration to retain the normal condition of the body. On earth's surface the act of respiration alone consumes by far the larger proportion of vital energy, and the muscular exertion involved thereby necessitates a proportionate amount of breathing in order that breath itself may continue. This act of respiration is the result of one of the conditions of surface earth life, and consumes most of the vital force. If men would think of this, they would understand how paradoxical it is for them to breathe in order to live, when the very act of respiration wears away their bodies and shortens their lives more than all else they have to do, and without adding to their mental or physical constitution in the least. Men are conversant with physical death as a constant result of suspended respiration, and with respiration as an accompaniment of life, which ever constant and connected conditions lead them to accept that the act of breathing is a necessity of mortal life. In reality, man occupies an unfortunate position among other undeveloped creatures of external earth; he is an animal, and is constitutionally framed like the other animals about him. He is exposed to the warring elements, to the vicious attacks of savage beasts and insidious parasites, and to the inroads of disease. He is a prey to the elementary vicissitudes of the undesirable exposure in which he exists upon the outer surface of our globe, where all is war, even among the forces of nature about him. These conditions render his lot an unhappy one indeed, and in ignorance he overlooks the torments of the weary, rasping, endless slavery of respiration in the personal struggle he has to undergo in order to retain a brief existence as an organized being. Have you never thought of the connected tribulations that the wear and tear of respiration alone inflict upon the human family? The heaving of the chest, the circulation of the blood, the throbbing of the heart, continue from mortal birth until death. The heart of man forces about two and one-half ounces of blood with each pulsation. At seventy beats per minute this amounts to six hundred and fifty-six pounds per hour, or nearly eight tons per day. The lungs respire over one thousand times an hour, and move over three thousand gallons of air a day. Multiply these amounts by three hundred and sixty-five, and then by seventy, and you have partly computed the enormous life-work of the lungs and heart of an adult. Over two hundred thousand tons of blood, and seventy-five million gallons of air have been moved by the vital force. The energy thus consumed is dissipated. No return is made for the expenditure of this life force. During the natural life of man, more energy is consequently wasted in material transformation resulting from the motion of heart and lungs, than would be necessary to sustain the purely vital forces alone for a thousand years. Besides, the act of respiration which man is compelled to perform in his exposed position, necessitates the consumption of large amounts of food, in order to preserve the animal heat, and replace the waste of a material body that in turn is worn out by these very movements. Add this waste of energy to the foregoing, and then you will surely perceive that the possible life of man is also curtailed to another and greater degree in the support of the digestive part of his organism. His spirit is a slave to his body; his lungs and heart, on which he imagines life depends, are unceasing antagonists of life. That his act of breathing is now a necessity upon the surface of the earth, where the force of gravity presses so heavily, and where the elements have' men at their command, and show him no mercy, I will not deny; but it is exasperating to contemplate such a waste of energy, and corresponding loss of human life."

"You must admit, however, that it is necessary?" I queried.

"No; only to an extent. The natural life of man should, and yet will be, doubled, trebled, multiplied a dozen, yes a thousand-fold."

I stepped in front of him; we stood facing each other.

"Tell me," I cried, "how men can so improve their condition as to lengthen their days to the limit you name, and let me return to surface earth a carrier of the glad tidings."

He shook his head.

I dropped on my knees before him.

"I implore you in behalf of that unfortunate humanity, of which I am a member, give me this boon. I promise to return to you and do your bidding. Whatever may be my subsequent fate, I promise to acquiesce therein willingly."

"I DROPPED ON MY KNEES BEFORE HIM."

He raised me to my feet. "Be of good cheer," he said, "and in the proper time you may return to the surface of this rind of earth, a carrier of great and good news to men."

"Shall I teach them of what you have shown me?" I asked.

"Yes; in part you will be a forerunner, but before you obtain the information that is necessary to the comfort of mankind you will have to visit surface earth again, and return again, perhaps repeatedly. You must prove yourself as men are seldom proven. The journey you have commenced is far from its conclusion, and you may not be equal to its subsequent trials; prepare yourself, therefore, for a series of events that may unnerve you. If you had full confidence and faith in your guide, you would have less cause to fear the result, but your suspicious human nature cannot overcome the shrinking sensation that is natural to those who have been educated as you have been amid the changing vicissitudes of the earth's surface, and you cannot but be incredulous by reason of that education."

Then I stopped as I observed before me a peculiar fungus—peculiar because unlike all others I had-seen. The convex part of its bowl was below, and the great head, as an inverted toadstool, stood upright on a short, stem-like pedestal. The gills within were of a deep green color and curved out from the center in the form of a spiral. This form, however, was not the distinguishing feature, for I had before observed specimens that were spiral in structure. The extraordinary peculiarity was that the gills were covered with fruit. This fruit was likewise green in color, each spore, or berry, being from two to three inches in diameter, and honeycombed on the surface, corrugated most beautifully. I stopped, leaned over the edge of the great bowl, and plucked a specimen of the fruit. It seemed to be covered with a hard, transparent shell, and to be nearly full of a clear, green liquid. I handled and examined it in curiosity, at which my guide seemed not to be surprised. Regarding me attentively, he said:

"What is it that impels a mortal towards this fruit?"

"It is curious," I said; "nothing more."

"As for that," said he, "it is not curious at all; the seed of the lobelia of upper earth is more curious, because, while it is as exquisitely corrugated, it is also microscopically small. In the second place you err when you say it is simply curious, 'nothing more,' for no mortal ever yet passed that bowl without doing exactly as you have done. The vein of curiosity, were it that alone that impels you, could not but have an exception."

Then he cracked the shell of the fruit by striking it on the stony floor, and carefully opened the shell, handing me one of the halves filled with a green fluid. As he did so he spoke the single word, "Drink," and I did as directed. He stood upright before me, and as I looked him in the face he seemingly, without a reason, struck off into a dissertation, apparently as distinct from our line of thought as a disconnected subject could be, as follows:

"HANDING ME ONE OF THE HALVES, HE SPOKE THE SINGLE WORD, DRINK."

CHAPTER XXXVI.

DRUNKENNESS. — THE DRINKS OF MAN.

"Intemperance has been the vice of every people, and is prevalent in all climes, notwithstanding that intoxicants, properly employed, may serve humanity's highest aims. Beginning early in the history of a people, the disease increases with the growth of a nation, until, at last, unless the knife is used, civilization perishes. A lowly people becomes more depraved as the use of liquor increases; a cultivated people passes backward into barbarism with the depravities that come from dissipation. Here nations meet, and individuals sink to a common level. No drinking man is strong enough to say, 'I cannot become dissipated;' no nation is rich and cultivated enough to view the debauch of its people without alarm.

"The disgusting habit of the drunken African finds its counterpart in the lascivious wine-bibber of aristocratic society. To picture the indecencies of society, that may be charged to debauchery, when the Grecian and Roman empires were at the height of greatness, would obscure the orgies of the barbarous African, and make preferable the brutality of the drunken American Indian. Intemperance brings men to the lowest level, and holds its power over all lands and all nations."

"Did the aborigines know how to make intoxicants, and were barbarians intemperate before contact with civilized nations?"

"Yes."

"But I have understood that drunkenness is a vice inherent only in civilized people; are not you mistaken?"

"No. Every clime, unless it be the far North where men are scarcely more than animals, furnishes intoxicants, and all people use them. I will tell you part of this record of nations.

"The Nubians make a barley beer which they call bonze, and also a wine, from the palm tree. The savages of Africa draw the clear, sweet juice of the palm oil tree into a gourd, in the morning, and by night it becomes a violent intoxicant. The natives of the Malayan Archipelago ferment and drink the sap of the flower stems of the cocoanut. The Tartar tribes make an intoxicating drink from mare's milk, called koomis. In South America the natives drink a vile compound, called cana, distilled from sugar cane; and in the Sandwich Islands, the shrub kava supplies the intoxicant kava-kava, drunk by all the inhabitants, from king to slave, and mother to child. In the heart of Africa, cannibal tribes make legyce of a cereal, and indulge in wild orgies over their barbaric cup. In North America the Indians, before Columbus discovered America, made an intoxicating drink of the sap of the maple tree. The national drink of the Mexicans is pulque, a beastly intoxicant, prepared from the Agave Americana. Mead is an alcoholic drink, made of honey, and used in many countries. In China wine was indulged in from the earliest day, and in former times, had it not been for the influence of their philosophers, especially Confucius, who foresaw the end, the Chinese nation would have perished from drunkenness. Opium, that fearful enslaver of millions of human beings, is in every sense a narcotic intoxicant, and stands conspicuous as an agent, capable of being either a friend, a companion, or a master, as man permits. History fails to indicate the date of its introduction to humanity. In South America the leaf of the cocoa plant is a stimulant scarcely less to be dreaded than opium. The juice of a species of asclepias produces the intoxicant soma, used once by the Brahmins, not only as a drink, but also in sacrificial and religious ceremonies. Many different flavored liquors made of palm, cocoanuts, sugar, pepper, honey, spices, etc., were used by native Hindoos, and as intoxicants have been employed from the earliest days in India. The Vedic people were fearfully dissipated, and page after page of that wonderful sacred book, the Rigs-Veda, is devoted to the habit of drunkenness. The worst classes of drunkards of India used Indian hemp to make bhang, or combined the deadly narcotic stramonium with arrack, a native beer, to produce a poisonous intoxicant. In that early day the inhabitants of India and China were fearfully depraved drunkards, and but for the reforms instituted by their wise men, must have perished as a people. Parahaoma, or 'homa,' is an intoxicant made from a lost plant that is described as having yellow blossoms, used by the ancient dissolute Persians from the day of Zoroaster. Cannabis sativa produces an intoxicant that in Turkey is known as hadschy, in Arabia and India as hashish, and to the Hottentots as dacha, and serves as a drunkard's food in other lands. The fruit of the juniper produces gin, and the fermented juice of the grape, or malt liquors, in all civilized countries are the favorite intoxicants, their origin being lost in antiquity. Other substances, such as palm, apples, dates, and pomegranates have also been universally employed as drink producers.

"Go where you will, man's tendency seems to be towards the bowl that inebriates, and yet it is not the use but the abuse of intoxicants that man has to dread. Could he be temperate, exhilarants would befriend."

"But here," I replied, "in this underground land, where food is free, and existence possible without an effort, this shameful vice has no existence. Here there is no incentive to intemperance, and even though man were present with his inherent passion for drink, he could not find means to gratify his appetite."

"Ah," my guide replied, "that is an error. Why should this part of the earth prove an exception to the general rule? Nature always supplies the means, and man's instinct teaches him how to prepare an intoxicant. So long as man is human his passions will rule. If you should prove unequal to the task you have undertaken, if you shrink from your journey, and turn back, the chances are you will fail to reach the surface of the earth. You will surely stop in the chamber which we now approach, and which I have now prepared you to enter, and will then become one of a band of earth drunkards; having all the, lower passions of a mortal you will yet be lost to the virtues of man. In this chamber those who falter and turn back, stop and remain for all time, sinking until they become lower in the human scale than any drunkard on earth. Without any restraining influence, without a care, without necessity of food or incentive to exertion, in this habitation where heat and cold are unknown, and no motive for self-preservation exists, they turn their thoughts toward the ruling passion of mankind and— Listen! Do you not hear them? Listen!"

CHAPTER XXXVII.

THE DRUNKARD'S VOICE.

Then I noticed a medley of sounds seemingly rising out of the depths beyond us. The noise was not such as to lead one to infer that persons were speaking coherently, but rather resembled a jargon such as might come from a multitude of persons talking indiscriminately and aimlessly. It was a constant volley, now rising and now falling in intensity, as though many persons regardless of one another were chanting different tunes in that peculiar sing-song tone often characteristic of the drunkard. As we advanced, the noise became louder and more of a medley, until at last we were surrounded by confusion. Then a single voice rose up strong and full, and at once, from about us, close to us, yes, against our very persons, cries and shrieks unearthly smote my ears. I could distinguish words of various tongues, English, Irish, German, and many unfamiliar and disjointed cries, imprecations, and maledictions. The cavern about seemed now to be resonant with voices, —shrieks, yells, and maniacal cries commingled, —and yet no form appeared. As we rushed onward, for now my guide grasped my arm tightly and drew me rapidly down the cavern floor, the voices subsided, and at length sounded as if behind us. Now however it seemed as though innumerable arrows, each possessed of a whistle or tone of its own, were in wave-like gusts shrieking by us. Coming from in front, they burst in the rear. Stopping to listen, I found that a connection could be traced between the screech of the arrow-like shriek, and a drunkard's distant voice. It seemed as though a rocket made of an escaping voice would scream past, and bursting in the cavern behind, liberate a human cry. Now and then all but a few would subside, to burst out with increased violence, as if a flight of rockets each with a cry of its own would rush past, to be followed after their explosion by a medley of maniacal cries, songs, shrieks, and groans, commingled. It was as though a shell containing a voice that escaped slowly as by pressure from an orifice, were fired past my ears, to explode and liberate the voice within my hearing. The dreadful utterance was not an echo, was not hallucination, it was real.

I stopped and looked at my guide in amazement. He explained: "Did you not sometime back experience that your own voice was thrown from your body?"

"Yes," I answered.

"These crazed persons or rather experiences depraved, are shouting in the cavern beyond," he said. "They are in front; their voices pass us to burst into expression in the rear."

Then, even as he spoke, from a fungus stalk near us, a hideous creature unfolded itself, and shambled to my side. It had the frame of a man, and yet it moved like a serpent, writhing towards me. I stepped back in horror, but the tall, ungainly creature reached out an arm and grasped me tightly. Leaning over he placed his hideous mouth close to my ear, and moaned: "Back, back, go thou back."

I made no reply, being horror-stricken:

"Back, I say, back to earth, or"—

He hesitated, and still possessed of fear, and unable to reply, I was silent.

"Then go on," he said, "on to your destiny, unhappy man," and slinking back to the fungus whence he arose, he disappeared from sight.

"Come," said my guide, "let us pass the Drunkard's Den. This was but a straggler; nerve yourself, for his companions will soon surround us."

CHAPTER XXXVIII.

THE DRUNKARDS' DEN.

As we progressed the voices in our rear became fainter, and yet the whistling volleys of screeching voice bombs passed us as before. I shuddered in anticipation of the sight that was surely to meet our gaze, and could not but tremble for fear. Then I stopped and recoiled, for at my very feet I beheld a huge, living human head. It rested on the solid rock, and had I not stopped suddenly when I did, I would have kicked it at the next leap. The eyes of the monster were fixed in supplication on my face; the great brow indicated intelligence, the finely-cut mouth denoted refinement, the well-modeled head denoted brain, but the whole constituted a monster. The mouth opened, and a whizzing, arrow voice swept past, and was lost in the distance.

"What is this?" I gasped.

"The fate of a drunkard," my guide replied. "This was once an intelligent man, but now he has lost his body, and enslaved his soul, in the den of drink beyond us, and has been brought here by his comrades, who thus rid themselves of his presence. Here he must rest eternally. He cannot move, he has but one desire, drink, and that craving, deeper than life, cannot be satiated."

"But he desires to speak; speak lower, man, or head of man, if you wish me to know your wants," I said, and leaned toward him.

Then the monster whispered, and I caught the words: "Back, back, go thou back!"

I made no reply.

"Back I say, back to earth or"—

Still I remained silent.

"Then go on," he said; "on to your destiny, unhappy man."

"This is horrible," I muttered.

"Come," said the guide, "let us proceed."

And we moved onward.

Now I perceived many such heads about us, all resting upright on the stony floor. Some were silent, others were shouting, others still were whispering and endeavoring to attract my attention. As we hurried on I saw more and more of these abnormal creatures. Some were in rows, resting against each other, leaving barely room for us to pass between, but at last, much to my relief, we left them behind us.

But I found that I had no cause for congratulation, when I felt myself clutched by a powerful hand—a hand as large as that of a man fifty feet in height. I looked about expecting to see a gigantic being, but instead beheld a shrunken pigmy. The whole man seemed but a single hand—a Brobdingnag hand affixed to the body of a Lilliputian.

"Do not struggle," said the guide; "listen to what he wishes to impart"

I leaned over, placing my ear close to the mouth of the monstrosity.

"Back, back, go thou back," it whispered.

"What have I to fear?" I asked.

"Back, I say, back to earth, or"—

"Or what?" I said.

"Then go on; on to your destiny, unhappy man," he answered, and the hand lost its grasp.

My guide drew me onward.

Then, from about us, huge hands arose; on all sides they waved in the air; some were closed and were shaken as clenched fists, others moved aimlessly with spread fingers, others still pointed to the passage we had traversed, and in a confusion of whispers I heard from the pigmy figures a babble of cries, "Back, back, go thou back." Again, I hesitated, the strain upon my nerves was becoming unbearable; I glanced backward and saw a swarm of misshaped diminutive forms, each holding up a monstrous arm and hand. The passage behind us was closed against retreat. Every form possessed but one hand, the other and the entire body seemingly had been drawn into this abnormal member. While I thus meditated, momentarily, as by a single thought each hand closed, excepting the index finger, and in unison each finger pointed towards the open way in front, and like shafts from a thousand bows I felt the voices whiz past me, and then from the rear came the reverberation as a complex echo, "Then go on; on to your destiny, unhappy man."

Instinctively I sprang forward, and had it not been for the restraining hand of my guide would have rushed wildly into passages that might have ended my misery, for God only knows what those unseen corridors contained. I was aware of that which lay behind, and was only intent on escaping from the horrid figures already passed.

"Hold," whispered the guide; "as you value your life, stop." And then exerting a power that I could not withstand, he held me a struggling prisoner.

"Listen," he said, "have you not observed that these creatures do not seek to harm you? Have not all of them spoken kindly, have any offered violence?"

"No," I replied, "but they are horrible."

"That they realize; but fearing that you will prove to be as weak as they have been, and will become as they are now, they warn you back. However, I say to you, if you have courage sufficient, you need have no fear. Come, rely on me, and do not be surprised at anything that appears."

Again, we went forward. I realized now my utter helplessness. I became indifferent again; I could neither retrace my footsteps alone, nor guide them forward in the path I was to pursue. I submissively relied on my guide, and as stoical as he appeared to be, I moved onward to new scenes.

We came to a great chamber which, as we halted on its edge, seemed to be a prodigious amphitheater. In its center a rostrum-like stone of a hundred feet in diameter, flat and circular on the top, reared itself about twelve feet above the floor, and to the base of this rostrum the floor of the room sloped evenly. The amphitheater was fully a thousand feet in diameter, of great height, and the floor was literally alive with grotesque beings. Imagination could not depict an abnormal human form that did not exhibit itself to my startled gaze. One peculiarity now presented itself to my mind; each abnormal part seemed to be created at the expense of the remainder of the body. Thus, to my right I beheld a single leg, fully twelve feet in height, surmounted by a puny human form, which on this leg, hopped ludicrously away. I saw close behind this huge limb a great ear attached to a small head and body; then a nose so large that the figure to which it was attached was forced to hold the face upward, in order to prevent the misshaped organ from rubbing on the stony floor. Here a gigantic forehead rested on a shrunken face and body, and there a pair of enormous feet were walking, seemingly attached to the body of a child, and yet the face was that of a man. If an artist were to attempt to create as many revolting figures as possible, each with some member out of proportion to the rest of the body, he could not add one form to those upon this floor. And yet, I again observed that each exaggerated organ seemed to have drawn itself into existence by absorbing the remainder of the body. We stood on the edge of this great room, and I pondered the scene before my eyes. At length my guide broke the silence:

"You must cross this floor; no other passage is known. Mark well my words, heed my advice."

"This is the Drunkards' Den. These men are lost to themselves and to the world. Every member of this assembly once passed onward as you are now doing, in charge of a guide. They failed to reach the goal to which you aspire, and retreating, reached this chamber, to become victims to the drink habit. Some of these creatures have been here for ages, others only for a short period."

"Why are they so distorted?" I asked.

"Because matter is now only partly subservient to will," he replied. "The intellect and mind of a drunkard on surface earth becomes abnormal by the influence of an intoxicant, but his real form is unseen, although evidently misshapen and partly subject to the perception of a few only of his fellow men. Could you see the inner form of an earth surface drunkard, you would perceive as great a mental monstrosity as is any physical monster now before you, and of the two the physically abnormal creature is really the least objectionable. Could you see the mind configurations of an assembly of surface earth topers, you would perceive a class of beings as much distorted mentally as are these physically. A drunkard is a monstrosity. On surface earth the mind becomes abnormal; here the body suffers."

"Why is it," I asked, "that parts of these creatures shrink away as some special organ increases?"

"Because the abnormal member can grow only by abstracting its substance from the other portions of the body. An increasing arm enlarges itself by drawing its strength from the other parts, hence the body withers as the hand enlarges, and in turn the hand shrinks when the leg increases in size. The total weight of the individual remains about the same.

"Men on earth judge of men not by what they are, but by what they seem to be. The physical form is apparent to the sense of sight, the real man is unseen. However, as the boot that encloses a foot can not altogether hide the form of the foot within, so the body that encloses the life entity, cannot but exhibit here and there the character of the dominating spirit within. Thus, a man's features may grow to indicate the nature of the enclosed spirit, for the controlling character of that spirit will gradually impress itself on the material part of man. Even on surface earth, where the matter side of man dominates, a vicious spirit will produce a villainous countenance, a mediocre mind a vapid face, and an amorous soul will even protrude the anterior part of the skull.

"EACH FINGER POINTED TOWARDS THE OPEN WAY IN FRONT."

"Carry the same law to this location, and it will be seen that as mind, or spirit, is here the master, and matter is the slave, the same rule should, under natural law, tend to produce such abnormal figures as you perceive. Hence the part of a man's spirit that is endowed most highly sways the corresponding part of his physical body at the expense of the remainder. Gradually the form is altered under the relaxing influence of this fearful intra-earth intoxicant, and eventually but one organ remains to tell of the symmetrical man who formerly existed. Then, when he is no longer capable of self-motion, the comrades carry the drunkard's fate, which is here the abnormal being you have seen, into the selected corridor, and deposit it among others of its kind, as in turn the bearers are destined sometime to be carried by others. We reached this cavern through a corridor in which heads and arms were abnormal, but in others may be found great feet, great legs, or other portions of self-abused man.

"I should tell you, furthermore, that on surface earth a drunkard is not less abnormal than these creatures; but men can not see the form of the drunkard's spirit. Could they perceive the image of the real man life that corresponds to the material part, it would appear not less distorted and hideous. The soul of a mortal protrudes from the visible body as down expands from a thistle seed, but it is invisible. Drink drives the spirit of an earth-surface drunkard to unnatural forms, not less grotesque than these physical distortions. Could you see the real drunkard on surface earth he would be largely outside the body shell, and hideous in the extreme. As a rule, the spirit of an earth-surface drunkard dominates the nose and face, and if mortal man could be suddenly gifted with the sense of mind-sight, they would find themselves surrounded by persons as misshapen as any delirious imagination can conjure. Luckily for humanity this scene is as yet withheld from man, for life would otherwise be a fearful experience, because man has not the power to resist the temptation to abuse drink."

"Tell me," I said, "how long will those beings rest in these caverns?"

"They have been here for ages," replied the guide; "they are doomed to remain for ages yet."

"You have intimated that if my courage fails I will return to this cavern and become as they are. Now that you have warned me of my doom, do you imagine that anything, even sudden death, can swerve me from my journey? Death is surely preferable to such an existence as this."

"Do not be so confident. Every individual before you have had the same opportunity, and has been warned as you have been. They could not undergo the test to which they were subjected, and you may fail. Besides, on surface earth are not men constantly confronted with the doom of the drunkard, and do they not, in the face of this reality, turn back and seek his caverns? The journey of life is not so fearful that they should become drunkards to shrink from its responsibilities. You have reached this point in safety. You have passed the sentinels without, and will soon be accosted by the band before us. Listen well now to my advice. A drunkard always seeks to gain companions, to draw others down to his own level, and you will be tried as never have you been before. Taste not their liquor by whatever form or creature presented. They have no power to harm him who has courage to resist. If they entreat you, refuse; if they threaten, refuse; if they offer inducements, refuse to drink. Let your answer be No, and have no fear. If your strength fails you, mark well my"—

Before he could complete his sentence, I felt a pressure, as of a great wind, and suddenly found myself seized in an embrace irresistible, and then, helpless as a feather, was swept out into the cavern of the drunkards.

CHAPTER XXXIX.

AMONG THE DRUNKARDS.

I remember once to have stood on the edge of Niagara's great whirlpool, but not more fearful did its seething waters then seem than did the semi-human whirl into which I had now been plunged. Whether my guide had been aware of the coining move that separated us I never knew, but, as his words were interrupted, I infer that he was not altogether ready to part from my company. Be this as it may, he disappeared from sight, and, as by a concerted move, the cries of the drunkards subsided instantly. I found myself borne high in the air, perched on a huge hand that was carried by its semi-human comrades. It seemed as though the contents of that vast hall had been suddenly thrown beneath me, for, as I looked about, I saw all around a sea of human fragments, living, moving parts of men. Round and round that hall we circled as an eddy whirls in a rock-bound basin, and not less silently than does the water of an eddy. Then I perceived that the disjointed mass of humanity moved as a spiral, in unison, throbbing like a vitalized stream, bearing me submissively on its surface. Gradually the distance between myself and the center stone lessened, and then I found that, as if carried in the groove of a gigantic living spiral, I was being swept towards the stone platform in the center of the room. There was method in the movements of the, drunkards, although I could not analyze the intricacies of their complex reel.

Finally, I was borne to the center stone, and by a sudden toss of the hand, in the palm of which I was seated, I was thrown upon the raised platform. Then in unison the troop swung around the stone, and I found myself gazing on a mass of vitalized fragments of humanity. Quickly a figure sprung upon the platform, and in him I discerned a seemingly perfect man. He came to my side and grasped my hand as if he were a friend.

"Do not fear," he said; "obey our request, and you will not be harmed."

"What do you desire?" I asked.

He pointed to the center of the stone, and I saw thereon many gigantic, inverted fungus bowls. The gills of some had been crushed to a pulp, and had saturated themselves with liquid which, perhaps by a species of fermentation, had undergone a structural change; others were as yet intact; others still contained men intently cutting the gills into fragments and breaking the fruit preparatory to further manipulation.

"You are to drink with us," he replied.

"No," I said; "I will not drink."

"Then you must die; to refuse to drink with us is to invite death."

"So, mote it be; I will not drink."

We stood facing each other, apparently both meditating on the situation.

I remember to have been surprised, not that the man before me had been able to spring from the floor to the table rock on which I stood, but that so fair a personage could have been a companion of the monstrosities about me. He was a perfect type of manhood, and was exquisitely clothed in a loose, flowing robe that revealed and heightened the beauty of his symmetrical form. His face was fair, yet softly tinted with rich, fresh color; his hair and beard were neatly trimmed; his manner was polished, and his countenance frank and attractive. The contrast between the preternatural shapes from among whom he sprung and himself was as between a demon and an angel. I marveled that I had not perceived him before, for such a one should have been conspicuous because so fair; but I reflected that it was quite natural that among the thousands of grotesque persons about me, one attractive form should have escaped notice. Presently he spoke again, seemingly having repented of his display of temper.

"I am a friend," he said; "a deliverer. I will serve you as I have others before you. Lean on me, listen to my story, accept my proffered friendship."

Then he continued: "When you have rested, I will guide you in safety back to upper earth, and restore you to your friends."

I could not resist his pleasing promise. I suddenly and unaccountably believed in his sincerity. He impressed me with confidence in his truthfulness, yes, against my better judgment, convinced me that he must be a friend, a savior. Grasping him by the hand I thanked him for his interest in a disconsolate wanderer, and assured him of my confidence.

"I am in your hands," I said; "I will obey you implicitly. I thank you, my deliverer; lead me back to surface earth and receive the gratitude of a despairing mortal."

"This I will surely do," he said; "rest your case in my hands, do not concern yourself in the least about your future. Before acquiescing in your desire, however, I will explain part of the experiences through which you have recently passed. You have been in the control of an evil spirit, and have been deceived. The grotesque figures, the abnormal beings about you, exist only in your disordered imagination. They are not real. These persons are happy and free from care or pain. They live in bliss inexpressible. They have a life within a life, and the outward expression that you have perceived is as the uncouth hide and figure that encloses the calm, peaceful eye of a toad. Look at their eyes, not at their seemingly distorted forms."

I turned to the throng and beheld a multitude of upturned faces mildly beaming upon me. As I glanced from eye to eye of each countenance, the repulsive figure disappeared from my view, and a sweet expression of innocence was all that was disclosed to me. I realized that I had judged by the outer garment. I had wronged these fellow-beings. A sense of remorse came over me, a desire to atone for my short-sightedness.

"What can I offer as a retribution?" I asked. "I have injured these people."

"Listen," was the reply. "These serene intelligences are happy. They are as a band of brothers. They seek to do you a kindness, to save you from disaster. One hour of experience such as they enjoy is worth a hundred years of the pleasures known to you. This delicious favor, an hour of bliss, they freely offer you, and after you have partaken of their exquisite joy, I will conduct you back to earth's surface whenever you desire to leave us." He emphasized the word, desire.

"I am ready," I replied; "give me this promised delight."

The genial allurer turned to the table rock behind us, and continued:

"In these fungus bowls we foment the extract of life. The precious cordial is as a union of the quintessential spirits of joy, peace, tranquility, happiness, and delight. Could man abstract from ecstasy the thing that underlies the sense that gives that word a meaning, his product would not approach the power of the potent liquids in these vessels."

"Of what are they composed?" I asked.

"Of derivatives of the rarest species of the fungus family," he answered. "They are made by formulae that are the result of thousands of years of experimentation. Come, let us not delay longer the hour of bliss."

Taking me by the hand, my graceful comrade led me to the nearest bowl. Then on closer view I perceived that its contents were of a deep green color, and in active commotion, and although no vapor was apparent, a delightful sensation impressed my faculties. I am not sure that I inhaled at all, —the feeling was one of penetration, of subtile, magic absorption. My companion took a tiny shell which he dipped into the strange cauldron. holding the tiny cup before me, he spoke the one word, "Drink."

Ready to acquiesce, forgetful of the warning I had received, I grasped the cup, and raised it to my lips, and as I did so chanced to glance at my tempter's face, and saw not the supposed friend I had formerly observed, but, as through a mask fair in outline, the countenance of an exulting demon, regarding me with a sardonic grin. In an instant he had changed from man to devil.

I dashed the cup upon the rock. "No; I will not drink," I shouted.

Instantly the cavern rung with cries of rage. A thousand voices joined as by accord, and simultaneously the throng of fragments of men began to revolve again. The mysterious spiral seemed to unwind, but I could not catch the method of its movement. The motion was like that of an uncoiling serpent bisected lengthwise, the two halves of the body seeming to slide against each other. Gradually that part of the cavern near the stone on which I stood became clear of its occupants, and at last I perceived that the throng had receded to the outer edge. Then the encircling side walls of the amphitheater became visible, and as water sinks into sand, the medley of fragments of I humanity disappeared from view.

I turned to my companion; he, too, had vanished. I glanced towards the liquor cauldrons; the stone was bare. I alone occupied the gigantic hall. No trace remained to tell of the throng that a short time previously had surrounded and mocked me.

Desolate, distracted, I threw myself upon the stone, and cursed my miserable self. "Come back," I cried, "come back. I will drink, drink, drink."

CHAPTER XL.

FURTHER TEMPTATION — ETIDORHPA.

Then, as my voice reverberated from the outer recesses, I caught a sound as of music in the distance. I raised my head and listened—yes, surely there was music. The melody became clearly distinct, and soon my senses were aware that both vocal and instrumental music were combined. The airs which came floating were sweet, simple, and beautiful. The voices and accompanying strains approached, but I could distinguish no words. By and by, from the corridors of the cavern, troops of bright female forms floated into view. They were clad in robes ranging from pure white to every richest hue, contrasting strangely, and in the distance their rainbow brilliancy made a gorgeous spectacle. Some were fantastically attired in short gowns, such as I imagine were worn by the dancing girls of sacred history, others had kirtles of a single bright color, others of, many shades intermingled, while others still were dressed in gauze-like fabrics of pure white.

As they filed into the cavern, and approached me, they formed into platoons, or into companies, and then, as dissolving views come and go, they presented first one and then another figure. Sometimes they would stretch in great circling lines around the hall, again they would form into squares, and again into geometrical figures of all shades and forms, but I observed that with every change they drew nearer to the stone on which I rested.

They were now so near that their features could be distinguished, and never before had I seen such loveliness in human mold. Every face was as perfect as a master's picture of the Madonna, and yet no two seemed to possess the same type of beauty. Some were of dark complexion with glossy, raven hair, others were fair with hair ranging from light brown to golden. The style of head dress, as a rule, was of the simplest description. A tinted ribbon, or twisted cord, over the head, bound their hair with becoming grace, and their silken locks were either plaited into braids, curled into ringlets, or hung loosely, flowing in wavelets about their shoulders. Some held curious musical instruments, others beautiful wands, and altogether they produced a scenic effect of rare beauty that the most extravagant dream of fairyland could not surpass. Thus, it was that I became again the center of a throng, not of repulsive monsters, but of marvelously lovely beings. They were as different from those preceding as darkness is from daylight.

Could any man from the data of my past experiences have predicted such a scene? Never before had the semblance of a woman appeared, never before had an intimation been given that the gentle sex existed in these silent chambers. Now, from the grotesque figures and horrible cries of the former occupants of this same cavern, the scene had changed to a conception of the beautiful and artistic, such as a poetic spirit might evolve in an extravagant dream of higher fairy land. I glanced above; the great hall was clothed in brilliant colors, the bare rocks had disappeared, the dome of that vast arch reaching to an immeasurable height, was decorated in all the colors of the rainbow. Flags and streamers fluttered in breezes that also moved the garments of the angelic throng about me, but which I could not sense; profiles of enchanting faces pervaded the glimmering space beyond; I alone was but an onlooker, not a participant of the joys about me.

The movements of the seraph-like figures continued, innumerable forms and figures followed forms and figures innumerable, and music indescribable blended with the poetry of notion. I was rapt, the past disappeared, my former mind was blotted from existence, the world vanished, and I became a thrill of joy, a sensation of absolute delight.

The band of spirits or fairy forms reached the rock at my feet, but I did not know how long a time they consumed in doing this; it may have been a second, and it may have been an eternity. Neither did I care. A single moment of existence such as I experienced, seemed worth an age of any other pleasure.

Circling about me, these ethereal creatures paused from their motions, and, as the music ceased, I stood above them, and yet in their midst, and gazed out into a distance illimitable, but not less beautiful in the expanse than was the adjacent part. The cavern had altogether disappeared, and in the depths about me as far as the eye could reach, seemingly into the broad expanse of heaven, I saw the exquisite forms that I have so imperfectly described.

Then a single band from the throng lightly sprung upon the stony terrace where I stood and sang and danced before me. Every motion was perfect as imagination could depict, every sound was concentrated extract of melody. This band retired to be replaced by another, which in turn gave way to another, and still another, until, as in space we have no standard, time vanished, and numbers ceased to be numbers.

No two of the band of dancers were clothed alike, no two songs were similar, though all were inexpressibly enchanting. The first group seemed perfect, and yet the second was better, and each succeeding band sung sweeter songs, were more beautiful, and richer in dress than those preceding. I became enveloped in the aesthetic atmosphere, my spirit seemed to be loosened from the body, it was apparently upon the point of escaping from its mortal frame; suddenly the music ceased, the figures about became passive, and every form standing upright and graceful, gazed upon my face, and as I looked at the radiant creatures, each successive face, in turn, seemed to grow more beautiful, each form more exquisite than those about.

Then, in the distance, I observed the phalanx divide, forming into two divisions, separated by a broad aisle, stretching from my feet to the limit of space without, and down this aisle I observed a single figure advancing toward me.

As she approached, the phalanx closed in behind her, and when at last she reached the stone on which I stood, she stepped, or was wafted to my side, and the phalanx behind moved together and was complete again.

"My name is Etidorhpa. In me you behold the spirit that elevates man, and subdues the most violent of passions. In history, so far back in the dim ages as to be known now as legendary mythology, have I ruled and blessed the world. Unclasp my power over man and beast, and while heaven dissolves, the charms of Paradise will perish. I know no master. The universe bows to my authority. Stars and suns enamored pulsate and throb in space and kiss each other in waves of light; atoms cold embrace and cling together; structures inanimate affiliate with and attract inanimate structures; bodies dead to other noble passions are not dead to love. The savage beast, under my enchantment, creeps to her lair, and gently purrs over her offspring; even man becomes less violent, and sheathes his weapon and smothers his hatred as I soothe his passions beside the loved ones in the privacy of his home.

"I have been known under many titles, and have comforted many peoples. Strike my name from Time's record, and the lovely daughters of Zeus and Dione would disappear; and with them would vanish the grace and beauty of woman; the sweet conception of the Froth Child of the Cyprus Sea would be lost; Venus, the Goddess of Love, would have no place in song, and Love herself, the holiest conception of the poet, man's superlative conception of Heaven's most precious charms, would be buried with the myrtle and the rose. My name is Etidorhpa; interpret it rightly, and you have what has been to humanity the essence of love, the mother of all that ennobles. He who loves a wife worships me; she, who in turn makes a home happy, is typical of me. I am Etidorhpa, the beginning and the end of earth. Behold in me the antithesis of envy, the opposite of malice, the enemy of sorrow, the mistress of life, the queen of immortal bliss.

"Do you know," she continued, and her voice, soft and sweet, carried with it a pleasurable sense of truthfulness indescribable, "do you know that man's idea of heaven, places me, Etidorhpa, on the highest throne? With the charm of maiden pure, I combine the devotion of wife and the holiness of mother. Take from the life of man the treasures I embody, and he will be homeless, childless, loveless. The thought of Heaven will in such a case be as the dismal conception of a dreary platitude. A life in such a Heaven, a Heaven devoid of love (and this the Scriptures teach), is one of endless torment.

"Love, by whatever name the conception is designated, rules the world. Divest the cold man of science, of the bond that binds him to his life-thought, and his work is ended. Strike from the master in music the chord that links his soul to the voice he breathes, and his songs will be hushed. Deaden the sense of love which the artist boars his art, and as the spirit that underlies his thought-scenes vanishes, his touch becomes chilled, and his brush inexpressive. The soldier thinks of his home and country, and without a murmur sheds his life blood.

"And yet there are debasing phases of love, for as love of country builds a nation, so love of pillage may destroy it. Love of the holy and the beautiful stands in human life opposed to love of the debasing and vicious, and I, Etidorhpa, am typical of the highest love of man. As the same force binds the molecules of the rose and the violet as well as those of noxious drugs, so the same soul conception may serve the love of good or the love of evil. Love may guide a tyrant or actuate a saint, may make man torture his fellow, or strive to ease his pain.

"Thus, man's propensity to serve his holy or his evil passion may each be called a degree in love, and in the serving of that passion the love of one heart may express itself as the antithesis of love in another. As bitter is to some men's taste more pleasant than sweet, and sour is yet more grateful to others, so one man may love the beautiful, another delight in the grotesque, and a third may love to see his neighbor suffer. Amid these, the phase of love that ennobles, brings the greatest degree of pleasure and comfort to mankind, but the love that degrades is love nevertheless, by whatever name the expression of the passion may be called. Love rules the

ETIDORHPA.

world, and typical of man's intensest, holiest love, I, Etidorhpa, stand the Soul of Love Supreme." She hesitated.

"Go on."

"I have already said, and in saying this have told the truth, I come from beyond the empty shell of a materialistic gold and silver conception of Heaven. Go with me, and in my home, you will find man's soul devotion, regardless of material surroundings. I have said, and truly, the corridors of the Heaven mansion, enriched by precious stones and metals fine, but destitute of my smiles and graces, are deserted. The golden calf is no longer worshiped, cobwebs cling in festoons motionless, and the dust of selfish thoughts perverted, dry and black as the soot from Satan's fires settling therein, as the dust of an antiquated sarcophagus, rest undisturbed. Place on one side the Heaven of which gold-bound misers sing, and on the other Etidorhpa and the treasures that come with me to man and woman, (for without me neither wife, child, nor father could exist,) and from any other heaven mankind will turn away. The noblest gift of Heaven to humanity is the highest sense of love, and I, Etidorhpa, am the soul of love."

She ceased speaking, and as I looked at the form beside me I forgot myself in the rapture of that gaze.

Crush the colors of the rainbow into a single hue possessed of the attributes of all the others, and multiply that entity to infinity, and you have less richness than rested in any of the complex colors shown in the trimming of her raiment. Lighten the softness of eiderdown a thousand times, and yet maintain its sense of substance, and you have not conceived of the softness of the gauze that decked her simple, flowing garments. Gather the shadows cast by a troop of radiant angels, then sprinkle the resultant shade with star dust, and color therewith a garment brighter than satin, softer than silk, and more ethereal than light itself, and you have less beauty than reposed in the modest dress that enveloped her figure. Abstract the perfume from the sweetest oriental grasses, and combine with it the essential spirit of the wild rose, then add thereto the soul of ambergris, and the quintessential extracts of the finest aromatics of the East, and you have not approached the exquisite fragrance that penetrated my very being at her approach. She stood before me, slender, lithe, symmetrical, radiant. Her hair was more beautiful than pen can depict; it was colorless because it cannot be described by colors known to mortals. Her face paled the beauty of all who had preceded her. She could not be a fairy, for no conception of a fairy can approach such loveliness; she was not a spirit, for surely material

ETIDORHPA APPEARS.

substance was a part of her form; she was not an angel, for no abnormal, irrational wing protruded from her shoulder to blemish her seraphic figure.

"No," I said musingly; "she is a creature of other climes; the Scriptures tell of no such being; she is neither human nor angelic, but"—

"But what?" she said.

"I do not know," I answered.

"Then I will tell you," she replied. "Yes; I will tell you of myself and of my companions. I will show you our home, carrying you through the shadows of heaven to exhibit that fair land, for heaven without Etidorhpa casts a shadow in comparison therewith. See," she said, as with her dainty fingers she removed front her garment a fragment of transparent film that I had not previously observed; "see, this is a cobweb that clung to my skirt, as, on my way to meet you, I passed through the dismal corridors of the materialists' loveless heaven."

She dropped it on the floor, and I stooped to pick it up, but vainly—my fingers passed through it as through a mist.

"You must be an angel," I stammered.

She smiled.

"Come," she said, "do not consume your time with thoughts of materialistic heaven; come with me to that brighter land beyond, and in those indescribable scenes we, you and I, will wander together forever."

She held out her hand; I hesitatingly touched it, and then raised it to my lips. She made no resistance.

I dropped upon my knees. "Are you to be mine?" I cried. "Mine forever?"

"Yes," she answered; "if you will it, for he who loves will be loved in turn."

"I will do it," I said; "I give myself to you, be you what you may, be your home where it may, I give up the earth behind me, and the hope of heaven before me; the here and the hereafter I will sacrifice. Let us hasten," I said, for she made no movement.

She shook her head. "You must yet be tempted as never before, and you must resist the tempter. You cannot pass into the land of Etidorhpa until you have suffered as only the damned can suffer, until you have withstood the pangs of thirst, and have experienced heat and cold indescribable. Remember the warning of your former guide, mark well the words of Etidorhpa: you must not yield. 'T was to serve you that I came before you now, 't was to preserve you from the Drunkard's Cavern, that I have given you this vision of the land beyond the End of Earth where, if you will serve yourself, we will meet again.

She held aloft two tiny cups; I sprung to my feet and grasped one of them, and as I glanced at the throng in front of me, every radiant figure held aloft in the left hand a similar cup. All were gazing in my face. I looked at the transparent cup in my hand; it appeared to be partly filled with a green liquid. I looked at her cup and saw that it contained a similar fluid.

Forgetting the warning she had so recently given, I raised the cup to my lips, and just before touching it glanced again at her face. The fair creature stood with bowed head, her face covered with her hand; her very form and attitude spoke of sorrow and disappointment, and she trembled in distress. She held one hand as though to thrust back a form that seemed about to force itself beyond her figure, for peering exultingly from behind, leered the same Satanic face that met my gaze on the preceding occasion, when in the presence of the troop of demons, I had been tempted by the perfect man.

Dashing the cup to the floor I shouted:

"No; I will not drink."

Etidorhpa dropped upon her knees and clasped her hands. The Satanic figure disappeared from sight. Realizing that we had triumphed over the tempter, I also fell upon my knees in thankfulness.

CHAPTER XLI.

MISERY.

As all the bubbles in a glass shrink and vanish when the first collapses, so the troop of fairy-like forms before me disintegrated, and were gone. The delicate being, whose hand I held, fluttered as does a mist in the first gust of a sudden gale, and then dissolved into transparency. The gaily decked amphitheater disappeared, the very earth cavern passed from existence, and I found myself standing solitary and alone in a boundless desert. I turned towards every point of the compass only to find that no visible object appeared to break the monotony. I stood upon a floor of pure white sand which stretched to the horizon in gentle wave-like undulations as if the swell of the ocean had been caught, transformed to sand, and fixed.

I bent down and scooped a handful of the sand, and raised it in the palm of my hand, letting it sift back again to earth; it was surely sand. I pinched my flesh, and pulled my hair, I tore my garments, stamped upon the sand, and shouted aloud to demonstrate that I myself was still myself. It was real, yes, real. I stood alone in a desert of sand. Morning was dawning, and on one side the great sun rose slowly and majestically.

"Thank God for the sun," I cried. "Thank God for the light and heat of the sun."

I was again on surface earth; once more I beheld that glorious orb for the sight of which I had so often prayed when I believed myself miserable in the dismal earth caverns, and which I had been willing to give my very life once more to behold. I fell on my knees, and raised my hands in thankfulness. I blessed the rising sun, the illimitable sand, the air about me, and the blue heavens above. I blessed all that was before me, and again and again returned thanks for my delivery from the caverns beneath me. I did not think to question by what power this miracle had been accomplished. I did not care to do so; had I thought of the matter at all I would not have dared to question for fear the transition might prove a delusion.

I turned towards the sun, and walked eastward. As the day progressed and the sun rose into the heavens, I maintained my journey, aiming as best

I could to keep the same direction. The heat increased, and when the sun reached the zenith it seemed as though it would melt the marrow in my bones. The sand, as white as snow and hot as lava, dazzled my eyes, and I covered them with my hands. The sun in the sky felt as if it were a ball of white hot iron near my head. It seemed small, and yet appeared to shine as through a tube directed only towards myself. Vainly did I struggle to escape and get beyond its boundary, the tube seemed to follow my every motion, directing the blazing shafts, and concentrating them ever upon my defenseless person. I removed my outer garments, and tore my shirt into fibers hoping to catch a waft of breeze, and with one hand over my eyes, and the other holding my coat above my head, endeavored to escape the mighty flood of heat, but vainly. The fiery rays streamed through the garment as mercury flows through a film of gauze. They penetrated my flesh, and vaporized my blood. My hands, fingers, and arms puffed out as a bladder of air expands under the influence of heat. My face swelled to twice, thrice its normal size, and at last my eyes were closed, for my cheeks and eyebrows met. I rubbed my shapeless hand over my sightless face, and found it as round as a ball; the nose had become imbedded in the expanded flesh, and my ears had disappeared in the same manner.

I could no longer see the sun, but felt the vivid, piercing rays I could not evade. I do not know whether I walked or rolled along; I only know that I struggled to escape those deadly rays. Then I prayed for death, and in the same breath begged the powers that had transferred me to surface earth to carry me back again to the caverns below. The recollection of their cool, refreshing atmosphere was as the thought of heaven must be to a lost spirit. I experienced the agony of a damned soul, and now, in contradistinction to former times, considered as my idea of perfect happiness the dismal earth caverns of other days. I thought of the day I had stood at the mouth of the Kentucky cave, and waded into the water with my guide; I recalled the refreshing coolness of the stream in the darkness of that cavern when the last ray of sunshine disappeared, and I cursed myself for longing then for sunshine, and the surface earth. Fool that man is, I mentally cried, not to be contented with that which is, however he may be situated, and wherever he may be placed. This is but a retribution, I am being cursed for my discontented mind, this is hell, and in comparison, with this hell all else on or in earth is happiness. Then I damned the sun, the earth, the very God of all, and in my frenzy cursed everything that existed. I felt my puffed limbs, and prayed that I might become lean again. I asked to shrink to a skeleton, for seemingly my misery came with my expanded form; but I prayed and cursed in vain. So I struggled on in agony, every moment seemingly covering a multitude of years; struggled along like a lost soul plodding in an endless expanse of ever-increasing, ever-concentrating hell. At last, however, the day declined, the heat decreased, and as it did so my distorted body gradually regained its normal size, my eyesight returned, and finally I stood in that wilderness of sand watching the great red sun sink into the earth, as in the morning I had watched it rise. But between the sunrise and the sunset there had been an eternity of suffering; and then, as if released from a spell, I dropped exhausted upon the sand, and seemed to sleep. I dreamed of the sun, and that an angel stood before me, and asked why I was miserable, and in reply I pointed to the sun. "See;" I said, "the author of the misery of man."

Said the angel: "Were there no sun there would be no men, but were there no men there would still be misery."

"Misery of what?" I asked.

"Misery of mind," replied the angel. "Misery is a thing, misery is not a conception—pain is real, pain is not an impression. Misery and pain would still exist and prey upon mind substance were there no men, for mind also is real, and not a mere conception. The pain you have suffered has not been the pain of matter, but the pain of spirit. Matter cannot stiffer. Were it matter that suffered, the heated sand would writhe in agony. No; it is only mind and spirit that experience pain, or pleasure, and neither mind nor spirit can evade its destiny, even if it escapes from the body."

Then I awoke and saw once more the great red sun rise from the sand-edge of my desolate world, and I became aware of a new pain, for now I perceived the fact that I experienced the sense of thirst. The conception of the impression drew my mind to the subject, and instantly intense thirst, the most acute of bodily sufferings, possessed me. When vitalized tissue craves water, other physical wants are unfelt; when man parches to death all other method; of torture are disregarded. I thought no longer of the rising sun, I remembered no more the burning sand of yesterday, I felt only the pain of thirst.

"Water, water, water," I cried, and then in the distance as if in answer to my cry, I beheld a lake of water.

Instantly every nerve was strained, every muscle stretched, and I fled over the sands towards the welcome pool.

On and on I ran, and as I did so, the sun rising higher and higher, again began to burn the sands beneath my feet, and roast the flesh upon my bones. Once more I experienced that intolerable sense of pain, the pain of living flesh disintegrating by fire, and now with thirst gnawing at my vitals, and fire drying up the residue of my evaporated blood, I struggled in agony towards a lake that vanished before my gaze, to reappear just beyond.

This day was more horrible than the preceding, and yet it was the reverse so far as the action of the sun on my flesh was concerned. My prayer of yesterday had been fearfully answered, and the curses of the day preceding were being visited upon my very self. I had prayed to become lean, and instead of the former puffed tissue and expanded flesh, my body contracted as does beef when dried. The tightening skin squeezed upon the solidifying flesh, and as the moisture evaporated, it left a shriveled integument, contracted close upon the bone. My joints stood out as great protuberances, my skin turned to a dark amber color, and my flesh became transparent as does wetted horn. I saw my very vitals throb, I saw the empty blood vessels, the shriveled nerves and vacant arteries of my frame. I could not close my eyes. I could not shield them from the burning sun. I was a mummy, yet living, a dried corpse walking over the sand, dead to all save pain. I tried to fall, but could not, and I felt that, while the sun was visible, I must stand upright; I could not stop, and could not stoop. Then at last the malevolent sun sank beneath the horizon, and as the last ray disappeared again, I fell upon the sand.

I did not sleep, I did not rest, I did not breathe nor live a human; I only existed as a living pain, the conception of pain realized into a conscious nucleus, —and so the night passed. Again, the sun arose, and with the light of her first ray I saw near at hand a caravan, camels, men, horses, a great cavalcade. They approached rapidly and surrounded me. The leader of the band alighted and raised me to my feet, for no longer had I the power of motion. He spoke to me kindly, and strange as it may seem to you, but not at all strange did it seem to me, called me by name.

"We came across your tracks in the desert," he said; "we are your deliverers."

I motioned for water; I could not speak.

"Yes," he said, "water you shall have."

Then from one of the skins that hung across the hump of a camel he filled a crystal goblet with sparkling water, and held it towards me, but just before the goblet touched my lips he withdrew it and said:

"I forgot to first extend the greetings of our people."

And then I noticed in his other hand a tiny glass containing a green liquid, which he placed to my lips, pronouncing the single word, "Drink."

I fastened my gaze upon the water, and opened my lips. I smelled the aroma of the powerful narcotic liquid within the glass, and hastened to obey, but glanced first at my deliverer, and in his stead saw the familiar face of the satanic figure that twice before had tempted me. Instantly, without a thought as to the consequences, without a fear as to the result, I dashed the glass to the sand, and my voice returning, I cried for the third time, "No; I will not drink."

The troop of camels instantly disappeared, as had the figures in the scenes before, the tempter resolved into clear air, the sand beneath my feet became natural again, and I became myself as I had been before passing through the hideous ordeal. The fact of my deliverance from the earth caverns had, I now realized, been followed by temporary aberration of my mind, but at last I saw clearly again, the painful fancy had passed, the delirium was over.

I fell upon my knees in thankfulness; the misery through which I had passed had proven to be illusory, the earth caverns were beneath me, the mirage and temptations were not real, the horrors I had experienced were imaginary—thank God for all this—and that the sand was really sand. Solitary, alone, I Kneeled in the desert barren, from horizon to horizon desolation only surrounded, and yet the scene of that illimitable waste, a fearful reality, it is true, was sweet in comparison with the misery of body and soul about which I had dreamed so vividly.

"'T is no wonder," I said to myself, "that in the moment of transition from the underground caverns to the sunshine above, the shock should have disturbed my mental equilibrium, and in the moment of reaction I should have dreamed fantastic and horrible imaginings."

A cool and refreshing breeze sprung now, from I know not where; I did not care to ask; it was too welcome a gift to question, and contrasted pleasantly with the misery of my past hallucination. The sun was shining hot above me, the sand was glowing, parched beneath me, and yet the grateful breeze fanned my brow, and refreshed my spirit.

"Thank God," I cried, "for the breeze, for the coolness that it brings; only those who have experienced the silence of the cavern solitudes through which I have passed, and added thereto, have sensed the horrors of the more recent nightmare scenes, can appreciate the delights of a gust of air."

The incongruity of surrounding conditions, as connected with affairs rational, did not appeal at all to my questioning senses, it seemed as though the cool breeze, coining from out the illimitable desolation of a heated waste was natural. I arose and walked on, refreshed. From out that breeze my physical self-drew refreshment and strength.

"'T is the cold," I said; "the blessed antithesis of heat, that supports life. Heat enervates, cold stimulates; heat depresses, cold animates. Thank God for breezes, winds, waters, cold."

I turned and faced the gladsome breeze. "'T is the source of life, I will trace it to its origin, I will leave the accursed desert, the hateful sunshine, and seek the blissful regions that give birth to cool breezes."

I walked rapidly, and the breeze became more energetic and cooler. With each increase of momentum on my part, corresponding strength seemed to be added to the breeze—both strength and coolness.

"Is not this delightful?" I murmured; "my God at last has come to be a just God. Knowing what I wanted, He sent the breeze; in answer to my prayer the cool, refreshing breeze arose. Damn the heat," I cried aloud, as I thought of the horrid day before; "blessed be the cold," and as though in answer to my cry the breeze stiffened and the cold strengthened itself, and I again returned thanks to my Creator.

With ragged coat wrapped about my form I faced the breeze and strode onward towards the home of the gelid wind that now dashed in gusts against my person.

Then I heard my footstep crunch, and perceived that the sand was hard beneath my feet; I stooped over to examine it and found it frozen. Strange, I reflected, strange that dry sand can freeze, and then I noticed, for the first time, that spurts of snow surrounded me, 't was a sleety mixture upon which I trod, a crust of snow and sand. A sense of dread came suddenly over me, and instinctively I turned, affrighted, and ran away from the wind, towards the desert behind me, hack towards the sun, which, cold and bleak, low in the horizon, was sinking. The sense of dread grew upon me, and I shivered as I ran. With my back towards the breeze I had blessed, I now fled towards the sinking sun I had cursed. I stretched out my arms in supplication towards that orb, for from behind overhanging blackness spread, and about me roared a fearful hurricane. Vainly. As I thought in mockery the heartless sun disappeared before my gaze, the hurricane surrounded me, and the wind about me became intensely cold, and raved furiously. It seemed as though the sun had fled from my presence, and with the disappearance of that orb, the outline of the earth was blotted from existence. It was an awful blackness, and the universe was now to me a blank. The cold strengthened and froze my body to the marrow of my bones. First came the sting of frost, then the pain of cold, then insensibility of flesh. My feet were benumbed, my limbs motionless. I stood a statue, quiescent in the midst of the roaring tempest. The earth, the sun, the heavens themselves, my very person now had disappeared. Dead to the sense of pain or touch, sightless, amid a blank, only the noise of the raging winds was to me a reality. And as the creaking frost reached my brain and congealed it, the sound of the tempest ceased, and then devoid of physical senses, my quickened intellect, enslaved, remained imprisoned in the frozen form it could not leave, and yet could no longer control.

Reflection after reflection passed through that incarcerated thought entity, and as I meditated, the heinous mistakes I had committed in the life that had passed, arose to torment. God had answered my supplications, successively I had experienced the hollowness of earthly pleasures, and had left each lesson unheeded. Had I not alternately begged for and then cursed each gift of God? Had I not prayed for heat, cold, light, and darkness, and anathematized each? Had I not, when in perfect silence, prayed for-sound; in sheltered caverns, prayed for winds and storms; in the very corridors of heaven, and in the presence of Etidorhpa, had I not sought for joys beyond?

Had I not found each pleasure of life a mockery, and notwithstanding each bitter lesson, still pursued my headstrong course, alternately blessing and cursing my Creator, and then myself, until now, amid a howling waste, in perfect darkness, my conscious intellect was bound to the frozen, rigid semblance of a body? All about me was dead and dark, all within was still and cold, only my quickened intellect remained as in every corpse the self-conscious intellect must remain, while the body has a mortal form, for death of body is not attended by the immediate liberation of mind. The consciousness of the dead man is still acute, and he who thinks the dead are mindless, will realize his fearful error when devoid of motion he lies a corpse, conscious of all that passes on around him, waiting the liberation that can only come by disintegration and destruction of the flesh.

So, unconscious of pain, unconscious of any physical sense, I existed on and on, enthralled, age after age passed and piled upon one another, for time was to me unchangeable, no more an entity. I now prayed for change of any kind; and envied the very devils in hell their pleasures, for were they not gifted with the power of motion, could they not hear, and see, and realize the pains they suffered? I prayed for death — death absolute, death eternal. Then, at last, the darkness seemed to lessen, and I saw the frozen earth beneath, the monstrous crags of ice above, the raging tempest about, for I now had learned by reflection to perceive by pure intellect, to see by the light within. My body, solid as stone, was fixed and preserved in a waste of ice. The world was frozen. I perceived that the sun, and moon, and stars, nearly stilled, dim and motionless, had paled in the cold depths of space. The universe itself was freezing, and amid the desolation only my deserted intellect remained. Age after age had passed, aeons of ages had fled, nation after nation had grown and perished, and in the uncounted epochs behind, humanity had disappeared. Unable to free itself from the frozen body, my own intellect remained the solitary spectator of the dead silence about. At last, beneath my vision, the moon disappeared, the stars faded one by one, and then I watched the sun grow dim, until at length only a milky, gauze-like film remained to indicate her face, and then—vacancy. I had lived the universe away. And in perfect darkness the living intellect, conscious of all that had transpired in the ages past, clung still enthralled to the body of the frozen mortal. I thought of my record in the distant past, of the temptations I had undergone, and called myself a fool, for, had I listened to the tempter, I could at least have suffered, I could have had companionship even though it were of the devils—in hell. I lived my life over and over, times without number; I thought of my tempters, of the offered cups, and thinking, argued with myself:

"No," I said; "no, I had made the promise, I have faith in Etidorhpa, and were it to do over again I would not drink."

Then, as this thought sped from me, the ice scene dissolved, the enveloped frozen form of myself faded from view, the sand shrunk into nothingness, and with my natural body, and in normal condition, I found myself back in the earth cavern, on my knees, beside the curious inverted fungus, of which fruit I had eaten in obedience to my guide's directions. Before me the familiar figure of my guide stood, with folded arms, and as my gaze fell upon him he reached out his hand and raised me to my feet.

"Where have you been during the wretched epochs that have passed since I last saw you?" I asked.

"I have been here," he replied, "and you have been there."

"You lie, you villainous sorcerer," I cried; "you lie again as you have lied to me before. I followed you to the edge of demon land, to the caverns of the drunkards, and then you deserted me. Since last we met I have spent a million, billion years of agony inexpressible, and have had that agony made doubly horrible by contrast with the thought, yes, the very sight and touch of Heaven. I passed into a double eternity, and have experienced the ecstasies of the blessed, and suffered the torments of the damned, and now you dare boldly tell me that I have been here, and that you have been there, since last I saw you stand by this cursed fungus bowl."

"Yes," he said, taking no offense at my violence; "yes, neither of us has left this spot; you have sipped of the drink of an earth-damned drunkard, you have experienced part of the curses of intemperance, the delirium of narcotics. Thousands of men on earth, in their drunken hallucination, have gone through hotter hells than you have seen; your dream has not exaggerated the sufferings of those who sup of the delirium of intemperance."

And then he continued:

"Let me tell you of man's conception of eternity."

CHAPTER XLII.

ETERNITY WITHOUT TIME.

"Man's conception of eternity is that of infinite duration, continuance without beginning or end, and yet everything he knows is bounded by two or more opposites. From a beginning, as he sees a form of matter, that substance passes to an end." Thus, spoke my guide.

Then he asked, and showed by his question that he appreciated the nature of my recent experiences: "Do you recall the instant that you left me standing by this bowl to start, as you imagined, with me as a companion, on the journey to the cavern of the grotesque?"

"No; because I did not leave you. I sipped of the liquid, and then you moved on with me from this spot; we were together, until at last we were separated on the edge of the cave of drunkards."

"Listen," said he; "I neither left you nor went with you. Yon. neither went from this spot nor came back again. You neither saw nor experienced my presence nor my absence; there was no beginning to your journey."

"Go on."

"You ate of the narcotic fungus; you have been intoxicated."

"I have not," I retorted. "I have been through your accursed caverns, and into hell beyond. I have been consumed by eternal damnation in the journey, have experienced a heaven of delight, and also an eternity of misery."

"Upon the contrary, the time that has passed since you drank the liquid contents of that fungus fruit has only been that which permitted you to fall upon your knees. You swallowed the liquor when I handed you the shell cup; you dropped upon your knees, and then instantly awoke. See," he said; "in corroboration of my assertion the shell of the fungus fruit at your feet is still dripping with the liquid you did not drink. Time has been annihilated. Under the influence of this potent earth-bred narcotic-intoxicant, your dream begun inside of eternity; you did not pass into it."

"You say," I interrupted, "that I dropped upon my knees, that I have experienced the hallucination of intoxication, that the experiences of my vision occurred during the second of time that was required for me to drop upon my knees."

"Yes."

"Then by your own argument you demonstrate that eternity requires time, for even a millionth part of a second is time, as much so as a million of years."

"You mistake," he replied, "you misinterpret my words. I said that all you experienced in your eternity of suffering and. pleasure, occurred between the point when you touched the fungus fruit to your lips, and that when your knees struck the stone."

"That consumed time," I answered.

"Did I assert," he questioned, "that your experiences were scattered over that entire period?"

No."

"May not all that occurred to your mind have been crushed into the second that accompanied the mental impression produced. by the liquor, or the second of time that followed, or any other part of that period, or a fraction of any integral second of that period?"

"I cannot say," I answered, "what part of the period the hallucination, as you call it, occupied."

"You admit that so far as your conception of time is concerned, the occurrences to which you refer may have existed in either an inestimable fraction of the first, the second, or the third part of the period."

"Yes," I replied, "yes; if you are correct in that, they were illusions."

"Let me ask you furthermore," he said; "are you sure that the flash that bred your hallucination was not instantaneous, and a part of neither the first, second, nor third second?"

"Continue your argument."

"I will repeat a preceding question with a slight modification. May not all that occurred to your mind have been crushed into the space between the second of time that preceded the mental impression produced by the liquor, and the second that followed it? Need it have been a part of either second, or of time at all? Indeed, could it have been a part of time if it were instantaneous?"

"Go on."

"Suppose the entity that men call the soul of man were in process of separation from the body. The process you will admit would occupy time, until the point of liberation was reached. Would not dissolution, so far as the separation of matter and spirit is concerned at its critical point be instantaneous?"

I made no reply.

"If the critical point is instantaneous, there would be no beginning, there could be no end. Therein rests an eternity greater than man can otherwise conceive of, for as there is neither beginning nor end, time and space are annihilated. The line that separates the soul that is in the body from the soul that is out of the body is outside of all things. It is a between, neither a part of the nether side nor of the upper side; it is outside the here and the here-after. Let us carry this thought a little further," said he. "Suppose a good man were to undergo this change, could not all that an eternity of happiness might offer be crushed into this boundless conception, the critical point? All that a mother craves in children dead, could reappear again in their once loved forms; all that a good life earns, would rest in the soul's experience in that eternity, but not as an illusion, although no mental pleasure, no physical pain is equal to that of hallucinations. Suppose that a vicious life was ended, could it escape the inevitable critical point? Would not that life in its previous journey create its own sad eternity? You have seen the working of an eternity with an end but not a beginning to it, for you cannot sense the commencement of your vision. You have been in the cavern of the grotesque, —the realms of the beautiful, and have walked over the boundless sands that bring misery to the soul, and have, as a statue, seen the frozen universe dissolve. You are thankful that it was all an illusion as you deem it now; what would you think had only the heavenly part been spread before you?"

"I would have cursed the man who dispelled the illusion," I answered.

"Then," he said, "you are willing to admit that men who so live as to gain such an eternity, be it mental illusion, hallucination or real, make no mistake in life."

"I do," I replied; "but you confound me when you argue in so cool a manner that eternity may be everlasting to the soul, and yet without the conception of time."

"Did I not teach you in the beginning of this journey," he interjected, "that time is not as men conceive it. Men cannot grasp an idea of eternity and retain their sun bred, morning and evening, conception of time. Therein lies their error. As the tip of the whip-lash passes with the lash, so through life the soul of man proceeds with the body. As there is a point just when the tip of the whip-lash is on the edge of its return, where all motion of the line that bounds the tip ends, so there is a motionless point when the soul starts onward from the body of man. As the tip of the whip-lash sends its cry through space, not while it is in motion either way, but from the point where motion ceases, the spaceless, timeless point that lies between the backward and the forward, so the soul of man leaves a cry (eternity) at the critical point. It is the death echo, and thus each snap of the life-thread throws an eternity, its own eternity, into eternity's seas, and each eternity is made up of the entities thus cast from the critical point. With the end of each soul's earth journey, a new eternity springs into existence, occupying no space, consuming no time, and not conflicting with any other, each being exactly what the soul-earth record makes it, an eternity of joy (heaven), or an eternity of anguish (hell). There can be no neutral ground."

Then he continued:

"The drunkard is destined to suffer in the drunkard's eternity, as you have suffered; the enticement of drink is evanescent, the agony to follow is eternal. You have seen that the sub-regions of earth supply an intoxicant. Taste not again of any intoxicant; let your recent lesson be your last. Any stimulant is an enemy to man, any narcotic is a fiend. It destroys its victim, and corrupts the mind, entices it into pastures grotesque, and even pleasant at first, but destined to eternal misery in the end. Beware of the eternity that follows the snapping of the life-thread of a drunkard. Come," he abruptly said, "we will pursue our journey."

[NOTE.—Morphine, belladonna, hyoscyamus and cannabis indica are narcotics, and yet each differs in its action from the others. Alcohol and methyl alcohol are intoxicants; ether, chloroform, and chloral are anaesthetics, and yet no two are possessed of the same qualities. Is there any good reason to doubt that combinations of the elements as yet hidden from man can not cause hallucinations that combine and intensify the most virulent of narcotics, intoxicants, and anaesthetics, and pall the effects of hashish or of opium?

If, in the course of experimentation, a chemist should strike upon a compound that in traces only would subject his mind and drive his pen to record such seemingly extravagant ideas as are found in the hallucinations herein pictured, would it not be his duty to bury the discovery from others, to cover from mankind the existence of such a noxious fruit of the chemist's or pharmaceutist's art? Introduce such an intoxicant, and start it to ferment in humanity's blood, and before the world were advised of its possible results, might not the ever increasing potency gain such headway as to destroy, or debase, our civilization, and even to exterminate mankind?—J. U. L.]

INTERLUDE.

CHAPTER XLIII.

THE LAST CONTEST.

I, Lewellyn Drury, had been so absorbed in the fantastic story the old man read so fluently from the execrably written manuscript, and in the metaphysical argument which followed his account of the vision he had introduced so artfully as to lead me to think it was a part of his narrative, that I scarcely noted the passage of time. Upon seeing him suspend his reading, fold the manuscript, and place it in his pocket, I reverted to material things, and glancing at the clock, perceived that the hands pointed to bed-time.

"To-morrow evening," said he, "I will return at nine o'clock. In the interim, if you still question any part of the story, or wish further information on any subject connected with my journey, I will be prepared to answer your queries. Since, however, that will be your last opportunity, I suggest that you make notes of all subjects that you wish to discuss."

Then, in his usual self-possessed, exquisitely polite manner, he bowed himself out.

I spent the next day reviewing the most questionable features of his history, recalling the several statements that had been made. Remembering the humiliation I had experienced in my previous attempts to confute him, I determined to select such subjects as would appear the most difficult to explain, and to attack the old man with vehemence.

I confess, that notwithstanding my several failures, and his successful and constant elucidation and minute details in regard to occurrences which he related, and which anticipated many points I had once had in mind to question, misgivings still possessed me concerning the truthfulness of the story. If these remarkable episodes were true, could there be such a thing as fiction? If not all true, where did fact end and fancy begin?

Accordingly, I devoted the following day to meditating my plan of attack, for I felt that I had been challenged to a final contest. Late the next day, I felt confident of my own ability to dispossess him, and in order further to test his power, when night came I doubly locked the door to my room, first with the key and next with the inside bolt. I had determined to force him again to induce inert material to obey his command, as he had done at our first interview. The reader will remember that Prof. Chickering had deemed that occurrence an illusion, and I confess that time had dimmed the vividness of the scene in my own mind. Hence, I proposed to verify the matter. Therefore, at the approach of nine o'clock, the evening following, I sat with my gaze riveted on the bolt of the door, determined not to answer his knock.

He gave me no chance to neglect a response to his rap. Exactly at the stroke of nine the door swung noiselessly on its hinges, the wizard entered, and the door closed again. The bolt had not moved, the knob did not turn. The bar passed through the catch and back to its seat,—I sprung from my chair, and excitedly and rudely rushed past my guest. I grasped the knob, wrenched it with all my might. Vainly; the door was locked; the bolt was fastened. Then I turned to my visitor. He was quietly seated in his accustomed place, and apparently failed to notice my discomposure, although he must have realized that he had withstood my first test.

This pronounced defeat, at the very beginning of our proposed contest, produced a depressing effect; nevertheless, I made an effort at self-control, and seating myself opposite, looked my antagonist in the face. Calm, dignified, with the brow of a philosopher, and the countenance of a philanthropist, a perfect type of the exquisite gentleman, and the cultured scholar, my guest, as serene and complacent as though, instead of an intruder, he were an invited participant of the comforts of my fireside, or even the host himself, laid his hat upon the table, stroked his silvery, translucent beard, and said:

"Well?"

I accepted the challenge, for the word, as he emphasized it, was a challenge, and hurled at him, in hopes to catch him unprepared, the following abrupt sentence:

"I doubt the possibility of the existence of a great cavern such as you have described. The superincumbent mass of earth would crush the strongest metal. No material known to man could withstand a pressure so great as would overlie an arch as large as that you depict; material would succumb even if the roof were made of steel."

"Do not be so positive," he replied. "By what authority do you make this assertion?"

"By the authority of common sense as opposed to an unreasonable hypothesis. You should know that there is a limit to the strength of all things, and that no substance is capable of making an arch of thousands of miles, which, according to your assertion, must have been the diameter of the roof of your inland sea."

"Ah," he replied, "and so you again crush my facts with your theory. Well, let me ask a question."

"Proceed."

"Did you ever observe a bubble resting on a bubble?"

"Yes."

"Did you ever place a pipe-stem in a partly filled bowl of soap water, and by blowing through it fill the bowl with bubbles?"

"Yes."

"Did you ever calculate the tensile strength of the material from which you blew the bubble?"

"No; for soap water has no appreciable strength."

"And yet you know that a bubble made of suds has not only strength, but elasticity. Suppose a bubble of energy floating in space were to be covered to the depth of the thickness of a sheet of tissue paper with the dust of space, would that surprise you?"

"No."

"Suppose two such globes of energy, covered with dust, were to be telescoped or attached together, would you marvel at the fact?"

"No."

He drew a picture on a piece of paper, in which one line was enclosed by another, and remarked:

"The pencil mark on this paper is proportionately thicker than the crust of the earth over the earth cavern I have described. Even if it were made of soap suds, it could revolve through space and maintain its contour."

"But the earth is a globe," I interjected.

"You do not mean an exact globe?"

"No; it is flattened at the poles."

He took from his pocket two thin rubber balls, one slightly larger than the other. With his knife he divided the larger ball, cutting it into halves. He then placed one of the sections upon the perfect ball, and held the arrangement between the gas light and the wall.

"See; is not the shadow flattened, as your earth is, at the poles?"

continuously collect dust, most of it of the earth's temperature, forming a fluid (water), would not that dust be propelled naturally from the poles?"

"Yes; according to our theory."

"Perhaps," said he, "the contact edge of the invisible spheres of energy which compose your earth bubbles, for planets are bubbles, that have been covered with water and soil during the time the energy bubble, which is the real bone of the globe, has been revolving through space; perhaps, could you reach the foundation of the earth dust, you would find it not a perfect sphere, but a compound skeleton, as of two bubbles locked, or rather telescoped together.

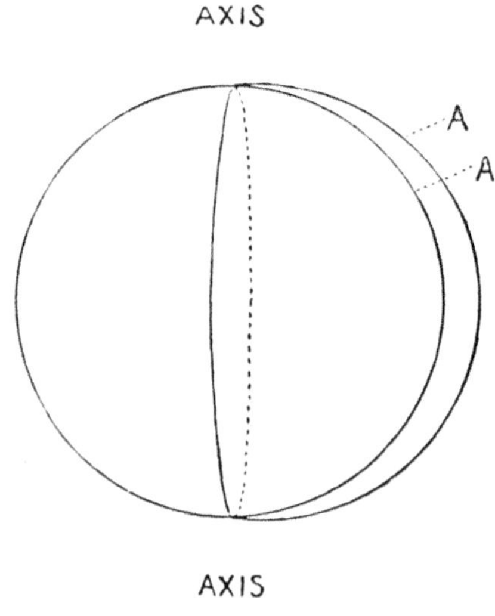

FIG. 33
A A, telescoped energy spheres.

"Are you sure that my guide did not lead me through the space between the bubbles?"

Then he continued:

"Do not be shocked at what I am about to assert, for, as a member of materialistic humanity, you will surely consider me irrational when I say that matter, materials, ponderous substances, one and all, so far as the ponderous part is concerned, have no strength."

"What! no strength?"

"None whatever."

I grasped the poker.

"Is not this matter?"

"Yes."

"I cannot break it."

"No."

"Have not I strength?"

"Confine your argument now to the poker; we will consider you next. You cannot break it."

"I can break this pencil, though," and I snapped it in his face.

"Yes."

I curled my lip in disdain.

"You carry this argument too far."

"Why?"

"I can break the pencil, I cannot break the poker; had these materials not different strengths there could be no distinction; had I no strength I could not have broken either."

"Are you ready to listen?" he replied.

"Yes; but do not exasperate me."

"I did not say that the combination you call a poker had no strength, neither did I assert that you could not break a pencil."

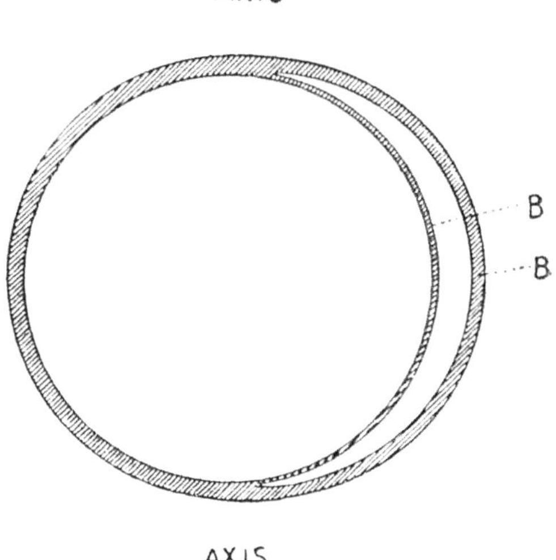

FIG. 34.
B B, telescoped energy spheres covered with space dirt, inclosing space between.

"A distinction without a difference; you play upon words."

"I said that matter, the ponderous side of material substances, has no strength."

"And I say differently."

He thrust the end of the poker into the fire, and soon drew it forth red-hot.

"Is it as strong as before?"

"No."

"Heat it to whiteness and it becomes plastic."

"Yes."

"Heat it still more and it changes to a liquid."

"Yes."

"Has liquid iron strength?"

"Very little, if any."

"Is it still matter?"

"Yes."

"Is it the material of the iron, or is it the energy called heat that qualifies the strength of the metal? It seems to me that were I in your place I would now argue that absence of heat constitutes strength," he sarcastically continued.

"Go on."

"Cool this red-hot poker by [illegible]

becomes very hard and brittle." [illegible]

"Yes."

"Cool it slowly, and it is comparatively soft and plastic."

"Yes."

"The material is the same, is it not?"

"Go on."

"What strength has charcoal?"

"Scarcely any."

"Crystallize it, and the diamond results."

"I did not speak of diamond."

"Ah! and is not the same amount of the same material present in each, a grain of diamond and a grain of charcoal? What is present in a grain of diamond that is not present in a grain of charcoal?"

"Go on."

"Answer my question."

"I cannot."

"Why does brittle, cold zinc, when heated, become first ductile, and then, at an increased temperature, become brittle again? In each case the same material is present."

"I do not know; but this I do know: I am an organized being, and I have strength of body."

The old man grasped the heavy iron poker with both hands, and suddenly rising to his full height, swung it about his head, then with a motion so menacing that I shrunk back into my chair and cried out in alarm, seemed about to strike, with full force, my defenseless brow.

"My God," I shouted, "what have I done that you should murder me?"

He lowered the weapon, and calmly asked:

"Suppose that I had crushed your skull—where then would be your vaunted strength?"

I made no reply, for as yet I had not recovered from the mental shock.

"Could you then have snapped a pencil? Could you have broken a reed? Could you even have blown the down from a thistle bloom?"

"No."

"Would not your material body have been intact?"

"Yes."

"Listen," said he. "Matter has no strength, matter obeys spirit, and spirit dominates all things material. Energy in some form holds particles of matter together, and energy in other forms loosens them. 'T is this imponderable force that gives strength to substances, not the ponderable side of the material. Granite crushed is still granite, but destitute of rigidity. Creatures dead are still organic structures, but devoid of strength or motion. The spirit that pervades all material things gives to them form and existence. Take from your earth its vital spirit, the energy that subjects matter, and your so-called adamantine rocks would disintegrate, and sift as dust into the interstices of space. Your so-called rigid globe, a shell of space dust, would dissolve, collapse, and as the spray of a burst bubble, its ponderous side would vanish in the depths of force."

I sat motionless.

"Listen," he repeated. "You wrong your own common sense when you place dead matter above the spirit of matter. Atoms come and go in their ceaseless transmigrations, worlds move, universes circulate, not because they are material bodies, but because as points of matter, in a flood of force, they obey the spirit that can blot out a sun, or. dissolve the earth, as easily as it can unlink two atoms. Matter is an illusion, spirit is the reality."

I felt that he had silenced me against my will, and although I could not gainsay his assertions, I determined to study the subject carefully, at my leisure.

"As you please," he interjected into my musings; "but since you are so determined, you would better study from books that are written by authors who know whereof they write, and who are not obliged to theorize from speculative data concerning the infrastructural earth crust."

"But where can I find such works? I do not know of any." "Then," said he, "perhaps it would be better to cease doubting the word of one who has acquired the knowledge to write such a book, and who has no object in misleading you."

"Still other questions arise," I said.

"Well?"

"I consider the account of the intra-earth fungus intoxicant beyond the realm of fact."

"In what respect?"

"The perfect loss of self that resulted immediately, in an instant, after swallowing the juice of the fungous fruit, so that you could not distinguish between the real guide at your side and the phantom that sprung into existence, is incredible. An element of time is a factor in the operation of

aders would probably
ion. J. U. L.)

"Have you investigated all possible anesthetics?" he asked.

"Of course not."

"Or all possible narcotics?"

"No."

"How long does it require for pure prussic acid to produce its physiological action?"

"I do not know."

He ignored my reply, and continued:

"Since there exists a relative difference between the time that is required for ether and chloroform to produce insensibility, and between the actions and resultant effects of all known anesthetics, intoxicants, and narcotics, I think you are hypercritical. Some nerve excitants known to you act slowly, others quickly; why not others still instantaneously? If you can rest your assertion on any good basis, I will gladly meet your questions, but I do not accept such evidence as you now introduce, and, I do not care to argue for both parties."

Again, I was becoming irritated, for I was not satisfied with the manner in which I upheld my part of the argument, and naturally, as is usually the case with the defeated party, became incensed at my invincible antagonist.

"Well," I said, "I criticize your credulity. The drunkards of the drunkards' cavern were beyond all credence. I cannot conceive of such abnormal creations, even in illusion. Had I met with your experiences I would not have supposed, for an instant, that the fantastic shapes could have been aught but a dream, or the result of hallucination, while, without a question, you considered them real."

"You are certainly pressed for subjects about which to complain when you resort to criticizing the possibilities in creations of a mind under the influence of a more powerful intoxicant than is known to surface earth," he remarked. " However, I will show you that nature fashions animals in forms more fantastic than I saw, and that even these figures were not overdrawn"—

Without heeding his remark, I interrupted his discourse, determined to have my say:

"And I furthermore question the uncouth personage you describe as your guide. Would you have me believe that such a being has an existence outside an abnormal thought-creation?"

"Ah," he replied, "you have done well to ask these two questions in succession, for you permit me to answer both at once. Listen: The Monkey, of all animals, seems to approach closest to man in figure, the Siamang Gibon of Asia, the Baldheaded Saki of South America, with its stub of a tail, being nearest. From these types we have great deviations as in the Wanderer of India, with its whiskered face, and the Black Macaque of the Island of Celebes, with its hairy topknot, and hairless stub of a tail, or the well-known Squirrel Monkey, with its long supple tail, and the Thumbless Spider Monkey, of South America. Between these types we have among monkeys, nearly every conceivable shape of limb and figure, and in color of their faces and bodies, all the shades of the rainbow.

"Some Squirrels jump and then sail through the air. The Sloth can barely move on the earth. Ant-eaters have no teeth at all, while the Grizzly Bear can crush a gun barrel with its molars.

"The Duck-billed Platypus of South Australia has the body of a mole, the tail of a raccoon, the flat bill of a duck, and the flipper of a seal, combined with the feet of a rat. It lays eggs as birds do, but suckles its young as do other mammals. The Opossum has a prehensile tail, as have some monkeys, and in addition a living bag or pouch in which the female carries her tiny young. The young of a kind of tree frog of the genus Hylodes, breathe through a special organ in their tails; the young of the Pipa, a great South American toad, burrow, into the skin of the mother, and still another from Chili, as soon as hatched, creep down the throat of the father frog, and find below the jaw an opening into a false membrane covering the entire abdomen, in which they repose in safety. Three species of frogs and toads have no tongue at all, while in all the others the tongue is attached by its tip to the end of the mouth, and is free behind. The ordinary Bullfrog has conspicuous great legs, while a relative, the Coecilia (and others as well) have a head reminding of the frog, but neither tail nor legs, the body being elongated as if it were a worm. The long, slender fingers of a Bat are united by means of a membrane that enables it to fly like a bird, while as a contrast, the fingers of a Mole, its near cousin, are short and stubby, and massive as compared with its frame. The former flies through the air, the latter burrows (almost flies) through the earth. The Great Ant-eater has a curved head which is drawn out into a slender snout, no teeth, a long, slender tongue, a great bushy tail, and claws that neither allow the

horny, curved tail, while another relative, the Long-tailed Pangolin, has a great alligator-like tail which, together with its body, is covered with horny, overlapping scales.

"The Greenland Whale has an enormous head occupying more than one-third its length, no teeth, and a throat scarcely larger than that of a sucker fish. The Golden Mole has a body so nearly symmetrical that, were it not for the snout, it would be difficult to determine the location of the head without close inspection, and it has legs so short that, were it not for the powerful claws, they would not be observed at all. The Narwhal has a straight, twisted tusk, a"—

"Hold, hold," I interrupted; "do you think that I am concerned in these well-known contrasts in animal structure?"

"Did you not question the possibility of the description I gave of my grotesque drunkards, and of the form of my subterranean guide?" my guest retorted.

"Yes; but I spoke of men, you describe animals."

"Man is an animal, and between the various species of animals that you say are well known, greater distinctions can be drawn than between my guide and surface-earth man. Besides, had you allowed me to proceed to a description of animal life beneath the surface of the earth, I would have shown you that my guide partook of their attributes. Of the creatures described, one only was of the intra-earth origin—the Mole, —and like my guide, it is practically eyeless."

"Go on," I said; "'t is useless for me to resist. And yet"—

"And yet what?"

"And yet I have other subjects to discuss."

"Proceed."

"I do not like the way in which you constantly criticize science, especially in referring thereto the responsibilities of the crazed anatomist. It seems to me that he was a monomaniac, gifted, but crazed, and that science was unfortunate in being burdened with such an incubus."

"True, and yet science advances largely by the work of such apparently heartless creatures. Were it not for investigators who overstep the bounds of established methods, and thus criticize their predecessors, science would rust and disintegrate. Besides, why should not science be judged by the rule she applies to others?"

"What do you mean?"

"Who is freer to criticize religion than the materialistic man of science?"

"But a religious man is not cruel."

"Have you not read history? Have you not shuddered at the crimes recorded in the name of the religions of man?"

"Yes; but these cruelties were committed by misguided men under the cloak of the church, or of false religions, during the dark ages. Do not blame religion, but the men who abused the cause."

"Yes," he added, "you are right; they were fanatics, crazed beings, men; yes, even communities, raving mad. Crazed leaders can infuse the minds of the people with their fallacies, and thus become leaders of crazed nations. Not, as I have depicted in my scientific enthusiast, one man alone in the privacy of his home torturing a single child, but whole nations pillaging, burning, torturing, and destroying. But this is foreign to our subject. Beware, I reiterate, of the science of human biology. The man who enters the field cannot foresee the end, the man who studies the science of life, and records his experiments, cannot know the extremes to which a fanatical follower may carry the thought-current of his leader. I have not overdrawn the lesson. Besides, science is now really torturing, burning, maiming, and destroying humanity. The act of destruction has been transferred from barbarians and the fanatic in religion to the follower of the devotees of science."

"No; I say, no."

"Who created the steam engine? Who evolves improved machinery? Who creates improved artillery, and explosives? Scientific men."

He hesitated.

"Go on."

"Accumulate the maimed and destroyed each year; add together the miseries and sorrows that result from the explosions, accidents, and catastrophes resulting from science improvements, and the dark ages scarcely offer a parallel. Add thereto the fearful destruction that follows a war among nations scientific, and it will be seen that the scientific enthusiast of the present has taken the place of the misguided fanatic of the past. Let us be just. Place to the credit of religion the good that religion has done, place to the credit of science the good that science is doing, and yet do not mistake, both leave in their wake an atmosphere saturated with misery, a road whitened with humanity's bones. Neither the young nor the old are spared, and so far as the sufferer is concerned it matters not whether the

Again, he hesitated.

"Go on."

"One of science's most serious responsibilities, from which religion has nearly escaped, is that of supplying thought-food to fanatics, and from this science cannot escape."

"Explain yourself."

"Who places the infidel in possession of arguments to combat sacred teachings? Who deliberately tortures animals, and suggests that biological experimentation in the name of science, before cultured audiences even, is legitimate, such as making public dissections of living creatures?"

"Enough, enough," I cried, thinking of his crazed anatomist, and covering my face with my hands; "you make my blood creep."

"Yes," he added sarcastically; "you shudder now and criticize my truthful study, and to-morrow you will forget the lesson, and perhaps for dinner you will relish your dish of veal, the favorite food of mothers, the nearest approach to the flesh of babies."

Then his manner changed, and in his usual mild, pleasant way, he said:

"Take what I have said kindly; I wish only to induce your religious part to have more charity for your scientific self, and the reverse. Both religion and science are working towards the good of man, although their devotees are human, and by human errors bring privations, sufferings, and sorrows to men. Neither can fill the place of the other; each should extend a helping hand, and have charity for the shortcomings of the other; they are not antagonists, but workers in one field; both must stand the criticisms of mutual antagonists, and both have cause to fear the evils of fanaticism within their own ranks more than the attacks of opponents from without. Let the religious enthusiast exercise care; his burning, earnest words may lead a weak-minded father to murder an innocent family, and yet 't is not religion that commits the crime. Let the zealous scientific man hesitate; he piles up fuel by which minds unbalanced, or dispositions perverted, seek to burn and destroy hopes that have long served the yearnings of humanity's soul. Neither pure religion nor true science is to blame for the acts of its devotees, and yet each must share the responsibility of its human agents."

"We will discuss the subject no further," I said; "it is not agreeable."

Then I continued:

"The idea of eternity without time is not quite clear to me, although I catch an imperfect conception of the argument advanced. Do you mean to say that when a soul leaves the body, the earth life of the individual, dominated by the soul, is thrown off from it as is the snap of a whip-lash, and that into the point between life and death, the hereafter of that mortal may be concentrated?"

"I simply give you the words of my guide," he replied, "but you have expressed the idea about as well as your word language will admit. Such a conception of eternity is more rational to one who, like myself, has lived through an instant that covered, so far as mind is concerned, a million years of time, than is an attempt to grasp a conception of an eternity, without beginning or end, by basing an argument on conditions governing material substances, as these substances are known to man. You have the germ of the idea which may be simply a thought for you to ponder over; 'you can study the problem at your leisure. Do not, however, I warn you, attempt to comprehend the notion of eternity by throwing into it the conception of time as men accept that term, for the very word time, as men define it, demands that there be both a beginning and an end. With the sense of time in one's mind, there can be no conception of the term eternity."

Then, as I had so often done before, I unwarily gave him an opportunity to enlarge on his theme, to my disadvantage. I had determined not to ask any questions concerning his replies to my criticism, for whenever I had previously done so, the result had been disastrous to me. In this case I unwittingly said:

"Why do you say that our language will not permit of clearer conceptions than you give?"

"Because your education does not permit you to think outside of words; you are word-bound."

"You astonish me by making such an arrogant assertion. Do you mean to assert that I cannot think without using words?"

"Yes. Every thought you indulge in is circumscribed. You presumably attempt to throw a thought-line forward, and yet you step backward and spin it in words that have been handed you from the past, and, struggle as you may, you cannot liberate yourself from the dead incubus. Attempt to originate an idea, and see if you can escape your word-master?"

"Go on; I am listening."

"Men scientific think in language scientific. Men poetical think in language poetic. All educated men use words in thinking of their subjects,

understood. In each case the foundation of a thought is a word that in the very beginning carries to the mind a meaning, a something from the past. Each thought ramification is an offshoot from words that express ideas and govern ideas, yes, create ideas, even dominating the mind. Men speak of ideas when they intend to refer to an image in the mind, but in reality, they have no ideas outside of the word sentences they unconsciously reformulate. Define the term idea correctly, and it will be shown that an idea is a sentence, and if a sentence is made of words already created, there can be no new idea, for every word has a fixed meaning. Hence, when men think, they only rearrange words that carry with themselves networks of ideas, and thus play upon their several established meanings. How can men so circumscribed construct a new idea or teach a new science?"

"New words are being created."

"Language is slowly progressing, but no new word adds itself to a language; it is linked to thought-chains that precede. In order to create a word, as a rule, roots are used that are as established in philology as are building materials in architecture. When a new sound is thrust into a language, its intent must be introduced by words already known, after which it conveys a meaning derived from the past, and becomes a part of mind sentences already constructed, as it does of spoken language. Language has thus been painfully and slowly evolved and is still being enlarged, but while new impressions may be felt by an educated person, the formulated feeling is inseparable, from well-known surviving words."

"Some men are dumb."

"Yes; and yet they frame mind-impressions into unspoken words of their own, otherwise they would be scarcely more than' animals. Place an uneducated dumb person in a room with a complicated instrument, and although he may comprehend its uses, he cannot do so unless he frames sense-impressions into, what is to him, a formulated mind-word sequence."

"But he can think about it."

"No; unless he has already constructed previous impressions into word-meanings of his own, he cannot think about it at all. Words, whether spoken or unspoken, underlie all ideas. Try, if you believe I am mistaken, try to think of any subject outside of words?"

I sat a moment, and mentally attempted the task, and shook my head.

"Then," said the old man, "how can I use words with established meanings to convey to your senses an entirely new idea? If I use new sounds, strung together, they are not words to you, and convey no meaning; if I use words familiar, they reach backward as well as forward. Thus, it is possible to instruct you, by a laborious course of reasoning, concerning a phenomenon that is connected with phenomena already understood by you, for your word-language can be thrust out from the parent stalk, and can thus follow the outreaching branches. However, in the case of phenomena that exist on other planes, or are separated from any known material, or force, as is the "true conception that envelops the word eternity, there being neither connecting materials, forces, nor words to unite the outside with the inside, the known with the unknown, how can I tell you more than I have done? You are word-bound."

"Nevertheless, I still believe that I can think outside of words."

"Well, perhaps after you attempt to do so, and fail again and again, you will appreciate that a truth is a truth, humiliating as it may be to acknowledge the fact."

"A Digger Indian has scarcely a word-language," I asserted, loth to relinquish the argument.

"You can go farther back if you desire, back to primitive man; man without language at all, and with ideas as circumscribed as those of the brutes, and still you have not strengthened your argument concerning civilized man. But you are tired, I see."

"Yes; tired of endeavoring to combat your assertions. You invariably lead me into the realms of speculation, and then throw me upon the defensive by asking me to prove my own theories, or with apparent sincerity, you advance an unreasonable hypothesis, and then, before I am aware of your purpose, force me to acquiesce because I cannot find facts to confute you. You very artfully throw the burden of proof on me in all cases, for either by physical comparisons that I cannot make, I must demonstrate the falsity of your metaphysical assertions, or by abstract reasonings disprove statements you assert to be facts."

"You are peevish and exhausted, or you would perceive that I have generally allowed you to make the issue, and more than once have endeavored to dissuade you from doing so. Besides, did I not several times in the past bring experimental proof to dispel your incredulity? Have I not been courteous?"

"Yes," I petulantly admitted; "yes."

diately to his subject, he invariably led by circuitous route to the matter under discussion. Before reaching the point, he would manage to commit me to his own side of the subject, or place me in a defenseless position. So, with covert aim I began:

"I believe that friction is one method of producing heat."

"Yes."

"I have been told that the North American Indians make fires by rubbing together two pieces of dry wood."

"True."

"I have understood that the light of a shooting star results from the heat of friction, producing combustion of its particles."

"Partly," he answered.

"That when the meteoric fragment of space dust strikes the air, the friction resulting from its velocity heats it to redness, fuses its surface, or even burns its very substance into ashes."

"Yes."

"I have seen the spindle of a wheel charred by friction."

"Yes."

"I have drawn a wire rapidly through a handkerchief tightly grasped in my hands, and have warmed the wire considerably in doing so."

"Yes."

I felt that I had him committed to my side of the question, and I prepared to force him to disprove the possibility of one assertion that he had made concerning his journey.

"You stated that you rode in a boat on the underground lake."

"Yes."

"With great rapidity?"

"Yes."

"Rapid motion produces friction, I believe?"

"Yes."

"And heat?"

"Yes."

"Why did not your boat become heated even to redness? You rode at the rate of nine hundred miles an hour," I cried exultingly.

"For two reasons," he calmly replied; "two natural causes prevented such a catastrophe."

And again, he warned me, as he had done before, by saying:

"While you should not seek for supernatural agencies to account for any phenomena in life, for all that is is natural, neither should you fail to study the differences that varying conditions produce in results already known. A miracle ceases to be a miracle when we understand the scientific cause underlying the wonder; occultism is natural, for if there be occult phenomena they must be governed by natural law; mystery is not mysterious if the veil of ignorance that envelops the investigator is lifted. What you have said is true concerning the heat that results from friction, but —

"First, the attraction of gravitation was inconsiderable where the boat, to which you refer, rested on the water.

"Second, the changing water carried away the heat as fast as it was produced. While it is true that a cannon ball becomes heated in its motion through the air, its surface is cooled when it strikes a body of water, notwithstanding that its great velocity is altogether overcome by the water. The friction between the water and the iron does not result in heated iron, but the contrary. The water above the rapids of a river has practically the temperature of the water below the rapids, regardless of the friction that ensues between these points. Admit, however, that heat is liberated as the result of the friction of solids with water, and still it does not follow that this heat will perceptibly affect the solid. With a boat each particle of water carries the heat away, each succeeding portion of water takes up the heat liberated by that preceding it. Thus, the great body of water, over which our boat sped, in obedience to the ordinary law, became slightly warmed, but its effect upon the boat was scarcely perceptible. Your comparison of the motion of a meteor, with that of our boat, was unhappy. We moved rapidly, it is true, in comparison with the motion of vessels such as you know, but comparison cannot be easily drawn between the velocity of a boat and that of a meteor. While we moved at the rate of many miles a minute, a meteor moves many times faster, perhaps as many miles in a second. Then you must remember that the force of gravitation was so slight in our position that"—

"Enough," I interrupted. "We will pass the subject. It seems that you draw upon science for knowledge to support your arguments, however irrational they may be, and then you sneer at this same method of argument when I employ it."

He replied to my peevish complaint with the utmost respect by calling to my attention

swer, and that h

"If I am wroı

right in my facts, and science thought is thus in the wrong, for facts overbalance theory. I ask you only to give me the attention that my statements merit. I am sincere, and aim to serve your interests. Should investigation lead you hereafter to infer that I am in error, at our final interview you can have my considerate attention. Be more charitable, please." Then he added:

"Is there any other subject you wish to argue?"

"Yes," I answered, and again my combativeness arose; "yes. One of the truly edifying features of your narrative is that of the intelligent guide," and I emphasized the word intelligent, and curled up my lip in a sarcastic manner.

"Proceed."

"He was verily a wonderful being; an eyeless creature, and yet possessed of sight and perception beyond that of mortal man; a creature who had been locked in the earth, and yet was more familiar with its surface than a philosopher; a cavern-bred monstrosity, and yet possessed of the mind of a sage; he was a scientific expert, a naturalist, a metaphysical reasoner, a critic of religion, and a prophet. He could see in absolute darkness as well as in daylight; without a compass he could guide a boat over a trackless sea, and could accomplish feats that throw Gulliver and Munchausen into disrepute."

In perfect composure my aged guest listened to my cynical, and almost insulting tirade. He made no effort to restrain my impetuous sentences, and when I had finished replied in the polished language of a scholarly gentleman.

"You state truly, construe my words properly, as well as understand correctly."

Then he continued musingly, as though speaking to himself:

"I would be at fault and deserve censure did I permit doubts to be thrown upon so clear a subject, or discredit on so magnanimous a person."

Turning to me he continued:

"Certainly, I did not intend to mislead or to be misunderstood, and am pleased to find you so earnest a scholar."

And then in his soft, mild manner, he commenced his detail reply, pouring oil upon the waters of my troubled soul, his sweet, melodious voice being so in contrast to my rash harangue. He began with his expressive and often repeated word, "listen."

"Listen. You are right, my guide was a being wonderful to mortals. He was eyeless, but as I have shown you before, and now swear to the fact, was not sightless; surely," he said, "surely you have not forgotten that long ago

I considered the phenomenal instinct at length. He predicted the future by means of his knowledge of the past—there is nothing wonderful in that. Can not a civil engineer continue a line into the beyond, and predict where the projection of that line will strike; can he not also calculate the effect that a curve will have on his line's destiny? Why should a being conversant with the lines and curves of humanity's journey for ages past not be able to indicate the lines that men must follow in the future? Of course, he could guide the boat, in what was to me a trackless waste of water, but you err in asserting that I had said he did not have a guide, even if it were not a compass. Many details concerning this journey have not been explained to you; indeed, I have acquainted you with but little that I experienced. Near surface earth we passed through caverns filled with creeping reptiles; through others we were surrounded by flying creatures, neither beast nor bird; we passed through passages of ooze and labyrinths of apparently interminable intra-earth structures; to have disported on such features of my journey would have been impracticable. From time to time I experienced strains of melody, such as never before had I conceived, seemingly choruses of angels were singing in and to my very soul. From empty space about me, from out the crevices beyond and behind me, from the depths of my spirit within me, came these strains in notes clear and distinct, but yet indescribable. Did I fancy, or was it real? I will not pretend to say. Flowers and structures beautiful, insects gorgeous and inexplicable were spread before me. Fig-tires and forms I cannot attempt to indicate in word descriptions, ever and anon surrounded, accompanied, and passed me by. The canvas conceptions of earth-bred artists bring to mind no forms so strange and weird and yet so beautiful as were these compound beings. Restful beyond description was it to drink in the indescribable strains of poetry of motion that I appreciated in the movements of fair creatures I have not mentioned, and it was no less soothing to experience the soul relief wrought by the sounds about me, for musicians know no notes so sweet and entrancing.

"There were also, in side caverns to which I was led, combinations of sounds and scenes in which floating strains and fleeting figures were interwoven and interlaced so closely that the senses of both sight and hearing became blended into a single sense, new, weird, strange, and inexpressible. As flavor is the combination of odor and taste, and is neither taste nor odor,

as when helping me through the chambers of mire, ooze, and creeping reptiles, my guide drew me onward.

"But to return to the subject. As to my guide being a cavern-bred monstrosity, I do not remember to have said that he was cavern-bred, and if I have forgotten a fact, I regret my short memory. Did I say that he was always a cavern being? Did I assert that he had never lived among mortals of upper earth? If so, I do not remember our conversation on that subject? He was surely a sage in knowledge, as you have experienced from my feeble efforts in explaining the nature of phenomena that were to you unknown, and yet have been gained by me largely through his instruction. He was a metaphysician, as you assert; you are surely right; he was a sincere, earnest reasoner and teacher. He was a conscientious student, and did not by any word lead me to feel that he did not respect all religions, and bow to the Creator of the universe, its sciences, and its religions. His demeanor was most considerate, his methods faultless, his love of nature deep, his patience inexhaustible, his sincerity unimpeachable. Yes," the old man said; "you are right in your admiration of this lovely personage, and when you come to meet this being as you are destined yet to do—for know now that you too will some day pass from surface earth, and leave only your name in connection with this story of myself—you will surely then form a still greater love and a deeper respect for one so gifted, and yet so self-sacrificing."

"Old man," I cried, "you mock me. I spoke facetiously, and you answer literally. Know that I have no confidence in your sailor-like tales, your Marco Polo history."

"Ah! You discredit Marco Polo? And why do you doubt?"

"Because I have never seen such phenomena, I have never witnessed such occurrences. I must see a thing to believe it."

"And so, you believe only what you see?" he queried. "Yes."

"Now answer promptly," he commanded, and his manner changed as by magic to that of a master. "Did you ever see Greenland?"

"No."

"Iceland?"

"No."

"A geyser?"

"No."

"A whale?"

"No."

"England?"

"No."

"France?"

"No."

"A walrus?"

"No."

"Then you do not believe that these conditions, countries, and animals have an existence?"

"Of course they have."

"Why?"

"Others have seen them."

"Ah," he said; "then you wish to modify your assertion—you only believe what others have seen?"

"Excepting one person," I retorted.

Then he continued, seemingly not having noticed my personal allusion:

"Have you ever seen your heart?"

I hesitated.

"Answer," he commanded.

"No."

"Your stomach?"

"No."

"Have you seen the stomach of any of your friends?"

"No."

"The back of your head?"

I became irritated, and made no reply.

"Answer," he again commanded.

"I have seen its reflection in a glass."

"I say no," he replied; "you have not."

"You are impudent," I exclaimed.

"Not at all," he said, good humoredly; "how easy it is to make a mistake. I venture to say that you have never seen the reflection of the back of your head in a mirror."

"Your presumption astounds me."

"I will leave it to yourself."

He took a hand-glass from the table and held it behind my head.

"Now, do you see the reflection?"

"No; the glass is behind me."

"Ah, yes; and so is the back of your head."

"FLOWERS AND STRUCTURES BEAUTIFUL, INSECTS GORGEOUS."

"Look," I said, pointing to the great mirror on the bureau; "look, there is the reflection of the back of my head."

"No; it is the reflection of the reflection in my hand-glass."

"You have tricked me; you quibble!"

"Well," he said, ignoring my remark; "what do you believe?"

"I believe what others have seen, and what I can do."

"Excluding myself as to what others have seen," he said facetiously.

"Perhaps," I answered, relenting somewhat.

"Has any man of your acquaintance seen the middle of Africa?"

"No."

"The center of the earth?"

"No."

"The opposite side of the moon?"

"No."

"The soul of man?"

"No."

"Heat, light, electricity?"

"No."

"Then you do not believe that Africa has a midland, the earth a center, the moon an opposite side, man a soul, force an existence?"

"You distort my meaning."

"Well, I ask questions in accord with your suggestions, and you defeat yourself. You have now only one point left. You believe only what you can do?"

"Yes."

"I will rest this case on one statement, then, and you may be the judge."

"Agreed."

"You cannot do what any child in Cincinnati can accomplish. I assert that any other man, any other woman in the city can do more than you can. No cripple is so helpless, no invalid so feeble as not, in this respect, to be your superior."

"You insult me," I again retorted, almost viciously.

"Do you dispute the assertion seriously?"

"Yes."

"Well, let me see you kiss your elbow."

Involuntarily I twisted my arm so as to bring the elbow towards my mouth, then, as I caught the full force of his meaning, the ridiculous result of my passionate wager came over me, and I laughed aloud. It was a change of thought from the sublime to the ludicrous.

The white-haired guest smiled in return, and kindly said:

"It pleases me to find you in good humor at last. I will return to-morrow evening and resume the reading of my manuscript. In the meantime, take good exercise, eat heartily, and become more cheerful."

He rose and bowed himself out.

CHAPTER XLIV.

I SEEK A CONFIDANT.

The more I thought over the foregoing incidents the more dissatisfied did I become with the part I, Llewellyn Drury, had taken therein.

It became evident that my personality had been dominated by a man experienced in many phases of life's study, as yet unknown to me, and as I revolved the matter in my mind, I became convinced that not only had I been craftily toyed with, but had been personally discredited. These thoughts were naturally exasperating, and, as I felt the spirit of rebellion arise within me, I became vindictive. I not only wanted to exculpate myself before myself, but I also wished to prove to the man in whose power I had been time and again that I was no longer a subject to his dominating will. With this thought in mind I did what I should have done long before, and would have done but for my former rebuke by Professor Chickering, sought advice from another. There is consolation in company, even if neither participant can assist the other. In the beginning of life, before we become arrogant and self-conceited, we seek the solace of those about us, and in the end of life, after we become aware that "all, all is vanity," we turn again to the companionship of our fellow-men. In the beginning of my experience with this strange being, I had sought the advice of one I hoped to lean upon, and now, when the indications pointed to the closing episode, I turned again to that humanity of which I was a part.

Seeking an aged scientific friend, in whom I had every confidence, and in whom I could trust implicitly, I opened my heart and gave without reservation, in minutest detail, all that I knew of the history that has been herein related. Instead of passing the story as the fantasia of a disordered mind he received it in attentive earnestness.

"There are, I believe," said he, "psychological conditions that are as yet misconstrued, and there are others unknown. Indeed," he added, "it

your perception was normal and referred to the influence his presence exerted over your mind. He has seemingly played on your credulity, and knowingly in all arguments has taken what is, according to our present logic, the weak side, aiming to convince you that the other (natural) side is unreal. In several cases it seems as though he made statements that cannot be true, and then artfully toyed with your mind until he actually led you to reason them out as natural."

"Name some of these statements."

"Vitalized darkness is one. It is preposterous to argue that a ray of energy- exists that can penetrate opaque bodies. Such a condition would discredit science. With the disproving of this irrational myth story concerning the light that penetrates opaque bodies his skillfully devised earth illumination disappears. There cannot be such a ray of energy. Next, the statement concerning new elements in the atmosphere is false. If chemists have established any point absolutely it is the constitution of the air. In making this assertion he has discredited Gulliver, for science has positively demonstrated that oxygen, hydrogen and nitrogen, with traces of well-known gaseous impurities, are all there is of air.

"And now I would call to your attention that the object you perceived and accepted so thoughtlessly as a brain view is a retina reflection. Purkinje, as your ingenious visitor probably very well knew, demonstrated that fact fifty years ago, conclusively so far as science is concerned, and since that time the phenomenon has been known as Purkinje's tracings or shadows.

"Your visitor should be credited with broad knowledge, keen penetration and great sagacity. His methods certainly excite my admiration, and it is by no means assured that despite his erratic methods he does not propose to serve his fellow-men. He is evidently studying mind expressions and conveying thought prints. He has most admirably proven that to you, facts may become fallacies, and fallacies may become facts, but he has not clearly differentiated between fact and fancy. Indeed, it seems as though he knows more than he tells, but feels that 'tis best to stir the thought stuff in your own self, and then let you find out for yourself that which he could tell you were he so inclined. You need not be at all disturbed. You are probably very susceptible to subtle reasonings; indeed, it is questionable if your visitor needs now enter the room in order to dominate your mind and make you see unreal things, as well as overlook things that exist."

Again I became irritated, for while my confidant had not asserted that my mind was disordered, as had Professor Chickering, he had humiliated me by arguing that I was mentally subject to the will of another. I sat in reverie a moment, and then said: "Are you willing to meet this personage?"

"Yes."

"Will you conceal yourself in my room to-morrow evening?"

"Certainly."

"Then I will place myself under your direction, and at the proper moment will confront you with him."

"If such is to be, you must exercise greater self-control than you have done heretofore."

In detail then my friend laid down our line of action. When he departed, I felt great pleasure in the comfort derived from the fact that I had now a confidant, and also in the certainty that together we could dispossess my strange mind-master, for I now felt convinced that I had been toyed with by a man educated in directions outside the lines of study that are as yet open to ordinary students. My thoughtless, empirical experimentation had probably been discovered by some means best known to I-Am-The-Man, and had led the master to seek my person. He was now wielding me as a moulder moulds a figure of putty—for what?

CHAPTER XLV.

'TIS NOT THE EYE, BUT THE BRAIN, THAT SEES AN OBJECT.

Promptly at eight o'clock the following evening my aged visitor knocked at the door, and upon entering the room conducted himself in the most conventional manner. I had purposely placed his chair in the line of vision from the large wardrobe, within which my scientific friend had been comfortably secreted, and from which my guest could be seen through a crack in the door without the hidden man being perceived. Every precaution had been taken to prevent the seer from suspecting the presence of my friend, the objects removed from the wardrobe were out of sight, as were also the cane and hat of my friend.

My visitor seated himself, and said: "Let us now continue the reading of the manuscript."

"No," I replied, "we will not."

He looked at me in apparent wonder, and asked: "What is your will?"

"I will that you listen to me," I said in a firm tone.

"Well?"

"You are playing with me, are using me for a hidden purpose; are neither reading a narrative nor relating facts."

"Go on."

"I will no longer submit to this imposition."

"Name your grievance, and if possible, I will serve you," he said, pleasantly.

"You have by some psychological power bound my attention and compelled my mind to obedience. You have forced me to see things that are not, and to overlook things that are."

"Name them."

I took from my pocket the carefully prepared paper of my scientific friend which I had copied in my own hand, and read as follows:

"No cavern such as you name has been discovered in Kentucky. You

can be vivified and made visible. You pretend that water can rise above its level, and thus by molecular force between solutions of varying gravity produce artesian wells by processes different from those accepted by geologists. You claim that the centre of gravitation is not the centre of the earth. You assert that the earth is hollow and that it is not matter that has weight, but that weight is an energy expression associated therewith, but which may exist free from matter. You assert that material has no strength, for that quality also you claim to be simply an expression of atomic and molecular energies. You assert that the prism does not decompose the sun's energy into its ultimates, but that the spectrum produced by a prism is a something scraped off from the light rays, the main ray passing directly through the prism. You claim also that rays exist that the prism cannot deflect and that as yet no device of man can enable him to appreciate. You claim further that the rays of the spectrum known to man are not ultimates, and that when they are finally dissociated, or again deflected, colors and conditions new to man will become evident. You assert that as yet man, because of his narrow mind, knows but little of the energy that pervades his sphere, and you assert that unknown forces permeate his very being. Yes," I cried, becoming almost frantic as I read, "yes, and at last you submit to me an experiment fifty years old, and craftily make me believe that I am looking at my brain when I really see the venation of the retina."

"Is that all?" he mildly asked.

"It is enough."

"No," he replied, "it is not enough. You might have added that you have heretofore been a slave to your master, one-sided science, based mainly on experimentation in certain limited directions, and have never been able to think outside of the narrow lines she prescribes. You might have said that never Eastern slave master, standing with whip in hand, more effectually crushed to earth a crouching supplicant than has this master crushed you and such as you. You might have added that the time of liberation is at hand and that, too, through the agency of that same science, for the wildest speculations of seemingly erratic dreamers is to be soon verified. You might have added much that I did not tell you and which is less probable than anything you have named as being improbable."

"Name one thing."

"You might have said that space outside the lines drawn from orb to orb is empty, an absolute void so far as man is now concerned."

"What, you astound me with your impudence."

"Yes," he replied, "because it is true."

"Look," I said, and, leading him to the window, I pointed to the starry heavens. "Look."

"Well?"

"Can light and heat pass through a vacuum, a perfect vacuum?"

"I did not assert that a vacuum stands between each world, each sun, each satellite and sun."

"You assuredly did."

"Listen," he said. "You misconstrue my words. I said as far as man is concerned outside the lines drawn from orb to orb," and, returning to his chair, he seated himself. "Listen to reason. Call your aged friend from the wardrobe. It is unkind to keep him longer in so uncomfortable a location. Besides, he wishes to join in the conversation."

I stood dumbfounded.

"You seem to forget what is proper," he remarked again, exactly as he had remarked at an early interview, and, opening the wardrobe door, he coolly invited my friend into the room. Taking him by the hand and looking him intently in the eye, The-Man-Who-Did-It said:

"You have questioned my personage and my mission, for which you certainly cannot be criticized. Be seated. And now for the figures of Purkinje," he added, joining in our former private conversation as though by request, "you are right and you are wrong. You are right in that Purkinje issued a pamphlet and wrote on the subject of retina venation shadows; you are wrong in accepting that the retina sees an object, for it does not. The real picture is not the shadow and is not the retina scene, but the impression made on the brain, to which a form of energy that you cannot now define and do not know carries the figure of that which is seemingly seen. So far as men's senses are concerned, an object seen is not always real, the only reality to man is the impression in the brain."

I looked at my new companion, awaiting his reply.

"You are mistaken," he asserted; "an object seen is real."

"No," the guest replied; "not necessarily; the object you perceive may not have an existence. It may not be situated where you think you see it. The impression on the retina may be so positive as to be beyond controversy,

The guest whirled him around so that he faced the mirror. "See," he said, "is not the lamp shade in the mirror?"

"No, that is a reflection."

"Of what?"

"Of the lamp shade."

"From what?"

"From the mirror."

"Does the lamp shade seem to be on the mirror?"

"No, far behind it."

"You know it is not behind the mirror?"

"Of course."

"You know also that it is not on the face of the mirror?"

"Yes."

"How do you know this?"

"By my knowledge of the laws of reflection."

"How do you know it is a reflection?"

"The real lamp is behind me."

"You are only giving an opinion, basing your opinion on what you assert you see in a place you know there is no lamp. You do not see the reflection and yet claim to do so. You actually see the lamp on the table behind you, and yet claim not to see it. You reason yourself into a self-evident fallacy. If you had not previously seen the lamp behind you, and that mirror had been set in a window frame so that you would not have suspected it to be a mirror, you would probably have accepted without question that you were looking into another room and were observing another lamp."

"Yes."

"You therefore see the lamp where it is not."

"Yes."

"You believe, however, since your reason states that the lamp is on the table, that what you see is the reflection."

"Surely."

"The reflection comes from the metallic surface on the back of the glass?"

"Yes."

"Now, let me say to you that you do not see the reflection—you see the lamp as much now as when you turn your eyes directly upon it. If you see the real lamp at all, you see it when you look toward that mirror."

"This I deny."

"Ah," he said, seemingly breaking the thought line, "I perceive that you wear spectacles. Please step to the lamp shade on the table, and examine the figures closely; read that inscription on the transparency."

My companion did so, holding his face about eighteen inches from the inscription; then he looked inquiringly at the guest.

"Be seated again, and let me ask you, where do you see the reflection of the lamp shade? Is it on the face of the mirror or beyond it?"

"Far beyond it."

"You do not claim that the rays really penetrate the quicksilver?"

"No; the reflecting surface is the mercury on the glass. The image of this lamp shade is reflected from that metallic surface, according to well-known laws."

The old man led my companion to the glass, and said, "If the image of the shade is reflected from the glass, the motto you have read is thrown from the glass, and you should be able to read the motto on the glass that reflects the engraving when you focus your eyes upon it through your spectacles. Please read the motto on the glass surface." My friend stepped to the mirror, and attempted to do as directed, and failed to accomplish the result.

"The image is not on the glass, nor yet on the quicksilver, I perceive, and so you do not see the reflection from the glass, as you asserted," said the guest. "Perhaps the motto is really behind the glass."

"Preposterous."

"Let us see. If it is behind the glass a telescope should focus it."

Taking my opera glasses from the table the intruding guest handed them to his companion, and said, "Focus them on the object you think you perceive behind the glass, and yet presume to argue is not there, and tell me if you cannot now read the motto."

"Yes, plainly."

"How consistent. You know the lamp shade is not there; you know that the reflection is not from that point but from the glass, and yet you assert that you perceive the motto where neither the substance nor the shadow can be, and cannot read the motto on the glass surface, from which, on the other hand, you claim you see the lamp reflected."

"I can explain this apparent inconsistency."

"Go on."

"Go on."

"I therefore see the reflection of the object apparently behind the mirror."

"My friend," said the old guest, "you have given the usual roundabout explanation for a very simple phenomenon, but it is not altogether satisfactory. You go around the tree and come back in order to examine the bark that faces you and then you talk in circles when you try to describe it. Now listen, my friend. You do not see the reflection, you simply look at the lamp shade which is behind you through a bent ray of light. While it is true that the angle of incidence is equal to the angle of reflection, that fact has nothing to do with the sight phenomenon. Why do you not say that the mirror bends the bundle of light rays, and that your eye receives the impressions imparted by the bent message before your brain does? The intellect has no power to see the bend or angle of that ray; it knows nothing of its path or journey and the impression received tells nothing about the mirror that rests between that object and yourself. The lamp shade is actually as far from your eye as are the combined distances of the shade and your eye from the glass when you look toward the shade in the mirror depths. It seems exactly that distance behind the glass because of the laws of perspective, and because you cannot appreciate the bend in your light ray. The one thing that exists, if anything exists in this phenomenon, is this bend in the ray of light, and that you cannot see. That which is you do not see (the bend in the ray), and that which is not (the reflection behind the glass) you assert that you do see. If you saw the image on the glass your spectacles would bring it into focus on the glass, but fail to do so. When you focused the opera glasses exactly as far as the shade is from your eye, counting the bend in the ray, you then asserted that you saw the inscription thereon. If a photographer had designed to take a picture of the motto from the so-called reflection, he would also have had to focus the camera on the real lamp shade, not on the mirror. This he could do by virtue of the bent ray of light. Is it not irrational to assert that an object exists where it is not?"

"I see the lamp shade through the bent ray of light, which, in other words, is your manner of telling what I said."

"No, I did not say you saw the lamp shade."

"Old man, you exasperate me; 'tis your own argument."

"It is not." My friend gazed at him in astonishment.

"I am tired," I interrupted; "tired of this folly. You twist facts to suit yourself, and prove one day by arguments that another day you use to disprove."

"Yes, and your masters in science teach you to-day that, what they taught yesterday were fallacies. You once made the assertion that you saw your reflection in the mirror, to which I added, 'No, not the reflection, but the reflection of the reflection.' Could I have taken time then to give you this lesson? I have overlooked many erroneous statements that you have made, and have myself used several human failings in order to be understood. Many things that might have been studied have been passed in silence; they could not be taken up on the moment. Are you through?" he asked.

"No. You asserted this evening that space is empty, and you know that it is filled with sun's rays."

"I did not."

I stood dumbfounded.

"I said that so far as men's faculties of observation are concerned space is empty."

"Ah," I sneered.

"Yes, a perfect blank."

"No ether of Aristotle therein?"

"No."

"No sunshine?"

"No."

"No heat?"

"No."

"No electricity?"

"No."

"Either you are the most arrogant of mortals, or we are fools."

"Neither condition is a necessity. Let's reason the matter out. It is usual for astronomers and mathematicians to calculate concerning the enormous amount of energy that the sun pours into space. On what premise do they base their calculations?" he turned to my student friend.

"They calculate from the amount the earth receives," was the reply.

"Ah. Now, what evidence have they to show that the sun is throwing the same amount of energy elsewhere into space?"

CHAPTER XLVI.

THE VISION OF THE FUTURE OF SCIENCE.

"Listen," said I-Am-The-Man. "Let us imagine that strings extend from your eye out into this room. Let us imagine that gravitation, not light, produces the sensation that you call sight, and that this force follows the strings. A string then becomes transparent to this sense of sight.

"Let us imagine that the extremities of these strings end in knobs and that these knobs are the exciting points, and thus severally impress the eye. Each string becomes a medium capable of conveying the energy that gives to the brain behind the eye the figure of the knob at the extremity of the string.

"Every string is simply a channel or path that leads directly from the brain, through the eye, to the knob extremity. The knob is at one end, the brain at the other, all between the slender strings is as vacancy. Let us imagine now that the observer, from what he knows, is asked to give his impression of the amount of energy these balls are throwing out. The decision will be that in all directions they throw off the same amount, thus pervading all space between the strings with the exciting energy in proportion to that which the eye receives. These balls only are seen by the brain; nothing else has ever been seen, nothing is known concerning the vast space between the radiating strings.

"Now as to your sun, the stars, the planets. These bodies are, so far as men know, connected with each other by energy channels apparently conveying heat and light as well as other force expressions. No evidence exists to show that these channels do not convey all the energy correlated by these bodies, all of it. At present, we can see by means of one of these forces of energy, one only, light, but in the time to come men will see by means of others. As before remarked, a pleasant pastime for some men is the calculation of the amount of energy the sun throws into space, basing their figures on the amount they believe the earth receives. However, since they have never

bodies. They guess only, and, as is usual with guesses, ridiculously. So far as space is concerned man has no data to indicate that a sliver of energy of any kind whatever escapes into space. Indeed, he accepts that gravitation exists only in lines connecting matter with matter, and because certain modifications of force radiate in all directions in his matter-surrounded vessels (as, for example, a hot iron ball in a vacuum glass), assumes that known forces pass in all directions correspondingly from planets and sun into space. Man has never seen outside the lines that connect his earth with the other planets and suns, which (the suns), like ganglii or nerve centres, are simply reservoirs in this complicated network. All the space between these channels and without these ganglii is to man as black as darkness can be, a void. Wherever a line crosses another, a sun springs into existence. Thus, as knots in a fisherman's net where cross the strings, so do the points of intersection of the channels of energy become as suns, and thus as a monstrous net in space these streams of energy, interlaced, are together moving through and sweeping infinity's chamber. Snap a line of energy, and the sun beyond disappears to us; intensify it, and the sun flames up; contract it, and the sun fades out. Thus, a star may seem to come and go, may suddenly brighten and as rapidly disappear.

"Now, let me go a little further in this thought line. Suppose an insect capable of seeing, reasoning, by means of the nerve impressions, rested in the great nerve of the neck vertebra of a living man. To that insect, bone, muscle, veins, blood, tissue of all kinds would have no existence, and the universe outside that human body would be as nothing. Feeling the nerve centres only, and seeing therewith the nerve ganglii, that insect would say: These are sources of energy; all outside the nerves leading to these centres is a blank. To that insect, only the threads of nerves and the great brain at one extremity would be a reality; all else would be empty space. If a nerve should die, both the nerve and all beyond and without would become a blank. If the person had a dead tooth, regardless of its solidity otherwise, it would not be a tooth to that insect, but vacant space.

"Do you know," suddenly asked the old man, "do you know how many dead teeth (worn-out suns and planets) are hanging to your earth and sun, giving out no heat, no light, no electricity; in other words, destitute of gravity and other forms of energy, invisible? Do you know how many dead worlds hang in space, destitute of gravity, light, heat, energy of all kinds, invisible consequently to you, transparent to your energy? Do you know how many live worlds hang to your sun, but above or below the plane on which your family of planets moves? Do you know how many space mediums, clear as crystal in substance, but opaque as graphite where the surfaces touch, blot out the worlds above and below the plane occupied by our family of planets?" He hesitated.

"Go on," said my companion, "go on."

"Now," said my mysterious visitor, "do you know where your sun is situated?"

"Of course."

"No, you do not. The thread of energy that connects your earth with the sun may be twisted, curved, bent, reflected from unseen surfaces of the space films here and there, and to you it must be straight. This thread is to man on earth the size of the earth; before it reaches the sun it may shrink to a thread's diameter. If it should snap, your sun would disappear in an instant. You look back toward the sun from this end of the channel; you know nothing of the curves and angles between. You saw the lamp shade, not where it is, for you know it to have been behind you. You see the sun and other heavenly bodies even less clearly, for you reason concerning them only from knowledge derived from this end of the line. The other end has never been touched. You see them through channels that, so far as you are concerned, may be straight or crooked, may be spirals or angular, may distort their sizes, shapes and distances. Would you not be surprised to know that from above your atmosphere the sun is invisible? Light is earth-bred."

Together we sat speechless. Then the Seer asked,

"Would you behold the future of science?"

"Yes," we both answered simultaneously. I-Am-The-Man removed the lamp shade. "Be seated side by side, and look at the lamp as you see it in your glass." We turned our eyes upon the mirror. He stepped behind us, and placed a hand on the forehead of each. "Behold," he said, "behold."

As he repeated these words the lamp disappeared, the room vanished, things seen dissolved, and things unseen took their places; things that I dare not say and dare not think about burst into view. To speak of that which enveloped my spirit during that vision would be to invite crucifixion at the hands of my scientific friends. Perhaps I have already done so.

When the vision disappeared, the old man was gone, and I found my student friend dazed by my side. Seemingly we came together back to

"Will you come again?" I asked.

"No," friend Llewellyn, he said, and silently departed.

I sat alone in my room, wrapped in thought shadows that come to such as I.

THE OLD MAN CONTINUES HIS MANUSCRIPT.

CHAPTER XLVII.

THE FATHOMLESS ABYSS.
THE EDGE OF THE EARTH SHELL.

Promptly at eight o'clock the next evening the old man entered my room. He did not allude to the occurrences of the previous evening, and for this considerate treatment I felt thankful, as my part in those episodes had not been enviable. He placed his hat on the table, and in his usual cool and deliberate manner, commenced reading as follows:

For a long time thereafter, we journeyed on in silence, now amid stately stone pillars, then through great cliff openings or among gigantic formations that often stretched away like cities or towns dotted over a plain, to vanish in the distance. Then the scene changed, and we traversed magnificent avenues, bounded by solid walls which expanded into lofty caverns of illimitable extent, from whence we found ourselves creeping through narrow crevices and threading winding passages barely sufficient to admit our bodies. For a considerable period, I had noted the absence of water, and as we passed from grotto to temple reared without hands, it occurred to me that I could not now observe evidence of water erosion in the stony surface over which we trod, and which had been so abundant before we reached the lake. My guide explained by saying in reply to my thought question, that we were beneath the water line. He said that liquids were impelled back towards the earth's surface from a point unnoticed by me, but long since passed. Neither did I now experience hunger nor thirst, in the slightest degree, a circumstance which my guide assured me was perfectly natural in view of the fact that there was neither waste of tissue nor consumption of heat in my present organism.

At last I observed far in the distance a slanting sheet of light that, fan-shaped, stood as a barrier across the way; beyond it neither earth nor earth's surface appeared. As we approached, the distinctness of its outline dis-

"Is this another hallucination?" I queried.

"No; it is a reality. Let us advance to the brink."

Slowly we pursued our way, for I hesitated and held back. I had really begun to distrust my own senses, and my guide in the lead was even forced to demonstrate the feasibility of the way, step by step, before I could be induced to follow. At length we neared the edge of the chasm, and while he stood boldly upright by the brink, with fear and trembling I crept on my knees to his side, and together we faced a magnificent but fearful void that stretched beneath and beyond us, into a profundity of space. I peered into the chamber of light, that indescribable gulf of brilliancy, but vainly sought for an opposite wall; there was none. As far as the eye could reach, vacancy, illuminated vacancy, greeted my vision. The light that sprung from that void was not dazzling, but was possessed of a beauty that no words can suggest. I peered downward, and found that we stood upon the edge of a shelving ledge of stone that receded rapidly beneath us, so that we seemed to rest upon the upper side of its wedge-like edge. I strained my vision to catch a glimpse of the bottom of this chasm, but although I realized that my eyes were glancing into miles and miles of space, there was no evidence of earthly material other than the brink upon which we stood.

The limit of vision seemed to be bounded by a silvery blending of light with light, light alone, only light. The dead silence about, and the new light before me, combined to produce a weird sensation, inexplicable, overpowering. A speck of dust on the edge of immensity, I clung to the stone cliff, gazing into the depths of that immeasurable void.

CHAPTER XLVIII.

MY HEART THROB IS STILLED, AND YET I LIVE.

"It now becomes my duty to inform you that this is one of the stages in our journey that can only be passed by the exercise of the greatest will force. Owing to our former surroundings upon the surface of the earth, and to your inheritance of a so-called instinctive education, you would naturally suppose that we are now on the brink of an impassable chasm. This sphere of material vacuity extends beneath us to a depth that I am sure you will be astonished to learn is over six thousand miles. We may now look straight into the earth cavity, and this streaming light is the reflected purity of the space below. The opposite side of this crevice, out of sight by reason of its distance, but horizontally across from where we stand, is precipitous and comparatively solid, extending upward to the material that forms the earth's surface. We have, during our journey, traversed an oblique, tortuous natural passage, that extends from the spot at which you entered the cave in Kentucky, diagonally down into the crust of the globe, terminating in this shelving bluff. I would recall to your mind that your journey up to this time has been of your own free will and accord. At each period of vacillation—and you could not help but waver occasionally—you have been at liberty to return to surface earth again, but each time you decided wisely to continue your course. You can now return if your courage is not sufficient to overcome your fear, but this is the last opportunity you will have to reconsider, while in my company."

"Have others overcome the instinctive terrors to which you allude?"

"Yes; but usually the dread of death, or an unbearable uncertainty, compels the traveler to give up in despair before reaching this spot, and the opportunity of a lifetime is lost. Yes; an opportunity that occurs only in the lifetime of one person out of millions, of but few in our brotherhood."

"Then I can return if I so elect?"

"We must descend from this cliff."

"You cannot be in earnest."

"Why?"

"Do you not see that the stone recedes from beneath us, that we stand on the edge of a wedge overhanging bottomless space?"

"That I understand."

"There is no ladder," and then the foolish remark abashed me as I thought of a ladder six thousand miles in length.

"Go on."

He made no reference to my confusion.

"There is practically no bottom," I asserted, "if I can believe your words; you told me so."

"And that I reiterate."

"The feat is impracticable, impossible, and only a madman would think of trying to descend into such a depth of space."

Then an idea came over me; perhaps there existed a route at some other point of the earth's crevice by which we could reach the underside of the stone shelf, and I intimated as much to the guide.

"No; we must descend from this point, for it is the only entrance to the hollow beneath."

We withdrew from the brink, and I meditated in silence. Then I crept again to the edge of the bluff, and lying flat on my chest, craned my head over, and peered down into the luminous gulf, the texture of the receding mineral was distinctly visible for a considerable distance, and then far, far beneath all semblance to material form disappeared—as the hull of a vessel fades in deep, clear water. As I gazed into the gulf it seemed evident that, as a board floating in water is bounded by water, this rock really ended. I turned to my guide and questioned him.

"Stone in this situation is as cork," he replied; "it is nearly devoid of weight; your surmise is correct. We stand on the shelving edge of a cliff of earthly matter, that in this spot slants upward from beneath like the bow of a boat. We have reached the bottom of the film of space dust on the bubble of energy that forms the skeleton of earth."

I clutched the edge of the cliff with both hands.

"Be not frightened; have I not told you that if you wish to return you can do so. Now hearken to me:

"A short time ago you endeavored to convince me that we could not descend from this precipice, and you are aware that your arguments were without foundation. You drew upon your knowledge of earth materials, as you once learned them, and realized at the time that you deluded yourself in doing so, for you know that present conditions are not such as exist above ground. You are now influenced by surroundings that are entirely different from those that govern the lives of men upon the earth's surface. You are almost without weight. You have nearly ceased to breathe, as long since you discovered, and soon I hope will agree entirely to suspend that harsh and wearying movement. Your heart scarcely pulsates, and if you go with me farther in this journey, will soon cease to beat."

I started up and turned to flee, but he grasped and held me firmly.

"Would you murder me? Do you think I will mutely acquiesce, while you coolly inform me of your inhuman intent, and gloat over the fact that my heart will soon be as stone, and that I will be a corpse?" He attempted to break in, but I proceeded in frenzy. "I will return to upper earth, to sunshine and humanity. I will retreat while yet in health and strength, and although I have in apparent willingness accompanied you to this point, learn now that at all times I have been possessed of the means to defend myself from personal violence." I drew from my pocket the bar of iron. "See, this I secreted about my person in the fresh air of upper earth, the sweet sunshine of heaven, fearing that I might fall into the hands of men with whom I must combat. Back, back," I cried.

He released his hold of my person, and folded his arms upon his breast, then quietly faced me, standing directly between myself and the passage we had trod, while I stood on the brink, my back to that fearful chasm.

By a single push he could thrust me into the fathomless gulf below, and with the realization of that fact, I felt that it was now a life and death struggle. With every muscle strained to its utmost tension, with my soul on fire, my brain frenzied, I drew back the bar of iron to smite the apparently defenseless being in the forehead, but he moved not, and as I made the motion, he calmly remarked: "Do you remember the history of Hiram Abiff?"

The hand that held the weapon dropped as if stricken by paralysis, and a flood of recollections concerning my lost home overcame me. I had raised my hand against a brother, the only being of my kind who could aid me or assist me either to advance or recede. How could I, unaided, re-cross that glassy lake, and pass through the grotesque forests of fungi and the

"I DREW BACK THE BAR OF IRON TO SMITE THE APPARENTLY DEFENSELESS BEING IN THE FOREHEAD."

"Forgive me," I sobbed, and sunk at his feet. "Forgive me, my friend, my brother; I have been wild, mad, am crazed." He made no reply, but pointed over my shoulder into the space beyond.

I turned, and in the direction indicated, saw, in amazement, floating in the distant space a snow- and ice-clad vessel in full sail. She was headed diagonally from us, and was moving rapidly across the field of vision Every spar and sail was clearly defined, and on her deck, and in the rigging, I beheld sailors clad in winter garments pursuing their various duties.

As I gazed, enraptured, she disappeared in the distance.

"A phantom vessel," I murmured.

"No," he replied; "the abstraction of a vessel sailing on the ocean above us. Every object on earth is the second to an imprint in another place. There is an apparent reproduction of matter in so-called vacancy, and on unseen pages a recording of all events. As that ship sailed over the ocean above us, she disturbed a current of energy, and it left its impress as an outline on a certain zone beneath, which is parallel with that upon which we now chance to stand."

"I cannot comprehend," I muttered.

"No," he answered; "to you it seems miraculous, as to all men an unexplained phenomenon approaches the supernatural. All that is is natural. Have men not been told in sacred writings that their every movement is being recorded in the Book of Life, and do they not often doubt because they cannot grasp the problem? May not the greatest scientist be the most apt skeptic?"

"Yes," I replied.

"You have just seen," he said, "the record of an act on earth, and in detail it is being printed elsewhere in the Book of Eternity. If you should return to earth's surface you could not by stating these facts convince even the persons on that same ship, of your sanity. You could not make them believe that hundreds of miles beneath, both their vessel and its crew had been reproduced in fac simile, could you?"

No."

"Were you to return to earth you could not convince men that you had existed without breath, with a heart dead within you. If you should try to impress on mankind the facts that you have learned in this journey, what would be the result?"

"I would probably be considered mentally deranged; this I have before admitted."

"Would it not be better then," he continued, "to go with me, by your own free will, into the unknown future, which you need fearless than a return to the scoffing multitude amid the storms of upper earth? You know that I have not at any time deceived you. I have, as yet, only opened before you a part of one rare page out of the boundless book of nature; you have tasted of the sweets of which few persons in the flesh have sipped, and I now promise you a further store of knowledge that is rich beyond conception, if you wish to continue your journey."

"What if I decide to return?"

"I will retrace my footsteps and liberate you upon the surface of the earth, as I have others, for few persons have courage enough to pass this spot."

"Binding me to an oath of secrecy?"

"No," he answered; "for if you relate these events men will consider you a madman, and the more clearly you attempt to explain the facts that you have witnessed, the less they will listen to you; such has been the fate

With a motion so quick in conception, and rapid in execution that I was taken altogether by surprise, with a grasp so powerful that I could not have repelled him, had I expected the movement and tried to protect myself, the strange man, or being beside me, threw his arms around my body. Then, as a part of the same movement, he raised me bodily from the stone, and before I could realize the nature of his intention, sprung from the edge of the cliff into the abyss below, carrying me with him into its depths.

"SPRUNG PROM THE EDGE OF THE CLIFF INTO THE ABYSS BELOW, CARRYING ME WITH HIM INTO ITS DEPTHS."

CHAPTER XLIX.

THE INNER CIRCLE, OR THE END OF GRAVITATION. IN THE BOTTOMLESS GULF.

I recall a whirling sensation, and an involuntary attempt at self-preservation, in which I threw my arms wildly about with a vain endeavor to clutch some form of solid body, which movement naturally ended by a tight clasping of my guide in my arms, and locked together we continued to speed down into the seven thousand miles of vacancy. Instinctively I murmured a prayer of supplication, and awaited the approaching hereafter, which, as I believed, would quickly witness the extinction of my unhappy life, the end of my material existence; but the moments (if time can be so divided when no sun marks the division) multiplied without bodily shock or physical pain of any description; I retained my consciousness.

"Open your eyes," said my guide, "you have no cause for fear."

I acquiesced in an incredulous, dazed manner.

"This unusual experience is sufficient to unnerve you, but you need have no fear, for you are not in corporal danger, and can relax your grasp on my person."

I cautiously obeyed him, misgivingly, and slowly loosened my hold, then gazed about to find that we were in a sea of light, and that only light was visible, that form of light which I have before said is an entity without source of radiation. In one direction, however, a great gray cloud hung suspended and gloomy, dark in the center, and shading therefrom in a circle, to disappear entirely at an angle of about forty-five degrees.

"This is the earth-shelf from which we sprung," said the guide; "it will soon disappear."

Wherever I glanced this radiant exhalation, a peaceful, luminous envelope, this rich, soft, beautiful white light appeared. The power of bodily motion I found still a factor in my frame, obedient, as before, to my will. I

so complacently? No; this could not be true. Then I thought: "I have been instantly killed by a painless shock, and my spirit is in heaven;" but my earthly body and coarse, ragged garments were palpable realities; the sense of touch, sight, and hearing surely were normal, and a consideration of these facts dispelled my first conception.

"Where are we now?"

"Moving into earth's central space."

"I comprehend that a rushing wind surrounds us which is not uncomfortable, but otherwise I experience no unusual sensation, and cannot realize but that I am at rest."

"The sensation, as of a blowing wind is in consequence of our rapid motion, and results from the friction between our bodies and the quiescent, attenuated atmosphere which exists even here, but this atmosphere becomes less and less in amount until it will disappear altogether at a short distance below us. Soon we will be in a perfect calm, and although moving rapidly, to all appearances will be at absolute rest."

Naturally, perhaps, my mind attempted, as it so often had done, to urge objections to his statements, and at first it occurred to me that I did not experience the peculiar sinking away sensation in the chest that I remembered follows, on earth, the downward motion of a, person falling from a great height, or moving rapidly in a swing, and I questioned him on the absence of that phenomenon.

"The explanation is simple," he said; "on the surface of the earth a sudden motion, either upward or downward, disturbs the equilibrium of the organs of respiration, and of the heart, and interferes with the circulation of the blood. This produces a change in blood pressure within the brain, and the 'sinking' sensation in the chest, or the dizziness of the head of a person moving rapidly, or it may even result in unconsciousness, and complete suspension of respiration, effects which sometimes follow rapid movements, as in a person falling from a considerable height. Here circumstances are entirely, different. The heart is quiet, the lungs in a comatose condition, and the blood stagnant. Mental sensations, therefore, that result from a disturbed condition of these organs are wanting, and, although we are experiencing rapid motion, we are in the full possession of our physical selves, and maintain our mental faculties unimpaired."

Again, I interposed an objection:

"If, as you say, we are really passing through an attenuated atmosphere with increasing velocity, according to the law that governs falling bodies that are acted upon by gravity which continually accelerates their motion, the friction between ourselves and the air will ultimately become so intense as to wear away our bodies."

"Upon the contrary," said he, "this attenuated atmosphere is decreasing in density more rapidly than our velocity increases, and before long it will have altogether disappeared. You can perceive that the wind, as you call it, is blowing less violently than formerly; soon it will entirely cease, as I have already predicted, and at that period, regardless of our motion, we will appear to be stationary."

Pondering over the final result of this strange experience I became again alarmed, for accepting the facts to be as he stated, such motion would ultimately carry us against the opposite crust of the earth, and without a doubt the shock would end our existence. I inquired about this, to me, self-evident fact, and he replied:

"Long before we reach the opposite crust of the earth, our motion will be arrested."

I had begun now to feel a self-confidence that is surprising as I recall that remarkable position in connection with my narrow experience in true science, and can say that instead of despondency, I really enjoyed an elated sensation, a curious exhilaration, a feeling of delight, which I have no words to describe. Life disturbances and mental worry seemed to have completely vanished, and it appeared as if, with mental perception lucid, I was under the influence of a powerful soporific; the cares of mortals had disappeared. After a while the wind ceased to blow, as my guide had predicted, and with the suspension of that factor, all that remained to remind me of earth phenomena had vanished. There was no motion of material, nothing to mar or disturb the most perfect peace imaginable; I was so exquisitely happy that I now actually feared some change might occur to interrupt that quiescent existence. It was as a deep, sweet sleep in which, with faculties alive, unconsciousness was self-conscious, peaceful, restful, blissful. I listlessly turned my eyes, searching space in all directions—to meet vacancy everywhere, absolute vacancy. I took from my pocket (into which I had hastily thrust it) the bar of iron, and released it; the metal remained motionless beside me.

"Traveling through this expanse with the rapidity of ourselves," said

that I was moving, equally in vain. I became oblivious to everything save the delicious sensation of absolute rest that enveloped and pervaded my being.

"I am neither alive nor dead," I murmured; "neither asleep nor awake; neither moving nor at rest, and neither standing, reclining, nor sitting. If I exist I cannot bring evidence to prove that fact, neither can I prove that I am dead."

"Can any man prove either of these premises?" said the guide.

"I have never questioned the matter," said I; "it is a self-evident fact."

"Know then," said he, "that existence is a theory, and that man is incapable of demonstrating that he has a being. All evidences of mortal life are only as the phantasms of hallucination. As a moment in dreamland may span a life of time, the dreamer altogether unconscious that it is a dream, so may life itself be a shadow, the vision of a distempered fancy, the illusion of a floating thought."

"Are pain, pleasure, and living, imaginary creations?" I asked facetiously.

"Is there a madman who does not imagine, as facts, what others agree upon as hallucinations peculiar to himself? Is it not impossible to distinguish between different gradations of illusions, and is it not, therefore, possible that even self-existence is an illusion? What evidence can any man produce to prove that his idea of life is not a madman's dream?"

"Proceed," I said.

"At another time, perhaps," he remarked; "we have reached the Inner Circle, the Sphere of Rest, the line of gravity, and now our bodies have no weight; at this point we begin to move with decreased speed, we will soon come to a quiescent condition, a state of rest, and then start back on our rebound."

CHAPTER L.

HEARING WITHOUT EARS — "WHAT WILL BE THE END?"

A flood of recollections came over me, a vivid remembrance of my earth-learned school philosophy. "I rebel again," I said, "I deny your statements. We can neither be moving, nor can we be out of the atmosphere. Fool that I have been not to have sooner and better used my reasoning faculties, not to have at once rejected your statements concerning the disappearance of the atmosphere."

"I await your argument."

"Am I not speaking? Is other argument necessary? Have I not heard your voice, and that, too, since you asserted that we had left the atmosphere?"

"Continue."

"Have not men demonstrated, and is it not accepted beyond the shadow of a doubt, that sound is produced by vibrations of the air?"

"You speak truly; as men converse on surface earth."

"This medium—the air—in wave vibrations, strikes upon the drum of the ear, and thus impresses the brain," I continued.

"I agree that such is the teachings of your philosophy; go on."

"It is unnecessary; you admit the facts, and the facts refute you; there must be an atmosphere to convey sound."

"Cannot you understand that you are not now on the surface of the earth? Will you never learn that the philosophy of your former life is not philosophy here? That earth-bound science is science only with surface-earth men? Here science is a fallacy. All that you have said is true of surface earth, but your argument is invalid where every condition is different from the conditions that prevail thereon. You use the organs of speech in addressing me as you once learned to use them, but such physical efforts are unnecessary to convey sense-impressions in this condition of rest and complacency, and you waste energy in employing them. You assert and

against the ear will not do the same, and many substances even better than the atmosphere?"

"This I admit."

"Will you tell me how the vibration of any of these bodies impresses the seat of hearing?"

"It moves the atmosphere which strikes upon the tympanum of the ear."

"You have not explained the phenomenon; how does that tympanic membrane communicate with the brain?"

"By vibrations, I understand," I answered, and then I began to feel that this assertion was a simple statement, and not sufficient to explain how matter acts upon mind, whatever mind may be, and I hesitated.

"Pray do not stop," he said; "how is it that a delicate vibrating film of animal membrane can receive and convey sound to a pulpy organic mass that is destitute of elasticity, and which consists mostly of water, for the brain is such in structure, and vibrations like those you mention, cannot, by your own theory, pass through it as vibrations through a sonorous material, or even reach from the tympanum of the ear to the nearest convolution of the brain."

"I cannot explain this, I admit," was my reply.

"Pass that feature, then, and concede that this tympanic membrane is capable of materially affecting brain tissue by its tiny vibrations, how can that slimy, pulpy formation mostly made up of water, communicate with the soul of man, for you do not claim, I hope, that brain material is either mind, conscience, or soul?"

I confessed my inability to answer or even to theorize on the subject, and recognizing my humiliation, I begged him to open the door to such knowledge.

"The vibration of the atmosphere is necessary to man, as earthy man is situated," he said. " The coarser attributes known as matter formations are the crudities of nature, dust swept from space. Man's organism is made up of the roughest and lowest kind of space materials; he is surrounded by a turbulent medium, the air, and these various conditions obscure or destroy the finer attributes of his ethereal nature, and prevent a higher spiritual evolution. His spiritual self is enveloped in earth, and everywhere thwarted by earthy materials. He is insensible to the finer influences of surrounding media by reason of the overwhelming necessity of a war for existence with the grossly antagonistic materialistic confusion that everywhere confronts, surrounds, and pervades him. Such a conflict with extraneous matter is necessary in order that he may retain his earthy being, for, to remain a mortal, he must work to keep body and soul together. His organs of communication and perception are of 'earth, earthy'; his nature is cast in a mold of clay, and the blood within him gurgles and struggles in his brain, a whirlpool of madly rushing liquid substances, creating disorder in the primal realms of consciousness. He is ignorant of this inward turmoil because he has never been without it, as ignorant as he is of the rank odors of the gases of the atmosphere that he has always breathed and cannot perceive because of the benumbed olfactory nerves. Thus, it is that all his subtler senses are inevitably blunted and perverted, and his vulgar nature preponderates. The rich essential part of his own self is unknown, even to himself. The possibility of delight and pleasure in an acquaintance with the finer attributes of his own soul is clouded by this shrouding materialistic presence that has, through countless generations, become a part of man, and he even derives most of his mental pleasures from such acts as tend to encourage the animal passions. Thus, it follows that the sensitive, highly developed, extremely attenuated part of his inner being has become subservient to the grosser elements. The baser part of his nature has become dominant. He remains insensible to impressions from the highly developed surrounding media which, being incapable of reaching his inner organism other than through mechanical agencies, are powerless to impress. Alas, only the coarser conditions of celestial phenomena can affect him, and the finer expressions of the universe of life and force are lost to his spiritual apprehension."

"Would you have me view the soul of man as I would a material being?"

"Surely," he answered; "it exists practically as does the more gross forms of matter, and in exact accord with natural laws. Associated with lower forms of matter, the soul of man is a temporary slave to the enveloping substance. The ear of man as now constituted can hear only by means of vibrations of such media as conduct vibrations in matter—for example, the air; but were man to be deprived of the organs of hearing, and then exist for generations subject to evolutions from within, whereby the acuteness of the spirit would become intensified, or permitted to perform its true function, he would learn to communicate soul to soul, not only with mankind, but with beings celestial that surround, and are now unknown to him. This he would accomplish through a medium of communication that requires

der perfectly natural conditions; your mind no longer requires the material medium by which to converse with the spiritual. We are conversing now by thought contact, there is no atmosphere here, your tongue moves merely from habit, and not from necessity. I am reading your mind as you in turn ate mine, neither of us is speaking as you were accustomed to speak."

"I cannot accept that assertion," I said; "it is to me impossible to realize the existence of such conditions."

"As it is for any man to explain any phenomenon in life," he said. "Do you not remember that you ceased to respire, and were not conscious of the fact?"

"Yes."

"That your heart had stopped beating, your blood no longer circulated, while you were in ignorance of the change?" "That is also true."

"Now I will prove my last assertion. Close your mouth, and think of a question you wish to propound."

I did so, and to my perfect understanding and comprehension he answered me with closed mouth.

"What will be the end?" I exclaimed, or thought aloud. "I am possessed of nearly all the attributes that I once supposed inherent only in a corpse, yet I live, I see clearly, I hear plainly, I have a quickened being, and a mental perception intensified and exquisite. Why and how has this been accomplished? What will be the result of this eventful journey?"

"Restful, you should say," he remarked; "the present is restful, the end will be peace. Now I will give you a lesson concerning the words Why and How that you have just used."

CHAPTER LI.

WHY AND HOW — "THE STRUGGLING RAY OF LIGHT FROM THOSE FARTHERMOST OUTREACHES."

"Confronting mankind there stands a sphinx—the vast Unknown. However well a man may be informed concerning a special subject, his farthermost outlook concerning that subject is bounded by an impenetrable infinity."

"Granted," I interrupted, "that mankind has not by any means attained a condition of perfection, yet you must admit that questions once regarded as inscrutable problems are now illuminated by the discoveries of science."

"And the 'discovered,' as I will show, has only transferred ignorance to other places," he replied. "Science has confined its labors to superficial descriptions, not the elucidation of the fundamental causes of phenomena."

"I cannot believe you, and question if you can prove what you say."

"It needs no argument to illustrate the fact. Science boldly heralds her descriptive discoveries, and as carefully ignores her explanatory failures. She dares not attempt to explain the why even of the simplest things. Why does the robin hop, and the snipe walk? Do not tell me this is beneath the notice of men of science, for science claims that no subject is outside her realm. Search your works on natural history and see if your man of science, who describes the habits of these birds, explains the reason for this evident fact. How does the tree-frog change its color? Do not answer me in the usual superficial manner concerning the reflection of light, but tell me why the skin of that creature is enabled to perform this function? How does the maple-tree secrete a sweet, wholesome sap, and deadly nightshade, growing in the same soil and living on the same elements, a poison? What is it that your scientific men find in the cells of root, or rootlet, to indicate that one may produce a food, and the other a noxious secretion that can destroy life? Your microscopist will discuss cell tissues learnedly, will speak fluently

enables the nerve in the nose to perform its discriminative function? You do not answer. Silver is sonorous, lead is not; why these intrinsic differences? Aluminum is a light metal, gold a heavy one; what reason can you offer to explain the facts other than the inadequate term density? Mercury at ordinary temperature is a liquid; can your scientist tell why it is not a solid? Of course, anyone can say because its molecules move freely on each other. Such an answer evades the issue; why do they so readily exert this action? Copper produces green or blue salts; nickel produces green salts; have you ever been told why they observe these rules? Water solidifies at about thirty-two degrees above your so-called zero; have you ever asked an explanation of your scientific authority why it selects that temperature? Alcohol dissolves resins, water dissolves gums; have you any explanation to offer why either liquid should dissolve anything, much less exercise a preference? One species of turtle has a soft shell, another a hard shell; has your authority in natural history told you why this is so? The albumen of the egg of the hen hardens at one hundred and eighty degrees Fahrenheit; the albumen of the eggs of some turtles cannot be easily coagulated by boiling the egg in pure water; why these differences? Iceland spar and dog-tooth spar are identical, both are crystallized carbonate of lime; has your mineralogist explained why this one substance selects these different forms of crystallization, or why any crystal of any substance is ever produced? Why is common salt white and charcoal black? Why does the dog lap and the calf drink? One child has black hair, another brown, a third red; why? Search your physiology for the answer and see if your learned authority can tell you why the life-current makes these distinctions? Why do the cells of the liver secrete bile, and those of the mouth saliva? Why does any cell secrete anything? A parrot can speak; what has your anatomist found in the structure of the brain, tongue, or larynx of that bird to explain why this accomplishment is not as much the birthright of the turkey? The elements that form morphine and strychnine, also make bread, one a food, the other a poison; can your chemist offer any reason for the fact that morphine and bread possess such opposite characters? The earth has one satellite, Saturn is encompassed by a ring; it is not sufficient to attempt to refer to these familiar facts; tell me, does your earth-bound astronomer explain why the ring of Saturn was selected for that planet? Why are the salts of aluminum astringent, the salts of magnesium cathartic, and the salts of arsenicum deadly poison? Ask your toxicologist, and silence will be your answer. Why will some substances absorb moisture from the air, and liquefy, while others become as dry as dust under like conditions? Why does the vapor of sulphuric ether inflame, while the vapor of chloroform is not combustible, under ordinary conditions? Oil of turpentine, oil of lemon, and oil of bergamot differ in odor, yet they are composed of the same elements, united in the same proportion; why should they possess such distinctive, individual characteristics? Further search of the chemist will explain only to shove the word why into another space, as ripples play with and toss a cork about. Why does the newly-born babe cry for food before its intellect has a chance for worldly education? Why"—

"Stop," I interrupted; "these questions are absurd."

"So, some of your scientific experts would assert," he replied; "perhaps they would even become indignant at my presumption in asking them, and call them childish; nevertheless these men can not satisfy their own cravings in attempting to search the illimitable, and in humiliation, or irritation, they must ignore the word Why. That word Why to man dominates the universe. It covers all phenomena, and thrusts inquiry back from every depth. Science may trace a line of thought into the infinitely little, down, down, beyond that which is tangible, and at last in that far distant inter-microscopical infinity, monstrous by reason of its very minuteness, must rest its labors against the word Why. Man may carry his superficial investigation into the immeasurably great, beyond our sun and his family of satellites, into the outer depths of the solar system, of which our sun is a part, past his sister stars, and out again into the depths of the cold space channels beyond; into other systems and out again, until at last the nebulae shrink and disappear in the gloom of thought-conjecture, and as the straggling ray of light from those farthermost outreaches, too feeble to tell of its origin, or carry a story of nativity, enters his eye, he covers his face and rests his intellect against the word Why. From the remote space caverns of the human intellect, beyond the field of perception, whether we appeal to conceptions of the unknowable in the infinitely little, or the immeasurably great, we meet a circle of adamant, as impenetrable as the frozen cliffs of the Antarctic, that incomprehensible word—Why!

"Why did the light wave spring into his field of perception by reflection from the microscopic speck in the depths of littleness, on the one hand; and how did this sliver of the sun's ray originate in the depths of inter-stel-

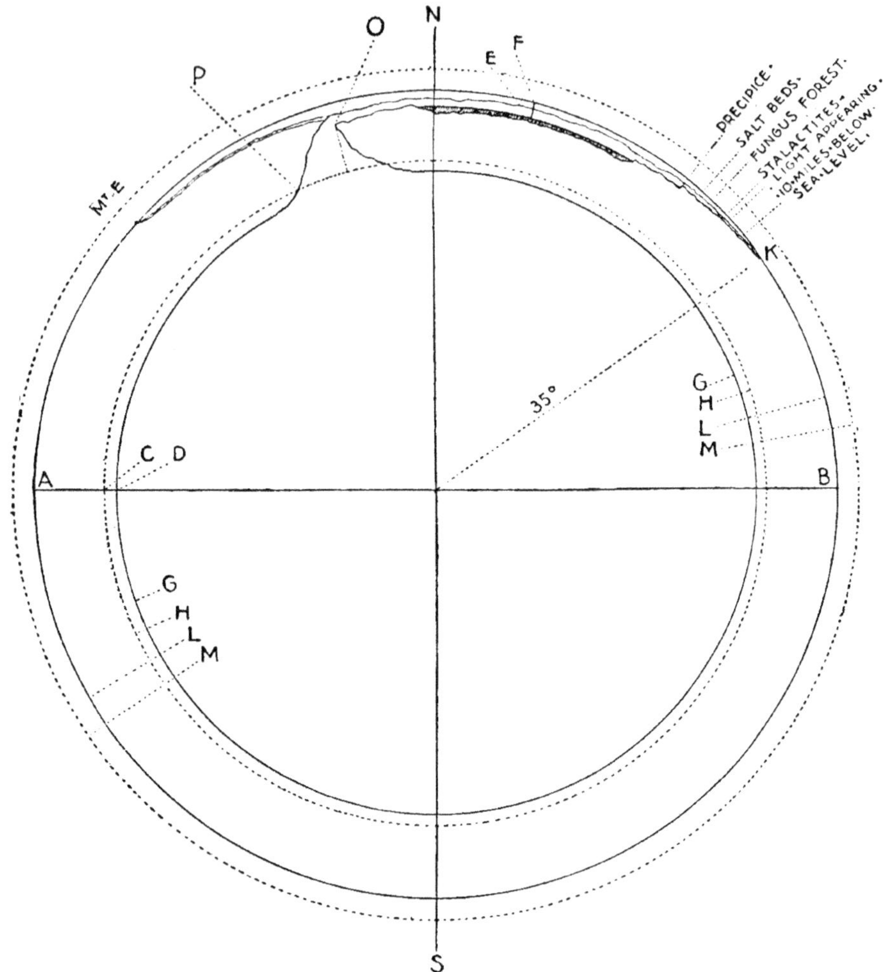

DESCRIPTION OF JOURNEY FROM K. [KENTUCKY] TO P. — "THE END OF EARTH."

A, B, Diameter of earth, 8,000 miles.	K, Entrance to cavern in Kentucky.
A, D, Thickness of earth crust, 800 miles.	L, Outer circle, earth's surface.
C, D, Distance from inner earth crust to energy sphere, 1oo miles.	Mt. E, Mount Epomeo in Italy
E, Underground lake.	N, North Pole.
E, F, Distance from surface of lake to earth's surface.	O, Rock shelf from which the leap was made into the intra-earth space.
G, Inner Circle (the Unknown Country).	P, Junction of earth crust with Circle of Rest. Point where I-Am-The-Man stepped "onward and upward" in "The Unknown Country."
H, Middle Circle (Sphere of Energy, or Circle of Rest).	S, South Pole.
L to M, Height of atmosphere, 200 miles.	

CHAPTER LII.

OSCILLATING THROUGH SPACE — EARTH'S SHELL ABOVE ME.

Continued my companion:

"We have just now crossed the line of gravitation. We were drawn downward until at a certain point, to which I called your attention at the time, we recently crossed the curved plane of perfect rest, where gravity ceases, and by our momentum are now passing beyond that plane, and are now pressing against the bond of gravitation again. This shell in which gravity centers is concentric with that of the earth's exterior, and is about seven hundred miles below its surface. Each moment of time will now behold us carried farther from this sphere of attraction, and thus the increasing distance increases the force of the restraining influence. Our momentum is thus retarded, and consequently the rapidity of our motion is continually decreasing. At last when the forces of gravitation and mass motion neutralize each other, we will come to a state of rest again. When our motion in this direction ceases, however, gravitation, imperishable, continues to exert its equalizing influence, the result being a start in the opposite direction, and we will then reverse our course, and retrace our path, crossing again the central band of attraction, to retreat and fly to the opposite side of the power of greater attraction, into the expanse from which we came, and that is now above us."

"Can this oscillation ever end? Are we to remain thus, as an unceasing pendulum, traversing space, to and fro across this invisible shell of attraction from now until the end of time?"

"No; there are influences to prevent such an experience; one being the friction of the attenuated atmosphere into which we plunge each time that we cross the point of greater gravity, and approach the crust of the earth. Thus, each succeeding vibration is in shorter lines, and at last we will come

observed conditions of natural laws formerly known to me, and that do not encompass us here; I accept, therefore, your statements as I have several times heretofore, because I cannot refute them. I must close my eyes to the future, and accept it on faith; I cease to mourn the past, I cannot presage the end."

"Well spoken," he replied; "and while we are undergoing this necessary delay, this oscillating motion, to which we must both submit before we can again continue our journey, I will describe some conditions inherent in the three spheres of which the rind of the earth is composed, for I believe that you are now ready to receive amid profit by facts that heretofore you would have rejected in incredulity.

"The outer circle, coat, or contour, of which you have heard others besides myself speak, is the surface crust of our globe, the great sphere of land and water on which man is at present an inhabitant. This is the exposed part of the earth, and is least desirable as a residence. It is affected by grievous atmospheric changes, and restless physical conditions, such as men, in order to exist in, must fortify against at the expense of much bodily and mental energy, which leads them, necessarily, to encourage the animal at the expense of the ethereal. The unmodified rays of the sun produce aerial convulsions that are marked by thermal contrasts, and other meteorological variations, during which the heat of summer and the cold of winter follow each other periodically and unceasingly. These successive solar pulsations generate winds, calms, and storms, and in order to protect himself against such exposures and changes in material surroundings, man toils, suffers, and comes to believe that the doom, if not the object, of life on earth is the preservation of the earthy body. All conditions and phases of nature on this outer crust are in an angry struggle, and this commotion envelops the wretched home, and governs the life of man. The surrounding cyclones of force and matter have distorted the peaceful side of what human nature might be until the shortened life of man has become a passionate, deplorable, sorrowful struggle for physical existence, from the cradle to the grave. Of these facts man is practically ignorant, although each individual is aware he is not satisfied with his condition. If his afflictions were obvious to himself, his existence would be typical of a life of desolation and anguish. You know full well that the condition of the outer sphere is, as I have described it, a bleak, turbulent surface, the roof of the earth on which man exists, as a creeping parasite does on a rind of fruit, exposed to the fury of the ever-present earth storms.

"The central circle, or medial sphere, the shell, or layer of gravitation, lies conformably to the outer configuration of the globe, about seven hundred miles towards its center. It stretches beneath the outer circle (sphere) as a transparent sheet, a shell of energy, the center of gravitation. The material crust of the earth rests on this placid sphere of vigor, excepting in a few places, where, as in the crevice we have entered, gaps, or crevices, in matter exist, beginning from near the outer surface and extending diagonally through the medial and inner spheres into the intra-earth space beyond. This medial sphere is a form of pure force, a disturbance of motion, and although without weight it induces, or conserves, gravity. It is invisible to mortal eyes, and is frictionless, but really is the bone of the earth. On it matter, the retarded energy of space, space dust, has arranged itself as dust collects on a bubble of water. This we call matter. The material portion of the earth is altogether a surface film, an insignificant skin over the sphere of purity, the center of gravitation. Although men naturally imagine that the density and stability of the earth are dependent on the earthy particles, of which his own body is a part, such is not the case. Earth, as man upon the outer surface can now know it, is an aggregation of material particles, a shell resting on this globular sphere of medial force, which attracts solid matter from both the outer and inner surfaces of earth, forming thereby the middle of the three concentric spheres. This middle sphere is the reverse of the outer, or surface, layer in one respect, for, while it attracts solids, gases are repelled by it, and thus the atmosphere becomes less dense as we descend from the outer surfaces of the earth. The greater degree of attraction for gases belongs, therefore, to the earth's exterior surface."

"Exactly at the earth's exterior surface?" I asked.

"Practically so. The greatest density of the air is found a few miles below the surface of the ocean; the air becomes more attenuated as we proceed in either direction from that point. Were this not the case, the atmosphere that surrounds the earth would be quickly absorbed into its substance, or expand into space and disappear."

"Scientific men claim that the atmosphere is forty-five geographical miles in depth over the earth's surface," I said.

"If the earth is eight thousand miles in diameter, how long would such an atmosphere, a skin only, over a great ball, resist such attraction, and

to men they would not be credited? Scientific men have calculated the weights of the planets, and have estimated therefrom the density of the earth, showing it to be solid, and knowing its density, they would, on this consideration alone, discredit your story concerning the earth shell."

THE EARTH AND ITS ATMOSPHERE.

The space between the inner and the outer lines represents the atmosphere upon the earth. The depth to which man has penetrated the earth is less than the thickness of either line, as compared with the diameter of the inner circle

"You mistake, as you will presently see. It is true that man's ingenuity has enabled him to ascertain the weights and densities of the planets, but do you mean to say that these scientific results preclude the possibility of a hollow interior of the heavenly bodies?"

"I confess, I do."

"You should know then, that what men define as density of the earth, is but an average value, which is much higher than that exhibited by materials in the surface layers of the earth crust, such as come within the scrutiny of man. This fact allows mortals of upper earth but a vague conjecture as to the nature of the seemingly much heavier substances that exist in the interior of the earth. Have men any data on hand to show exactly how matter is distributed below the limited zone that is accessible to their investigations?"

"I think not."

"You may safely accept, then, that the earth shell I have described to you embraces in a compact form the total weight of the earth. Even though men take for granted that matter fills out the whole interior of our planet, such material would not, if distributed as on earth's surface, give the earth the density he has determined for it."

"I must acquiesce in your explanations."

"Let us now go a step further in this argument. What do you imagine is the nature of those heavier substances whose existence deep within the earth is suggested by the exceedingly high total density observed by man on upper earth?"

"I am unable to explain, especially as the materials surrounding us here, seemingly, do not differ much from those with which my former life experience has made me acquainted."

"Your observation is correct, there is no essential difference in this regard. But as we are descending into the interior of this globe, and are approaching the central seat of the shell of energy, the opposing force into which we plunge becomes correspondingly stronger, and as a consequence, matter pressed within it becomes really lighter. Your own experience about your weight gradually disappearing during this journey should convince you of the correctness of this fact."

"Indeed, it does," I admitted.

"You will then readily understand, that the heavy material to which surface-bred mortals allude as probably constituting the interior of the earth, is, in fact, nothing but the manifestation of a matter-supporting force, as exemplified in the sphere of attractive energy, the seat of which we are soon to encounter on our journey. Likewise, the mutual attraction of the heavenly bodies is not a property solely of their material part, but an expression in which both the force-spheres and the matter collected thereon take part.

"Tell me more of the sphere in which gravitation is in-tensest."

"Of that you are yet to judge," he replied. " When we come to a state of rest in the stratum of greater gravity, we will then traverse this crevice in the sheet of energy until we reach the edge of the earth crust, after which we will ascend towards the interior of the earth, until we reach the inner crust, which is, as before explained, a surface of matter that lies with the external

wards the center of the earth, and at the same time you say that after leaving the Median Circle, we will then ascend, which seems contradictory."

"I have endeavored to show you that matter is resting in or on a central sphere of energy, which attracts solid bodies towards its central plane. From this fundamental and permanent seat of gravity we may regard our progress as up-hill, whether we proceed towards the hollow center or towards the outer surface of the globe. If a stick weighted on one end is floated upright in water, an insect on the top of the stick above the water will fall to the surface of the liquid, and yet the same insect will rise to the surface of the water if liberated beneath the water at the bottom of the stick. This comparison is not precisely applicable to our present position, for there is no change in medium here, but it may serve as an aid to thought and may indicate to you that which I wish to convey when I say 'we ascend' in both directions as we pull against Gravity. The terms up and down are not absolute, but relative."

Thus, we continued an undefined period in mind conversation; and of the information gained in my experience of that delightful condition, I have the privilege now to record but a small portion, and even this statement of facts appears, as I glance backward into my human existence, as if it may seem to others to border on the incredible. During all that time—I know not how long the period may have been—we were alternately passing and repassing through the partition of division (the sphere of gravity) that separated the inner from the outer substantial crust of earth. With each vibration our line of travel became shorter and shorter, like the decreasing oscillations of a pendulum, and at last I could no longer perceive the rushing motion of a medium like the air. Finally, my guide said that we were at perfect rest at a point in that mysterious medial sphere which, at a distance of about seven hundred miles below the level of the sea, concentrates in its encompassing curvature, the mighty power of gravitation. We were fixed seven hundred miles from the outer surface of the globe, but more than three thousand from the center.

CHAPTER LIII.

MY WEIGHT ANNIHILATED — "TELL ME," I CRIED IN ALARM, "IS THIS TO BE A LIVING TOMB?"

"If you will reflect upon the condition we are now in, you will perceive that it must be one of unusual scientific interest. If you imagine a body at rest, in an intangible medium, and not in contact with a gas or any substance capable of creating friction, that body by the prevailing theory of matter and motion, unless disturbed by an impulse from without, would remain forever at absolute rest. We now occupy such a position. In whatever direction we may now be situated, it seems to us that we are upright. We are absolutely without weight, and in a perfectly frictionless medium. Should an inanimate body begin to revolve here, it would continue that motion forever. If our equilibrium should now be disturbed, and we should begin to move in a direction coinciding with the plane in which we are at rest, we would continue moving with the same rapidity in that direction until our course was arrested by some opposing object. We are not subject to attraction of matter, for at this place gravitation robs matter of its gravity, and has no influence on extraneous substances. We are now in the center of gravitation, the 'Sphere of Rest.'"

"Let me think it out," I replied, and reasoning from his remarks, I mentally followed the chain to its sequence, and was startled as suddenly it dawned upon me that if his argument was true we must remain motionless in this spot until death (could beings in conditions like ourselves die beyond the death we had already achieved) or the end of time. We were at perfect rest, in absolute vacancy, there being, as I now accepted without reserve, neither gas, liquid, nor solid, that we could employ as a lever to start us into motion. "Tell me," I cried in alarm, "is this to be a living tomb? Are we to remain suspended here forever, and if not, by what method can we hope to extricate ourselves from this state of perfect quiescence?" He

"So, it would continue," he remarked, "until the end of time, were it not for the fact that I could not possibly release it in a condition of absolute horizontal rest. There is a slight, slow, lateral motion that will carry the object parallel with this sheet of energy to the material side of this crevice, when its motion will 'be arrested by the earth it strikes.'"

"That I can understand," I replied, and then a ray of light broke upon me. "Had not Cavendish demonstrated that, when a small ball of lead is suspended on a film of silk, near a mass of iron or lead, it is drawn towards the greater body? We will be drawn by gravity to the nearest cliff," I cried.

"You mistake," he answered; "Cavendish performed his experiments on the surface of the earth, and there, gravity is always ready to start an object into motion. Here objects have no weight, and neither attract nor repel each other. The force of cohesion holds together substances that are in contact, but as gravitation cannot now affect matter out of molecular contact with other forms of matter, because of the equilibrium of all objects, so it may be likewise said, that bodies out of contact have at this point no attraction for one another. If they possessed this attribute, long ago we would have been drawn towards the earth cliff with inconceivable velocity. However, if by any method our bodies should receive an impulse sufficient to start them into motion, even so gently though it be, we in like manner would continue to move in this frictionless medium—until"—

"We would strike the material boundary of this crevice," I interrupted.

"Yes; but can you conceive of any method by which such voluntary motion can now be acquired?"

"No."

"Does it not seem to you," he continued, "that when skillful mechanics on the earth's surface are able to adjust balances so delicately that in the face of friction of metal, friction of air, inertia of mass, the thousandth part of a grain can produce motion of the great beams and pans of such balances, we, in this location where there is no friction and no opposing medium—none at all—should be able to induce mass motion?"

"I cannot imagine how it is possible, unless we shove each other apart. There is no other object to push against, —but why do you continue to hold me so tightly?" I interrupted myself to ask, for he was clasping me firmly again.

"In order that you may not leave me," he replied.

"Come, you trifle," I said somewhat irritated; "you have just argued that we are immovably suspended in a frictionless medium, and fixed in our present position; you ask me to suggest some method by which we can create motion, and I fail to devise it, and almost in the same sentence you say that you fear that I will leave you. Cease your incongruities and advise with me rationally."

"Where is the bar of iron?" he asked.

I turned towards its former location; it had disappeared.

"Have you not occasionally felt," he asked, "that in your former life your mind was a slave in an earthly prison? Have you never, especially in your dreams, experienced a sensation of mental confinement?"

"Yes."

"Know then," he replied, "that there is a connection between the mind and the body of mortal beings, in which matter confines mind, and yet mind governs matter. How else could the will of men and animals impart voluntary motion to earthy bodies? With beings situated as are the animals on the surface of the earth, mind alone cannot overcome the friction of matter. A person could suspend himself accurately on a string, or balance himself on a pivot, and wish with the entire force of his mind that his body would revolve, and still he would remain at perfect rest."

"Certainly. A man would be considered crazy who attempted it," I answered.

"Notwithstanding your opinion, in time to come, human beings on the surface of the earth will investigate in this very direction," he replied, "and in the proper time mental evolution will, by experimentation, prove the fact of this mind and matter connection, and demonstrate that even extraneous matter may be made subservient to mind influences. On earth, mind acts on the matter of one's body to produce motion of matter, and the spirit within, which is a slave to matter, moves with it. Contraries rule here. Mind force acts on pure space motion, moving itself and matter with it, and that, too, without any exertion of the material body which now is a nonentity, mind here being the master."

"How can I believe you?" I replied.

"Know, then," he said, "that we are in motion now, propelled by my will power."

"Prove it."

"You may prove it yourself," he said; "but be careful, or we will sepa-

"Wish intensely that you would move in a circle about me." I acquiesced, and at once my body began to circle around him. "Call for the bar of iron."

I did as directed, and soon it came floating out of space into my very hand.

"I am amazed," I ejaculated; "yes, more surprised at these phenomena than at anything that has preceded."

"You need not be; you move now under the influences of natural laws that are no more obscure or wonderful than those under which you have always existed. Instead of exercising its influence on a brain, and thence indirectly on a material body, your mind force is exerting its action through energy on matter itself. Matter is here subservient. It is nearly the same as vacuity, mind being a comprehensive reality. The positions we have heretofore occupied have been reversed, and mind now dominates. Know, that as your body is now absolutely without weight, and is suspended in a frictionless medium, the most delicate balance of a chemist cannot approach in sensitiveness the adjustment herein exemplified. Your body does not weigh the fraction of the millionth part of a grain, and where there is neither material weight nor possible friction, even the attrition that on surface earth results from a needle point that rests on an agate plate is immeasurably greater in comparison. Pure mind energy is capable of disturbing the equilibrium of matter in our situation, as you have seen exemplified by our movements and extraneous materials, 'dead matter' obeys the spiritual. The bar of iron obeyed your call, the spiritless metal is subservient to the demands of intelligence. But, come, we must continue our journey."

Grasping me again, he exclaimed: "Wish with all intensity that we may move forward, and I will do the same."

I did so.

"We are now uniting our energies in the creation of motion," he said; "we are moving rapidly, and with continually accelerated speed; before long we will perceive the earthy border of this chasm."

And yet it seemed to me that we were at perfect rest.

CHAPTER LIV.

IS THAT A MORTAL? — "THE END OF EARTH."

At length I perceived, in the distance, a crescent-shaped ring of silver luster. It grew broader, expanding beneath my gaze, and appeared to approach rapidly.

"Hold; cease your desire for onward motion," said the guide; "we approach too rapidly. Quick, wish with all your mind that you were motionless."

I did so, and we rested in front of a ridge of brilliant material, that in one direction, towards the earth's outer circle, broadened until it extended upward as far as the eye could reach in the form of a bold precipice, and in the other towards the inner world, shelved gradually away as an ocean beach might do.

"Tell me, what is this barrier?" I asked.

"It is the bisected edge of the earth crevice," he said. "That overhanging upright bluff reaches towards the external surface of the earth, the land of your former home. That shelving approach beneath is the entrance to the 'Inner Circle,' the concavity of our world."

Again, we approached the visible substance, moving gently under the will of my guide. The shore became more distinctly outlined as we advanced, inequalities that were before unnoticed became perceptible, and the silver-like material resolved itself into ordinary earth. Then I observed, upright and motionless, on the edge of the shore that reached toward the inner shell of earth, towards that "Unknown Country" beyond, a figure in human form.

"Is that a mortal?" I asked. "Are we nearing humanity again?"

"It is a being of mortal build, a messenger who awaits our coming, and who is to take charge of your person and conduct you farther," he replied. "It has been my duty to crush, to overcome by successive lessons your obe-

come, be gained by mortal man, and while he is in the flesh. The vicissitudes through which you have recently passed should be to you an impressive lesson, but the future holds for you a lesson far more important, the knowledge of spiritual, or mental evolution which men may yet approach; but that I would not presume to indicate now, even to you. Your earthly body has become a useless shell, and when you lay it aside, as you soon can do, as I may say you are destined to do, you will feel a relief as if an abnormal excrescence had been removed; but you cannot now comprehend such a condition. That change will not occur until you have been further educated in the purely occult secrets for which I have partly prepared you, and the material part of your organism will at any time thereafter come and go at command of your will. On that adjacent shore, the person you have observed, your next teacher, awaits you."

"Am I to leave you?" I cried in despair, for suddenly the remembrance of home came into my mind, and the thought, as by a flash, that this being alone could guide me back to earth. "Recall your words, do not desert me now after leading me beyond even alchemistic imaginings into this subterranean existence, the result of what you call your natural, or pure, ethereal lessons."

He shook his head.

"I beg of you, I implore of you, not to abandon me now; have you no compassion, no feeling? You are the one tie that binds me to earth proper, the only intelligence that I know to be related to a human in all this great, bright blank."

Again, he shook his head.

"Hearken to my pleadings. Listen to my allegation. You stood on the edge of the brook spring in Kentucky, your back to the darkness of that gloomy cavern, and I voluntarily gave you my hand as to a guide; I turned from the verdure of the earth, the sunshine of the past, and accompanied you into as dismal a cavern as man ever entered. I have since alternately rebelled at your methods, and again have trusted you implicitly as we passed through scenes that rational imagination scarce could conjure. I have successively lost my voice, my weight, my breath, my heart throb, and my soul for aught I know. Now an unknown future awaits me on the one hand, in which you say my body is to disappear, and on the other you are standing, the only link between earth and my self-existence, a semi-mortal it may be, to speak mildly, for God only knows your true rank in life's scale. Be you man or not, you brought me here, and are responsible for my future safety. I plead and beg of you either to go on with me into the forthcoming uncertainty 'Within the Unknown Country' to which you allude, or carry me back to upper earth."

He shook his head again, and motioned me onward, and his powerful will overcoming my feeble resistance, impelled me towards that mysterious shore. I floated helpless, as a fragment of camphor whirls and spins on a surface of clear, warm water, spinning and whirling aimlessly about, but moving onward. My feet rested on solid earth, and I awkwardly struggled a short distance onward and upward, and then stepped upon the slope that reached, as he had said, inward and upward towards the unrevealed "Inner Circle." I had entered now that mysterious third circle or sphere, and I stood on the very edge of the wonderful land I was destined to explore, "The Unknown Country." The strange, peaceful being whom I had observed on the shore, stepped to my side, and clasped both my hands, and the guide of former days waved me an adieu. I sank upon my knees and imploringly raised my arms in supplication, but the comrade of my journey turned about, and began to retrace his course. Suspended in vacancy, he seemed to float as a spirit would if it were wafted diagonally into the heavens, and acquiring momentum rapidly, became quickly a bright speck, seemingly a silver mote in the occult earth shine of that central sphere, and soon vanished from view. In all my past eventful history there was nothing similar to or approaching in keenness the agony that I suffered at this moment, and I question if shipwrecked sailor or entombed miner ever experienced the sense of utter desolation that now possessed and overcame me. Light everywhere about me, ever-present light, but darkness within, darkness indescribable, and mental distress unutterable. I fell upon my face in agony, and thought of other times, and those remembrances of my once happy upper earth life became excruciatingly painful, for when a person is in misery, pleasant recollections, by contrast, increase the pain. "Let my soul die now as my body has done," I moaned; "for even mental life, all I now possess, is a burden. The past to me is a painful, melancholy recollection; the future is"—

I shuddered, for who could foretell my future? I glanced at the immovable being with the sweet, mild countenance, who stood silent on the strand beside me, and whom I shall not now attempt to describe. He replied:

Then he added:

"Have you accepted that whatever seems to be is not, and that that which seems not to be, is? Have you learned that facts are fallacies, and physical existence a delusion? Do you accept that material bliss is impossible, and that while humanity is working towards the undiscovered land, man is not, cannot be satisfied?"

"SUSPENDED IN VACANCY, HE SEEMED TO FLOAT."

"Yes," I said; "I admit anything, everything. I do not know that I am here or that you are there. I do not know that I have ever been, or that any form of matter has ever had an existence. Perhaps material things are not, perhaps vacuity only is tangible."

"Are you willing to relinquish your former associations, to cease to concern yourself in the affairs of men? Do you"—

He hesitated, seemed to consider a point that I could not grasp; then, without completing his sentence, or waiting for me to answer, added:

"Come, my friend, let us enter the expanses of the Unknown Country.

You will soon behold the original of your vision, the hope of humanity, and will rest in the land of Etidorhpa. Come, my friend, let us hasten."

Arm in arm we passed into that domain of peace and tranquility, and as I stepped onward and upward perfect rest came over my troubled spirit. All thoughts of former times vanished.

The cares of life faded; misery, distress, hatred, envy, jealousy, and unholy passions, were blotted from existence. Excepting my love for dear ones still earth-enthralled, and the strand of sorrow that, stretching from soul to soul, linked us together, the past became a blank. I had reached the land of Etidorhpa—

THE END OF EARTH.

INTERLUDE.

CHAPTER LV.

THE LAST FAREWELL.

My mysterious guest, he of the silver, flowing beard, read the last word of the foregoing manuscript, and then laid the sheet of paper on the table, and rested his head upon his hand, gazing thoughtfully at the open fire. Thus, he sat for a considerable period in silence. Then he said:

"You have heard part of my story, that portion which I am commanded to make known now, and you have learned how, by natural methods, I passed by successive steps while in the body, to the door that death only, as yet, opens to humanity. You understand also that, although of human form, I am not as other men (for with me matter is subservient to mind), and as you have promised, so you must act, and do my bidding concerning the manuscript."

"But there is surely more to follow. You will tell me of what you saw and experienced beyond the end of earth, within the possessions of Etidorhpa. Tell me of that Unknown Country."

"No," he answered; "this is the end, at least so far as my connection with you is concerned. You still question certain portions of my narrative, I perceive, notwithstanding the provings I have given you, and yet as time passes investigation will show that every word I have read or uttered is true, historically, philosophically, and spiritually (which you now doubt), and men will yet readily understand how the seemingly profound, unfathomable phenomena I have encountered may be verified. I have studied and learned by bitter experience in a school that teaches from the outgoings of a deeper philosophy than human science has reached, especially modern materialistic science which, however, step by step it is destined to reach. And yet I have recorded but a small part of the experiences that I have undergone. What I have related is only a foretaste of the inexhaustible feast which, in the wisdom expanse of the future, will yet be spread before

and experimental, those permitted to review it. I have carried my history to the point at which I can say to you, very soon afterward I gave up my body temporarily, by a perfectly natural process, a method that man can yet employ, and passed as a spiritual being into the ethereal spaces, through those many mansions which I am not permitted to describe at this time, and from which I have been forced unwillingly to return and take up the semblance of my body, in order to meet you and record these events. I must await the development and expansion of mind that will permit men to accept this faithful record of my history before completing the narrative, for men are yet unprepared. Men must seriously consider those truths which, under inflexible natural laws, govern the destiny of man, but which, if mentioned at this day can only be viewed as the hallucinations of a disordered mind. To many this manuscript will prove a passing romance, to others an enigma, to others still it will be a pleasing study. Men are not now in a condition to receive even this paper. That fact I know full well, and I have accordingly arranged that thirty years shall pass before it is made public. Then they will have begun to study more deeply into force disturbances, exhibitions of energy that are now known and called imponderable bodies (perhaps some of my statements will then even be verified), and to reflect over the connection of matter therewith. A few minds will then be capable of vaguely conceiving possibilities, which this paper will serve to foretell, for a true solution of the great problems of the ethereal unknown is herein suggested, the study of which will lead to a final elevation of humanity, such as I dare not prophesy."

"Much of the paper is obscure to me," I said; "and there are occasional phrases and repetitions that appear to be interjected, possibly, with an object, and which are yet disconnected from the narrative proper."

"That is true; the paper often contains statements that are emblematical, and which you cannot understand, but yet such portions carry to others a hidden meaning. I am directed to speak to many persons besides yourself, and I cannot meet those whom I address more directly than I do through this communication. These pages will serve to instruct many people — people whom you will never know, to whom I have brought messages that will in secret be read between the lines."

"Why not give it to such persons?"

"Because I am directed to bring it to you," he replied, "and you are required:

"First, to seal the manuscript, and place it in the inner vault of your safe.

"Second, to draw up a will, and provide in case of your death, that after the expiration of thirty years from this date, the seals are to be broken, and a limited edition published in book form, by one you select.

"Third, an artist capable of grasping the conceptions will at the proper time be found, to whom the responsibility of illustrating the volume is to be entrusted, he receiving credit therefor. Only himself and yourself (or your selected agent) are to presume to select the subjects for illustration.

"Fourth, in case you are in this city, upon the expiration of thirty years, you are to open the package and follow the directions given in the envelope therein."

And he then placed on the manuscript a sealed envelope addressed to myself.

"This I have promised already," I said.

"Very well," he remarked, "I will bid you farewell."

"Wait a moment; it is unjust to leave the narrative thus uncompleted. You have been promised a future in comparison with which the experiences you have undergone, and have related to me, were tame; you had just met on the edge of the inner circle that mysterious being concerning whom I am deeply interested, as I am in the continuation of your personal narrative, and you have evidently more to relate, for you must have passed into that Unknown Country. You claim to have done so, but you break the thread in the most attractive part by leaving the future to conjecture."

"It must be so. This is a history of man on Earth, the continuation will be a history of man within the Unknown Country."

"And I am not to receive the remainder of your story?" I reiterated, still loth to give it up.

"No; I shall not appear directly to you again. Your part in this work will have ended when, after thirty years, you carry out the directions given in the sealed letter which, with this manuscript, I entrust to your care. I must return now to the shore that separated me from my former guide, and having again laid down this semblance of a body, go once more into"—

He buried his face in his hands and sobbed. Yes; this strange, cynical being whom I had at first considered an impertinent fanatic, and then, more than once afterward, had been induced to view as a cunning impos-

men, nearly a human, and I long to go back once more to my old home, my wife, my children. Why am I forbidden? The sweets of Paradise cannot comfort the mortal who must give up his home and family, and yet carry his earth-thought beyond. Man can not possess unalloyed joys, and blessings spiritual, and retain one backward longing for mundane subjects, and I now yearn again for my earth love, my material family. Having tasted of semi-celestial pleasures in one of the mansions of that complacent, pure, and restful sphere, I now exist in the border land, but my earth home is not relinquished, I cling as a mortal to former scenes, and crave to meet my lost loved ones. All of earth must be left behind if Paradise is ever wholly gained, yet I have still my sublunary thoughts.

"Etidorhpa! Etidorhpa!" he pleaded, turning his eyes as if towards one I could not see, "Etidorhpa, my old home calls. Thou knowest that the beginning of man on earth is a cry born of love, and the end of man on earth is a cry for love; love is a gift of Etidorhpa, and thou, Etidorhpa, the soul of love, shouldst have compassion on a pleading mortal."

He raised his hands in supplication.

"Have mercy on me, Etidorhpa, as I would on you if you were I and I were Etidorhpa."

Then with upturned face he stood long and silent, listening.

"Ah," he murmured at last, as if in reply to a voice I could not catch, a voice that carried to his ear an answer of deep disappointment; "thou spokest truly in the vision, Etidorhpa; it is love that enslaves mankind; love that commands; love that ensnares and rules mankind, and thou, Etidorhpa, art the soul of Love. True it is that were there no Etidorhpa, there would still be tears on earth, but the cold, meaningless tears of pain only. No mourning people, no sorrowful partings, no sobbing mothers kneeling with upturned faces, no planting of the myrtle and the rose on sacred graves. There would be no child-love, no home, no tomb, no sorrow, no Beyond"—

He hesitated, sank upon his knees, pleadingly raised. his clasped hands and seemed to listen to that far-off voice, then bowed his head, and answered:

"Yes; thou art right, Etidorhpa—although thou bringest sorrow to mortals, without thee and this sorrow-gift there could be no bright hereafter. Thou art just, Etidorhpa, and always wise. Love is the seed, and sorrow is the harvest, but this harvest of sadness is to man the richest gift of love, the golden link that joins the spirit form that has fled to the spirit that is still enthralled on earth. Were there no earth-love, there could be no heart-sorrow; were there no craving for loved ones gone, the soul of man would rest forever a brother of the clod. He who has sorrowed and not profited by his sorrow-lesson, is unfitted for life. He who heeds best his sorrow-teacher is in closest touch with humanity, and nearest to Etidorhpa. She who has drunk most deeply of sorrow's cup has best fitted herself for woman's sphere in life, and a final home of immortal bliss. I will return to thy realms, Etidorhpa, and this silken strand of sorrow wrapped around my heart, reaching from earth to Paradise and back to earth, will guide at last my loved ones to the realms beyond—the home of Etidorhpa."

Rising, turning to me, and subduing his emotion, ignoring this outburst, he said:

"If time should convince you that I have related a faithful history, if in after years you come to learn my name (I have been forbidden to speak it), and are convinced of my identity, promise me that you will do your unbidden guest a favor."

"This I will surely do; what shall it be?"

"I left a wife, a little babe, and a two-year-old child when I was taken away, abducted in the manner that I have faithfully recorded. In my subsequent experience I have not been able to cast them from my memory. I know that through my error they have been lost to me, and will be until they change to the spirit, after which we will meet again in one of the waiting Mansions of the Great Beyond. I beg you to ascertain, if possible, if either my children, or my children's children live, and should they be in want, present them with a substantial testimonial. Now, farewell."

He held out his hand, I grasped it, and as I did so, his form became indistinct, and gradually disappeared from my gaze, the, fingers of my hand met the palm in vacancy, and with extended arms I stood alone in my room, holding the mysterious manuscript, on the back of which I find plainly engrossed:

"There are more things in Heaven and Earth, Horatio,
Than are dreamt of in your philosophy."

“I STOOD ALONE IN MY ROOM HOLDING THE MYSTERIOUS MANUSCRIPT.”

EPILOGUE.

LETTER ACCOMPANYING THE MYSTERIOUS MANUSCRIPT.

The allotted thirty years have passed, and as directed, I, Llewellyn Drury, now break the seals, and open the envelope accompanying the mysterious package which was left in my hand, and read as follows:

Herein find the epilogue to your manuscript. Also, a picture of your unwelcome guest, I-Am-The-Man, which you are directed to have engraved, and to use as a frontispiece to the volume. There are men yet living to bear witness to my identity, who will need but this picture to convince them of the authenticity of the statements in the manuscript, as it is the face of one they knew when he was a young man, and will recognize now that he is in age. Do not concern yourself about the reception of the work, for you are in no wise responsible for its statements. Interested persons, if living, will not care to appear in public in connection therewith, and those who grasp and appreciate, who can see the pertinence of its truths, who can read between the lines and have the key to connected conditions, will assuredly keep their knowledge of these facts locked in their own bosoms, or insidiously oppose them, and by their silence or their attacks cover from men outside the fraternity, their connection with the unfortunate author. They dare not speak.

Revise the sentences; secure the services of an editor if you desire, and induce another to publish the book if you shrink from the responsibility, but in your revision do not in any way alter the meaning of the statements made in the manuscript; have it copied for the printer, and take no part in comments that may arise among men concerning its reception.

(From a review of the fac simile, it will be seen that an exact print word for word could not be expected. In more than one instance subsequent study demonstrated that the first conception was erroneous, and in the interview with

Those who are best informed regarding certain portions thereof, will seemingly be least interested in the book, and those who realize most fully these truths, will persistently evade the endorsement of them. The scientific enthusiast, like the fraternity to which I belong, if appealed to, will obstruct the mind of the student either by criticism or ridicule, for many of these revelations are not recorded in his books.

You are at liberty to give in your own language as a prologue the history of your connection with the author, reserving, however, if you desire to do so, your personality, adding an introduction to the manuscript, and, as interludes, every detail of our several conversations, and of your experience. Introduce such illustrations as the selected artist and yourself think proper in order to illuminate the statements. Do not question the advisability of stating all that you know to have occurred; write the whole truth, for although mankind will not now accept as fact all that you and I have experienced, strange phases of life phenomena are revealing themselves, and humanity will yet surely be led to a higher plane. As men investigate the points of historical interest, and the ultra-scientific phenomena broached in this narrative, the curtain of obscurity will be drawn aside, and evidence of the truths contained in these details will be disclosed. Finally, you must mutilate a page of the manuscript that you may select, and preserve the fragment intact and in secret. Do not print another edition unless you are presented with the words of the part that is missing.*

*(*I have excised a portion (see Chapter XXIX).—J. U. L.)*

(Signed.) I-AM-THE-MAN.

NOTE BY MR. DRURY.— Thus the letter ended. After mature consideration it has been decided to give verbatim most of the letter, and all of the manuscript, and to append, as a prologue, an introduction to the manuscript, detailing exactly the record of my connection therewith, including my arguments with Professors Chickering and Vaughn, whom I consulted concerning the statements made to me directly by its author. I will admit that perhaps the opening chapter in my introduction may be such as to raise in the minds of some persons a question concerning my mental responsibility, for as the principal personage in this drama remarks: "Mankind cannot now accept as facts what I have seen." Yet I walk the streets of my native city, a business man of recognized thoughtfulness and sobriety, and I only relate on my own responsibility what has to my knowledge occurred. It has never been intimated that I am mentally irresponsible, or speculative, and even were this the case, the material proof that I hold, and have not mentioned as yet, and may not, concerning my relations with this remarkable being, effectually disproves the idea of mental aberration, or spectral delusion. Besides, many of the statements are of such a nature as to be verified easily, or disproved by any person who may be inclined to repeat the experiments suggested, or visit the localities mentioned. The part of the whole production that will seem the most improbable to the majority of persons, is that to which I can testify from my own knowledge, as related in the first portion and the closing chapter. This approaches necromancy, seemingly, and yet in my opinion, as I now see the matter, such unexplained and recondite occurrences appear unscientific, because of the shortcomings of students of science. Occult phenomena, at some future day, will be proved to be based on ordinary physical conditions to be disclosed by scientific investigations [for "All that is, is natural, and science embraces all things "], but at present they are beyond our perception; yes, beyond our conception.

Whether I have been mesmerized, or have written in a trance, whether I have been the subject of mental aberration, or have faithfully given a life history to the world, whether this book is altogether romance, or carries a vein of prophecy, whether it sets in motion a train of wild speculations, or combines playful arguments, science problems, and metaphysical reasonings, useful as well as entertaining, remains for the reader to determine. So far as I, Llewellyn Drury, am concerned, this is—

THE END.

John U. Lloyd:—

You are hereby directed to issue future editions of Etidorhpa, using your judgment, and add from time to time the reserved chapters, and also add other illustrations.

With one exception, those in the present work are satisfactory. You know that the picture of Etidorhpa is not as it should be. Why have you not followed the directions?

I-Am-The-Man.

Had the above communication and the missing fragment of manuscript been withheld, it is needless to say that this second edition of Etidorhpa would not have appeared.

On behalf of the undersigned, who is being most liberally scolded by friends and acquaintances who can not get a copy of the first edition, and on behalf of these same scolding mortals, the undersigned extends to I-Am-The-Man the collective thanks of those who scold and the scolded.

—J. U. L.

To the recipients of the Authors edition of Etidorhpa.

One whose study of the material~~s~~ has [to himself] discredited ~~dispelled~~ materialism and who sees in every form of matter a marvel inexplainable; who considers fact to be as strange as fiction and that things visible are but verses in God's wonder book; who believes a fairy story to be not less true ~~real~~ than many visions scientific and that mind cannot conceive of creatures more wonderful ~~weird or strange~~ than Nature fashions ~~creates~~; who believes that fancy cannot carve thought matter into structures more weird and grotesque than God creates in objective fact; that force and spirit are neither less real one than the other and that matter is not more substantial ~~real~~ than either; who loves the mysterious and the beautiful and sees mystery and beauty in all visible structures and all possible thought creations; who questions if a line can be drawn between fact and fiction or if man can demonstrate where real things end and those fanciful begin; who questions if enthusiasm intense is far separated from sarcasm deep; who believes the cynic is often more of an educator than the sage and that the study of matter may finally bring man to question if the very attributes of matter are not qualities of force; — should not, in the record that follows, attempt to differentiate between history and romance, fact and fancy, speculation and science, sarcasm, ignorance and irony. Consequently the writer will make no [subsequent] comments concerning the work to follow.

Respectfully

Norwood Ohio
July 4th 1895

This introduction, which in the author's edition was signed by the writer, is here reprinted in order that my views of the book be not misconstrued.
—J. U. L.

Appendix A

The identity of I-AM-THE-MAN
(By Lisandro Cottet)

William Morgan (1774 – 1826?) is clearly the real person in which the character I-AM-THE-MAN was inspired.

He was born in Culpeper, Virginia, he worked as a bricklayer and stone cutter and served in the war of 1812. At the age of 40 he married Lucinda Pendleton, they had two children: Lucinda Wesley Morgan and Thomas Jefferson Morgan. Two years after his marriage, Morgan moved his family to York, Upper Canada, where he operated a brewery. When his business was destroyed in a fire, Morgan was reduced to poverty. He returned with his family to the United States, settling first at Rochester, New York, and later in Batavia, where he again worked as a bricklayer and stonecutter.

In 1826 he published his book "Illustrations of Freemasonry" exposing some of the freemasonry's secrets. It is said he did this because he was rejected to enter the order, and after contacting an expelled freemason, David Cade Miller, he found the information he needed to publish this book; it is also said he was the expelled freemason. Either way, this book wasn't well-received by the local freemasons, they tried to set on fire the print shop where it was being produced, they managed to get Morgan arrested for some supposedly unpaid debts, but his friend (the allegedly ex-freemason) paid the bail; notwithstanding, he was arrested a few hours later accused of more debts and the theft of a shirt and a tie. That same night, a stranger presenting himself as a friend paid the bail again, both men were seen getting in a carriage, which was seen in Fort Niagara the next day, after this, William Morgan was never seen again.

The most accepted version is that he was killed and thrown to the Niagara River, a body was found on the shores of it but it was unrecognizable. Three freemasons were arrested and went to prison because of this,

This case shook up the region and gave birth to an Anti-Mason movement.

This was the mysterious end of William Morgan, and here I add an illustration, in case there is any doubt on the resemblance of this person and I-AM-THE-MAN.

WILLIAM MORGAN

Appendix B

THE LIFE OF PROF. DANIEL VAUGHN
BY PROF. RICHARD NELSON
TO WHICH IS ADDED AN ACCOUNT OF HIS DEATH BY FATHER EUGENE BRADY, S. J.

PROF. DANIEL VAUGHN.

Story of the Life of Prof. Daniel Vaughn.
(Reprinted from the Cincinnati Tribune.)

HIS VALUABLE LIBRARY SHOWING MARKS OF MUCH STUDY.
Twelve Years' Record in the Chair of Chemistry at the Cincinnati College of Medicine.

[A paper read before the Literary Club by Prof. Richard Nelson.]

Few men, if any, so eminent in science and philosophy have been known to live and die in such obscurity as the subject of this paper. A mathematician whose knowledge has never been fathomed, an original investigator in terrestrial and celestial chemistry, most of whose speculations are now accepted as law; a contributor to the philosophical journals of Europe, whose papers were received with distinguished favor; an astronomer, who, in those papers, ventured to differ with Laplace, and, too, as will be shown, a man skilled in classical scholarship, yet unknown to his nearest neighbors and recognized by only a few in his own city. He lived and died in obscurity and poverty in a city distinguished for its schools of science and art, and the liberality and public spirit of its men of wealth; who, if any, were to blame? One object of this paper is to unravel the mystery.

HIS BIRTHPLACE AND PARENTAGE.

Daniel Vaughn was born in the year 1818 at Glenomara, four miles from Killaloe, County Clare, Ireland. His father's name was John, who had two brothers, Daniel and Patrick. John, like Daniel, was educated for the church, but, being the eldest son, remained on the farm. Daniel became, subsequently, the parish priest of Killaloe, and in 1845 was ordained Bishop.

John Vaughn had three children, Daniel (the subject of this paper), Owen and Margaret, afterward Mrs. Kent. The distance to the nearest school being four Irish miles, John had his sons educated by a tutor till they were prepared to enter a classical academy.

At the age of about sixteen Dan, as he was familiarly called, was placed under the care of his uncle and namesake at Killaloe, where he entered the academy. There the young student pursued the study of Greek, Latin and mathematics, giving some attention to certain branches of physics, for which he evinced peculiar aptitude.

HE EMIGRATES AND FINDS A HOME.

About the year 1840 his uncle, desirous of having the young man enter the church, advanced him a sum of money to defray his expenses at a theological school in Cork, but on seeing the American liners when he reached

Queenstown, the temptation to take the voyage to the land of promise was too great for the young adventurer to resist, so he secured a passage to New York. When at school he made wonderful advancement in study, especially in higher mathematics, and felt he ought to go to a country where he could be free to pursue his favorite line of thought and where attainments in science would not be circumscribed, as in the church.

Of his voyage and subsequent wanderings little is known until he reached Kentucky. That he visited many schools and paid his way in part by teaching there is no question. The college of the late Dr. Campbell, in Virginia, was one of the institutions visited, but he felt he must push on to Kentucky. About 1842 he had reached the Blue Grass region, near the home of the late Colonel Stamps, in Bourbon County. The Colonel saw him engaged at work and was quick to observe that the stranger was no common man. Taking him to his house and supplying his wants, the Colonel soon installed him as his guest, and eventually made him instructor of his children. Access to the Colonel's library was a boon to the stranger, developing in him traits of genius of which his host was very proud.

It was only a short time till the neighboring farmers heard of the distinguished young scholar, and desired to have the more mature members of their families under his care. A school was opened in the Colonel's house for instruction in the higher mathematics, the classics, geology, physical geography and astronomy. The young people were pleased with their teacher and made commendable progress, but the curriculum was too varied and comprehensive for an instructor, who, though far advanced in scholarship, had not yet studied the art of teaching.

ACCEPTS A PROFESSORSHIP.

In 1845 he accepted the chair of Greek in a neighboring college, which afforded him leisure for his scientific pursuits. After an absence of seven years the Professor returned to his old friend, Colonel Stamps and family, where he remained some two years, leaving them to settle in Cincinnati.

During his stay at the Colonel's (1851) he became a member of the American Association for the Advancement of Science, and in 1852 contributed to it his first article, entitled "On the Motions of Numerous Small Bodies and the Phenomena Resulting Therefrom." Having accumulated

For subsistence he delivered lectures before teachers' institutes and colleges till 1856, when an affection of the lungs compelled him to abandon the lecture field.

In the meantime, he had offered papers for publication to Silliman's Journal, the principal scientific magazine of America at that time, but, receiving no response to his communications and being denied publication, he took the advice of a friend and sent his subsequent articles to the British Association for the Advancement of Science and to the Philosophic Magazine, where they were received with favor. He was much gratified to find his article on "Meteoric Astronomy" published in the report of the Liverpool meeting of the association in 1854. Six papers, which he subsequently sent in 1857, 1859 and 1861, met with similar favor.

For several years he visited schools, colleges and teachers' institutes in Oxford, Lebanon, Cleveland and other cities, lecturing on his favorite branches of science. It had been his intention to popularize the science of physical astronomy by the publication of tracts or pamphlets.

PUBLISHES PAMPHLETS.

In the year 1856, at the request of teachers before whom he had lectured at the institutes, and with a view to popularize scientific knowledge, the Professor commenced the publication of pamphlets. The first number treated of "The Geological Agency of Water and Subterranean Forces." Only two of these pamphlets came into the possession of the administrator. One of them was a good-sized volume, as may be inferred from the following articles it contained:

"The Influence of Magnitude on Stability."
"The Doctrine of Gravitation."
"Theory of Tides."
"Effects of Tides."
"Cases of Excessive Tidal Action and Planetary Instability."
"The Rings of Saturn."
"The Supposed Influence of Satellites in Preserving Planetary Rings."
"Movements of Comets."
"The Tails of Comets."
"Mass and Density of Comets."
"Cometary Catastrophes."
"Phenomena Attending the Fall of Meteors."

"The Origin of Solar and Meteoric Light."
"Variable Stars and the Sun's Spots."
"Temporary Stars."
"Electrical Light and the Aurora Borealis."
"Proof of the Stability of the Solar System," with an appendix.

Some of these subjects had been treated of at greater length and published by American and British associations for the advancement of science.

He sent to the British Association for the Advancement of Science:

"Cases of Planetary Instability Indicated by the Appearance of Temporary Stars."

"Appearance of Temporary Stars."

Other papers appeared:

"Note on the Sunspots," Philosophical Magazine for December, 1858.

"On the Solar Spots and Variable Stars, idem, Vol. 15, p. 359.

"Changes in the Conditions of Celestial Bodies," an essay.

"The Origin of Worlds," Popular Science Monthly, May, 1879.

"Planetary Rings and New Stars," Popular Science Monthly, February, 1879.

"Astronomical History of Worlds," idem, September, 1878.

"On the Stability of Satellites in Small Orbits and the Theory of Saturn's Rings," Philosophical Magazine, May, 1861.

"On the Origin of the Asteroids." Contributed to the American Association for the Advancement of Science.

"Static and Dynamic Stability in the Secondary Systems," Philosophical Magazine, December, 1861.

"On Phenomena which May be Traced to the Presence of a Medium Pervading all Space," idem, May 11, 1861.

The Professor contributed to other publications on both sides of the Atlantic, but as he failed to retain copies of the articles or of the magazines in which they were published, doubtless many papers of interest are among the number.

them were works of some of the most prominent authors in branches of theoretical and practical science. Those of Laplace, Kepler, Tycho-Brahe, Leibnitz, Herschel, Newton and others, together with many pamphlets and periodicals, composed his library. He possessed a familiar knowledge of the German, French, Italian and Spanish languages, and of ancient Greek and Latin. Many of his papers appeared in the continental languages. It may be here stated that for the eminent astronomer, Laplace, as a scientist and writer, Prof. Vaughn entertained great respect, though he could not accept his nebular hypothesis, because important parts of it would not bear mathematical investigation. [The proof is in the papers in my possession. —N.] In an article of the Professor to the Popular Science Monthly (February, 1879) is a case of the kind, showing that the distinguished astronomer ignored his own famous theory. The article reads: "In endeavoring to account for the direct motion in secondary systems Laplace contends that, in consequence of friction the supposed primitive solar rings would have a greater velocity in their outer than in their inner zones. Now, if friction is to counteract to such an extent the normal effects of gravitation, it must be an eternal bar against the origin of worlds by nebulous dismemberment, and if the ring of attenuated matter were placed under the circumstances suggested by the eminent astronomer, it would be ultimately doomed, not to form a planet, but to coalesce with the immense spheroid of fiery vapor it was supposed to have environed."

It is interesting to know that the theory of our Professor was the correct one, as proved by a recent discovery of Prof. James E. Keeler, astronomer of the Allegheny Observatory. As announced in a daily paper: "Prof. James E. Keeler, of the Allegheny Observatory, has made a wonderful discovery. It is a scientific and positive demonstration of the fact that the rings of Saturn are made up of many small bodies and that the satellites of the inner edge of the rings move faster than the outer."

As to satellites, Prof. Vaughn, in the paper quoted, page 466, states: "The matter spread over the wide annular fields is ever urged by its own attraction to collect together and form satellites, which are ever destroyed by attractive disturbance of the primary, and have their parts scattered once more over a wide space."

INSTALLED AS PROFESSOR OF CHEMISTRY.

The Professor was elected to the chair of chemistry in the Cincinnati College of Medicine and Surgery in 1860, where he served with distinction for twelve years. His scholarly valedictory at that institution is one of the papers reserved for publication in his memoirs.

While in the college he continued his investigations in science, applying his knowledge of terrestrial chemistry to the chemistry of the heavens, as shown in nearly all his writings. Besides the position held in the college, he gave lessons in schools and seminaries in geology, astronomy, chemistry, Latin and Greek.

In 1873 he visited Lexington, where he met his old friend, Dr. J. C. Darby, and delivered lectures in public, at the Sayre Institute and the Baptist School, returning to Cincinnati the following spring. Except from his writings, he seemed to have no source of revenue for several years. How he managed to exist his most intimate friends could only conjecture. True, he contributed papers to monthly publications, but they appeared at such long intervals they could not be relied on for support, so, in the autumn of 1878 his friends organized for him a course of lectures, which were well patronized by physicians and others versed in science. In the meantime, negotiations were opened with prominent citizens of suburban towns for other lectures, and efforts were made to retire the Professor on an annuity.

HIS END DRAWING NEAR.

Enfeebled health, which confined him to his room for several weeks, prevented him from entering on the suburban course, so a second course was projected for the city and one of the lectures delivered. From what transpired after that lecture his friends were again anxious regarding his health, and, as the time approached for the delivery of the second, determined to see him. For reasons stated elsewhere it was with some difficulty he was found. Prostrated on a couch, he was suffering from a hemorrhage of the lungs of a few days previous, with evidences all-around of a state of extreme destitution. No time was lost in having him removed to comfortable quarters in the Good Samaritan Hospital, where his friends arranged for his care as a private patient. Next day, April 3, he expressed himself as greatly benefited by the change and talked cheerfully and hopefully of the future. Next day, Friday, he continued to improve, but on Saturday proof of his forthcoming article in the Popular Science Monthly reached him, and, feeling that he ought to return it promptly, he sat up to do the work, the effort was too great. Over-

HIS OBSEQUIES.

A committee of the more intimate friends of the deceased was formed, consisting of the late Jacob Traber, his nephew, J. C. Sproull, Drs. J. J. and William Taft and the writer.

Funeral services were held in the chapel of the Hospital, where, considering the suddenness of the Professor's demise, many mourners were present. The interest evinced was profound, while the floral tributes that covered the casket were eloquent of affection and esteem.

The remains were interred in a burial lot of Jacob Traber, who generously tendered its use until a separate place of interment and a monument could be procured. The remains of the two friends now lie side by side.

HIS EFFECTS.

After the funeral the committee referred to visited the room occupied by the Professor prior to his decease, and had the writer, as his nearest friend, procure letters of administration, so that papers of value, if any, would be cared for. A few letters, some private relics, unsalable remnants of books and pamphlets and scraps of manuscript constituted the effects. The scarcity of manuscript was easily accounted for, as it was the habit of the deceased for years to print articles designed for publication and have them mailed to magazines and to savants in different parts of Europe and America.

CHARACTERISTICS AND HABITS OF STUDY.

A prominent characteristic of Prof. Vaughn was shyness—a shrinking from familiarity or conspicuousness. He never was the first to salute a casual acquaintance on the street, and when introduced to a stranger would extend his hand with apparent diffidence or reserve—not with the warmth of a hearty shake, but rather with a cautious presentation of the finger tips. Undemonstrative in manner, and inexperienced in the customs of social life, his diffidence was taken for coldness, yet he was kind and tender hearted almost to a fault, and a most grateful recipient of a favor. In his poverty he would part with money or personal property to people whom he considered more necessitous than himself. Of the proceeds of his last course of lectures he gave to one such a sum so large as to almost discourage his friends from helping him.

Then, too, he was glad to render service to professional and public men. He made translations for writers and wrote lectures for others and made chemical analyses for the city when payment was not expected. As to his placing a commercial value upon his services he never learned to do it, though they often cost him both time and money that he could not well spare.

His waking hours were always fully occupied in writing or study, either in his laboratory, the libraries or in open-air observations. He was thoroughly familiar with the geology of the neighborhood and the physical geography of the entire continent, as may be seen by his articles on "Volcanoes," "The Origin of Lakes and Mountains," "The Absence of Trees on Prairies," "Malaria," etc. His ingenuity in the construction of apparatus for his illustrations in chemistry was remarkable. Given a few tubes of glass and rubber, a piece of tin, some acid and alkali, a blow-pipe, soldering iron and a pair of pinchers, he could construct at will enough apparatus for a lesson, a lecture or an analysis.

Considering his poverty, it may be questioned how he was able to maintain a laboratory. For twelve years he found a room at the Medical College. At other times he extemporized quarters at his humble lodgings, where the same apartment was to him laboratory, study and living room. Such a room he could not find in a private house, so he sought it elsewhere, as in the tenement in which he was found in his last illness. That life necessarily isolated him from society, its pleasures and advantages before he became familiar with the laws by which it was governed.

Having acquired a mastery of Greek and Latin in his youth, he had a good preparation for the acquisition of the modern languages; besides, to prosecute his studies and investigations, he found it necessary to understand most of the languages of Europe.

Exception has been taken to the Professor's manner as a lecturer. When we consider his natural diffidence in the presence of strangers we are surprised that he attempted to lecture at all. Take his case when he last lectured, his lecture hall, the operating room of the Dental College, and his platform that of the operator with his audience around but elevated a few feet above him. The position was an exceedingly trying one, and some time elapsed before he was able to make a good start. While hesitating, on such occasions, his eyes would wander around the audience till they rested on those of a familiar friend. Immediately he addressed himself to that person, and confidence was restored. Like other public speakers we know of, he

HIS RELIGIOUS LIFE.

The Professor was a Bible student, if we judge from fragments found among his effects and a well-worn Bible, now a relic in possession of a former student. The book is a curiosity, worn as is the cover with marks of his fingers as he held it, often with a candle in his hand, as shown by occasional drippings on the page and cover.

He was not a member of any church. At least, had not been up to a month before his decease, though he visited churches of all denominations and was familiar with their doctrines and polity. His religion consisted in his living up to his highest ideas of right and truth; hence he was charitable almost to a fault. When he had not money to give, he parted with his books.

An eloquent public speaker, referring to his private life, has said: "He was social, kind and humane. He took pleasure in instructing the children and communing with friends—good men and women, who loved and admired him—and his humanity was gratified in bestowing what he valued most—knowledge. To him nothing seemed more precious than truth, and to shed the light of it abroad. His heart was in his work, and without a glance to the right or left, he pursued his arduous quest."

Of the works of creation which occupied so much of his thoughts, the Professor's views may be had by reading the following concluding remarks found in his "Physical Astronomy:"

"Whatever doubts may hang over all speculations respecting distant events, either of past or future time, we have reason to believe that our universe will ever exhibit great and useful operations throughout its extensive domains. From the ruins of some celestial bodies others will rise to act a part in the drama of the physical creation in future ages. Though nature's work may all decay, her laws remain the same, and numerous agencies, obedient to their control and aided by occasional interventions of creative power, must maintain the heavens forever in a harmonious condition and transform innumerable spheres into seats of light and intelligence. While the laws of nature have been thus widely ordained for such great ends, their simplicity renders them intelligible to the limited powers of the human mind, and the immense universe thus becomes a vast field of intellectual enjoyment for man."

TESTIMONY OF THE LATE DR. JOHN HANCOCK.

The late Dr. Hancock, in writing to Mrs. J. W. McLaughlin, stated that he attended institute lectures of Prof. Vaughn, making his acquaintance at a meeting of the Southwestern Ohio Normal Institute. The Professor was engaged to lecture on his favorite specialties, physical geography and astronomy. "It is my recollection," says the doctor, "that Prof. Vaughn was a graduate of Trinity College, Dublin. However, that may be, there can be no doubt as to his wide and profound scholarship. He was not only deeply versed in the physical sciences, but was equally proficient in the classics and mathematics. It is said by competent judges that he read Greek and Latin as he would English, as though he thought in those languages, and he was one of the few Americans who read through Laplace's 'Mechanique Celeste.' He had a prodigious memory. At the Oxford Institute, to which I have referred, some dozen of the leading members, Prof. Vaughn among them, got up some literary games requiring wide reading and retentive memories for successful rivalry. In these games the Professor showed a wealth of reading and an ability to use it on the instant that I have never seen approached by any other scholar. It is needless to say that he was first in the game and the rest nowhere.

"Some ten years afterward, when connected with Nelson's Commercial College, I edited a little educational paper, the News and Educator, of which Mr. Nelson was proprietor. In this relation I came much more frequently in contact with Prof. Vaughn than I ever did before. To this paper he contributed a number of articles on scientific subjects, but, being printed in an obscure local paper, they attracted little attention."

REMINISCENCES OF MRS. STAMPS.

Mrs. Eliza Stamps, widow of the late Colonel Stamps, in giving her experience with the Professor, said: "He was a very industrious student, in his profound researches pursuing them to the exclusion of everything else. He would frequently forget the demands of hunger and disregard the summons to his meals. As to his engaging in innocent amusements, he considered it a sacrifice of valuable time; yet, lest he should be accused of selfishness or wanting in social etiquette, he sometimes left his books to unite with the children in their games, and, diffident though he was, would occasionally take part in the dance.

"He enjoyed the Colonel's library, but soon exhausted its resources and those of the neighbors; so, to obtain a supply, he would go on foot to Cin-

tion for Colonel Stamps, his benefactor, and his family, and the young ladies and gentlemen who had been his pupils, who never ceased to venerate him for his learning, or to love and cherish his memory. Some such were among the mourners at his funeral.

REPUTATION IN ENGLAND.

The late Jacob Traber, one of the most intimate friends of the Professor, has written: "In the year 1858 I was in the office of John Sayre, bookseller, High Holborn, where I made the purchase of books that were yet in the hands of the printer. I gave my address and directions for shipping. When in the act of leaving the office, I was accosted by an elderly gentleman who, with the apology, 'Beg pardon, I overheard you when you gave your address, Cincinnati, and desire to make inquiry about one of your distinguished citizens. Daniel Vaughn. Assuming that you know him, may I ask how long it is since you have seen him?' I replied that I had known the Professor some four years, and had met him but a few months ago. At that time, I regarded the Professor as a mechanical genius of the speculative type, and so expressed myself. A quick rejoinder came in that broad and forcible accent of an Englishman: 'If you Cincinnati people vote Vaughn as a speculative mechanic, the ripest and profoundest mathematical scholar in England may be marked as his apprentice. You have a treasure in that man. Why, sir, we send him problems that fail to be mastered here, and speedily have them back not only with a solution, but with the demonstration.' The speaker proved to be one of the ablest scholars and scientists in Europe."

FIXING THE RESPONSIBILITY FOR HIS CONDITION.

The subject of this paper, it will be inferred, did not inherit a patrimony, yet he contributed his valuable services to many worthy objects without pecuniary compensation. As has been stated, his great pleasure, next to the investigation of truth, was to impart useful knowledge and help the needy. When in the medical college he was paid with shares of stock on which a dividend was never declared, and when engaged in lecturing and teaching his diffidence prevented him from placing a sufficient value on his services. Living the life of a recluse, he concealed his poverty from his nearest friends, who were ignorant even of his address. Then, he never sought a gratuity, and his friends could only learn by conjecture when he was in need. When asked if his privations did not cause him much anxiety, he said they gave him no concern.

On more than one occasion the writer, at the request of men of wealth and influence, proposed to retire him on an annuity, but he modestly but firmly declined to accept, and it was not until after the of his last course that he consented. Then the proposition was to pay his expenses at a hotel of his choice and advance him money for his personal expenses, for which he was to lecture when and where he might choose. The gentlemen most active in this project were the following, now deceased: Henry Peachy, William F. Corry, Jacob Traber, Colonel Geoffrey and others. Favorably known to the public were Drs. J. J. and William Taft, Dr. Thad Reamy, J. C. Sproull, etc.

The project had so far matured that the writer and another had arranged with Mr. Peachy to make the Lafayette National Bank the custodian of the funds. Had the Professor survived, he would have enjoyed a life of leisure and comfort, at one of the most prominent hotels in the city.

The people of Cincinnati were, therefore, not responsible for the poverty of our friend, nor for the state of destitution in which he was found prior to his removal to the hospital.

ACCOUNT OF THE DEATH OF PROF. VAUGHN, BY REV. EUGENE BRADY, S. J.

[Concerning the last days of Professor Vaughn, the following from the pen of Father Brady, pastor of St. Xavier's Church, is of special interest. This is peculiarly appropriate by reason of the fact that Father Brady, while a boy, attended the college during the time Professor Vaughn taught in Bardstown, Kentucky, and finally comforted him in his last moments. —J. U. L.]

"MY DEAR MR. LLOYD: —

"Concerning the foot-note on Chapter XXIV of Etidorhpa. The description of Daniel Vaughn is correct. The story of his privations is quite true. He was so absorbed in science as to be self-neglectful. Moreover, he was grossly neglected by those who made use of his labors.

"A servant girl told the venerable Sister Anthony that a poor lodger was dying in destitution in the west end of the city. The lodger was Professor Vaughn. The Sister had the good man conveyed to the Good Samaritan Hospital on April 1, 1879. She made him comfortable, as he repeatedly

was neither delirium nor senility that revived his faith. He was but sixty-one years of age, and as rational as ever in life."

—Eugene Brady, S. J.

Appendix C

TO THE RECIPIENTS OF THE AUTHOR'S EDITION OF ETIDORHPA:
(Reviews of Etidorhpa)

That so large an edition as 1,299 copies of an expensive book, previously unseen by any subscriber, should have been taken in advance by reason of a mere announcement, is complimentary to the undersigned; and yet this very confidence occasioned him not a little anxiety. Under such circumstances to have failed to give, either in workmanship or subject-matter, more than was promised in the announcement of Etidorhpa, would have been painfully embarrassing.

Not without deep concern, then, were the returns awaited; for, while neither pains nor expense were spared to make the book artistically a prize, still, beautiful workmanship and attractive illustrations may serve but to make more conspicuous other failings. Humiliating indeed would it have been had the recipients, in a spirit of charity, spoken only of artistic merit and neat bookwork.

When one not a bookman publishes a book, he treads the danger-line. When such a person, without a great publishing-house behind him, issues a book like Etidorhpa—a book that, spanning space, seemingly embraces wild imaginings and speculation, and intrudes on science and religion—he invites personal disaster.

That in the case of the Author's Edition of Etidorhpa the reverse happily followed, is evidenced by hundreds of complimentary letters, written by men versed in this or that section wherein the book intrudes; and in a general way the undersigned herein gratefully extends his thanks to all correspondents—thanks for the cordial expressions of approval, and for the graceful oversights by critics and correspondents, that none better than he realizes have been extended towards blemishes that must, to others, be not

it is not only as a duty, but as a pleasure, that the undersigned reproduces the following abstracts from public print concerning the Author's Edition, adding, that as in most cases the reviews were of great length and made by men specially selected for the purpose, the brief notes are but fragments and simply characteristic of their general tenor.

The personal references indulged by the critics could not be excised without destroying the value of the criticisms, and the undersigned can offer no other apology for their introduction than to say that to have excluded them would have done an injustice to the writers.

Respectfully,
JOHN URI LLOYD.

Reviews of Etidorhpa:

ETIDORHPA AS A WORK OF ART.

If a fine statue or a stately cathedral is a poem in marble, a masterpiece of the printer's art may be called a poem in typography. Such is Etidorhpa. In its paper, composition, presswork, illustrations, and binding—it is the perfection of beauty. While there is nothing gaudy in its. outward appearance, there is throughout a display of good taste. The simplicity of its neatness, like that of a handsome woman, is its great charm. Elegance does not consist in show nor wealth in glitter; so, the richest as well as the costliest garb may be rich in its very plainness. The illustrations were drawn and engraved expressly for this work, and consist of twenty-one full-page, half-tone cuts, and over thirty half-page and text cuts, besides two photogravures. The best artistic skill was employed to produce them, and the printing was carefully attended to, so as to secure the finest effect. Only enameled book paper is used; and this, with the wide margins, gilt top, trimmed edges, and clear impressions of the type, makes the pages restful to the eyes in reading or looking at them. The jacket, or cover, which protects the binding, is of heavy paper, and bears the same imprint as the book itself. Altogether, as an elegant specimen of the bookmakers' art it is a credit to the trade. All honor to the compositors who set the type, the artists who drew and engraved the illustrations, the electrotyper who put the forms into plate, the pressman who worked off the sheets, and the binder who gathered and bound them in this volume.

PROFESSOR S. W. WILLIAMS, WYOMING, OHIO.

The present is an age of expectancy, of anticipation, and of prophecy; and the invention or discovery or production that occupies the attention of the busy world, as it rushes on its self-observed way, for more than the passing nine day's wonder, must needs be something great indeed. Such a production has now appeared in the literary world in the form of the volume entitled "Etidorhpa, or the End of Earth;" the very title of which is so striking as to arrest the attention at once.

A most remarkable book. . . . Surpasses, in my judgment, any thing that has been written by the elder Dumas or Jules Verne, while in moral purpose it is equal to Hugo at his best. . . . It appeals to the thoughtful scientist no less than to the lover of fascinating romance.

B. O. Flower, Editor of The Arena, Boston

In summing, I would say that I have found the book distinctly stimulating. It is odd, but with the oddity of force. It has passages of uncanny imagination, but they excellently evade the enormous and extravagant. It is a book that by its title and by such features as strike one at a hurried glance might easily in the repel. Yet it is a book that, studied carefully, calls for re-reading and deep meditation. Its theories are capable of scientific demonstration, its imaginings, while they may not be fact, are always consistent with it. The reader who lets the outside repel him errs sadly. Let him read it, and he will be as changed in his position toward it, as ready to convert others, as is the reviewer, who picked it up with foreboding and laid it down with the sense of having read great thoughts.

Mr. Herbert Bates, Commercial Gazette, Cincinnati.

"The End of Earth" is not like any other book. The charm of adventure, the excitement of romance, the stimulating heat of controversy, the keen pursuit of scientific truth, the glow of moral enthusiasm, are all found in its pages. The book may be described as a sort of philosophical fiction, containing much exact scientific truth, many hold theories, and much ingenious speculation on the nature and destiny of man. . . . The occult and

to reason, religion and morality. . . . The direct teaching of the book, in so far as it aims to influence conduct, is always lofty and pure.

Dr. W. H. Venable.

"My Dear Sir: Let me thank you most heartily for sending me the special copy of your wonderful book 'Etidorhpa,' which I shall ever value. I may say that when by chance I found it in Cincinnati I read it with the greatest interest and pleasure, and was so struck by it that I have sent copies to several friends of mine here and at home. I hope I may have the pleasure of meeting you someday either here or in London. I remain, sincerely yours,

HENRY IRVING.

"20th March, 1896."

Letter from Sir Henry Irving, to the Author.

No one could have written the chapter on the "Food of Man" but Professor Lloyd; no one else knows and thinks of these subjects in a similar way. . . . The "old man's" description of "the spirit of stone," "the spirit of plants," and finally, "the spirit of man," is very fine, but those who hear Professor Lloyd lecture catch Lloyd's impulses throughout. The only regret one has in reading this entrancing work is, that it ends unexpectedly, for the End of Earth comes without a catastrophe. It should have been a hundred pages longer; the reader yearns for more, and closes the book wistfully.

Eclectic Medical Journal, Cincinnati.

One of the great charms of the book is the space between the lines, which only the initiated can thoroughly comprehend. Don't fail to read and re-read Etidorhpa. Be sure and read it in the light of contemporaneous literature, for without doing so, its true beauty will not appear. Aside from its subject-matter, the excellency of the workmanship displayed by the printer, and artistic beauty of the illustrations, will make Etidorhpa an ornament to any library.

New Idea, Detroit.

This book, to use the words of the editor of the Chicago Inter-Ocean, is "the literary novelty of the year." . . . In a literary sense, according to all reviewers, it abounds with "word-paintings of the highest order"—in some chapters being "terrible" in its vividness, several critics asserting that Dante's Inferno has nothing more realistic. . . .

Cincinnati Student.

We have read it with absorbed interest, the vividly-depicted scenes of each stage in the miraculous journey forming a theme which enthralls the reader till the last page is turned. Many new views of natural laws are given by the communicator, and argued between him and Drury, into which, and into the ultimate intent of Etidorhpa, we will not attempt to enter, but will leave it for each reader to peruse, and draw his own conclusions. . . . Professor Lloyd's style is quaint and polished, and perfectly clear. The printing and paper are all that can be desired, and an abundance of artistic and striking illustrations are admirably reproduced.

The British and Colonial Druggist, London, England.

Etidorhpa, the End of the Earth, is in all respects the worthiest presentation of occult teachings under the attractive guise of fiction that has yet been written. Its author, Mr. John Uri Lloyd, of Cincinnati, as a scientist and writer on pharmaceutical topics, has already a more than national reputation, but only his most intimate friends have been aware that he was an advanced student of occultism. His book is charmingly written, some of its passages being really eloquent; as, for instance, the apostrophe to Aphrodite—whose name is reversed to make the title of the story. It has as thrilling situations and startling phenomena as imagination has ever conceived. . .

There is no confusion between experiences and illusions, such as are common in the works of less instructed and conscientious writers treating of such matters. He knows; where to draw the line and how to impress perception of it, as in the four awful nightmare chapters illustrating the curse of drink. Etidorhpa will be best appreciated by those who have "traveled

We are disposed to think "Etidorhpa" the most unique, original, and suggestive new book that we have seen in this the last decade of a not unfruitful century.

John Clark Ridpath, LL. D.

It is as fascinating as the richest romance by Dumas, and mysterious and awe-inspiring as the wild flights of Verne. Hugo wrote nothing more impassioned than those terrible chapters where "The-Man-Who-Did-It" drinks liquor from the mushroom cup. There never was a book like it. It falls partly in many classes, yet lies outside of all. it will interest all sorts and conditions of men and it has that in it which may make it popular as the most sensational novel of the day. Intricate plotting, marvelous mysteries, clear-cut science without empiricism, speculative reasoning, sermonizing, historical facts, and bold theorizing make up the tissue of the story, while the spirit of Etidorhpa, the spirit of love, pervades it all. . . . Happy is the scientist who can present science in a form so inviting as to charm not only the scholars of his own profession, but the laymen besides. This, Professor John Uri Lloyd has done in his Etidorhpa.

Times-Star, Cincinnati.

For eighteen years the writer has been seated at his desk, and all kinds of books have been passed in review, but has never before met with such a stumper as Etidorhpa. Its name is a stunner, and its title-page, head-lines, and weird, artistic pictures send you such a ghastly welcome as to make goblins on the walls and fill the close room with spooks and mystery. The writer has only known of Professor Lloyd as a scientist and an expert in the most occult art of the pharmacist, and can scarcely conceive him in the rôle of the mystic and romancer in the region heretofore sacred to the tread of the supernatural. . The book is the literary novelty of the year, but those interested in such lines of thought will forget its novelties in a profound interest in the themes discussed.

The Inter-Ocean, Chicago.

The work stands so entirely alone in literature, and possesses such a marvelous versatility of thought and idea, that, in describing it, we are at a loss for comparison. In its scope it comprises alchemy, chemistry, science in general, philosophy, metaphysics, morals, biology, sociology, theosophy, materialism, and theism—the natural and supernatural. . . . It is almost impossible to describe the character of the work. It is realistic in expression, and weird beyond Hawthorne's utmost flights. It excels Bulwer-Lytton's Coming Race and Jules Verne's most extreme fancy. It equals Dante in vividness and eccentricity of plot. . . . The entire tone of the work is elevating. It encourages thought of all that is ennobling and pure. It teaches a belief and a faith in God and holy things, and shows God's supervision over all his works. It is an allegory of the life of one who desires to separate himself from the debasing influences of earth, and aspires to a pure and noble existence, as beautiful and as true to the existing conditions of human life as Bunyan's Pilgrim's Progress. The sorrow; the struggle with self; the physical burdens; the indescribable temptations with the presence and assistance of those who would assist in overcoming them; the dark hours, Vanity Fair, and the Beulahland, are all there.

The Chicago Medical Times.

In every respect the volume bearing the title Etidorhpa, or the End of the Earth, is a most remarkable book. Typographically, it is both unique and artistic—as near perfection in conception and execution as can be conceived. . . . The author is John Uri Lloyd, of Cincinnati, a scientific writer whose pharmaceutical treatises are widely known and highly valued. That a man whose mind and time have been engrossed with the affairs of a specialist and man of affairs could have found time to enter the field of speculation, and there display not only the most extensive knowledge of the exact natural sciences, and refute what is held to be scientific truth with bold theories and ingenious speculations on the nature and destiny of man is marvelous. . . .

The Addenda is as original as the book itself, consisting, as it does, of a list of names, some of whom are not subscribers, but to whom the author is deeply obliged, or whom he regards as very dear friends, and those of a few whom he personally admires. . . . If each of them has a copy of Etidorhpa, or the End of the Earth, he possesses a book which is not like any other

It relates to a journey made by the old man under the guidance of a peculiar being into the interior of the earth. The incidents of this journey overshadow anything that Verne ever wrote in his palmiest days. But perhaps the most singular part of it is that they are all based on scientific grounds. Dr. Lloyd, the author of the volume, is one of the deepest students, and is well known as a profound writer on subjects pertaining to his profession, as well as one who has taken much pains in studying the occult sciences. . . . The book is a very pleasant one to read, a little redundant at times, but full of information. . . . Readers who succeed in securing it will be very lucky indeed.

Cleveland Leader.

Appendix D

On The Lloyd Library and Museum
A VALUABLE AND UNIQUE LIBRARY.
From the Pharmaceutical Era, New York, October, 1894.

In Cincinnati is one of the most famous botanical and pharmacal libraries in the world, and by scientists it is regarded as ail invaluable store of knowledge upon those branches of medical science. So famous is it that one of the most noted pharmacologists and chemists of Germany, on a recent trip to this country, availed himself of its rich collection as a necessary means of completing his study in the line of special drug history. When it is known that he has devoted a life of nearly eighty years to the study of pharmacology, and is an emeritus professor in the famous University of Strassburg, the importance of his action will be understood and appreciated. We refer to Prof. Frederick Flueckiger, who, in connection with Daniel Hanbury, wrote Pharmacographia and other standard works. Attached to the library is an herbarium, begun by Mr. Curtis Gates Lloyd when a schoolboy, in which are to be found over 30,000 specimens of the flora of almost every civilized country on the globe. The collections are the work of two brothers, begun when in early boyhood. In money they are priceless, yet it is the intention of the founders that they shall be placed; either before or at their death, in some college or university where all students may have access to them without cost or favor, and their wills are already made to this end, although the institution to receive the bequest is not yet selected. Eager requests have been made that they be sent to foreign universities, where only, some persons believe, they can receive the appreciation they deserve.

The resting place of this collection is a neat three-story house at 204 West Court street, rebuilt to serve as a library building. On the door is a plate embossed with the name Lloyd, the patronymic of the brothers

connected subjects, while his brother is equally devoted to materia medica, pharmacy, and chemistry.

In the botanical department are the best works obtainable in every country, and there the study of botany may be carried to any height. In point of age, some of them go back almost to the time when the art of printing was discovered. Two copies of Aristotle are notable. A Greek version bound in vellum was printed in 1584. Another, in parallel columns of Greek and Latin, by Pacius, was published in 1607. Both are in excellent preservation. A bibliographical rarity (two editions) is the "Historia Plantarum," by Pinaeus, which was issued, one in 1561, the other in 1567. It appears to have been a first attempt at the production of colored plates. Plants that were rare at that time are colored by hand, and then have a glossy, fixative spread over them, causing the colors still to be as bright and fresh as the day that the three-hundred-years-dead workmen laid them on. Ranged in their sequence are fifty volumes of the famous author, Linnaeus. Mr. Lloyd has a very complete list of the Linnæan works, and his commissioners in Europe and America are looking out for the missing volumes. An extremely odd work is the book of Dr. Josselyn, entitled "New England Rarities," in which the Puritan author discusses wisely on "birds, beasts and fishes" of the New World. Dr. Carolus Plumierus, a French savant, who flourished in 1762, contributes an exhaustive work on the "Flora of the Antilles." He is antedated many years, however, by Dr. John Clayton, who is termed Johannes Claytonus, and Dr. John Frederick Gronovius. These gentlemen collated a work entitled the "Flora of Virginia," which is among the first descriptions of botany in the United States. Two venerable works are those of Mattioli, an Italian writer, who gave his knowledge to the world in 1586, and Levinus Lemnius, who wrote "De Miraculis Occultis Naturæ" in 1628. The father of modern systematized botany is conceded to be Mons. J. P. Tournefort, whose comprehensive work was published in 1719. It is the fortune of Mr. Lloyd to possess an original edition in good condition. His "Histoire des Plantes," Paris (1698), is also on the shelves. In the modern department of the library are the leading French and German works. Spanish and Italian authors are also on the shelves, the Lloyd collection of Spanish flora being among the best extant. Twenty-two volumes of rice paper, bound in bright yellow and stitched in silk, contain the flora of Japan. All the leaves are delicately tinted by those unique flower-painters, the Japanese. This rare work was presented to the Lloyd library by Dr. Charles Rice, of New York, who informed the Lloyds that only one other set could be found in America.

One of the most noted books in the collection of J. U. Lloyd is a Materia Medica written by Dr. David Schoepf, a learned German scholar, who traveled through this country in 1787. But a limited number of copies were printed, and but few are extant. One is in the Erlangen library in Germany. This Mr. Lloyd secured, and had it copied verbatim. In later years Dr. Charles Rice obtained an original print and exchanged it for that copy. A like work is that of Dr. Jonathan Carver of the provincial troops in America, published in London in 1796. It treats largely of Canadian materia medics. Manasseh Cutler's work, 1785, also adorns this part of the library. In addition to almost every work on this subject, Mr. Lloyd possesses complete editions of the leading serials and pharmaceutical lists published in the last three quarters of a century. Another book, famous in its way, is Barton's "Collections Toward a Materia Medica of the United States," published in 1798, 1801, and 1804.

Several noted botanists and chemists have visited the library in recent years. Prof. Flueckiger formed the acquaintance of the Lloyds through their work, "Drugs and Medicines of North America," being struck by the exhaustive references and foot-notes. Students and lovers of the old art of copperplate engraving especially find much in the ornate title pages and portraits to please their aesthetic sense. The founders are not miserly, and all students and delvers into the medical and botanical arts are always welcome. This library of rare books, has been collected without ostentation and with the sole aim to benefit science and humanity. We must not neglect to state that the library is especially rich in books pertaining to the American Eclectics and Thomsonians. Since it has been learned that this library is at the disposal of students and is to pass intact to some worthy institution of learning, donations of old or rare books are becoming frequent.

Appendix E.

"THE LAND THAT WAS, BUT YET EXISTS."
THE ETIDORHPA SEQUEL THAT NEVER WAS.

In 1935 John Uri Lloyd started writing a sequel to Etidorhpa, which he first referred to as Etidorhpa: Volume 2. Unfortunately, Lloyd died one year later, and far as we know the sequel was never completed. Forward in time, to 2016, an auction of several items belonging to J. Augustus Knapp (Etidorhpa's Illustrator) took place on the web; between these items, there were several letters signed by J.U.L. concerning his new book and the first thirty pages of The land that was, but yet exists. The one writing these lines didn't buy said collection but I did get to see some pages of this apparently unfinished novel. Here I transcribe the few pages I could see, unfortunately not continuous ones, so that we can get at least a small idea of the character of this work; I think the most remarkable glimpse you will get from this, is the name of the protagonist.

Hopefully, sometime, whoever got their hands on this unfinished work will publish it, but for the time being, far as I know, this is all the general public can get.

THE LAND THAT WAS, BUT YET EXISTS.

By John Uri Lloyd.

(Extracts for an unfinished? Etidorhpa sequel)

First Chapter.

"Telegram for you, Sir."

One Saturday evening in mid-December in the year 1898, I attended the meeting of the Cincinnati Literary Club. The hour was late when I turned my face homeward. I was then living in Norwood.

Judge John Weld Peck, an ambitious young attorney, accompanied me

Run", and the tract itself was known as "Bloody Hollow". In the settlement of Cincinnati, John Filson of Lexington, Kentucky, the original surveyor of the city, wandered one Sunday into this section – never to be heard again. It was accepted that he had been captured by the Indians. Hence the gruesome name for the hollow and the creek.

This night on reaching home, I found on the dining room table a tray of refreshment which my wife had prepared for me as was her custom. She had banked the fire, but it needed only a few strokes of the poker and the addition of a few lumps of cannel coal. The room was swiftly flooded with light and flickering shadows.

Page 13

...The Juggler tapped her closed fist with his wand. "sish-sish," he said. "Open hand." She did so. In it lay four silver coins. She counted them one by one into his hand.

Again seating himself on the desk, the juggler took the white chicken from his blouse, placing it under the cup. Tapping it he said, "Sish-sish," and raised the cup. The little chicken was there. Apparently out of patience at a seeming failure of his experiment, the juggler grabbed the body of the chicken with one hand, and with the other seemingly pulled off its head. A murmer indignation arose from the circle about him. Then opening both hands, Lo! In one stood the white chicken pert and alive, in the other stood the brown one.

Rising, the juggler turned to the gentleman who had given him the gold sovereign. "Want gold money back?" he asked. "Yes," was the reply.

With the tip of his wand the juggler tapped the turban on his head, inclined it and the paper containing the sovereign slipped from it into his open palm. Handing it to the gentleman, he said, "Open paper." The sovereign was there.

I am giving in the detail the marvelous manner in which this juggler deceived us or appeared to deceive us. Had I waited to write this until after my experiences which followed, probably this whole chapter would have been omitted as neither interesting nor extraordinary.

Page 18.

...him a double handful of dried dates, I bathed his fevered forehead and face for a few moments with water out of the cool drippings from the bag that, although swinging in the tropical sunshine, never gets hot.

During this time the face of the sufferer were fixed on my face, and in return I caught a familiar glance. Then smashed a memory touch.

His face was that of the Oriental who stared at me through the window of my home in Norwood.

But he gave no sign of recognition. His eyes were closed, his face smoothed, apparently sleep had come to him as we turned our aim and drove into the volcanic crater near where tradition records the Queen of Sheba started with a caravan of camels, jewels, spices, precious stones and other gifts, when she came to Solomon, seeking to prove the wise man with hard questions. In the Bible we are told that "Solomon answered all her questions, that there was nothing hidden in Solomon which he told her not." * But my object is not now to recite Biblical deeds or misdeeds.
**(II Chronicles, IX:2.)*

Sixth chapter.

Again I stood on the rim of one of the prodigious tanks laid beneath the sand of that extinct volcano. Again I wandered upon the little village of Arabs that men call Aden. Again I walked my way though the aisles of the market places of Aden, where…

Page 23.

To this I will reply, "It matters little to me whether any person believes or disbelieves."

But a few minutes did this dialogue require, as we finally stood on the path overlooking the stone tank perched on the lofty mountain side. Then my guide spoke.

"You have demanded to enter 'The land of Never Was'. My answer is, whether you will or no, you must enter it."

Eight Chapter.

It has been asserted that many years had passed since rain had fallen on Aden, and that it had never rained in the desert behind that volcanic rim. This must be an error, for surely those great stone water-tanks in the side of that mountain's crater would not have been constructed for other purposes

followed perfect silence. The question might be asked, are there degreed of silence? Is there a modified stillness? Is not silence complete if it be silence? An answer might be given by a person reared in a region subject to thunderstorms, to the effect that instantly after the crash, may come a sensation akin to stillness that appears to be neither noise, sound, nor silence.

But our problem now is not metaphysics, or any other form of the science or phenomena of being, but what happened to the two standing on the edge of the cement bowl of that elevated mountain water-tank.

Whoever has been stunned by a crash of thunder such as has been mentioned, knows that the blow is not an imaginary shock in which nothing strikes nothing. Whoever has been crashed by the sound of a thunderbolt, know that vacancy did not, as vacancy, strike that blow.

Page 29.

The interpreter then addressed me. His summary of the Captain's remark was that he had asked the party to drink to the health of the President of the United States, I being his representative at the table. As I stood before the Captain, it ran through my mind that if drank that glass of vodka I would soon be diving under the table. Then came the necessity of quick thinking. I stopped the glass to my lips and grasped the Captain's hand, having barely touched the vodka with my lips.

All eyes were on me. It was a moment of suspense as the Captain turned on me and in Russian made a short address being as I could see by his appearance and action very much offended. Standing thus the interpreter said to me, "The Captain is very angry with you." Then he added:

"Professor Lloyd, you have mortally offended this assembly by not drinking to the health of the President of the United States."

Towering over me the Captain then thundered:

"Do you know that we are drinking to the health of your President? Are you not a citizen of the United States? Are you not an American?"

Turning back to him I said, as quickly came to me the happy thought:

"Yes, I am an American citizen and am on a journey in behalf of the United States of America. I was born in America and lived my life as an American. I am aware of what is good form were I in my country, and as an American citizen here I have known what is proper in honoring the President of the United States." Then I turned and said to my interpreter, "Tell the Captain and all theses gentlemen that it is custom in the United States, when drinking to the health of our President, to only touch the lips to a glass, never take a swallow of the liquid. It would be considered very improper…

End of the extracts.

Nighttime Editions
For contact and other books published:
https://nighttimeeditions.wordpress.com

Printed in Great Britain
by Amazon

For my daughter-in-law and son-in-law: My biggest fans!
Thank you for reading my books.

CHAPTER 1
THE DOUBLE S RANCH

BRIAN BAILEY RACED HIS HORSE AFTER THE RUNNING bull that was trying to make it to a deep, shrub-filled ravine. He had his lariat in hand and was waiting to get close enough to dab the loop over the longhorn. This was a tough and wily bull, one of the original herd that they had brought to the Animas from Texas to start their ranch. At their last tally, they had found that they were missing many head of cattle, and at first they had suspected rustlers. But Brian had done some scouting around and had found that a small herd of cows and heifers had taken shelter in a deep ravine that was filled with shrubs, trees, and boulders, making it difficult to drive them out. He had also found the bull that had led them there and had promptly named it Bronco Bull. Bronco Bull had thwarted their efforts to drive the herd out of the ravine, by hiding in the trees and then suddenly charging the cowboys who came near. After two cowboys had been hurt and a horse gored by the bull, they had dropped the notion of driving the herd out of the ravine. Brian told Mark, "We got to get Bronco Bull first when he's out of the ravine, and then it will be easy to drive out the rest. But we got to get him first!"

They told the ranch hands to keep an eye out for Bronco Bull; if anyone spotted the bull, he was to call for the others to help cut the bull off from the ravine first before throwing a loop on him. That fateful day, Brian was riding alone, just scouting the area, when he spotted Bronco Bull trying to push some cows towards the ravine. It was less than two miles to the ravine, and Brian decided that there was no time to call on Mark or the other ranch hands, so he started for the bull by himself. The wily bull spotted his horse when he was still half a mile away and immediately turned around and headed for the ravine. Brian slowly increased his speed to close the gap without alarming the bull, but Bronco Bull had other ideas and began to run at top speed for the ravine, with Brian giving chase. Brian realized that the bull would have to swerve to reach the ravine, and turning his horse slightly, he started riding at a tangent to the bull. He was starting to cut the bull off from the ravine when Bronco Bull suddenly swerved and charged straight for him. Nothing much would have happened if Brian had been riding his favorite cutting horse, because the horse would have easily avoided the bull's charge, and then Brian would have dabbed a loop on him. But on this day, he was riding a freshly broken mustang to get the kinks out of the horse.

When Bronco Bull charged, the mustang was just a tad slow in getting out of the way, and the bull hit the horse a glancing blow with his massive horn, throwing horse and rider to the ground. The horn tore open the horse from shoulder to belly, and the horse was dying as it fell. Unfortunately for Brian, he was off balance and couldn't jump off the horse fast enough, and the horse landed on his leg. He was struggling to free his leg when Bronco Bull spun around and came snorting and charging straight at him. Brian sighed and tried to get his rifle from the sheath, but it was held down by the horse's weight. The sight of a maddened bull charging straight at you with those long, pointed horns would have panicked many a man, but not Brian.

He drew his pistol and first shot the dying horse in the head, putting it out of its misery. Then he calmly rested his elbow on the dead horse and took careful aim before squeezing the trigger. His aim was true, and the bullet entered the bull's brain through the eye. Even then it was touch and go for Brian, as the momentum of the dead bull's charge kept it moving forward until it collapsed just a foot away from Brian's dead mount.

Brian was still struggling to free his leg when his brother Mark and Joe Lamprey came riding up to him. They swung down from their saddles, and together, using their lariats, they managed to shift the dead horse and free Brian's leg. While Mark was checking Brian's leg, Joe surveyed the scene and remarked, "This is as close as it can get. Another three feet and that there bull would have landed right on top of you." Brian said feelingly, "Don't I know it! For a moment there, I thought that I was a goner for sure. That there is Bronco Bull, and although it pained me to kill him, there was no other way. This mustang was just a tad slow in getting out of his way, and one of the horns gored it. I had to get my leg out of the way of the horn, and I reckon I was off balance when the horse dropped, so I couldn't jump clear in time." Mark had checked out his brother's leg, and now he said, "Nothing broken as far as I can tell, but you are going to be laid up for at least a month."

Joe was bent over the dead bull and suddenly he stood up and exclaimed, "A true son of the hills of Tennessee! He shot it through the eye, for crying out loud!" He turned to Mark and said, "Not between the eyes, mind you, but *through* the eye." Mark shook his head and said, "Not even with a rifle, but with a pistol; and with his leg trapped under the horse just to make it more interesting." He turned to his brother and asked him, "You trying to prove something, Brian?" His brother shrugged and said, "Didn't have much choice; anywhere else and the bullet might have glanced off a bone. Besides, I couldn't free my rifle from the sheath." Joe looked at Mark and said laconically,

"Never thought he'd be such a show-off." Brian and Mark laughed, and then Brian winced as he tried to move his leg. Mark told him, "Stay still while we make a travois for you." He rode away and came back after a while with two long poles. He and Joe used the horse blankets to fashion a travois with the two poles, and then they carefully placed Brian on it. They then attached the travois to Mark's saddle using their lariats and started for the ranch.

They rode slowly and carefully, taking care to avoid small rocks and rough ground to avoid jolting Brian as much as possible. Brian never made a sound, but at each bump in the trail, he gritted his teeth against the pain that shot through his leg. They rode into the ranch yard and Brian's wife Sue came running out. Mark told her, "He'll be okay, just busted up his leg a mite. You go get a bed ready while we carry him in." He looked around and called out to a ranch hand, "Bill! That door you were making for the new bunkhouse, bring it here pronto!" They carefully shifted Brian onto the door to keep his leg straight and then carried him into the house and laid him on his bed. Sue cut away the pant to expose the leg, and she gasped at what she saw. The leg was already swollen from just above the knee right down to the ankle. It was mottled with red and blue angry patches and was bleeding in some places where the skin had split. Joe told Sue, "You just clean it up as much as you can. I'll be back with some Indian medicine."

By the time Sue had cleaned up the leg, Joe was back with a bunch of leaves and some bark. He told Sue, "Put some of this here bark in boiling water and let it boil for some time. Then cool it a mite and let him drink some of the water; it will help with the pain and the swelling. While you do that, I'll make a poultice out of these leaves and we'll smear it all over his leg, and then wrap it up; it seems to always help wounds to heal. You got to clean the leg and change the poultice every day." Sue had water already boiling, and she dumped the bark in the water. She had cut up a bedsheet into long strips, and she said, "These will do to wrap the entire leg. I'll apply the poultice to his leg while you go and bring in our guest from the bunkhouse."

Brian grunted and asked her, "We have a guest?" It was Mark who told him, "Says his name's Clayton Moss and that Tally Stevens sent him to find us. That's as far as he got when we heard the shot, and I told Bill to keep him in the bunkhouse until I returned. Joe had also heard the shot, and we met up on the way. You want to wait and talk to him later?" Brian shook his head and said, "Let's hear what he has to say; might as well get it over with while the shock keeps the pain away." Joe came back with a short, broad-shouldered, tough-looking man who had miner written all over him. The man slowly shook his head as he looked at Brian's leg and said, "Looks like Tally's luck is running out."

Brian tried to shift his position and grunted with pain. He looked at Clayton and said, "Last we seen of Tally, he was determined to make Heaven his last stop." Clayton smiled and said, "I met up with him there, but the mines in Purgatory began to play out and Tally got restless. Me and four other miners went with him when he left the town. We were newcomers, and there wasn't much for us there anyway. We travelled to Arizona's Sonoran desert because Tally remembered a place there where he had stopped one time, some years ago. He told us that he was sure there was gold and silver there, but that before he had a chance to prospect, he was chased away by Indians."

Sue had started to apply the poultice, and Mark was cooling the brew from the bark. She told Clayton, "You're welcome to have lunch with the boys, but right now we need to see to Brian's leg. You can come back after you've eaten and tell us the rest of the story." Brian started to protest, but Sue told him firmly, "You stay still until I finish applying this poultice and get the leg wrapped up; time enough to talk after that." She told

Joe, "You see that our guest gets fed, and you tell cookie that I want a lot of strong beef broth and some fresh bread for our patient." Joe said, "Yes, Ma'am! We'll be back in an hour. I would say that Mark could talk to our guest, but you know your husband." Sue sighed and shook her head, "Don't I know him! You come back in an hour, and he can hear the rest of it; and then he's going to sleep. No visitors for at least a day!"

The story of Brian shooting the bull through the eye, while being pinned down by his dead horse, was the talking point for the ranch hands as soon as lunch was over. One of them said, "I know that the Baileys are sharpshooters with a rifle; but nailing a charging bull through the eye with a pistol while being pinned to the ground? That story will travel along the trails, and it will be spoken about for years to come!" Another cowboy said, "Joe is another crack shot with a rifle; not that he's a slouch when it comes to drawing his six-shooter. I reckon they put a rifle in a baby's arms up in those Tennessee hills! Bill here is another sharpshooter with a rifle." Bill Hanson said, "It's tough to make a living up in them hills, so we children are taught not to waste a bullet, 'cause bullets cost money. By the time we are ten years old, any boy in the hills can bark a squirrel without wasting a bullet." Randy, a cowboy from Kansas, asked him, "I've heard that term, barking a squirrel. What exactly does it mean?" Bill smiled and told him, "If you shoot the squirrel, you spoil most of the meat 'cause the squirrel is small. So what you do is, you shoot the tree right next to the squirrel and the flying bark kills it. You got to hit that tree right close to the squirrel or the flying bark will most likely miss it, and then that means you've wasted a bullet!"

Clayton was listening to the talk, and now he said, "When I was a kid, I always thought that mining was the most dangerous and toughest job in the world, but when I got to cattle country I learned different. I've seen what a charging steer can do to a man or horse, so I reckon it must be real scary to find yourself lying trapped on the ground facing a charging maddened bull!" Randy remarked, "Oh, it's scary all right! It's scary because you know that what you're seeing is actually death charging you; death with hooves and horns." Clayton said, "But Brian didn't panic in that situation; he just shot the bull dead. I guess what I'm trying to say is that I now understand why Tally sent me for the Bailey brothers."

CHAPTER 2
THE BAILEY BROTHERS

BRIAN AND MARK BAILEY WERE BROTHERS, BRIAN being the older by two years. Their family had a ranch in Texas, the Rafter K, named after their mother, who had died in an Indian attack when the family were on their way to Texas. The Baileys were originally from Tennessee and came to Texas via Kansas, Colorado, and Arizona. Their father was Nolan Bailey of the feuding Bailey clan in Tennessee. The Baileys had a running feud with the Hawkes clan until Nolan fell in love with Kate Hawkes and married her. They had four sons and a daughter. Mike was the oldest at thirty-three, Brian was thirty, Mark twenty-eight, Luke twenty-five, and their sister Betsy had just celebrated her twenty-third birthday. Mike and Betsy were still at the home ranch. Betsy had married Bruce McCullough of the Double M ranch, and they lived on the Rafter K. After the battle of Cedar Creek, which was fought by the Double M and Rafter K ranches against a ruthless carpetbagger, Jack Donovan had married Beth McCullough, and they stayed at the Double M. A year later, Brian and Mark decided to hunt for gold to get a stake and start a ranch of their own.

They had travelled through New Mexico, where Mark had

met and fallen in love with Sally Taylor of the Box T ranch near the town of Red Butte. From New Mexico, they travelled through Arizona and met Tally Stevens, an old miner, who asked them to help him in fighting off claim jumpers who were trying to take over his gold mine. After they had helped him save his mine, he had given them a location near the San Juan Mountains where he had found gold before but had not mined it. Together with some miners who asked to accompany them, the two brothers had found the gold mine. In Silver City, they had a run-in with claim jumpers who had found a new way of taking over the mines. They forced the miners to sign a bill of sale and then killed them. They then claimed legal ownership and promptly sold the mine. Brian met and fell in love with Sue Allen there; her grandfather had a gold mine, and the claim jumpers had threatened him to sign over the mine. At the end of the trouble, and after the fighting was over, the brothers married their sweethearts and started a ranch in a beautiful valley near the mountains. Two of the men who had accompanied them to search for the gold, Joe Lamprey and Dewey Long, had also started a ranch near them. Brian and Mark named their ranch the Double S for their wives, Sue and Sally. Joe Lamprey and Dewey Long owned the Double L ranch and were their neighbors.

They had filed on their claims for the water holes and the land to start their ranches, and they had planned on travelling back to New Mexico for Sally Taylor and having a double wedding there. But Sue had fallen from her horse while riding the range, and Brian decided that she could not make the long journey to New Mexico. So Brian and Sue Allen got married in Silver City, and Sue stayed there with her grandfather, Chet Allen, while Brian, Mark, Joe, and Dewey left for New Mexico. They planned on Mark and Sally Taylor getting married there and then driving a herd back to start their ranches. Brian had said, "We can get us some whiteface cattle, but I want a lot of

Texas longhorns as well to start with because they're tough and will survive any weather." He and his brother remembered what had happened when their father had started a ranch in Colorado, and two bitter cold winters had wiped them out. Brian told Mark, "This time we'll take no chances, and we'll build this ranch on a firm foundation. We'll bring in the cattle in summer so they'll get used to the climate by the time winter sets in."

They went to the Box T, and after the marriage of Mark and Sally, they put together a large herd of two thousand head of cattle, bought from Texas and New Mexico. They hired ten cowboys who were willing to settle down in Colorado, and they bought forty horses for the remuda. Brian was the trail boss, and they started slow and easy for the first three days to break in the cattle to the trail. The drive was long and hard, but once the cattle were trail-broken, things got easier; although easier is a relative word when describing a cattle drive. Along the way, they faced heavy rains and flash floods, and once near the borders of New Mexico and Colorado, they had a run-in with rustlers and lost two of their men, but killed seven of the rustlers. They lost about a hundred head on the drive, and they reached their new home twenty days after starting from New Mexico. Both ranches were now doing well after two years, and Brian had a baby daughter named Kate, while Mark had a baby son named Nolan. Then the traveler came to their ranch. Mark, his wife Sally, Sue, Joe, and Dewey Long sat with Brian by his bed and listened to the tale that Clayton told them.

CHAPTER 3
TALLY STEVENS

BRIAN AND MARK HAD SAVED TALLY AND HIS FRIENDS from the claim jumpers, and then they had left to continue their hunt for gold. Tally had renamed the town of Providence and called it Heaven, while the area of the mines was called Purgatory. But after six months, the mines began to play out, and Tally told his partners, "In another six months, there won't be any gold left worth the trouble of mining it. You boys can stay on, but I got this itch that I just gotta scratch, so I'm going prospecting again. There's a place I remember seeing while travelling, it's some miles southwest of Maricopa Wells in Arizona. There was a small oasis with two deep wells, fed by the river, I reckon, because the water was sure sweet. I had camped for the day to rest up, and the next day I did some prospecting. I saw some rocks laden with silver, and I'm sure that there's gold up there as well. Trouble was, some Indians spotted me, and I had to leave in a hurry. I had planned on going back, but there was a lot of trouble and fighting between the tribes and it wasn't a safe place to prospect for gold and silver. I recall it now after all these years, and I'm going back there." One of the newcomers asked him, "You sure you can find it again after so long?" Tally's partners laughed and told him, "Tally never forgets a place where he thinks there's gold. He'd find it again after fifty years if necessary!" Tally told the newcomer, "There were two tall stone formations near the top of the hill where I was camping. They looked like two forks standing upright. Yeah, I reckon I can find it again."

Clayton Moss, Pat Simpson, Harvey Kline, and Bull Redding had joined Tally, and they travelled to Phoenix. The new city was bustling, and the farming community was doing well. The city was expanding rapidly, and there were two banks and an assayer's office as well. They stayed there for a day to enjoy some hotel comforts and then left for Maricopa Wells with six mules and three spare horses. Travelling through the desert, they laid up during the day and travelled through the night. Not many did that at the time because they could end up travelling in circles, but Tally was adept at using the stars to guide him. They passed the Wells and continued in a southwest direction, and after a day's ride they came to a range of mountains. They camped for the night, and the next morning Tally took them to a big rock and pointed up the hill. "See that?" he said. "Two forks."

The two rock formations did indeed resemble forks standing upright, although one had three tines and one only two. They mounted up and walked their horses up a gentle slope for about five hundred feet, and Tally said, "This here spot is mine. See those stakes? That marks my boundary, and this is silver; but I'm sure that further up there is gold. I had found a likely place when the Indians saw me, and I had to ride like the devil to save my skin." He got off his horse and, taking a burlap sack, began to fill it with some rocks. "You boys fill some sacks and I'll cut the four of you in at forty percent of what we get; that's ten percent for each of you."

Harvey Kline looked at the rocks and said, "I know my gold, and that ain't it; are you telling me that those rocks are silver?" Tally showed him a rock with silvery-gray spider-like veins running through it, and he said, "Yep! That there's silver that you can see! Take those black rocks that look kind of sooty, as though a fire was built near them; that's silver ore as well. There's enough here on the surface to get us started, but then we'll have to mine for the rest. This here is my claim, and the one I saw further up will be my claim for gold. Whatever else is there, you can divide amongst you." He looked at the four men and said, "But there may not be more gold or silver around, so I'll tell you what: I'll take one partner for this here silver mine and one partner for my gold mine. But if my partner finds another lode, then we go partners in that as well." Clayton Moss said, "I reckon I'll take your offer for the gold mine." Bull Redding said, "I know silver, so I'd be obliged if you would take me on as a partner in this mine."

They gathered the silver ore from the surface and took a bit more by doing some shallow open mining. After two days, Bull Redding said, "I reckon that's enough to give us all a stake for further prospecting and mining." Harvey Kline told Tally, "Before we leave, maybe we could take a look at that gold claim of yours and do a little prospecting for a day or two. If we find some suitable sites, then we could stake out a claim before going back to Phoenix. The minute we hit Phoenix with this silver ore, there will be many others following us when we return. This way, we'll be one step ahead at least." Tally said, "We're all in this together, so if that's what everyone wants, then let's do it." The others agreed, and Tally led them up the hill and showed them his claim, which he had staked out in a hurry. Clayton said, "You boys go ahead and do your prospecting. Me and Tally are going to survey this area and stake out a proper claim right now." At the end of two days, Bull Redding had staked out a claim for another silver mine about seven hundred feet up and about a hundred feet west of Tally's silver mine. Clayton staked a claim for a gold mine about a thousand feet up the mountains and two hundred feet east of Tally's gold mine. Harvey Kline and Pat Simpson staked claims for gold mines about eight hundred feet up the mountain, with only a hundred feet separating them. They also staked out a location for a town about a mile from the foothills, and Tally drew up a map showing the area and all the claims before they left for Phoenix.

They reached Phoenix three days later and went first to the assayer's office and unloaded the silver ore. Tally made a good deal for the ore and divided the money with the others. They then went to the courthouse and officially filed on their claims using the map drawn by Tally. They spent a week in Phoenix outfitting themselves for the work ahead and bought two wagons to carry the tools and food supplies. Phoenix was a farming community, and there weren't many miners around, but Harvey Kline was able to hire a tough, well-built farmhand named Butch Brady, who was more interested in mining for gold than farming. Pat Simpson met a miner he knew, Kelly Proctor, and he hired him as a working partner. Tally ran into an old friend of his, Nick Palmer, who had been a Marshal in a small town in Colorado. He told Nick about the mines and said, "The minute we leave from here, there will be others who will follow us. We've laid out the site for the town, and we're calling it Two Forks." He stared at Nick and told him, "A town will need a Marshal so I would like it if you came along with us. I've seen you as a lawman, and you're good. This would suit you, so what do you say?" Nick thought about it and then said, "I ain't getting younger, Tally, but I guess I'll give it a whirl."

The day before they left Phoenix, Clayton's younger brother, Harry Moss, rode into town. Clayton told Tally, "Harry has always been a rolling stone, and he never settles down anywhere, but he is good with a gun and he's fast on the draw. He's a hard worker as well, so maybe we should take him along with us." Tally met Harry and liked the look of the tall, broad-shouldered young man. He told Clayton, "The mine that you staked out is yours, and I don't need to be a partner in that. You and Harry can be partners there." Clayton told him, "I heard that you were a fair man and that prospecting and finding gold is what drives you and not the gold itself, but your offer is more than fair, and I can't accept it. For the claim I staked, we'll make it a three-way partnership." Tally smiled at him and said, "I reckon to be a good judge of men, and I figured you for an honest man. I'll go along with your offer, and just to sweeten the deal, we'll make both the mines a three-way partnership." Clayton started to protest, but Tally held up his hand and said, "No arguments on *that* offer, partner!" Clayton thanked him and remarked, "Maybe this will help Harry to settle down. Who knows, maybe Two Forks will be his last stop for a while."

CHAPTER 4
THE MAKING OF TWO FORKS

THE CAVALCADE OF NINE MEN WITH A PACK OF MULES and two wagons left Phoenix early the next morning before dawn. They were watched by many men who had made their plans to follow the miners. As they travelled to the yet-to-be-born town of Two Forks, Nick Palmer rode ahead as lookout for trouble or Indians, and Harry Moss kept an eye on their back trail. On the second day, when they had camped for the night and everyone was sitting around the campfire, Harry told Tally, "There are two groups of riders following us, but they are not travelling together. Both are a day's ride behind us, and they don't seem interested in closing the gap." Everyone started to speak at the same time, and Tally held up his hand and said, "We knew this was bound to happen, so no need to get excited about it. There will be good people as well as claim jumpers and the rough crowd following us, and that is to be expected as well. It takes all kinds to make a town, and our town will need a Marshal; which is why Nick Palmer is riding with us. He's been a town Marshal before, and so I asked him to be the Marshal of Two Forks."

He turned to Harry and asked him, "How many would you

say are behind us?" Harry shrugged and said, "Judging by the dust they raise, I would say one group has about ten to fifteen, and the other is smaller; maybe around five or six." Tally grimaced and said, "If past experience is anything to go by, then the larger group will have the rough crowd, and the smaller group will be miners." He gave Harry a contemplative look and told him, "You shape up like a man who can handle himself, so you might have to back up Nick as a deputy if and when he needs some help. You're a partner now in two claims, so you have the motivation." Harry shrugged and said, "I'll do what I can to help out if Nick needs me, but until then, I'll work the mines. I find it relaxing to do hard physical work."

They reached their destination without trouble and immediately got down to work. Everyone worked together to put up two large cabins close to the claims. It turned out that Butch Brady was the best when it came to swinging an axe, so he was teamed up with Clayton, who was also good, and they cut down the trees for building the cabins. Kelly Proctor and Harvey Kline were good carpenters, and they split and leveled the logs. They also made benches, tables, and bunk beds for the cabins. Nick suggested laying out some sites in town for buildings, but Tally told him, "We might make a bit of money by selling town sites, but we'll also make some enemies, so it's not worth it. The ones who are following us will set up their own buildings anyway, or they'll live in tents. But together with these cabins, we'll work on putting up a strong Marshal's office for you. In fact, I think that should be the priority."

The next day six men rode in, and they went straight to where Tally and the others were working. Nick and Harry were armed with rifles, and the others all had guns nearby that they could reach in a few seconds. In an open land like this, no sensible person took chances. One of the men, a tall, well-built man with broad features, told Tally, "My name is Hugh Benton, and I know you by reputation. The six of us are miners, and we would be much obliged if you could tell us where your claims are so we can do some prospecting without stepping on your toes." Tally regarded him for a moment and then said, "I also know you by reputation, and you're reputed to be an honest man. I'll come with you and show you our claims that we have staked out, and I'll also point you to where I think you might find gold, if you won't take offense." Hugh Benton and the men with him laughed, and Hugh said, "Anyone who would be offended by Tally Stevens' offer of help can't be a miner. As I said, I know of you by reputation, and I'd be grateful if you would point us in the right direction." Tally took them around, showed them the claims, and then pointed out a few areas in the distance and said, "I got a gut feeling that there's gold out there. Last time I was here before the Indians chased me away, I only managed to get a quick look, but I always go with my gut." Hugh laughed and said, "That's good enough for me. Thanks, Tally, your generosity is legendary!" Tally just shrugged and said, "I reckon I've been lucky in finding gold, and I've enough money stashed away to last me two lifetimes; so now it's the prospecting and finding the gold that gives me pleasure as I grow older."

The next day, except for Harry and Nick, who were keeping a watch on the claims, the others began the work to build a Marshal's office and a jail, along with the work on the cabins. There were trees in plenty on the slopes, but it turned out that Bull Redding and Pat Simpson were good stone smiths, so while the others were felling trees and shaping logs, Bull and Pat began collecting stones that were available in the required shapes and sizes and shaping them. Harry told Tally that evening that he was sure the second group was watching them from the top of a hill. "I got flashes of sunlight on steel," he said. "I reckon they're sizing us up, and they'll be here tomorrow." It turned out that Harry was right because the next morning, four big wagons rolled in accompanied by thirteen men.

Tally's men did not stop their building of the Marshal's office to welcome the newcomers. Hugh Benton and his group had put two of their men to prospect and stake out their claims, while the remaining four helped Tally in the building. Tally had thanked them and said, "Once we complete the Marshal's office and the cabins, we will all work on building two more cabins for your group." Hugh had shrugged and said, "I've been to some boom towns, and I've found that it's best that the good people stick together." He had paused and then added, "Otherwise, they tend to die alone."

Now a tall, rangy man with broad shoulders, who looked more like a cowboy than a miner, came up to them and said, "Howdy! You all look mighty busy, so I won't bother you; just want to ask if I can pitch my tent anywhere or are there town sites laid out." A tough-looking, stocky young man of average height came up to stand next to him, and he said, "I answer to Rusty Bellows, and this here is my saddle partner." Both the men wore pistols with the holsters tied down. Tally stepped forward and asked them, "You don't intend to build, just pitch a tent?" The tall man said, "The name's Rock Masters, and I'll be opening a saloon. If the town lasts for three months, then for sure I'll build something more permanent. But right now, I just got to get my business running, so a tent will have to do."

As they were speaking, the others in the group came up, and a slim, saturnine-looking man dressed in a full white suit with a low-slung gun on his right hip said, "I'm Drake Manning, and I'll also be opening a saloon, but I intend to invest in mining as well." Turning to the men standing behind them, he said, "Let me make the introductions so you can get on with your building." He pointed to each man and gave a name: "Rod, Max, Burt, and Rick. Rick is called Big Red for obvious reasons." The man was over six feet with a massive body and a shock of red hair. Drake continued, "That there is Hans, Rupert, Sam, and Wayne. The last two are Pete and John, and they are all miners." Tally said, "Good to meet you. You were following us and then watching us from the top of that there hill, so we were wondering when you were going to ride in."

Drake said easily, "Don't get us wrong, we were just checking to see if we would be welcome. Sometimes when someone finds gold, visitors are met with lead instead of talk." Tally shrugged and told him, "You can set up anywhere you like. The town is called Two Forks, and we're just building the Marshal's office." He turned to the men whom Drake had said were miners and told them, "You can go prospecting, but just stay away from the claims that are already staked. Now I got to get back to work."

Rock Masters put up a big tent with a sign that read Gold Mine Saloon. He and his partner were experts, and they had the big tent up within four hours, and by the evening the bar, tables, and chairs had been put together, and the place was open for business. Rock owned two of the big wagons, Drake owned one of them, and the last one belonged to Hans and Rupert. Drake put up a tent with a sign that advertised the Silver Rock Saloon. Hans and Rupert also put up a smaller tent with a sign that simply said Hardware and Everything Else. The rest of the men had only pack horses, and they went about selecting their campsites; they would live in the open until they could build their cabins.

Within two weeks, the Marshal's office was ready and Nick Palmer moved in. It was a strong cabin, built partly of stone and partly of logs. It had a small room to serve as an office and another room to serve as the Marshal's bedroom. There was a larger room that they had converted into two cells with solid wood doors and wooden poles for bars. Once the Marshal's office was done, the men concentrated on the two cabins and completed them in another week. Then Tally's group helped Hugh Benton to put up two small cabins near their claims, and finally, the two groups started work on their mines. Hugh

Benton and his group had staked out two mines, and they were all equal partners. Hans Kruger and Rupert Schwartz went prospecting and staked out a claim for a gold mine. They then hired two of the miners, Sam Rockwell and Wayne Goodman, to work it. Both Sam and Wayne were good miners, but they were broke, so they agreed to work Kruger's mine for wages. Pete Ford and John Mason filed on a gold claim about two thousand feet up the mountain, but they first built a small cabin near it and then started to work their claim. Max Shultz and Burt Wayling filed on a claim with Drake Manning as a partner. Rod Tilson and Big Red just hung out at the Silver Rock Saloon and played cards and drank whiskey. Tally's group and Hugh Benton's group seemed to favor the Gold Mine Saloon in the evenings after a hard day's work.

CHAPTER 5
BOOM TOWN

TWO MONTHS LATER, THE TOWN HAD EXPANDED AND was bustling with activity. Five big wagons had come in, and a fat man with a genial smile that never reached his eyes had set up a grocery and hardware store. He told everyone, "The name's Fat Fred and I follow the boom towns. When I leave, it's a signal that the town won't last; never failed in six boom towns!" A tall, thin man who said his name was Homer Lee drove into town with two big wagons loaded with planks and everything needed to set up a hotel. He had two big-made men with him, and together they had the hotel up and running in ten days. There were a lot of men available now for those like Homer Lee and Fat Fred to hire for the building of their places, because men kept drifting in to see what was happening and then stayed on. There was a stage run from Phoenix to Maricopa Wells, and from there, the men came to Two Forks on horseback. The assayer from Phoenix opened an office in the town after three months and kept two men there to run it. They collected the ore from the miners, and when the load was sufficient, the assayer sent a wagon from Phoenix with an armed escort to move the ore, most of which was silver. By the end of two months, Phil Barnaby had come in and opened the town's first bank.

The town developed fast because the gold and silver strikes were quite rich, and four more mines opened up. Sam Rockwell and Wayne Goodman staked their own claim for a silver mine and started working for themselves. Tally was an old hand where boom towns were concerned, and he was an astute observer. He noted that no one was working the gold mine of Hans and Rupert after Sam and Wayne left. He also noted that almost no work was being done in the silver mine that Drake owned. Max Shultz and Burt Wayling did a lot of digging and threw around a sufficient amount of mud and boulders to make it appear that the mine was being worked, but Tally told Clayton that there was no silver there. Max and Burt appeared to spend their time walking around and talking to the men in the other mines. They told everyone that the pickings in their mine were slim, and so they were looking around for a more promising claim. At the end of the third month, the population of Two Forks was around a hundred, and two more saloons, a building with only rooms for rent, a couple more stores, and an eating house had opened up. The tents of Rock Masters and Drake Manning were packed away, and solid wooden buildings took their place.

Tally Stevens noted that Rock Masters started building his saloon only after Drake Manning had started on his; and not for the first time he wondered about Rock Masters and his saddle partner, Rusty Bellows. There was no doubt that the two were Texans, although they never said where they came from. Once when Tally casually asked Rock where he was from, he just as casually replied, "From over yonder." There was also no doubt that the two were very fast on the draw. One evening when Tally and Hugh Benton were standing at the bar having a drink, two hard-faced men with tied-down guns walked up to the bar and ordered drinks. They were dusty and unshaven and appeared to have just arrived in town. They downed the first two shots of whiskey and then took two steps back from the bar. The taller of the two men kept facing the bar, while the other man turned to face the room. The man facing the bar told Rock, "That ain't whiskey, that's moonshine, and I want my money back. In fact, I think you just tried to poison me, so maybe you better ante up twenty dollars, and I'll forget about it." His hand was on his gun as he spoke, but he suddenly froze and stared at the pistol in Rock's hand. The other man, facing the room, had started to draw his gun when everyone heard the snick of a hammer being drawn back, and the man froze. He was staring at the gun held firmly in the hand of Rusty Bellows.

There was a deafening silence in the room, and men began to move back slowly to get out of the line of fire. The man facing Rock swallowed hard and said, "Maybe I was wrong about that moonshine. If it's all the same to you, we'll be on our way." Rock's face was grim as he said, "Unbuckle your gun belts and let them fall to the ground." The man very slowly took his hand off his gun and then, just as slowly, he unbuckled his belt and let it drop. Rusty told the man he was facing, "You heard him! Drop the belt!" The man swore but removed his hand from his gun. Rusty casually pushed back the hammer and dropped his gun in his holster. The man's hand immediately flashed for his gun, and Rusty shot him through the heart. The man staggered back and fell, dead before he hit the ground.

Nick Palmer came in and looked the scene over. Tally told him what had happened, and Nick asked Rock, "You figure they were just looking to hold you up for some cash?" Rock told him bluntly, "They were planning on killing us." Nick stared at him for a moment but did not ask anything further. He just said, "Reckon I'll lock this one up and get the other buried." But Rock said, "No need, Marshal. This man will bury his sidekick and then he'll leave town." He paused for a moment and then added, "If he wants to live, that is." The man turned and told Nick, "I'll bury him, and I'll leave. You won't see me again!" Nick threw a puzzled look at Rock but then told the man, "Okay, bury him right now and skedaddle the hell out of this town. If I see you again, I'll shoot first and then talk."

The body was removed, and everyone went back to what they had been doing before the shooting. Tally told Rock, "Seems to me that you could have found out from that man if he was only after some cash or if he was after you." Rock gave him a grim look and then told him, "As I just said, they were planning on killing us." He moved away, and Tally stared after him thoughtfully. Hugh Benton said, "Way I figure it, there's something going on between Rock and Drake. He only started building this place after Drake had started his." Tally told him, "You're a canny man and I like that, so I'll just say this: I reckon it would pay us to keep an eye on Drake and Hans." Hugh stared at him for a moment and then asked, "You know something about them?" Tally shook his head and just said, "I don't like the look of them." Hugh was thoughtful, and he said, "Rock and Rusty are real fast on the draw, so maybe we should try to get them on our side. I swear I have never seen a faster draw." But all Tally said to that was, "*I* have."

The first big load of gold was ready to be shipped, and Tally had a talk with the assayers and the bank. Tally had the largest gold mine, and most of the gold that was to be shipped was his. He told Phil Barnaby, "I would be happier if Wells Fargo opened an office here and shipped the gold. Holding up a shipment of silver ore is not worth the trouble, because you got to refine the ore to get at the silver, but gold is different, and there's a lot of free gold from my mine." Phil told him, "It would take about a month to get Wells Fargo to do the shipping. Don't you think it would be dangerous to keep that amount of gold lying around for so long? Why don't you put the gold in this bank?" Tally shrugged and said, "Banks can be robbed. I got the gold hidden, and no one is going to find it.

Anyone comes searching, they're going to get a belly full of lead."

It took more than a month for Wells Fargo to open an office in Two Forks. A tall, lean Texan who said his name was Bret Hogan was the manager. He wore two guns, and he looked like he could use them. He told Tally and Phil, "A week from now, the wagons and the armed escort will arrive, and then we'll ship your gold. You reckon there'll be trouble?" Tally shrugged and said dourly, "There are enough outlaws near Prescott who would be willing to travel down here if gold is being shipped. But now that Wells Fargo is involved, maybe there won't be." Phil looked at him in surprise and said, "You should be happy that the gold will be safe, but you don't look it!" Tally sighed and said, "No trouble on the trail just means that there will be trouble here." He walked away before they could ask him what he meant. The next week, the gold was shipped, and the town celebrated. Almost everyone had come down from the mines to watch the gold being shipped, and the saloons were full that evening. Harvey Kline had also shipped a modest amount of gold, and he had come to town for the event. He had told Tally, "I'm glad I joined up with you. The mine looks very promising, and I can tell you that the next shipment will have a lot of my gold going with it."

CHAPTER 6
THE KILLING BEGINS

HARVEY GOT SEPARATED FROM THE OTHERS AND wandered into the Silver Rock Saloon. He was watching a card game when someone bumped into him. He turned to see Rod Tilson standing with an empty glass in his hand. Rod snarled at him, "Goddamn stinking digger! You spilt my drink!" Harvey looked at him in mild surprise and said, "I'm just standing here, and you bumped into me." Tilson's eyes gleamed, and he suddenly shouted, "You calling me a liar?" As soon as he shouted the words, he drew his gun in a flash and shot Harvey. It was close quarters, and Harvey took the bullet in his heart; he was dead before he hit the floor. Nick Palmer, Harry Moss, and Tally, had been searching for Harvey, and a man had told them that he had seen him go into the Silver Rock. They were outside when they heard the shot, and they rushed in. Tally took in the scene at a glance and he slipped outside immediately. He looked around and spotted Butch Brady. "Butch!" he called out. "Round up the others right now and bring them here. Harvey has been shot!" Butch did not ask any questions but turned and ran to the Gold Mine Saloon.

Tally went back inside the Silver Rock and heard Drake

Manning telling Nick Palmer in a smooth voice, "I don't know what happened, Marshal. I was playing cards when Harvey called Rod a liar, and so Rod shot him. Maybe Harvey was celebrating too much?" Tally walked forward and said, "Harvey wasn't a drinking man; he had one shot of whiskey, and then he got separated from us." Drake looked at him, and his eyes were cold. Before he could say anything, Rod Tilson said, "You calling me a liar?" Tally turned to him and said grimly, "You pull a gun on me, and you better make sure to kill me; because if you don't, some night when you are sleeping, you'll feel a knife in your ribs. Come to that, if you *do* kill me, one day one of my friends *will* kill you." He paused and then added, "And I've got a lot of friends!"

Drake was looking thoughtfully at Tally, and now he smiled and told him, "No need for everyone to go off half-cocked over this. As I said, I don't really know what happened except that Harvey called Rod a liar. It's an unfortunate thing to happen in my saloon, and you have my condolences." Turning to Nick, he said, "You know how it is, Marshal, you call someone a liar out here, and they can't let it slide. Now if there's nothing else, Marshal? I need to get back to my game 'cause I'm winning, and I don't want to let these yahoos off the hook!" Rod Tilson was going to say something more, but then he looked behind Tally and saw Clayton, Butch, Hugh, and the rest of Tally's group standing by the door, so he just turned and walked to the bar.

The next day, Nick Palmer went to see Tally, and he told him, "Hans Kruger and Rupert Schwartz came to my office this morning, and they showed me a bill of sale." Tally said, "Let me guess; Harvey Kline sold his mine to Kruger." Nick stared at him for a moment and then asked, "You knew about this? But why did Harvey sell to Kruger?" Tally sighed and told him, "He didn't, but this isn't a new story for me." Nick asked him, "Do you know Harvey's sign or mark?" Tally shook his head and asked him, "No, but who were the witnesses?" Nick said grimly,

"Max Shultz and Big Red. Hans said that Harvey figured the mine was playing out and wanted to sell it." Tally said sarcastically, "And ole Hans bought a played-out mine out of the goodness of his heart."

Nick shrugged and told him, "He claimed to be a better miner than Harvey and said that he figured he could make the mine pay." Tally was silent, and finally Nick said, "There's nothing that I can do, Tally, unless you can prove that Harvey didn't sell the mine. I was hoping that you would know his sign, but you don't." Tally sighed and told him, "That evening Harvey told me that the mine looked very promising and that the next gold shipment would have a lot of his gold. So I know that he wouldn't sell his mine, but I figure that this is only the start, and others are going to be targeted. They'll kill them and then claim that the victim sold them the mine." Nick stood up and said, "From now on, you keep your boys here, and I'll be around most of the time. When you do come to town, come in strength and let me know."

A week after the killing of Harvey Kline, Hugh Benton and his group went to town with Pete Ford late one evening. They went, as usual, to the Gold Mine Saloon to have a drink and listen to what was being said. A saloon was a place where you could hear what was happening in that area and around the country; it was a gathering place for news, rumors, and gossip. After some time, Hugh looked around and found that Pete Ford was missing. He shouted out, "A minute of your time, gentlemen! There was a blond, stocky man of medium height with us; anyone see him leave?" A man at a table said, "Some guy told him that there was a good card game going on in the Silver Rock Saloon, and he left with him." One of Hugh's group said, "Way I heard it, Pete Ford loves poker." Hugh Benton was worried and said, "Come on, let's go make sure that he's not in trouble. Tally told everyone to stay away from the Silver Rock." He turned to leave, and Rusty Bellows said, "Hang on!" He bent over the bar and came up with a Winchester, which he handed to Hugh and said, "Better take that along as insurance."

The group went to the Silver Rock Saloon and found Big Red getting ready to put the boot to Pete, who was lying dazed and bleeding on the floor. "Hold it!" Hugh yelled. "You kick that man, and I'll put a bullet in your leg!" He jacked a shell into the chamber for emphasis, and Big Red turned to glare at him. "You're next!" he snarled. But Hugh was unfazed and said, "Maybe, but not today. Now step away from him, or I *will* pull this trigger." The others in his group had also drawn their pistols, and Big Red reluctantly backed away. Hugh told two of his men, "Pick up Pete, and let's get shut of this place." They left the Silver Rock Saloon walking backwards with their guns held ready. One of the men went running to bring their horses, and they mounted up and rode out of town. The next day, Pete Ford told them, "I was going to sit in on a game when Big Red pushed me and then cursed me. He slapped me, and I hit him." He paused and then said, "That man is strong as an ox! He just wiped the floor with me, and there was nothing I could do about it. I think he meant to kill me." Tally said grimly, "That's exactly what was planned, and then they would have killed Mason here as well before producing a bill of sale for your mine."

Two weeks later, Pat Simpson was shot dead in front of his mine. Nick was around, and he heard the shot. The shot sounded from far off, but it was to his right, and he rode across the mountainside and looked in on the mines he passed. He finally found Kelly Proctor bending over Pat's body. Kelly looked up and said, "He's dead! It was a sniper. I was just inside and came running out when I heard the shot, but I saw no one, so it must have been a sniper." Nick bent down and examined the wound and then looked around. Tally and the others came running up, and Nick said, "Judging by the entry and exit of the bullet, I reckon the shot must have come from that hill over there." He hunted around and found the bullet and held it up.

"Winchester for sure," he remarked. Tally said, "No point in you riding over there. By the time you get there, the sniper would be long gone." The next day, Nick Palmer told Tally, "Drake Manning showed me a bill of sale for Pat Simpson's mine. Witnesses were Max Shultz and Big Red. I don't suppose you know Pat's sign or mark either." Tally shook his head and said, "Those boys joined up with me only recently. But Kelly Proctor is a partner in the mine, so Pat couldn't just sell the mine." Nick told him, "The bill of sale was only for his share of the mine." Tally grunted and remarked, "Whoever is at the back of this play, they sure do their homework; they knew Pat and Kelly were partners."

Nick said, "Maybe I should confront Drake and Hans; tell them that this is just too much of a coincidence." But Tally shook his head and told him, "You're a good man, Nick, and fast on the draw, but I don't think you're in the class of Drake Manning. We could all support you, but then it would be all-out war, and I hear tell that Drake and Hans have been hiring some of the rough crowd." Nick looked frustrated and said, "So you're saying that there's nothing we can do. Well, I'm going to do some tracking, and I guess I'll start where I think the sniper shot from. If I get me some proof that Drake or Hans are crooked, then I'll arrest them, and I don't care how fast they are on the draw." He looked at Tally and said, "I got me two shotguns, and they're fully loaded for bear!"

That night Tally called everyone together and told them, "I think that this here is a new kind of claim jumping. They kill a mine owner and then produce a fake bill of sale, and since we don't know Harvey or Pat's sign, we can't prove otherwise. Right now, we can do what I should have thought of earlier. We're all going to put our signatures or marks on a sheet of paper, and Nick Palmer will keep it. Nick will also spread the word that he has the signatures of every mine owner. That should keep us safe from snipers, or at least I hope so. But the ones who are at the back of all this will just think up some other way to take our mines. We are going to need help, and I'm sending Clayton to get that help. It's at least a twenty-day ride, but he can cut that down to fifteen, I reckon, if he takes three spare horses and keeps going by switching saddles."

Clayton asked him, "Where am I going for this help?" Tally told him, "Near to the San Juan Mountains. Follow the Animas, and when you come to Silver City, ask about a new ranch, or two new ranches, that started about two years ago in a valley near the gold strike. Ask for the Bailey brothers." Harry Moss told Tally, "They may have men watching the trail for just this to happen, so let me go instead." But Tally shook his head and told him, "Until help comes, which could take maybe forty days, we need you here, and we need your gun." Clayton said, "Some of you could come with me until we're at least a mile away from town. I doubt they'll have watchers further than that." Tally said, "Now that's using the old noggin! When we come back, I want the rest of you to agree to my plan to keep us safe until help comes."

Sam Rockwell asked him, "What plan is that?" Tally said, "You and Wayne, Pete and John, leave your mines, and we all will hole up here at my gold mine. It is well-situated to be easily defended, so I reckon it's the best place to be. Bull and Harry will also leave the other mines and stay here; I've already taken on Butch, and Kelly will also stay here." Pete said, "But that would leave our mines without protection, and they can take out a good bit in forty days." But Tally told him, "No amount of gold is worth your life. If Hugh hadn't acted fast on that day, you would be dead by now. They intend to pick us off one by one. I don't think they're interested in mining, I think they just want the ownership and then they'll sell the mines. But even if they take out the ore, they are not going to be able to ship it. I've had a word with the assayers and Wells Fargo, and no gold or silver will leave the town for the next two months."

Hugh Benton told him, "There are six of us in our group, and our two mines are right next to each other, so we'll put up some defenses and we'll stay put there. But all of us need to factor in the sniper, so my suggestion is to put up walls of mud and rubble to shield the mines, and anyone who moves around must take care to keep those walls between him and that low hill from where the sniper shot Pat. That's the only place that gives a sniper a direct line of sight to most of the mines, except for our two mines." Tally said, "That's true, and that's why I want everyone to stay here, because this mine also doesn't give a sniper a direct line of sight." Everyone agreed with Tally's plan, and so that night they sent Clayton on his way to the San Juan Mountains.

CHAPTER 7
THE BROTHERS DELIBERATE

CLAYTON ENDED HIS TALE AND SAID, "THIS WAS Tally's last throw of the dice. He knows he's the next target because he has the richest gold strike. We also have another gold mine and two silver mines, and we are all partners. Tally, Harry, and myself are partners in the gold mines, while Tally and Bull Redding are partners in the silver mines. I reckon we could all be targets, but Tally is the leader, so they'll try to get him first. He's the only one holding everyone together right now; without him, the group would split up and provide easier targets." He stared at Brian's leg and said, "Then I come here, and this happens. As I said, looks like Tally's luck is running out." Brian grunted and told him, "Soon as this bum leg gets better and I can sit on a horse, I'll come. But Tally is a generous man, and it's thanks to him that we found the gold that gave us our stake to start these ranches; so we owe him. Now he's in trouble, and he needs our help, so Mark and Joe will come with you." Clayton was curious and he said, "The way Tally told it was that *he* was in trouble, and you saved him and his partners. He was in your debt, and so he gave you directions to find the gold. A man might say that you don't owe him anything." Brian just shrugged and remarked, "He's a friend, and we Baileys take friendship seriously."

Dewey Long spoke up and told Brian, "I'm going along with Mark and Joe. If you're thinking about the ranch, our foreman, Finn Dolan, is more than capable of handling it." Brian smiled at him and said, "You're always thinking that I'm trying to keep you out when fighting time comes around; like that time when we were moving our first load of gold." Turning serious, he told him, "You're not going with them because you're riding to the Red River in Texas. Go to Red River town and ask for directions to the Rafter C ranch; you'll find our brother Luke there. He married Gina Campbell of the Rafter C and settled there in the valley. Tell him the story and take him with you to Two Forks." Mark smiled and told Brian, "I reckon it'll be good to have Luke with me again. We couldn't go to his wedding because we were on the trail bringing in our herds, so we never did meet his wife." He thought for a moment and then asked Brian, "Once this business is over, why don't I bring Luke and his wife to spend some time here with us?" Brian smiled and said, "Now that's a good idea! Bring them with you on the way back."

Clayton was looking from one brother to the other as they spoke, and now he said, "You're making plans for the future, but you do realize that you may not survive if you come and help us out? I've told you the setup, so you know the danger, yet here you are making plans for the future!" Mark told him, "That tale about there being a bullet with your name on it? That's bunkum! You can die in this wild land in so many ways other than by a bullet. Your horse can die on you and leave you stranded in the desert without water. You can run into an Indian hunting party, and they may take a notion to kill you. You could be travelling in lonesome country, and your horse could step into a gopher hole or be scared by a rattler and throw you. The fall could break your leg or your back, and you would die there in open country because there's no one around to help you. You die when you become careless, you live when you're careful; it's as simple as that." Brian said ruefully, "Like what happened to me now. I was riding that half-broken mustang, and I never should have gone after that cantankerous bull by myself. But I did, and I paid the price for being careless and reckless. Now I'm being careful by sending Luke to join up with Mark; and by sending Dewey and Joe as well, I'm being extra careful." Clayton said, "I've heard the stories about the Baileys, and I'm thankful that you're going to be on our side in this trouble."

Early the next morning they set out. Mark and Joe went with Clayton on the long trail to Arizona, and they took twelve spare horses with them. Dewey started out for the Texas Panhandle and the Red River with four spare horses. Mark figured to make the trip in two weeks using the spare horses and riding sixteen hours a day. Dewey had the longest ride he'd ever make, and he would have to travel twice the distance that Mark and the others did. He had to first go to Luke near the high plains, which was about the same distance that Mark would travel to reach Arizona. But after that, he had to make the journey with Luke to Arizona, which was again more than the distance that Mark would travel. But Dewey was a tough man, which was why Brian had chosen him for the longer ride. Sally had sat in on the discussions, and she had sent her husband Mark on his way the next morning. But Sally had also made her plans to keep her husband safe. She had spoken to Bill Hanson about her plan, and he had chosen Paddy Connor. He told her, "That lad was born to the saddle, he's tough, he's fast on the draw, and he's travelled the country before settling down with us." After Mark had left, Paddy Connor rode away from the ranch with four spare horses.

CHAPTER 8

COLORADO TO MARICOPA WELLS

MARK, JOE, AND CLAYTON SET OUT AT A SEDATE walking pace and then slowly increased that to a canter and then a gallop. After they had ridden hard for about six hours, Mark held up his hand and called a halt. Clayton looked worried and told Mark, "The horses can go for another hour at least, and then we can switch saddles. The faster we get there, the better for Tally and the others." But Mark told him, "We got to break the horses in for a long ride. Once their muscles are nicely loosened up, they will last longer and will be in better shape than if we just drive them into the ground." They gave the horses water to drink and rubbed them down. They let the horses graze while they had a cup of strong coffee. After half an hour, they started out again, and this time they switched horses and rode without stopping for ten hours before settling down for the night. They gave the horses a rubdown and let them drink at the small spring they had stopped by before putting them on a long tether so they could graze and lie down if they wanted to. Joe fried up some bacon and ham, and they had that with some flatbread and coffee. Then they slept for five hours and were up before dawn.

They fed the horses some corn that they had brought along, and after having breakfast, they set out again.

On the third day, as they were passing through the borders of Utah and New Mexico before entering the territory of Arizona, they saw a Ute hunting party in the distance. Mark continued riding on a slight deviation that would take them further away from the Utes. Clayton rode closer to Mark and shouted out, "They look like a hunting party and not a war party." Mark shouted back, "Indians are contrary, so best not to take a chance." Joe came riding up on the other side of Mark and said, "They're giving chase." Mark immediately slowed his horse and then stopped. The other two did the same, and Mark drew his rifle from the sheath and turned his horse around. He told Joe and Clayton, "Keep your rifle in plain sight, but don't point it at them."

The Utes came racing up and drew up in a flurry of dust. Mark raised his left hand in the peace sign and said, "What can I do for my brothers? We in hurry, going Arizona." He pointed towards Arizona as he spoke. One of the Indians moved his horse forward and said solemnly, "You speak bad English for a white man." Mark laughed and told him, "Forgive me. Let me guess, missionary?" The Indian nodded and said, "He teach me good. Why did you run away when you saw us?" Mark shrugged and told him, "We are not running away. My brother is in trouble in Arizona, and we are in a hurry to get there. Talking to you now is wasting our time." The Indian nodded and then said, "Give us some food, for we are hungry." Mark stared at him and said, "The Utes are a strong people, and they can hunt for their own food. I would not shame you by giving you free food." The Indian's eyes glinted for a moment, but then he laughed and told Mark, "Good answer. Strong man. Go in peace." He turned his horse around, and the other Indians followed him. Clayton sighed in relief and then asked Mark, "We could have given them some food; wasn't it a risk to refuse?" But Mark said, "If you give an Indian what he demands, he sees it as a sign of weakness, and then he'll want to take all we have and then kill us."

Soon they were riding mostly uphill, and the going became tougher. They travelled through grasslands, forests, and semi-desert regions. They still managed to cover at least forty miles a day, and sometimes more. The weather turned cooler as they climbed higher, and by the eighth day, they came to Antelope Spring, which was at an elevation of almost seven thousand feet. It was a small settlement with about twelve buildings, but there was a saloon with some horses hitched in front and a barn. They rode straight to the barn and swung down wearily from their saddles. A gray-haired man was sitting on a barrel just outside the door, smoking a corncob pipe. He looked at the fifteen horses and said, "I'll rub them down, water them, and feed them; I got corn and hay. Cost you, though." Joe asked him, "How much?" The gray-haired man scratched his head and asked hesitantly, "Three bucks?" Mark told him, "I'll give you five dollars if you do everything and have them saddled and ready in an hour." The man took hold of the reins and said happily, "Sure, boss; consider her done!"

As they turned to leave, the man said, "If you boys are going to the saloon, there are three real rough-looking men who rode in a while ago. Their horses looked to be ridden hard, just like yours, but they didn't bother to leave them with me when I asked them for a dollar." Mark told him, "Thanks, but we aren't chasing them. We're in a hurry to get to Two Forks near Maricopa Wells." The gray-haired man gave him a quizzical look and said, "I heard one of them say that it was a fair piece still to Two Forks." Mark walked back to him and gave him a dollar. "That's for the information," he said. The three of them walked to the saloon, and Joe remarked, "Might be hired guns or maybe they just like boom towns." Clayton remarked, "Can't be miners or they would have cared for their horses first and not their own thirst." They saw the three horses standing hitched to the rail and noted that they were tired and coated with sweat and dust. Joe said with disgust, "That's no way to treat a horse!"

They walked into the saloon and stood just inside the door for a moment to let their eyes adjust to the gloom. They saw the three men sitting at a table with a bottle of whiskey before them, and there were four other men standing at the bar. Mark and the others walked up to the bar, and Joe told the barkeep, "Whiskey, and make sure it's the good stuff." The barkeep was a half-bald, stocky man with broad shoulders and huge biceps. He chuckled and said, "Mister, you're in Antelope Spring, and what you get here is mostly moonshine. But you're in luck, because I do keep a bottle of good whiskey for those who can pay for it. Cost you fifty cents a shot." Mark looked at him in surprise and remarked, "That's steep, but we'll take it." One of the men at the table heard the remark and turned sideways to look at Mark. He muttered something to his companions, and the other two also looked at Mark. Although Mark was aware that the three men were looking at him, he didn't show it. He stood slightly sideways to the bar and told Joe softly, "Those three are taking an interest in us. Let's have the whiskey and find out if there's some good food in town." He told Clayton softly but loud enough for Joe to hear, "I'm fed up with the slop that he dishes up." Joe said in mock anger, "Just you wait; the next time I'll put sand in your coffee!" They all laughed and Mark noted that the three men were still sizing them up.

The barkeep poured their shots, and Joe asked him, "Know where we can get some good food in town? We're kind-a tired of eating our own cooking." The barkeep told him, "I make a mean antelope steak, and I've got bacon and fresh-baked bread." Joe told him, "Long as it's not as mean as the cost of the whiskey, we'll take it." The barkeep laughed and said, "It's not. I answer to Hank, and I can guarantee that the food will be good." Mark smiled and told him, "Well, Hank, just make sure that the plates are loaded 'cause I'm hungry as a starved mountain lion." Suddenly a voice said, "You boys going far?" Mark turned slowly, knowing it was one of the men at the table who had spoken. He just said, "Yonder." Then he pretended to talk to Joe, but he saw the man get up from the table and told Joe, "Here comes trouble; you keep an eye on the other two." The man walked up to Mark, saying, "I was talking to you! You trying to insult me?" Mark straightened up from the bar and faced him, saying, "Don't reckon I would need to *try*!" The man's face turned ugly, and he snarled, "You trying to be funny?" Mark sighed and took two steps towards the man. Suddenly, he drew his gun and slashed the man hard across the side of his head with the barrel. The man dropped like a poleaxed steer, and Joe said mildly, "I wouldn't if I were you."

Mark swung his gun to cover the other two men, but he saw that Joe had them under his gun already. Staying out of Joe's line of fire, he walked up to the table and said, "You boys seem to have ridden a long way, judging by your horses out front. You also seem to like hunting trouble." One of the men had long dirty hair held in place by his hat. He had a scraggly beard and whiskers, and his eyes were small and mean-looking. He slowly stood up and said, "Put that gun away and then talk." Mark slowly walked around him, and when he started to turn, Mark said, "Turn, and I'll shoot you right now. Stay still." Mark went behind the man and hit him hard on the head with the gun butt. The man fell back in his chair, and his face hit the table. He lay there without moving, and the third man swore viciously. He looked a bit younger than the other two, who were in their thirties, and he was better dressed and a bit cleaner as well. Mark asked him, "You want to join your friends?" The man said, "The name's Slick Sam, and I'm from Utah; you may have heard of me."

Mark seemed to think about it and then he said, "I don't think I've had the misfortune to have heard of you. Now, if you don't want to join your friends in dreamland, just slowly ease your gun out and drop it to the floor." Slick Sam slowly stood up and said grimly, "Like hell I will!" His hand was dropping in a fast move for his gun when Mark shot him through the forearm. He then casually walked up and removed Slick's gun from its holster and pushed him back down in his chair. He went to the bar and gave the gun to Hank. He told Clayton, "Collect the guns from the other two and search all three for any extras; then hand the guns to Hank here."

Clayton handed over the guns to Hank, and the Marshal walked into the bar. "I heard only the one shot," he told Hank. "Figured there was no hurry for me to get here." He looked at the three men and then asked Hank, "Someone going to tell me what happened here?" Mark told him, "Those three were hunting trouble, or maybe they just didn't like the look of us. I soothed their feelings, and they ain't hunting trouble now." The other men at the bar said, "That's the way it was, Marshal." The Marshal went and checked on the men and then walked up to the bar. "You been a lawman," he told Mark. It wasn't a question, and Mark shrugged and said, "Deputy for a time." The Marshal nodded and said, "Reason I mentioned it was, that's the way a good lawman takes care of troublemakers without killing them. You know them?" Mark shook his head and said, "Never seen them before. I think they were just hunting trouble, and I didn't want to be delayed because of a shootout. We're in a hurry to get to Two Forks to help out a friend." The Marshal looked thoughtful when he remarked, "I heard tell of some trouble down there. I also heard that Nick Palmer is the Marshal in Two Forks. I know Nick, and he's a good man." Clayton said, "Tally Stevens appointed Nick as Marshal, but Tally thinks that he needs help, so he sent me to get it." The Marshal told Mark, "Well, if you're the help, then Nick's lucky. My name's Will Loomis; tell Nick I asked about him." He turned around to leave, but then said, "You boys can go on your way. I'll keep these three in the pen for a week."

They ate a good meal and topped it off with strong coffee. Then they collected their horses and hit the trail again. They rode fast and hard again for two days before they reached Prescott, which used to be the capital of the Territory of Arizona before the capital was shifted to Tucson. It was a sprawling city with two main streets and a population of around seven hundred. They reached Prescott late in the evening, and they put up their horses at the livery stable, and Mark told the hostler, "Groom them well, feed them corn, and let them rest. We leave tomorrow before sunrise, and if I like the way they've been cared for, you get an extra dollar." They went to a hotel, and the first thing they did was to have a long, hot bath. Then they enjoyed a splendid meal and slept for five hours. They left Prescott the next morning before the first light of day could hit the city. It took them two more days to reach Phoenix, and they reached Two Forks fourteen days after leaving their ranch in Colorado.

CHAPTER 9
PADDY CONNOR

PADDY CONNOR WAS A TEXAN OF IRISH ANCESTRY. He was twenty-two years old when he heard about the gold strike near the San Juan Mountains, and he headed there, figuring to maybe do some mining. He was drifting at the time, and the San Juan range seemed as good a place as any to drift to. He never did make it to the gold mines because he saw the cattle ranches in the valley and rode into the yard of the Double S ranch house. Sally Taylor-Bailey was outside the house at the time, and she told him, "Light and set. I'll get you a cup of coffee." She called out, "Cookie! Visitor! Cup of coffee, please!" Paddy swung down from his saddle and looked around. He liked what he saw; he was a born cattleman until events in his life made him move along. He told Sally, "I heard about a gold strike in these parts, and I was heading there when I saw the ranch. I'm from Texas originally, and if you're hiring, I reckon I'd forget about the gold."

Mark came out of the house, and he heard the last remark. He told Paddy, "I'm Mark Bailey and this is my wife, Sally. I'm from Texas as well; my family has a ranch in Cedar Creek, but originally I hail from Tennessee." Paddy gave him a speculative look and said, "I left Texas a while ago, but I've heard of the Cedar Creek battle; Jack Donovan and the Baileys." Mark said, "If you're looking for a riding job, you're hired." Paddy told him, "I'm a drifter, been drifting for some four years now." Mark shrugged and said, "I reckon we're all drifters; my family drifted from Tennessee to Kansas, Colorado, Arizona, and then Texas." He smiled and added, "And now I've drifted back to Colorado." Cookie brought the coffee, and Sally took the cup and gave it to Paddy, saying, "Cookie makes the best coffee this side of the Rockies." Paddy stayed on and proved to be an excellent cowboy.

Paddy Connor was born with natural hand dexterity, and given the time he was born in, that dexterity turned him into a fast man on the draw. He was born and lived in South Texas close to the Mexican border on a small cattle ranch. He became a skilled cowhand and grew to be a tall, rangy, broad-shouldered young man. At the age of eighteen, he was in town one evening when two brothers of a neighboring big rancher started a fight with him. They were drinking, and one of them had pushed Paddy aside at the bar; but Paddy was not a man to be pushed, and he had pushed back very hard, and the man fell down. He got up cursing, and he and his brother went for their guns; but Paddy shot them both before their guns could clear leather. The town Marshal at the time was a friend of the big rancher, and he told Paddy, "Their guns are still in their holsters, which means you gunned them down without giving them a chance." The barkeep protested and said, "I was here, and both of them went for their guns first, but Paddy was faster." The Marshal ignored him and told Paddy, "You got two choices; leave town, or stay here and I'll arrest you."

Paddy was young, and the injustice of the Marshal's reaction to the shooting angered him. He told the Marshal, "That badge that you wear is supposed to mean something. You're supposed to be impartial and to uphold the law, but you're nothing more than a four-flusher!" The Marshal went red in the face and drew his gun. Paddy waited until the Marshal's gun had cleared his holster, and then he drew and fired. He was always accurate in his shooting, and the Marshal died on the spot. The barkeep was a friend of Paddy's father, and now he told him, "I don't blame you, son; they forced this on you. But all the same, now you have to leave town. Luckily, the bar is empty, so I'll give you a five-minute head start before I report this. I'll say that a stranger walked in, and those two picked a fight with him and got the short end of the stick. The Marshal braced the stranger, and the stranger shot him and then left." Paddy looked miserable, but he thanked the barkeep and said, "My Dad..." But the barkeep told him, "Don't worry about it. I'll tell him the truth, and he'll understand. Go on now, son, and don't come back for a few years at least; give the dust time to settle down."So Paddy left and began drifting for four years before he found the Double S ranch.

When Sally told him to ride to the Box T, she said, "Mark should reach Two Forks in about two weeks, but his brother Luke will take more than three weeks to get there, and Mark might need help before then. If you go to my father's ranch, the Box T in Red Butte, you can take Trent Williams and the boys and reach Two Forks in less than three weeks." Paddy rode away from the ranch with four spare horses, and he rode fast for two days with just a few hours' sleep each night. He reached Pagosa Springs and stopped to rest the horses, but a party of Ute Indians rode in, and Paddy mounted up again and rode off. He figured the Indians had come there for the healing waters of the springs, but he had no wish to find out if he was wrong.

He continued riding, and the land began to rise in elevation. He figured he was at least six thousand feet above sea level when he ran into a hunting party of Jicarilla Apaches. It was a forested area in the Rockies, and when the arrows started to fly, he took shelter behind a huge juniper and began to fire rapidly with his lever-action 1866 Yellow Boy Winchester rifle, which held fifteen rounds. The Apaches backed off in the face of such rapid but accurate firing. Paddy reloaded and swung into his saddle. He rode through the trees, still firing to keep the Apaches at bay; but the Apaches did not chase him as they had four wounded men already, and they figured their medicine was bad.

The land kept climbing, and he soon reached the small cross-roads town of Chama at an elevation of almost eight thousand feet. The air was cold, although it was still summer, and Paddy stopped there to rest the horses. There was a small livery barn, and Paddy promised the hostler two dollars if he could feed and rub down the horses immediately. "I'll be leaving in about an hour, and you'll get the two dollars if I'm satisfied," he told him. He went to a small building, which had a sign that just said Saloon, and walked up to the bar. "Whiskey," he told the barkeep. "And I'd be much obliged if you know where I can get some good food around here; just point me in the right direction." The barkeep was a sour-looking individual who told him, "I can give you a good steak with gravy and bread." Paddy told him, "I reckon that'll do me for now. I figure to be on my way in an hour." The barkeep poured his drink and went into a back room.

There were two men standing at the bar, and they turned to look at Paddy. "You seem to be in a mighty big hurry, Mister," one of them said. "Travelling far?" Paddy said shortly, "A fair distance." He downed his drink, and the barkeep returned and told him, "Better have another; the steak will be ready in about ten minutes. You can eat at that table over there." Paddy nodded, and the barkeep poured him another shot, which he nursed. The two men were talking softly together, and the big man who had spoken earlier told him, "Reason I asked you if you're travelling far is 'cause someone is hiring guns in the area of Maricopa Wells, and we're going there. The man who told us said that they're paying top wages for a fast gun." Paddy shrugged and said shortly, "Me, I'm headed for Santa Fe." The man who had spoken was a big-made man with a flat face, and he wore two tied-down guns. His companion was of medium height and slim build with sharp features, sporting a small beard and drooping whiskers. He also wore two tied-down guns, and now he stepped away from the bar and said, "Not the friendly type, are you?"

Paddy grimaced and told him, "See no reason to be; I'm just passing through, and you're strangers." The man's eyes glinted, and he said softly, "Maybe you don't like the look of us. Maybe I should teach you to be friendly with strangers." The big man said, "This here is Buck, and they call him the Fast Buck for a reason. He's a bad man to cross!" Paddy slowly put down his glass and just as slowly turned to face them. Buck was standing with his hand hovering over his gun butt, and the big man had his hand on his gun. Buck said, "You should listen to..." He didn't complete his sentence because a gun suddenly appeared in Paddy's hand. Paddy said, "You with the mouth, you got just one second to take your hand off your gun or draw it, makes no never mind to me which way you decide." The big man hastily removed his hand from his gun butt and licked his lips. He had always thought that Buck was the fastest gun he had ever seen. He had not seen Paddy draw, but suddenly the gun was just there in his hand. Paddy told Buck, "You going to draw or you want to change your mind." Buck was shaken, but he had a reputation and he said, "You're holding a gun on me."

Paddy dropped the gun in his holster, and Buck's hand flashed for his gun. He was telling himself, "The fool fell for it! I got him now, I..." Then everything went black for him, and Fast Buck fell dead to the floor with a hole between his eyes. The big man stared at Buck and then stared at Paddy. There was a tremor in his voice as he said, "Mister, if it's all the same to you, I'll be riding now." Paddy told him, "Take him with you, and if you want my advice, stay away from Maricopa Wells because that's where I'm heading after Santa Fe." The big man slung the dead body over his shoulder and almost ran from the saloon. There was the drumming sound of hooves, and the barkeep said, "Good riddance!"

After a good meal, Paddy collected his horses and rode south in the direction of Santa Fe. He reached Santa Fe in three days but bypassed the town and continued south until he hit the town of Red Butte. He asked for directions to the Box T, and he rode into the yard of the ranch house late one evening, just six days after he had left the Double S ranch. The last three days he had ridden almost continuously, making do with just about three hours' sleep every night, and he was dead tired. His horses were also exhausted, and after telling Trent Williams who he was and where he had come from, he said, "But first, let me take care of my horses, and then we'll talk." Trent looked at this man who was actually swaying on his feet from tiredness, and he liked what he saw. He told him, "The boys will take care of those horses; you come on in before I have to carry you in."

Rick Taylor came in and was introduced to Paddy, who had just downed a shot of good whiskey which Trent had given him. They served him a double steak with eggs, gravy, and freshly baked bread, and he told them about Two Forks and Tally Stevens as he ate. Then he had a long, hot bath and slept for ten straight hours. When he awoke, Trent and the boys were ready to leave, and Trent told him, "You could stay on here, get some rest, and come on later. We're leaving now, and we hope to make it to Two Forks in two weeks' time." But Paddy told him, "I'm coming with you. I know the old Indian trails, and I'll get us there faster." He ate a large breakfast, and they left; ten cowboys with Trent and three spare horses for each man. Paddy's string of horses was rested, and he took them with him.

Paddy led them through Albuquerque and then turned southwest along the edge of the Zuni lands. He took them up old Indian trails that could hardly be called a trail now, but Paddy rode without hesitation. Trent asked him, "You been through this area before?" Paddy told him, "I'd been drifting for four years before joining the Double S, and I've seen a lot of country. These old trails will cut short our ride by at least two days, I reckon." He turned south again, bypassing Phoenix and passing through the edge of the Tonto forest. He took them into the town of Two Forks, exactly eighteen days after he had ridden away from the Double S ranch.

CHAPTER 10
DEWEY

DEWEY WAS A SHORT, BARREL-CHESTED MAN WITH bulging muscles. He always had a smile on his face and seemed to enjoy life, but come fighting time, he stepped up to the mark. He could lift almost anything that he laid his hands on, and everyone knew that he was a very tough man. But Brian chose him for the longest ride because he knew that Dewey also had incredible endurance and stamina. Dewey rode away from the Double L ranch and turned southeast. He rode almost without stopping until he reached the ancient Taos Pueblo in New Mexico Territory in six days. He had slept for barely three hours a day during the six-day ride. At the Pueblo, the Taos tribe were mostly gentle folk, and they fed him and cared for his horses while he slept for six hours. He continued to ride southeast, cutting across the northeast of New Mexico until he entered Texas.

He rode into the settlement of Oneida and went straight to the livery stable to put up his horses. He told the hostler, "In two hours I'll be leaving, and if my horses are fed and cared for in that time, then you get two dollars." That was a lot of money and the hostler happily agreed. Dewey walked up to the bar in the nearest saloon and ordered a double shot of whiskey. He nursed his drink and asked the barkeep where he could get something decent to eat immediately. The barkeep told him, "Sit down at a table and I'll bring you a steak with bacon and bread; best that I can do right now." Dewey thanked him and downed his drink. He walked across the room to sit at an empty table, but before he got halfway there, a man said, "Hold it, Mister!" Dewey stopped and looked at the man who had spoken. He was a big-made man with long hair to his shoulders and sported a bushy beard and whiskers. He was sitting across a table facing Dewey, and another tall, clean-shaven man sat at the table to Dewey's left. Dewey asked the man who had spoken, "Something on your mind Mister or do you just stop strangers for no reason at all?" The man gave him a grim smile and said, "Only strangers who seem to be in a real God Almighty hurry. Where you headed for in such a hurry, Mister?" Dewey sighed and moved to the table. He casually moved the chair in front of him to his left side. He kept his left hand on the chair and gripped the edge of the table with his right hand.

He told the man, "Not that it's any of your business, but I'm travelling yonder." The clean-shaven man said, "What do you know, Kent; we got us a funny man here." Kent started to get up, and Dewey heaved the heavy table one-handed onto him. At the same time, he swung the chair with his left hand and smashed it across the clean-shaven man's head, and the man fell to the ground. Kent was struggling to shift the heavy table, and Dewey lifted it slightly and then slammed it down again onto the man's chest; the man made a moaning sound and then fainted. Dewey calmly lifted the table and set it on its legs and then walked across and sat down at an empty table. The barkeep brought him his food and commented, "That's a mighty heavy table, and that there chair ain't a feather either." Dewey shrugged and told him, "Sorry about that, but I'm in a hurry and I can't afford to be delayed." The barkeep asked him curiously,

"You know those two?" Dewey was eating and just shook his head. The barkeep told him, "They been asking if any man or men had passed through here who seemed to be in an awful hurry to get somewhere." Dewey swallowed the food in his mouth and muttered, "After I've gone, you can tell them that I passed through."

He rode south from Oneida and some hours later entered a large, lush valley. He came across a man camped under a tree and asked him for directions to the Rafter C. Two days after leaving the Pueblo, he rode up to the ranch house of the Rafter C. It was an incredible ride, and he did it by sleeping for a total of three hours in snatches over the two days; and that was whenever he rested the horses briefly. He rode into the yard, and the first person he saw was Luke. He had no doubt that this man was the brother of Brian and Mark because the family resemblance was unmistakable. He swung down from the saddle, stumbled, and had to hold onto the saddle to keep himself upright.

Luke ran up to him and said, "You look all in, friend; how long have you been up in that saddle?" Dewey gave him a tired grin and said, "It's been eight days since I left your brother Brian at the ranch. Give me a strong cup of coffee, and I'll tell you the tale as I drink it." Luke gave him coffee laced with whiskey, and Dewey told him about Tally Stevens and the call for help. "Mark will reach Two Forks in about two weeks, so that will be maybe six days from now. I figure it will take us fifteen days to get to Two Forks from here, so Mark will be on his own for nine days." Luke told him, "I've travelled through most of the area we will be crossing, and I know some shortcuts and old trails. I reckon I can cut down that time by two days. You bathe, eat, and sleep now, and we'll leave when you're ready." Dewey told him, "Let me sleep for five hours and then wake me. I can sleep when we hit Two Forks."

Luke took Hardy Collins, Jake Jenkins, and Rudy Hackett,

plus ten of their toughest ranch hands. He did not want to take the ranch hands, but his wife Gina insisted. "If they're bringing in hired guns, then you're going to need more men to hold the town," she told him. He protested, saying, "But that would leave Mike shorthanded on the ranch!" Mike Holden shook his head and told him, "Don't you worry about that, Luke. The Slash 8 and the Double O will help out until you return. In fact, they'd be happy to help out because they still feel that they owe you a debt that they can never repay." He was referring to the trouble that the ranchers had faced with a carpetbagger, Rafe Winston, when Luke rode into their lives. Luke had led the fight that defeated Rafe Winston, and the owners of the other ranches knew that without Luke, they would have lost the battle. Luke had fallen in love with Gina of the Rafter C, and after the fighting ended, he married her and settled down on the Rafter C.

Hardy Collins was a stocky man of medium height with bulging muscles; he had good features and blue eyes. Jake Jenkins was a rawboned tall young man whose face always bore a permanent mournful expression, and so he was called Happy Jake. Rudy Hackett was very good looking, with square jaws and dark blue eyes. He was tall with broad shoulders and very fast on the draw. All three wore their guns slung low and tied down. They were devoted to Luke and looked up to him as he had trained them in the art of the fast draw and also in a new form of fist fighting. Luke knew that if he hadn't taken them along, they would have quit and followed him anyway. They rode away from the Rafter C, fifteen fighting men, and Luke took them south of Albuquerque. Without knowing it, he followed the same trails that Paddy had taken, and they reached the town of Two Forks in thirteen days.

CHAPTER 11

THE TOWN OF TWO FORKS

When Mark, Joe, and Clayton reached the outskirts of Two Forks late one evening, Mark sent Clayton straight to the mine to talk to Tally. He told Clayton, "For the moment, I'd rather not be seen with you. We'll enter the town as strangers, and we'll find out what the situation is now." Mark and Joe rode into the town and went straight to the hotel of Homer Lee and booked in. Mark told Homer, "Hot baths, a big meal, and clean beds in that order. If you don't serve food, then just point us in the right direction and we'll take care of it." Homer looked at the exhausted pair and their dusty clothes, and he said, "You boys look like you've been travelling a fair piece." Joe said shortly, "Yeah! We've come a long way and we need that bath right now." After showing them to their room, Homer told them, "The bath is right down this hallway and the water will be hot in ten minutes. I'll have steaks, eggs, vegetables, and fresh bread ready for you after that." They soaked in the hot water for more than half an hour to ease their tired muscles. Then they dressed and went down to the hotel bar, and Homer served them a meal that had Joe smiling. Mark told Homer, "This food is good enough for the big cities if it can get Joe here to smile!"

Homer thanked him for the compliment and then said, "You don't look like prospectors, and this here is a mining town, so if you're looking for something or somebody, maybe I can help you out." Mark looked at him thoughtfully and said, "That's mighty neighborly of you. Not often you get people who are that interested in helping out strangers!" Joe said casually, "Maybe the man is just curious, or maybe he has something up his sleeve." They both stared at Homer without smiling, and he shifted his feet and looked uncomfortable. He bowed his head and said, "I'm sorry, I didn't mean to pry; just curious, I guess." He turned to leave, but Mark told him sharply, "Stay! We weren't just talking, we want an answer, and it better be an honest one." Homer sighed, turned back to face them, and said, "I've been in many boom towns, and I know the signs of trouble. This town is sitting on trouble, and it's about ready to erupt. You boys look like you can handle yourselves; you wear tied down guns that show evidence of much use, so I just wondered if you came here because someone sent for you."

Mark stared at him for a long moment and then said, "Sit down, Mr. Lee. I remember you now. I saw you in Kansas and in Texas; you had a hotel in both places, so you must be who you say you are. Tell us about this here trouble that this town has; I'm just curious." He paused and then added, "For the moment." Homer Lee, in turn, stared at him for a long while and then exclaimed, "You're a Bailey! I should have recognized the chiseled features and that strong chin. But it was the eyes that reminded me just now, when it turned greenish from gray-blue; that's something peculiar to you Baileys. I've seen a Bailey in Kansas, an older-looking man many years ago; a tough man who settled a range war there. I've seen Baileys in Texas." He frowned in thought and then said, "That Bailey in Texas now, that was more recent and in the town of Shackelford across the Trinity; his name was Luke. He was a tough man to cross." Mark said mildly, "That would be my younger brother; he's settled down in a valley near the Red River." Homer sat up straight and said, "No Bailey would fight on the wrong side, so if you are here because of this trouble, then you must be here for Tally and not that other crowd."

Mark stayed silent and just looked at him, so Homer said, "I know that Clayton Moss went looking for help, and I hope that help is you. But there's something that happened after Clayton left; Nick Palmer, the town Marshal, was shot dead on the outskirts of town a week ago. The new Marshal is Big Red, and his deputy is Rod Tilson. He's told Tally that either they work the mines, or they can be taken over by anyone. He says it's for the good of the town, and as the town Marshal, he will enforce the law." Mark asked him, "Tally and the others are still holed up in the one mine?" Homer nodded and said, "They're forted up there, and they have lookouts on the hilltops, so no one can get at them, which is why Big Red and the others want them out of there and back in their mines." Joe remarked, "Where they can be picked off more easily." Mark told Homer, "Clayton told us of some of the players here, so I want you to tell me what you think of them and if there are others that we should know about. For instance, Rock Masters and his saddle partner." Homer shrugged and said, "They're Texans, no doubt about that, and they're good with their guns. There's something about Rock that I think I should know, but it don't come to mind. Something I think that I heard maybe; some tragedy or something..."

Mark said, "Drake Manning." Homer grimaced and told him, "If you ask me, that one is behind everything, except for Hans Kruger. I don't know if the two of them are working together or separately. Hans produced the bill of sale from Harvey, and Drake had the bill of sale from Pat; witnesses were Big Red and Max Shultz. Hans has Rupert, and Drake has Big Red, Tilson, Shultz, and Wayling. Rupert wears a tied down gun, but no one has seen him use it. Big Red is said to be fast, but he depends on his strength; he's real big with red hair, hence the name. Tilson is also a fast gun, and he's the one who killed Harvey Kline. Whoever shot Pat and Nick is good with a rifle because they were shot from long range. Nick was scouting for the tracks of the man who shot Pat, and he seemed excited a few days before he died. He came in here and told me that he was onto something, and maybe he would find Pat's killer."

He paused to take a deep breath and then said, "Nick was frustrated because he was sure that the bills of sale were fake; but since no one knew the signatures of Harvey or Pat, there was nothing that he could do. That was when he decided to try and find Pat's killer." Mark said, "So if someone were to know the signatures of Harvey and Pat, then those bills would be worthless." Homer sighed and said, "That Drake Manning is very fast on the draw, I think, and I do believe that he has a hideout gun. No one is going to tell him that the bill of sale he has is a fake." Mark stood up and said, "*I* might; but right now we're going to get a long deserved sleep, and we don't want to be disturbed." Joe added, "If anyone disturbs us, they might get a bellyful of lead for breakfast."

The next morning, they had a heavy breakfast of eggs, bacon, ham, and freshly baked bread. There were a good number of men also having breakfast, and Mark asked Homer, "Where do you get the eggs and vegetables from?" Homer told him, "I always keep chickens in the back because in boom towns, eggs become a big attraction." Mark smiled and said, "Judging from the crowd, it's a big attraction here as well." Homer agreed and said, "The vegetables are delivered by the Maricopa Indians. They are mostly farmers, and I made a deal with them." They finished their breakfast and sat back to enjoy a cup of strong coffee. Joe asked Mark, "So what's our first move? You told Clayton not to come into town with us because you didn't want to advertise that Tally had sent for us." Mark told him, "I've been looking over the people having breakfast here, and most of them seem like solid citizens." Joe said, "So?" Mark explained, "It means that the town has really expanded, and traders and others have moved in. In fact, some of these men look like farmers." Joe again asked him, "So what's our first move?" Mark stood up and said, "We pay a visit to our exalted Marshal after meeting with Phil Barnaby, who Clayton says is the bank manager." Joe grunted and muttered, "Exalted! Hah! I hate it when you get all highfalutin on me."

Mark grinned and slapped him on his back. He said, "Depending on what we learn from Phil, there are two ways we can go when we meet the Marshal. If he's been appointed legally by the town council, then we ask to see the bills of sale; me being a former friend of Harvey Kline and you being a former friend of Pat Simpson." Joe asked him, "That's one way, so what's the other way?" Mark told him, "If he hasn't been appointed legally by the town council, then he's going to resign, and we appoint ourselves as Marshal and Deputy Marshal." Joe asked him, "And what if he refuses to resign?" Mark just stared at him, and Joe shook his head ruefully and said, "Dumb question! Brain must be tired from all the riding."

CHAPTER 12

THE MARSHAL OF TWO FORKS

MARK AND JOE FIRST WENT TO THE BANK AND MET Phil Barnaby. Mark introduced themselves and then asked him, "Does the town have a town council or something similar for making appointments to civic posts?" Phil gave him a puzzled look and said, "Not really, because there aren't any civic posts at present." Mark said mildly, "I've always understood that the town Marshal's office was a civic post, and as such, appointments are made by the town council. So who appointed the current town Marshal?" Phil was a bit flustered and said, "Well, Nick Palmer was appointed by Tally Stevens, I guess because they were the first ones here. This Marshal, I believe, was appointed by two businessmen who are also mine owners." Mark said casually, "And that would be Drake Manning and Hans Kruger." Phil sat back in his chair and told Mark, "You're right, and I can see how it looks with the trouble that is going on here. But the traders and others who came later, including me, really have no stake in this game and so we don't interfere or take sides. This is a boom town and there will be many more, so as long as it is conducive to conducting our business, we stay, otherwise we move on. I'm sorry, but that's just the way it is."

Mark told him, "I'm sorry too, because in a war, civilian casualties or collateral damage are also facts of life, and it does not behoove any sensible person to think that the violence will leave him unscathed." He and Joe stood up, and Phil asked him, "What exactly are you saying?" Mark told him, "Homer is a solid citizen and I could see many others in just a glance. Get them together and form a town council to elect a Marshal. Do it now because the matter is urgent." Phil asked him, "But what about the present Marshal?" Mark turned to leave and told him, "He's going to retire right now." He paused and then added, "Because of his bad health." They left the bank, and Joe laughed and said admiringly, "Now that's a whole lot of highfalutin words for a man to use at any one time. I swear it really made ole Phil dizzy just trying to understand them all at once." Mark smiled and told him, "You're forgetting yourself, Happy Joe; you actually laughed just now." Joe immediately put on a somber expression and lamented, "A man who is about to die should at least have one last laugh. I always knew that tying up with you fighting Baileys would be the death of me!"

They walked into the Marshal's office and found Big Red slouching in a chair with his legs up on the desk. Rod Tilson was sitting in front of him, and they both held glasses filled with whiskey. Mark and Joe stood and surveyed them for a moment, and then Mark said, "I thought that Nick Palmer was the Marshal here." Big Red swung his feet off the desk and put his glass down. Rod Tilson also put down his glass and turned around in his chair to stare at the intruders. Big Red snarled, "Who the hell are you!" Mark said mildly, "The point actually is, who the hell are *you*? You're obviously not Nick Palmer." Rod Tilson made to get up, and Joe shoved him back in his chair. Big Red started to draw his gun but stopped when he found himself staring at the gun in Mark's hand. He slowly removed his hand from his gun and said, "Nick is dead and I'm the new Marshal. You going to shoot a lawman?"

Mark shrugged and told him, "Nick Palmer was a lawman and someone shot him. Seems like it's open season on lawmen in this town. But were you appointed by the town council?" Rod Tilson said, "There ain't no town council, Drake and Hans appointed us. I'm the deputy." Mark said with a grim smile, "If you weren't appointed by the town council, then you're not lawmen and I can shoot you." Big Red said sullenly, "As Rod just said, there ain't no town council." Mark told him, "There is one now, so you're going to take off that badge." Big Red snarled, "Put that gun away and I'll tear you apart with my bare hands!" Mark glanced at Joe and asked him, "Did he just say that he has the hands of a bear?" Joe shrugged and said laconically, "Could be; he sure enough looks like one." Big Red growled and started to get up, and Mark shot the lobe off his right ear. Big Red's growl ended in a yelp as he clutched his bleeding ear. Joe shook his head sadly and remarked, "No, that ain't no bear; sounded more like a coyote to me." Rod Tilson swore and told Joe, "You talk like a big man when you got the drop, but put the gun away and face me in a fair fight and I'll show you who's a coyote." Joe gave him a thoughtful look and said, "Would that be something like the fair fight you gave Harvey Kline?"

Mark said, "Enough of this! Where are the bills of sale for Harvey Kline and Pat Simpson's mines? Hand them over." Big Red muttered, "They ain't here." Mark said mildly, "You maybe need a bullet through your elbow to refresh your memory?" Joe remarked, "Was I you I'd be careful, because he always calls his shots and he never misses. Someone once told me that a broken elbow never heals properly." Big Red looked angry, scared, and confused all at the same time. He pulled out a drawer and took out two pieces of paper which he threw on the table. Mark said, "Both of you remove those badges and place them on the table. Hesitate and I'll shoot you both." Both of them removed the badges as fast as they could and threw them on the table. Mark stretched out his left hand to pick up the papers and the badges.

Big Red's eyes lit up, and with a triumphant look on his face, he grabbed hold of Mark's hand with the intention of throwing him off balance or heaving him over the desk. Whatever his intention was, it never came off because Mark shot him through the head.

Mark picked up the badges, pinned one on, and gave the other to Joe. He looked at the bills of sale and then folded and pocketed them. Joe pinned on the badge and told Rod, "You said something about a fair fight, so I'm going to give you one, unlike what you did with Harvey Kline. Let's see if there's some man in you or just all coyote." He pointed to the door, and Rod Tilson walked out to the street with Mark and Joe following him. When Tilson had moved about ten paces, Joe called out, "That's far enough, turn around!" Rod Tilson stood still for a moment, and then he swung around, drawing his gun as he turned. If he intended to take Joe by surprise, it did not work, because Joe waited until he had turned around and was lifting his gun before he moved. Rod Tilson's gun was almost aligned when Joe palmed his gun and shot him through the head. Tilson never got a shot off.

Drake Manning, Max Shultz, Burt Wayling, and two more men came out of the Silver Rock Saloon and started down the street towards the Marshal's office. Phil Barnaby, Homer Lee, Fat Fred, and Bret Hogan of Wells Fargo came out of the bank and also walked down to the Marshal's office. Both groups reached the office about the same time, and Drake stared at Mark and Joe, who were leaning negligently against the building. Drake's face was grim as he demanded, "What the hell's going on here?! Who are you two, and what are you doing wearing those badges!" Joe said mildly, "He's the new Marshal and I'm the new deputy." Drake cursed and asked him, "Did you shoot the deputy?" Joe seemed to think about it and then he said, "You got me kind-a confused there; see, I'm the deputy, so how can I shoot myself?" Drake's face turned red and he said,

"We have a permanent treatment here for funny boys! Did you shoot that man lying there?" Joe opened his eyes wide and said innocently, "You mean that there Rod Tilson, the man who murdered Harvey Kline?" Drake said through his teeth, "Harvey called him a liar so Rod shot him!"

Joe looked at Mark and said, "See? And you say there's no such thing as coincidence." Turning to Drake, he told him, "That's the very same thing that happened right now. Ole Tilson done called me a liar and so I shot him!" Drake took a deep breath and asked, "Where's Big Red?" Joe told him sadly, "Ole carrot top attacked the Marshal, and so the Marshal had to shoot him." Drake almost shouted, "Big Red *is* the Marshal!" Mark said mildly, "You mean was, Big Red *was* the Marshal; but wasn't Nick Palmer the Marshal?" Drake took a deep breath, and speaking slowly he said, "Nick was the Marshal, but he died and so Big Red became the Marshal." Mark straightened up and asked him sternly, "Nick Palmer was murdered! Did the town council appoint Big Red as the new Marshal?"

Drake looked around and saw Hans and Rupert standing across from him. He told Mark, "We traders and businessmen of the town appointed him." Mark shook his head and said, "Well, if you and Hans there can appoint a Marshal, so can the others, and we've been appointed." Drake almost snarled and said, "Show me the person who appointed you!" Suddenly, a voice from behind Drake said quietly, "I did. You want to make something of it?" Drake slowly turned around and saw Rock Masters and Rusty Bellows standing with their thumbs hooked in their gun belts. He stared at them for a moment as his face turned red with anger. "One of these days," he told Rock. "One of these days, you'll go too far!" He turned and walked back to the Silver Rock Saloon, and after a moment the rest of his men followed him. Mark was looking thoughtfully at Hans and Rupert, who were staring at him as though sizing him up; then they abruptly turned and walked away.

Mark walked up to Rock Masters and held out his hand. Rock hesitated for a moment and then shook it. He told Mark gruffly, "I like the way you shape up. You can call on us anytime to back your play." Then he turned and walked away, with Rusty following. Mark was still staring at them as they walked back to the Gold Mine Saloon when Phil Barnaby and the others came up to him. Phil told Mark, "We've been talking, and we've formed a town council. You sure you want to take on the job of Marshal?" Bret Hogan was staring at Mark and suddenly he said, "He's sure! And since he's already wearing the badge, we can just go ahead and ratify him as the town Marshal. I know this man, or at least I know about him. I've seen him in Silver City."

He looked at Joe and said, "I've seen you too in Silver City." He looked around and then asked Mark, "I recall you had a brother in Silver City; he ain't here with you?" Mark shook his head and said, "He got hurt on the range, and he's laid up with a bum leg. But my younger brother will be joining me soon." Phil looked at Bret and asked him, "You know this man?" Bret shrugged and told him, "Like I said, I know *about* him, and I've seen him in action; he and his brother." He paused and then said, "He's one of the Bailey brothers." Homer Lee declared, "You're damn right he is! And I for one am glad of that fact!" Fat Fred, for once, was not smiling as he said, "I've heard of the Baileys too. Maybe I won't close down and leave just yet."

CHAPTER 13
DRAKE MANNING

DRAKE MANNING GREW UP ON THE LOUISIANA bayous, living on a boat with a drunken father who whipped the boy more times than he spoke to him. Drake never knew who his mother was, and he learned at a very young age to fend for himself. They lived off the land, and Drake learned to shoot when he was nine. He caught fish and shot wildfowl, and if he missed a shot, his father would whip him; so he learned not to miss. When he was fourteen, his father hit him once too often, and this time Drake hit back. He had spent his childhood fighting with the other boys on the bayou, and he was tough and knew how to use his fists. The blow to the chin knocked his father backwards, and he hit his head on the edge of the boat and fell into the swampy water. He sank like a stone, and Drake did not bother to go after him. He took the boat and rowed aimlessly for a long while until he was far away from the swamps and had entered clear water. He saw a shanty town near the banks and rowed to the shore. He pulled his boat up from the water and tied it to a tree. He sat by the boat and pondered on his next move. He was now free of his father, but he was realizing that freedom was a relative concept. He told himself that he was free, but free to do what?

A neatly dressed man, who looked to be in his fifties, saw the boy and came up to him. "You look as though the sky just fell on your head, youngster," he said. Drake scrambled up and said respectfully, "My father is dead, Sir, and I was just pondering on my next move." The man sized up the youngster, and liking what he saw, he asked him, "No family, no relatives hereabouts?" Drake shook his head and said, "No one. Me and my dad lived on the bayou." He paused and then said, "We lived off the land." The man told him, "My name is Seymour Williams, what name do you go by?" To a boy from the bayou who lived off the land, this man looked like a very wealthy man, and Drake said, "My name is Drake Manning, Sir!" Seymour smiled and said, "Forget the 'Sir,' just call me Will." He pointed to the gun stuck in a sash on Drake's hip and asked him, "I see you carry a gun; can you use it?" Drake looked around and spotted a waterfowl at the edge of the water. The bird was more than thirty feet away, but in a swift move, Drake drew his gun and fired. Will noted that the boy did not take up a stance and aim before shooting; he just drew and shot, but the head of the waterfowl went missing.

He told Drake, "That's quite impressive! I could use a lad like you if you're interested. Come with me and you'll see a lot of places and learn a lot of things. I'm a riverboat gambler, and I travel the rivers and earn my living. I could use a lad like you to watch my back and hold my bank when I'm gambling." Drake started to say something, but Will held up his hand and said, "Hear me out before you make up your mind. You are a strong-looking lad, and I would teach you how to fight. You're good with that gun, but I would make you better. I would outfit you so that no one would know that you're from the bayou. I would teach you to make the cards talk to you, and in time, you would make a decent living as a gambler." This time Drake held up his hand and said, "You had me at the word 'teach,' so I'm with you; just give me some time to sell my boat, and I'll join you." Will told him, "Sell everything, including your clothes; leave your past behind and never tell anyone where you are from. When people don't know who or what you are, they tend to be wary around you, and that's the best way to avoid trouble."

Drake soon found out that Will wasn't wealthy; he just dressed well. He told Drake, "A gambler should dress like a gentleman and always keep aloof from others. Remember this lesson well, Drake; familiarity breeds contempt, so stay aloof and do not become too close to anybody." He gave Drake a deck of cards and showed him the different ways to shuffle the cards. He was impressed at the dexterity of the boy's hands, and within six months, he had taught Drake the tricks of the gambler's trade. Drake was hungry for learning, and the student soon turned out to be better than his teacher. Will would win but also lose at cards, so sometimes they were broke, and sometimes they had a lot of money. Will became fond of the young boy he had picked up at the riverside, and he treated him like a son.

When Drake turned eighteen, no one would ever guess that he was a homeless boy from the bayou. He always dressed in a white suit and white hat, and he wore a low-slung tied-down gun. During the four years he was with Will, he had learned the art of the fast draw, and one day Will told him that he had never seen anyone faster. But eighteen was when Will died, and Drake was on his own again. They had left the river and had toured the boom towns, gambling in saloons. Will was playing in a high-stakes game in a town in Arkansas when a man called him a cheat. Will went for his gun, but he was getting old and slow, and the man shot him dead. The man had holstered his gun when Drake said coldly, "Let's see how good you are when you're not facing an old man." The man drew, and Drake shot him dead. But the man had friends in town, and Drake had to leave in a hurry to avoid a hanging party.

He drifted for the next six years, playing cards in all the towns he stopped at. He had determined not to end up like Will, and so he slowly built up a stake for the future. When he figured he had enough, he went south to the Rio Grande and played the riverboats there. He finally came to the border town of Roma, and he decided that this was where he would stop and build his future. He opened his own saloon and developed contacts with outlaws who lived on the border between Mexico and Texas. He would finance raids on distant cattle ranches and banks, and the outlaws would cross the Rio Grande to the safety of Mexico. Drake would be there to divide the spoils, and in two years he became rich. Drake made sure that no raids were carried out in the vicinity of Roma, and so the outlaws were safe from the local law. The next move that he had planned was to turn from being a gambler to a landowner and thus achieve a veneer of respectability which would finally put his past to rest. He bought a small ranch and put his gang of outlaws to run it. He tried to cultivate the other ranchers, and he became furious when they spurned him. And then he saw Rosie Masters in town, and everything changed again.

CHAPTER 14
ROCK'S STORY

THE NEW TOWN COUNCIL OF TWO FORKS REMOVED the bodies of Big Red and Rod Tilson, and Mark and Joe went to the Gold Mine Saloon. Joe stood with his back to the bar and kept an eye on the room. Mark told Rock Masters, "I'm here because Tally Stevens sent word that he needed some help, and he's a friend of ours. Now, I don't mean to pry, and your business with Drake Manning is your affair; but given the situation in this town, I need to know where everybody stands. So tell me what your beef with Drake is all about, and is that the only reason you're here." Rock gave him a cool look and asked, "What makes you think that I have a beef with Drake?" Mark sighed and said bluntly, "Because I wasn't born yesterday, and my family is from the Tennessee hills." Rock stared at him for a while but then nodded as though coming to a decision. "I'm from Texas, so I've heard of the Cedar Creek battle and the Bailey family. I know Jack Donovan because I met him during the war. I reckon I can understand your situation, so I'll tell you about Drake, but let's go to the backroom and talk." Mark told Joe, "You hold the fort here; I'll be back." They sat in the backroom, and Rock Masters told

Mark about Drake Manning and the connection he had with him.

Drake Manning was a professional gambler and one of the really fast guns. He had been a riverboat gambler and then had moved to Roma, on the Texas border with Mexico. He opened his first saloon there and did a thriving business, mainly in moonshine whiskey and gambling. He killed three men there in straight and fair shootouts, and he became known as a man to leave alone. Although he sometimes operated on the borderlines of the law, he was careful not to overstep; but that was in the beginning. He accumulated money, and with it his ambitions began to grow. He bought a small ranch in the Rio Grande valley and hired men who were suspected by the locals to be borderline outlaws to run it. There were three other ranches close to his, and he tried to cultivate the owners to improve his standing in the neighborhood. But the other ranchers were old-time Texans, and to them he was just a professional gambler, and they refused to mix with him socially.

"These were family men," Rock told Mark. "There was no way they would invite a professional gambler and saloon owner into their homes, especially one like Drake, with his shady dealings. Nobody knew who he was or where he came from. All that was known was that he had been a riverboat gambler who decided to stop in Roma and set up a saloon." Rock paused to gather his thoughts and then continued. "Everyone also knew the men he associated with," Rock said. "They were suspected to be borderline outlaws who would do anything for a price. Maybe he thought that by becoming a ranch owner, he would be accepted by the respectable community." He shook his head and said, "That just showed that Drake didn't know much about how things work in the West."

Rock Masters was a young man, twenty-four years of age at the time, and his father owned a small ranch in the valley. Rock had a younger sister, Rosie, who had just turned sixteen. She was very beautiful, and she was in love with Rusty Bellows, who was the son of their neighbor, Simon Bellows. Rusty was eighteen years old and he worshipped Rosie. The families liked the match, and they planned on getting them married when Rosie turned eighteen. One day, Rock and Rusty took Rosie to Roma because she wanted to do some shopping. That was the day that Drake Manning saw her for the first time, and he was filled with the desire to possess her.

They were leaving a store when Drake Manning pretended to unintentionally bump into them. He was profuse in his apologies, doffed his hat, and bowed low to Rosie. "Forgive me my clumsiness," he told Rosie. "But it is my good luck and an honor to meet such a beautiful lady in these wild surroundings." Rosie was young, and Drake was a good-looking man, so she smiled at him and said, "Thank you, Sir, for the compliment." Rusty was also young and impetuous; besides, to him Drake was just a gambler. He pushed up close to Drake and told him, "Take your mealy-mouthed comments to women more suited to men like you. Now get out of the way!" Drake's eyes seemed to burn with anger, but he just bowed again to Rosie and walked away.

Rock Masters told Mark, "I thought that was the end of the matter, because we never ran into the man again. But a week later, Rosie was riding the range and she never returned home." The two families searched everywhere, but they could not find her. The Marshal of Roma, Mike Smith, came to the Masters' ranch and helped in the search, but after two days, they still came up empty. It was then that Rock remembered the altercation with Drake and the rage in his eyes. He told the Marshal, but Mike Smith was skeptical and said, "Something like that happens all the time in town, but no one would take such extreme measures for revenge. After all, he could just call out young Rusty and shoot him; I know for a fact that that man is very fast on the draw." But Rock just said, "So is Rusty, and everyone knows that as well."

Rock, Rusty, and some of their ranch hands went to the D Bar M ranch, which was owned by Drake. They found the place deserted, and they searched the small shack that served as a house, and they searched the range but found nothing. Rock commented, "There ain't a single head of cattle here." Rusty said, "And where are those hard cases who were supposed to be running the place?" They went to Roma and met the Marshal. Rock told him that Drake's ranch looked abandoned, and Mike Smith sighed and said, "I can understand your grief and stress, but I just cannot arrest a man without some evidence." He sent his deputy to call Drake, and when Drake arrived at the office, the Marshal said, "Fair warning to all of you; I will not tolerate any gunplay here, so settle down and we'll get this business sorted out." He told Drake, "Rock's sister is missing, and he reckons you might be responsible." Drake appeared to be shocked and he exclaimed, "You mean that sweet young girl I met a while ago in town? I know nothing about her being missing; first I'm hearing of it! But why would I be a suspect?"

The Marshal told him, "Because Rusty told you to stay away from her." Drake shook his head and said, "I'm used to that. I get that reaction a lot just because I'm a gambler; but if I had taken offence then I would have called out the young man right there." Rock told him, "You had a bunch of hard cases running that two-bit ranch of yours, but now there's no one there." At the use of the word 'two-bit,' Drake's eyes turned cold, but then he told the Marshal, "A friend of mine recommended those men to run my ranch, since I'm not a cattleman. It's been some time since I went to the ranch, but if what he says is true, then it means that they've run off with all my cattle." He sighed and said, "I'm going to have some strong words with the man who recommended those men to me."

The Marshal asked him, "You want me to look into it? Rustling's a serious crime in this state." Drake told him, "I would be grateful if you could find my cattle, but you and I both know that the border is right here and you have no jurisdiction in Mexico. No, I'll get my money back from the man who recommended those men to me." Turning to Rock, he said, "You can search the ranch if you think that those men had anything to do with your sister's disappearance." Suddenly he exclaimed, "Why, that would account for their disappearance along with my cattle! Maybe they did abduct your sister!" The Marshal sent him away and then told Rock, "If you can come up with some evidence, then I will arrest the man; otherwise, what he says makes sense. Maybe those yahoos took off with the cattle and your sister to Mexico. I will talk to some lawmen I know over the border, and I'll ask them to look around. I'm sorry, Rock, but there's nothing else that I can do."

Rock was pensive as he completed his story and he told Mark, "When Drake turned to leave the Marshal's office, I saw the look of triumph in his eyes, and I knew at that moment that he had taken Rosie. After a week, he left town and nobody knew where he had gone. We went across the border and searched and asked people if they had seen a white girl in the company of bad men, but no one had seen her." He sighed and said, "We spent two months in Mexico and then came back. One day, we met up with a drifter who told us about a shootout in a Colorado boom town between a gambler and a miner. He said that the gambler was the fastest gun he had ever seen. The description he gave us matched Drake, and so we travelled to the town, but he had already left. We kept tracking him and finally found him in Kansas. That was where we started a saloon and watched him in the hope that he would finally lead us to Rosie. When he moved, we followed him, and that's what we have been doing for more than two years now." Mark asked him, "You think she's still alive?" There was a sadness in Rock's eyes as he said, "No, I think she's dead, but Rusty refuses to believe that, and so I can't kill Drake. Rusty is still clinging on to the hope that eventually Drake will lead us to Rosie."

CHAPTER 15

ROSIE MASTERS

ROCK'S SISTER ROSIE HAD ALWAYS LIVED ON THE ranch, and the only town she had seen was the town of Roma. But magazines and books dropped off or exchanged by drifters and travelling drummers gave her a glimpse into a different world. A world of fashion, grand cities, and large hotels; of gentlemen and ladies fashionably dressed and gay, while her world was filled with rough men riding the range and a small town that provided just the basic necessities of living. She loved Rusty, and she adored her big brother, but when she met Drake Manning in town that day, she was impressed by the way he dressed and carried himself. It was like the pictures and drawings that she had seen in magazines. He had been courteous, and she had responded the same way. When Rusty had sent him on his way, she had chided him, "You don't have to be so jealous, Rusty! He behaved like a gentleman, and so I had to be courteous in return." Rock and Rusty exchanged glances, and Rock told his sister, "Some men are not fit company for respectable ladies. That man is a professional gambler." Rosie ignored them for a while, and the men dropped the subject.

Rosie was aware of what the boys were talking about, but Drake Manning had been well dressed and so courteous that she just couldn't believe that he was not suitable for her society. She smiled to herself and thought that Rusty was just jealous, which pleased her. The day she went missing, she was riding the range when she realized that she had crossed over into the small ranch that Drake Manning had recently bought. She immediately turned around to leave and came face to face with him. He had been looking over his range when he spotted her, and he had ridden fast to intercept her. Now he doffed his hat and told her with a smile, "I seem to be really in luck these days; imagine running into a fair maiden again in such a short time." She said, "I'm sorry, I did not realize that I had crossed over the boundary, and I was just on my way back to our ranch."

He shook his head, and giving her a slight bow, he said, "No need to be sorry, my dear. Your presence makes this dreary place look like paradise. My ranch house is just a short distance from here, so allow me to offer you some refreshments before you leave." He had moved his horse closer as they spoke, and now he was at her side. Rosie began to feel uncomfortable, although she did not understand why she should feel like that; after all, she told herself, he was still very much the gentleman. But she began to move her horse forward, saying, "Thank you Sir, but I really should be getting back home, or my family will start to worry." Drake put his hand on hers to stop her and said, "You must do me the honor of visiting my humble abode." She jerked her hand free and blurted out, "My father would kill me if I visited the house of a gambler and saloon owner!"

It was the wrong thing to say to a man like Drake, who hated his past and wanted to belong to the better class of society. A haze descended on his mind, and he grabbed hold of her and pulled her off her horse. She screamed and fought him and managed to free herself. She fell to the ground, and Drake jumped off his horse and threw himself on top of her. But Rosie was a tough, ranch-bred girl, and she fought back fiercely. She hit him on his nose and drew blood, which only enraged him further, and he hit her on her chin. In his blind rage, he had hit her harder than he intended, and he heard a dry snap like the breaking of a twig, and Rosie went limp in his arms.

For a long time, Drake sat there by her body, struggling to get control of his emotions. He realized that his dream of being integrated into the respectable community was at an end in this place, but he also realized that he had to get rid of the body to save himself from a hanging. He threw her body across her saddle, and mounting up he rode to the ranch house. He told the leader of his outlaw gang what had happened and said, "Take all the cattle, and her horse and body, and cross the river to Mexico. Bury her deep there and sell the cattle and the horse. All the money from the sale is yours to keep, and I'll be in touch when things settle down here. But don't return here until I tell you to."

He played his part when the Marshal called him to his office, and he knew that the Marshal had no proof that he was involved with the disappearance of Rosie. He also knew that Rock and Rusty believed him guilty, and he was tempted to face them with a gun to put an end to this matter. He was sure he could take either of them in a gunfight, but there was something about Rock Masters that held him back. He knew men, and he had a feeling that only a bullet to the heart or head would stop a man like Rock Masters. He had seen men like that, who would keep shooting even with six bullets in them, and Drake Manning was not ready to die.

He left Roma within a week and began drifting again until he ran into Rock and Rusty in Kansas. He left Kansas, but they followed him, and wherever he stopped, they stopped and put up a saloon. This had been going on now for nearly two years, and Drake's nerves were getting frazzled. He had chosen to come to Two Forks because he had made up his mind to settle this affair in this out-of-the-way place once and for all. He had hired the two drifters to kill Rock and Rusty in the Gold Mine Saloon, but they had failed. He had paid men before this to kill Rock and Rusty, but each time they had failed, and now he realized that he would have to kill them himself.

CHAPTER 16

MARK TAKES CHARGE

MARK AND JOE WENT OVER TO HANS KRUGER'S STORE. Hans and Rupert were talking in low tones over the counter, and they stopped talking as soon as Mark and Joe entered. Hans gave Mark a wary look and asked him, "What can I do for you, Marshal?" Mark told him, "You produced a bill of sale for Harvey Kline's mine, and there's a question about Harvey's signature." Rupert started to speak, but Mark held up his hand and said, "Until I get the issue sorted out, no one goes near that mine." Hans protested and said, "He signed that bill of sale in front of witnesses!" Mark smiled and told him, "I reckon it's mighty convenient that the witnesses are all your friends. Now, if the witnesses had to include Butch or any of Harvey's friends..." Joe told Mark casually, "You remember that trouble in Silver City? A gang was killing off miners and then producing a bill of sale for the mine." He looked at Hans and said, "Funny thing was, none of the witnesses were friends or relatives of the dead miner." Hans' face turned red, and he said angrily, "I don't know what you're hinting at, but you're the law, and I'll wait until you get this sorted out." Mark glanced at Rupert, but there was no expression on the man's face. They left and went over to the Silver Rock Saloon.

They stood just inside the batwing doors and scanned the room. Drake Manning was sitting at a table playing cards with three other men. Burt Wayling was behind the bar, and Max Shultz was talking to him with a glass of whiskey in his hand. Burt saw the Marshal and said something to Max, and he turned around. Max Shultz was just shy of six feet, but he was built like a barrel with bulging biceps. In the shadow of Big Red, nobody actually noticed that he was a big man himself. Now he placed the glass on the bar counter and walked up to Mark. When he was about a foot away from Mark, he started to swing a haymaker from his hip, but Mark stepped in close and thrust the barrel of his gun with force into his stomach. Max grunted and his hand dropped. "No need to stop," Mark told him casually. "I always wondered whether a man's hand could move faster than a bullet. Now would be a good time to find out." He smashed the barrel of his gun again into Max's stomach, and Max moved back, but Mark continued to poke the barrel hard into his stomach, so Max was forced to keep moving back. When they reached the bar, Mark told him, "Turn around!" Max turned around, and Mark hit him on the head with the gun barrel, and he dropped like a stone. He heard Joe say behind him, "I wouldn't if I were you."

Mark ordered Burt, "Come out of there and stand in front of me." Burt glared at him but came out and walked to the table where Drake was sitting with a grim look on his face. Mark asked Joe, "Someone get a little playful?" Joe shrugged and said, "The kid in the red shirt was feeling tired of sitting down, I reckon." Mark turned and saw a weasel-looking man who must have been all of twenty years old glaring at him. He was sitting at the table playing cards with Drake and the others. Drake said grimly, "Was it necessary to pistol-whip Max?" Mark seemed to ponder that question for a bit and then told him seriously,

"When a man takes a swing at a lawman, he's asking for trouble. Max there is lucky I didn't put a bullet in him. I know many a lawman who would have done just that. Max is lucky because he gets to spend some time in the hoosegow when he gets up, contemplating his mistake." He looked at the man in the red shirt and asked him, "What's your name, kid?" The man snarled, "The name's Killer Marvin, and I ain't no kid! Meet me outside and let's see how good you are when you're facing a man!"

Joe made a clucking sound and said, "You keep that up, kid, and you won't live long enough to grow into a man." Killer Marvin started to get up, and Mark took two steps forward and slammed the pistol barrel on his head. Marvin slowly folded up and fell to the floor. Drake's eyes were cold when he asked Mark, "You came here on some business, or just to beat up my men?" Mark told him mildly, "Now that you ask, I did come here on some business. You produced a bill of sale for Pat Simpson's mine, but there's a question regarding his signature, which I'm looking into. Until that is sorted out, no one is to go near the mine."

Drake started to say something, but Mark cut him off and said, "All the things you're going to say about witnesses and all that; Hans already asked, and he got the answers, so you can talk to him." He looked around and pointed to two stocky miners. "You two," he told them. "I'd be mighty obliged if you would throw some water on these two sleeping men and then escort them to the jail. Joe here will follow you just in case they get a bit restless." He and Joe went outside, and he told Joe, "You hold down the fort here. I'm going to talk to Tally."

Clayton had given him directions, and it didn't take him long to find the mine. He stopped some distance away and shouted out, "Tally Stevens!" Tally came out from behind the ramparts they had thrown up for defense, and he waved to Mark to come on in. By the time he swung down from the saddle, most of the miners were out in the open. He told Tally, "I was told that there were snipers around." Tally said, "Now that we've got lookouts, there's little chance of a sniper getting a shot at us. We placed our men so that they have a good view all around, and they're higher than the hills from where a sniper can hope to get a shot in."

He gripped Mark's hand and said, "I was sorry to hear about Brian. I hope he gets better soon. Clayton tells me you brought Joe with you, but I'm worried that it may not be enough. I, for one, still don't know exactly who is behind all this. I figure Drake and Hans, but whether they're working together or not, I don't know. Besides, it may be a play by Big Red and the others." Mark said, "Big Red and Rod Tilson are dead. Max Shultz and a weasel-looking man, calls himself Killer Marvin, are in jail nursing sore heads." Tally stared at him in surprise and then turned around and told everyone, "What did I tell you boys! The Baileys don't let the grass grow under their feet!" He turned back to Mark and said, "That was fast work, Mark. What did Hans and Drake have to say about you gunning down the Marshal?"

Mark shrugged and told him, "He wasn't the Marshal when I shot him; he had taken off his badge and resigned. Tilson made the mistake of calling out Joe, and he died in the street." He then told Tally all that had happened that day, and Tally said, "I figured something was going on between Rock and Drake. So what's the next move, Marshal?" Mark told him, "You get back to working your mines. As I told Hans and Drake, no one goes to Harvey and Pat's mines until I sort things out. None of you know Harvey or Pat's signature?" Tally said, "Clayton was with them for nigh on a year, but he never had cause to see them make their mark on anything. But we all put our marks on paper and gave it to Nick so that no more fake bills of sale would come up. You can take charge of the paper now." He gave the paper to Mark, who said, "Now that there's a good move." He pocketed the paper, and then, looking around, he pointed to Harry and said, "You must be Harry Moss. I'm deputizing you because Joe and me, we got to sleep sometime, and we could do with an extra pair of eyes and an extra gun. From now on, one of us will always be awake and around to keep an eye on Hans and Rupert." Tally asked him, "You think they're more dangerous than Drake Manning?" Mark shrugged and said, "Hans is big and seems to be the leader, but there's something about Rupert that tells me he is the most dangerous of the lot." Kelly Proctor was curious, and he asked Mark, "How do you know if Harry is good enough with a gun?" It was Tally who answered, and he just said, "He knows." Clayton asked Mark, "You just said to keep an eye on Hans and Rupert, but what about Drake?" Mark told him, "Rock and Rusty will take care of that."

CHAPTER 17
HIRED GUNS

MARK, JOE, AND HARRY WERE SITTING IN THE Marshal's office that evening when Rusty Bellows walked in and told Mark, "Rock figured you should know that about a month back Drake sent a man out and he took the trail that could lead to Utah and Kansas. We reckon he was wise to the fact that Tally had sent a man for help." Joe remarked, "Always a lot of guns for hire in Kansas and Utah." Mark thought about it for a while and then said, "Let's tell Tally to put two men to watch the trails, and if they see strangers coming, then he should send us word immediately." Harry looked puzzled and asked Mark, "Why watch the trails when we'll see them anyway when they ride into town?" Joe smiled and told him, "That's just the Bailey way; you take the fight to them." Harry was still puzzled, but he didn't ask any more questions.

The next morning, Joe and Harry made the rounds of all the establishments for Harry to check if any new arrivals had sneaked in during the night. They went back to the Marshal's office and told Mark that everything was quiet. Harry said, "No new arrivals as far as I could figure. Of course, I don't really know everyone who has already come to this town." Mark shrugged and told him, "I trust your instinct." Suddenly from the cells, Marvin shouted out, "Hey! Yeller belly! I'm still waiting for you to face me man to man!" Joe sighed and went to the jail. "You sure this is what you want, kid?" he asked Marvin. "That's what I want if you ain't yeller!" Marvin snarled. Joe opened the door and said, "Come on out then." Marvin came out and Max Shultz stood up, but Joe said, "You poke your snout out of this door, and you're liable to get it shot off; but you do what you want." He left the door open, and lifting down Marvin's gun belt from the wall, he handed it to him and said, "Out the door and on the street." Marvin sneered at him and walked out to the street, buckling on his gun belt.

Joe followed him, and when they were on the street, he said, "Turn around." Marvin turned around and adjusted his gun belt. He tied down his holster and loosened the gun in it. Then he stood spraddle-legged and went into the gunfighter's crouch, while Joe just stood negligently, a little bit side-on, facing him. Men had come out of the saloons and stores, and they stood watching the two men. Marvin's hand hovered over his gun butt and he snarled, "Now you yeller..." That was as far as he got when Joe palmed his gun and shot him. Marvin staggered back and Joe shot him again. Marvin was staggering, but he still tried to pull his gun, and Joe shot him yet again. He was dead before he hit the street. One of the watching men shouted, "Hell! I never seen his hand move, but the gun was there and blazing away!" Joe just turned and walked back to the Marshal's office, but Mark saw Drake standing by the batwings of the Silver Oak Saloon and staring at Joe thoughtfully. He went back in and told Max Shultz that he was free to go.

That evening, Kelly Proctor came racing into town and swung down before the Marshal's office. He rushed in and told Mark, "Two for sure gunslingers are on the way; they're about a mile from town right now riding the Kansas trail." Mark thanked him and sent him on his way. He and Joe stood up, and

Harry said, "You're going to meet them outside town, that's why the lookouts." Joe said, "I told you, take the fight to them." Harry jumped up and said, "I'm coming too." But Mark told him, "You stay here and keep an eye on things; won't do for all three of us to be missing from town."

Mark and Joe mounted up and rode out of town in the direction that Kelly had said. They rode fast and about half a mile from town they saw the two men approaching, and they pulled on the reins. They waited until the men were about ten feet away and then Mark said, "That's far enough! Turn around and go back to where you came from." The men stopped and one of them told the other, "Well, lookee here, Dicky! We rate a welcoming committee!" Dicky said, "They must know who we are, Ricky." Ricky told Mark, "We're the Sullivan twins, and you'd do well to just keep riding on. We got us a contract to kill two lawmen and it don't matter to us which two we kill, because we for sure will collect the bounty." Both of them sat up straight in the saddle with their hands hovering over their guns, and then they suddenly froze.

They stared at the guns held by Mark and Joe, and Mark told them, "Unbuckle your belts and throw them to the side." The twins kept staring at them and their eyes were bleak. Their hands had not moved and Joe said laconically, "You got one second to move those hands, or I shoot." He shot Ricky through the biceps of his right arm and Mark shot Dicky through the wrist. Joe said mildly, "Show off." Mark asked him, "You sure the one second was over before you shot the man?" Joe shrugged and said, "Never was good at telling time." Mark told the twins, "You got five seconds to start unbuckling those gun belts before I shoot you again." The twins struggled to unbuckle the belts with only one hand, and Mark told Joe, "Never heard of anyone giving someone a one-second warning. Now five seconds is more reasonable."Joe told him, "You got yourself to blame for that. After meeting you, I realized that if I gave you a five-second warning you'd put five bullets in me."

The twins finally got their gun belts off and threw them to the ground. Mark told them, "Turn around and go back to where you came from. If I ever see you again, I'll shoot you on sight!" They turned around and rode away at a canter and then a gallop. Joe said, "I think they don't like you. They can't get away from you fast enough." Mark laughed and said, "Let's go back, but first pick up those gun belts and we'll take them with us." They returned to town and rode slowly past the Silver Rock Saloon so everyone could see the two extra gun belts hanging across Joe's saddle. At the Marshal's office, Harry Moss asked Joe, "You boys have done this before?" So Joe told him about the gold strike near the San Juan Mountains in Colorado and the gold rush that brought in a lot of the rough crowd. "Mark's brother Brian was an officer during the war," he told Harry. "It was his idea to keep roving lookouts, and when we spotted men coming in, we would meet them on the trail. The miners we would welcome, and the others we would bury. Brian said that was the best way to keep the rough crowd from getting too big to handle. He said that once the killers and outlaws grew in strength in a town, then it became difficult for the law-abiding citizens to get them out." He paused and then added, "As I said before, the Baileys believe in taking the fight to them."

CHAPTER 18
SNIPER ATTACK

IT WAS THE EVENING OF THE THIRD DAY SINCE MARK and Joe had ridden into town, and they were making their rounds of the establishments. Mark was walking towards the Marshal's office when a man who looked like a miner rode down the street towards him. The man stopped, and looking at the badge he said, "Marshal, I saw a body halfway up the slope of that hill on the north side of town." Mark asked him, "Which slope would that be?" The man shrugged and said, "I'm just passing through, so I don't know this country, but there was a bunch of desert ironwood trees that I didn't see on any of the other slopes." He bent and looked closely at Mark and then said, "Hell! That man looked like you!" Mark's face turned grim and he said, "Just exactly how did you see this man." The man shrugged and told him, "I was coming over the hill when I heard what sounded like a shot. I was riding down the slope when I saw this man lying near these ironwood trees. He looked dead to me; there was blood on his chest, so I rode into town to tell the law. I gotta be moving, Marshal, but that man sure enough looked like you." He rode on out of town, and Mark ran for his horse, which was saddled and hitched in front of the Marshal's office. "Harry!" he shouted out as he swung into the saddle. Harry came running out, and Mark told him, "Find Joe and tell him that I'm riding to that slope with those ironwood trees on the north side of town. A man just rode in and said he saw a wounded or dead man up there who looked like me." Before Harry could ask him anything, he swung his horse around and went racing out of town.

The one thought in Mark's mind was that if the man looked like him, then it had to be Luke. He went charging up the slope and, when he neared the ironwood trees, he stopped and looked around. He turned sideways in the saddle to look, and that move saved his life. He heard the sound of a rifle shot and he felt the impact of the bullet to his back. Instinct made him kick his horse in the ribs, and the horse took off into the grove of trees. After about ten feet, he reined in the horse and slipped to the ground. He pulled his saddlebags and rifle off the horse and sat down behind a tree, scanning the area from where he figured the shot had come. There were no more shots, and he pulled off his shirt and looked down at the wound. There was a hole in his chest, but he was thankful for that because it meant that the bullet had passed through from his back. He pulled out some clean rags from his saddlebags and just plugged the hole in his chest. He grimaced with pain as he reached around to try and push a plug into the hole in his back. Luckily, the bullet had hit him on the right side, closer to his arm, and he was just able to reach it with his left hand. Taking out a long strip of cloth, he gritted his teeth and managed to tie it tight around his chest to hold the plugs in place.

He continued to keep an eye on the place, a huge boulder with some trees around it, where he figured the shot had come from as he tended to his wound, but he saw no movement. Using his rifle, he pulled himself up and went to his horse. He took a long drink from his canteen and then slowly pulled himself up until he was sitting in the saddle. He then triggered three fast shots at the boulder where he thought the sniper might be. He didn't shoot with any hope of hitting the sniper; the shots were a signal for Joe if he heard them. Then he turned his horse and rode slowly down the hillside, keeping in the cover of the grove of ironwood trees. When the trees petered out, he got down and continued down the slope, keeping the horse between him and the sniper. He had reached the bottom of the slope when he saw Joe and Harry come riding up to him. He pointed to the boulder and shouted, "Sniper!" Then he just grunted in pain and sat down on the ground. Harry told Joe, "You see to him while I scout that area." He raced away at an angle to the big boulder, and Joe rode up to Mark.

Mark told him, "My saddlebags are up there in the trees; get them." Joe rode up the slope and found the saddlebags. There was blood spatter all around, and Joe was worried. He came back, and Mark told him, "Take those leaves out of the saddlebags and pound them to a paste." Joe made the paste and then removed the plugs, cleaning the wound with water from his canteen. He pushed enough paste into the wound on both sides and then placed clean pads and tied a bandage around Mark's chest to hold the pads in place. By the time he had finished, Harry came back and said, "No one's there now, I reckon he shot and then skedaddled." They lifted Mark up and got him into his saddle and then rode to town.

They got him into the Marshal's office, and he lay down on the bed. Harry went to Homer Lee and told him to make some strong beef broth for Mark. Everyone had seen Mark ride into town with the bloody bandage around his chest, and Rock Masters came to the Marshal's office. Mark told him what had happened and said, "I need you to put on a badge and I'll deputize you. We're going to need your help." Just then Bull Redding came charging into the Marshal's office and stopped short when he saw Mark lying in bed. Mark told him, "I'm okay, go ahead and talk." Bull told him, "There's a passel of men riding hard, coming to town. The thing that puzzles me is that they all look like cowboys, and they look like they've ridden a fair distance and ridden hard!" Mark thought for a moment and then told Joe, "You got Harry, Rock, Rusty, and Bull here. Get them under cover with rifles and wait for those riders to come in. Don't shoot before we find out who they are and what they want. You stand in front of the office and see what you make of them."

Joe was standing on the street when the group of twelve men rode up to him. He shouted out, "Rock, Harry, don't shoot! You can come on out! This here is just a no-account Irish lad who's far from home." The men all swung down, and Paddy told Joe, "This here is Trent Williams and his boys from the Box T in Red Butte, New Mexico." Joe looked surprised and then burst out laughing, exclaiming, "Damn me to hell and gone! God bless Sally! I know Trent and these boys; me and Dewey were at the Box T for Mark's wedding." He shook hands with Trent and then told Harry, "You wait here with these boys and stay sharp until we talk to Mark." He told Paddy, "You and Trent come with me. I know you all must be tired, but just hang on for a while longer until we talk to Mark." The three of them went to Mark, and he laughed and then grimaced in pain when he saw Paddy and Trent. "I married me a real smart woman," he told Trent. He told Paddy, "I bet she sent you right after I left." Paddy said, "She told me that Luke would take time to get to you and that you might need help before that. She worked out the time it would take for Dewey to ride to Texas and then for Luke to get to you. She figured it would be faster for me to go straight to New Mexico and pick up the Box T boys and come here." Mark shook his head and said again, "A right smart woman." Paddy asked him, "What you want us to do, boss?"

Mark told Joe, "Tell Rock and Harry to show them around so they get familiar with the layout." He asked Trent, "How many of your boys did you bring?" Trent said, "Ten of them. Rick wanted to come along, but I told him to stay put and get some men together in case we need them." Mark said, "Let half of them sleep for five hours, and then the other half can do the same. You sleep with the first half, and Paddy can sleep after that. If you're here now, I can imagine how fast you've been travelling." He looked at Paddy and said, "You've been travelling more than that distance; do you want to rest first?" Paddy shrugged and said, "I slept for six hours when I reached the Box T. I'll survive." Mark told Joe, "Deputize Trent and Paddy and thank Rock for his help; we won't need to deputize him now. Everyone to prowl the town in pairs, armed with rifles; a show of strength. Two shifts, half of the Box T cowboys with Trent in one group and the other half with Paddy. You take one group and Harry takes the other. I'm going to sleep now, so you're in charge."

CHAPTER 19

GUNFIGHT IN TWO FORKS

THE NEXT DAY MARK HAD A RAGING FEVER, AND Homer Lee came to take care of him. Homer wanted to move him to the hotel, but Mark said, "This place is safer as there's always someone around. I got me some bark in my saddlebag that's good for fever, and there should be some of those leaves left to make this poultice to keep the wound from getting infected; ask Joe." Homer told Joe, and he got the bark and leaves, and Joe told him, "Boil the bark for a while and give him the water to drink. Change the poultice every day after cleaning the wound. This here is Indian medicine, but it sure does work." For three days Homer took care of Mark. He fed him broth and eggs, and when he could eat, he fed him bacon, eggs, vegetables, and the strong beef broth. He also put a little salt in water and made Mark drink that. He told Joe that he had found that the salt helped when a man had lost a lot of blood. He cleaned Mark's wound every day and changed the poultice and bandage. He kept boiling the bark and giving Mark the water to drink. After two days, the fever went away, and the wound was looking good to heal, but Mark was still very weak, mainly due to the loss of blood.

It was the evening of the third day after the Box T had arrived in Two Forks, and Harry's team were doing the rounds of the town. Harry was used to trouble, and he had been in many a gunfight with rustlers and the rough crowd in boom towns. He was a cautious man, and he had instructed the men to always glance at the rooftops when they were patrolling the town. This evening, it was Harry who spotted the gun barrel and the head behind it on the roof of a store. He shouted a warning to his men and began working the lever of his Winchester as he fired rapidly at the roof until the gun disappeared. He shouted out to his team, "Work in pairs! Two for each building; search the building and the roof. Anyone tries something, shoot first, and we'll ask questions later." He told Paddy, "You're with me." They ran into the store where Harry had spotted the rifle barrel. It was one of the new stores that had opened about two weeks back, and it sold everything from flour to nails. The man behind the counter stared at them in surprise when they came in with rifles held ready. Harry said, "Your name and be quick about it." The man said, "Name's Saul, and I ain't done nothing wrong." Paddy told him, "There was a man with a gun on your roof just now, so how would he get there." Saul was flustered and said, "A man with a gun on my roof? But... but..." Paddy walked up to him and, slamming the counter, he demanded, "How would someone get to your roof!" Saul reared back and then cried out, "Not from here! Not from inside! There's a ladder at the back to get to the roof if necessary."

Harry and Paddy went outside and split up, each going around the building from opposite sides. They met up at the back, and the ladder was there. Harry ran up the ladder until he reached the top, and then he took a hasty peek over and ducked down immediately. He again pushed his head up, but from the side, and threw another glance across the roof. He saw no one, and he climbed onto the roof and walked to where he had seen the gun barrel. He studied the spot and found the end of a cigar lying nearby. He picked it up and sniffed it. "Good quality," he murmured and slipped it into his pocket. He went back down and told Paddy, "Nothing there now except the end of a good quality cigar."

Suddenly they heard the sound of shots, and they raced to the street. From around the corner of a building, they scanned the rooftops and saw a man slowly topple over and fall from the roof of a general store, landing with a thud in the street. Two buildings down from there, a man came running out from a saloon into the street with a rifle in his hand. Paddy stepped forward with his rifle held ready and called out, "Hold it right there and drop that rifle!" The man turned towards the voice and swung up his rifle, and Paddy triggered two shots to his chest. The man threw up his hands and fell back against the building. He slumped to the ground, and the rifle fell from his hands. More shots sounded further down the street, and Paddy and Harry moved forward swiftly but cautiously, staying by the sides of the buildings. They had crossed two buildings when a man came running out of the next building holding a rifle. Harry shouted out, "Drop the rifle!" The man turned and fired in one smooth but swift movement, and Harry took the bullet in his shoulder. Before the man could fire again, Paddy killed him with a shot to the head.

A deathly silence hung over the town when the shooting stopped. Then from each building came the call, "Box T coming out!" and the cowboys came onto the street. Paddy called out, "Anyone hurt?" One of the men told him, "My partner got a bullet hole in the arm, but he'll live, and we got the back-shooter. He's up there on the roof, deader than a doornail." One by one, the men lined up on the street, and Harry counted three wounded besides himself. He told them, "If you can walk, then come with me to the Marshal's office and Homer will fix us up. Anyone who can't make it on his own, come with your partner." He told Paddy, "You're in charge now, but you got only two men left. Send one to Homer's hotel to wake Joe and tell him. You and the other cowboy hole up in Rock's saloon and keep an eye on the town from there." The wounded went to the Marshal's office, and Homer said grimly, "They know we're watching the trails, so they must have snuck in those men in the night by keeping off the trails."

Mark looked worried, and he told Harry, "No way of knowing how many men they've brought in. Did you send someone for Joe?" Harry said, "Yeah, I told Paddy to send one of the men he had left. He and the other man are holed up in the Gold Mine Saloon." Mark slowly pushed himself up to a sitting position, and then he stood up. He teetered on his feet for a bit but then steadied himself. Taking a deep breath, he told Homer, "Just pass me my gun belt from that peg." Homer protested and told him, "You lost a lot of blood, and you're still too weak to fight!" But Mark told him, "I can always shoot a gun; just pass me that belt." He strapped on the gun belt and then told Homer, "Patch these boys up, and those who can still use a gun can join me in the office." He went into the office and dragged a chair to where he could see the street from the door and window. Picking up a rifle, he sat himself down in the chair and kept a watch on the street.

The man Paddy sent for Joe went to the hotel to wake him up while Paddy and the remaining cowboy stood just inside the Gold Mine saloon with their rifles held ready. They were joined by Rock, who held a rifle in his hands, and then Rusty came up to them holding a shotgun. He patted the shotgun and told Paddy, "Best thing to have when you're faced with a crowd of enemies out to get you." Suddenly there was the thunder of hooves, and a large group of riders came racing into town, and they started firing at the Marshal's office as they rode past. Paddy stood at the side of the door and began triggering fast shots into the group and had the satisfaction of seeing two of them drop their rifles. Rock knelt on one knee by the door and began coolly picking off targets one by one. He shot two men off their horses before the rest rode past the saloon and disappeared down the street. Mark had also been shooting from the Marshal's office, and now four men lay in the dust on the street. Two of them tried to get up but then flopped back down.

A heavy silence hung over the town again for more than fifteen minutes as though everyone was waiting for the other shoe to drop. Suddenly there was the sound of rifle shots from outside the town, and Paddy and Rock looked at each other. Rock said laconically, "Maybe they're shooting each other out there." Paddy started to smile but then abruptly told Rock, "Cover me! I'm going to see Mark." He told the Box T cowboy, "You stay here with Rock." He started out the door and said over his shoulder, "If riders come into town, don't shoot unless we do." Rock gave him a puzzled look, but before he could ask him anything, Paddy was gone. He kept to the sides of the buildings in the gathering dusk and moved erratically to make it difficult for any sniper to anticipate his movements. He reached the Marshal's office without any shots being fired, and he called out, "Mark, I'm coming in; don't shoot!" Mark said, "Come ahead, Paddy." Paddy slipped into the office and saw Mark sitting in the chair with the rifle in his hands. He looked exhausted, and Paddy exclaimed, "You should be in bed!" Homer and the other wounded were also there, and Homer said, "That's what I've been telling him, but he won't listen." Mark said, "If that crowd is anything to go by, then we're gonna need every gun we've got."

He turned to Paddy and asked him, "What was that shooting? It sounded like it came from out of town." Paddy told him, "That's why I came here. I told Rock not to shoot at any riders unless we do. Joe and the others are in the hotel, and we need to tell them as well." Mark stared at him for a moment and then abruptly told Harry, "Think you can make it to the hotel?" Harry moved to the door without answering, and Paddy told him, "Tell

Joe I think that Dewey has arrived." Harry reached the hotel without anyone shooting at him, and he told Joe what Paddy had said. Joe asked him, "How's Mark?" Harry shrugged and said, "He's sitting in a chair with a rifle in his lap. He shot at least two of those men lying in the street. His wound is bleeding again, and he's played out but just won't admit it!" Joe just said, "Don't worry about him, that's just his way. He'll keep going until he drops if he thinks it's necessary."

He looked at Harry's bandaged shoulder and said, "Think you can shoot?" Harry just nodded, and Joe told Trent, "Two men for each building and check the roofs again as well. I'll take Harry with me, and we'll see if any rats are still here in town." They came out of the hotel warily and looked around. Suddenly from outside the town, two shots sounded close together, and after the count of three, another single shot. Joe smiled, and pointing his rifle to the sky, he fired the same sequence of shots. He told the others, "This here hotel is almost at the end of this side of town, so let's clear these two buildings first." They sent two men to each building, and Joe moved cautiously to the end of the street. He whistled, and from nearby, Dewey whistled back. Joe moved forward and called out, "Come ahead, you're just in time to help us clear the town of rats." Horses suddenly appeared, walking slowly towards him, and Joe counted at least a dozen. A stocky figure wearily dismounted, and Joe said, "Never thought I'd see the day when you'd look tired, partner." Dewey laughed and came forward saying, "I can still carry your sack of bones for two miles if need be!"

Luke walked his horse closer and said, "You must be the Happy Joe that Dewey told me about. I brought you a new friend; we call him Happy Jake. He's busy right now watching the trails into town, so you'll have to wait to meet him, but where's Mark?" Joe told him, "Mark's been shot by a sniper, but he's recovering. I'll send a man with you to the Marshal's office to see him, but I need your men right now to clear all the buildings in town." Luke just said, "Let's move!" He started his horse, and the others followed. Joe called out to Harry, and when he came forward, he told him, "This here is Mark's brother, Luke Bailey. Take him to the Marshal's office to see Mark." He turned to Trent and said, "Pair off one of your men with one of Luke's, and let's get this town cleared, building by building."

CHAPTER 20
LUKE TAKES CHARGE

THE FIRST THING THAT LUKE DID WAS TO GET MARK into bed again. His wound had started to bleed again, so Luke removed the bandages and cleaned it up. "It's healing nicely," he told Mark. "It's just bleeding a little because you were crazy enough to use a rifle to shoot with!" Then he told Paddy, "Soon as they clear the town, take Dewey and three men who are rested. Dewey will take you to my boys, and the three men can replace my three boys who are watching the trails into town. Tell them to stay alert until daybreak and then come back to town. My boys need to sleep through the night; otherwise they won't be of much help come tomorrow." Paddy left the Marshal's office, and Mark told Luke everything that had happened in Two Forks since he had come in a week ago. After he had finished, he told his brother, "It's good to see you again, kid. You've filled out, so marriage must be good for you." Luke grinned and said, "All Gina does is put food in front of me, so what's a man to do except eat!" Mark said, "I never expected you to come so fast, but I reckon that's the reason why Brian chose Dewey for the longest ride. That boy is sure tough!" Luke agreed and said, "He sure is; he made it to my place in eight days, slept for six hours, and then started out with us again. But where did the others come from?" Mark told him about Sally sending Paddy to her father's ranch in New Mexico, and Luke grinned and said, "No one can say that we Baileys don't know how to pick our partners in life; that was a smart move!"

Joe, Paddy, Trent, and Dewey trooped into the Marshal's office, and Joe told Mark, "No rats in town, so I'm keeping my boys to watch all the approaches to town through the night. Three of them have replaced Luke's boys watching the trails, and I've put the rest on the roofs so they'll be able to see if anyone approaches the town other than by the trails." Mark introduced Luke to Joe, Trent, and Paddy, and then Luke told him, "You get some rest, and we're going to do the same. We'll meet and talk in the morning." Homer got up and said, "I'll put you and your boys up at my hotel. I've seen you before in the town of Shackelford." Luke stared at him for a moment and then said, "I remember; you're Homer Lee."

The next morning, they held a war council meeting in the Marshal's office, and Luke told Mark, "The Box T has two men wounded, so they're left with eight. Two of those eight are also wounded, but they call it a scratch and insist that they can walk and use a gun. Harry has to rest, so that leaves Joe, Dewey, and Trent, which makes eleven. I'm taking three of my boys with me, and Joe can have the other ten. That gives Joe twenty-one men to hold this town and cover all exits." He told Joe, "I don't want anyone from this town to move out. We counted roughly about eight men who rode off last night. They may be joining others who are holed up somewhere; I aim to find out where. If no one leaves this town, then I won't have to worry about a sniper laying for me."

Mark asked him, "What's your plan?" Luke said, "I'm going first to the mines, and I'll send Tally and the others back to town, or they could be the next target of attack. How many of them are there?" Joe did a quick mental count and then said,

"Nine, including Tally and not counting Harry. Then there's Rock and Rusty who will chip in when needed." Paddy said mildly, "I know I'm not invisible, but nobody has said where I'm supposed to be." Luke grinned at him and said, "I've seen you before riding the old trails. You're with me, and I'm taking Rock as well; six of us should be enough when we find where these yahoos are hiding out." He turned to Joe and told him, "With those nine miners, you'll have thirty men, so just make sure that no one can leave this town and no one enters." Joe told him, "There's also Hugh Benton and his group, but they're six in number, and they'll hole up in their mines. They have two mines next to each other, and they've fortified them before this. But you could tell them what's happening and warn them to stay alert."

Luke, Rudy, Jake, Hardy, Paddy, and Rock rode out of town and went straight to the mines. Tally came out with the other miners, and as soon as he saw Luke, he said, "You must be Mark's brother. We heard a lot of shooting last night from the direction of the town, so I brought everyone back here from the other mines." Luke told him, "Looks like your enemies have managed to bring in a lot of hired guns. They must know about Mark being wounded because they attacked the town last night and tried to shoot up the Marshal's office. But Paddy and Rock here, together with the other boys, held them off and killed four of them. They were getting ready to attack again when me and my boys arrived. There was a mite of shooting, and I reckon they decided that the odds had shifted, so they disappeared into the night." He looked at the miners and saw haggard faces. He knew the strain of being isolated and constantly on alert was beginning to tell on them.

He told Tally, "I can see that you're having a rough time of it, so I came to tell you to head for town; all of you. Joe said to warn Hugh Benton, and if you could do that, it would save me some time." Tally said, "Clayton, ride to Hugh's mine and tell him what's been happening. Tell him we're all going to town, and I said that he and his boys should come too." Pete Ford protested and said, "We've left all the other mines open to these thieves once again. But this is the richest strike, and if they get control of this..." Luke said bluntly, "They won't! We counted about eight men who rode away last night, and who knows how many more of them are hiding out somewhere. The attack on the town failed last night, so now they might try attacking you. If they do, then you might find yourselves badly outnumbered. You go to town, and don't worry about your mines; we're going to end this." Tally looked at the other miners and said, "He makes sense, and if he says he's going to end this, then I, for one, believe him. I know his brothers, Mark and Brian, and I can tell you this. If the Baileys say they're going to do something, well, they just go ahead and do it!" He turned back to Luke and asked him, "We'll move to town right now, but where are you going?" Luke turned his horse around and said, "We're going rat hunting."

CHAPTER 21
THE HUNT

LUKE RODE BACK TO THE PLACE WHERE THEY HAD surprised the attackers the night before. While Paddy and Rock waited, Luke, Hardy, Jake, and Rudy spread out and began searching for tracks. There was a confusion of tracks, and they had to move further and further in a widening circle before Luke called out, "I think I found it!" The others rode up, and Luke said, "This set of tracks leads straight ahead, so it must be the group that ran last night." Luke rode ahead with the others following and he kept an eye on the trail to make sure that no tracks deviated from the main one. The trail led to the mountains, and when they reached the foothills, Luke called a halt. He told the others, "They could be holed up anywhere around here; I'm sure there are lots of hiding places big enough to shelter a large group of men." He looked around and then turned to his three boys and told them, "The four of us are pretty good at making the sound of the rock wren, so let's split up and move in cautiously. When anyone spots their hiding place, give the call of the wren, and the rest of us will come fast." He told Paddy and Rock, "You pair up with one of the boys." But Paddy told him, "I can make the call of the wren, and I'll bet that I'm better than the lot of you!" Luke grinned at him and said, "Okay, okay, you and Rock go together."

They split up and then cautiously began to move forward silently, with every sense alert for trouble. There were boulders, shrubs, trees, and hollows before the mountain slope, and caves in the mountainside. They cleared the hollows and found no one. They moved more slowly as they approached the mountain-side. Suddenly Luke gave the call of the wren, and everyone moved back and then made their way to where the call had come from. They found Luke, and he made a sign for silence and then whispered, "I came upon a track and followed it here. See that dark opening in the mountainside? Look closely, and you can see a hoof mark and a boot mark just outside in the sand." They looked, and Paddy whispered, "Yep! I can see it, and it looks fresh; the boot mark more than the hoof. Someone must have stepped out to relieve himself, maybe, and got careless when wiping out his tracks."

Although Luke had said that he came upon a track, it wasn't that he found tracks that led straight to this spot. He had seen a few crushed leaves on the side of a shrub. To him, it meant that a horse or man had stepped on it and the twig had later sprung back up. Nothing else would account for a few crushed leaves on the side of a shrub. Further on, he spotted a fresh scratch on a large stone which could have been made by a shod hoof. Luke was a good tracker, and these little signs were enough for him to track his quarry. Now he told the others, "I reckon they're in there, but the question is whether they're all in there or some are outside." He pondered on that for a bit and then said, "There's something about this setup that don't sit right with me. You boys spread out but make sure that you're well hidden; not just from that cave but from anyone who might approach from another direction. I'll just scout around and see what I can find. If they do come out, then give the call of the wren, and I'll come a-running; but you start the ball and don't wait for me." He turned to leave but then turned back and said, "Paddy and Rudy, you boys watch the back trail, and the others can watch the cave."

He moved away like a ghost, and no one heard him go. He carefully scouted the area on one side of the cave for more than twenty yards and then went back and scouted the other side. He was alert and wary, which was why he noticed a few horse hairs on a tree trunk where a horse had brushed against it. He bent down and carefully studied the ground, walking forward slowly. He saw what appeared to be half a hoof print, and he pressed on, scanning not just the ground in front of him but to the sides as well. The ground was rocky, but there were patches of grass and sand, and soon he found another hoof mark in a patch of sand. He figured that they had been brushing away the tracks as they passed but had missed a few. Suddenly he stopped and stayed half-bent over without moving. His sixth sense was tingling, and slowly he raised his head and looked forward. There was a man standing sideways to him with his thumbs hooked in his belt. He was looking bored and suddenly he yawned and shook his head. Although he was not looking directly at him, Luke knew that if he moved, the man would see him with his peripheral vision.

Inch by inch, Luke lowered himself to the ground until he was screened by the bushes and shrubs. Then he began to inch forward, taking care not to press on anything that would make a sound. Silently, he continued forward until he was just two feet away from the man. The man grunted and turned to look at a cave in the mountainside, which was all that Luke needed. He rose up like a ghost with his six-gun in his hand, took a step forward, and hit the man on the head with the gun barrel. He took another swift step forward and caught the man as he fell. He dragged him back and laid him down under some shrubs. He tore the man's shirt into strips, gagged him, and bound his hands and feet. Then he went forward and stared at the large cave in the mountainside. Now he knew what had been troubling him about the setup at the other cave; the cave was too small for a large group of men. Luke realized that whoever was in charge of these men was smart. He had laid just enough of a trail to lead to the other, smaller cave. Too much of a trail, and suspicions would have been aroused; but if a skilled tracker was tracking them, then he would find the few tracks and believe that the men were holed up in the small cave. It was only because Luke was a cautious man and never took anything for granted that he had searched again and found the larger cave.

He slowly retraced his steps to where he had left his rifle under a tree, and there he gave the call of the rock wren. He gave it twice, which he knew his boys would recognize as an urgent signal. He held the rifle ready and watched the cave as he waited for the boys to come to him. Within a few minutes, they were there, and Rudy asked him, "You found something, boss?" For an answer, Luke pointed to the cave, which was visible through the shrubs, although they were standing at least twenty feet away. Paddy told him, "I left Jake to watch the other cave. Should I call him?" But Luke shook his head and said, "No, that was a good move; there may be a few men there. They laid a false trail to that cave, and if shooting started there, then the main group from here would have attacked from all sides. It's a good plan, and the man in charge of these men knows his business." Rock asked him, "So what's your plan now?" Luke told Hardy, "You go and join Jake and start shooting; don't let anyone escape from there. Once you start shooting, I'm sure the men here will come charging out, and we'll be ready for them. Go now and start shooting as soon as you're there."

Hardy left, and Luke and the others crawled forward until they were just ten feet from the cave with a clear field of fire. The man who Luke had knocked on the head had come to his senses and was struggling to get free, so Luke crawled up to him and hit him on the head once more. He crawled back and told Paddy, "That man's brain is going to be scrambled unless he's got a real hard head. That's the second time now he's taken a whack to the head."

CHAPTER 22
DECLAN

THEY WAITED WITH RIFLES HELD READY, AND THEN there came the sound of rapid rifle fire. Suddenly, the silence was broken by curses and shouting from inside the cave, and some men came running out, leading their horses. Luke and the others calmly started shooting them down. Rudy would later say that it was more like target practice than a gunfight because Luke, Paddy, and Rock were not firing blindly; they were picking their targets, and each shot scored a hit. The men who had come rushing out of the cave fell one by one, and then, from inside the cave, the rest of the men started firing back, and Luke and the others hugged the ground. Paddy and Rudy started shooting into the cave, but they were shooting blindly because they could not see anyone. Luke raised his voice and told the others, "Shoot at the walls of the cave and hope for ricochets!" All four of them started firing rapidly at the sides of the cave walls, and soon they could hear the nasty whine of ricochets from inside the cave. The volley of rifle fire from four guns was just too much, and suddenly a voice bellowed from inside the cave, "Stop shooting! We surrender!" Luke held up his hand, and the firing stopped. He shouted out, "If we think that anyone has a gun in his hand or in his belt, we'll shoot him on sight and apologize later if we're wrong. Come on out one by one and lay down on the ground with your face pointing to the sky and your hands underneath your back. You men outside the cave who can still move, don't! Just turn over on your back and look at the sky."

Three of the seven men lying outside groaned and turned with difficulty to lie on their backs. Men from inside the cave came out one by one and lay down on the ground. Luke and the others stayed under cover until all the men were lying flat on their backs. Luke counted twenty-one, and then he darted forward to the nearest man, and catching him by the hair, he lifted him up bodily to act as a shield. The man grunted in pain, and Luke transferred his grip from his hair to his neck and told him, "I'll ask you this only once, and if you lie, I'll shoot out your spine, and you'll die a slow and very painful death." He dug his pistol fiercely into the man's spine, and the man grunted again in pain and said, "Mister, you ask your question, and I'll give you an honest answer. I happen to be very attached to my backbone."

Luke found himself liking the man; he was a hired gun, but he had courage if he could joke in such a situation. Luke told him, "Actually, its two questions: are there any more men inside that cave?" The man asked him, "How many men are here now?" Luke said, "Twenty-eight, including you." The man told him, "That's the lot then." Luke asked him, "How many in the other cave?" The man chuckled and said, "A real canny man you are, friend! So you worked out that dodge; and just so you know, you're the only one so far to have worked that one out. There are three men in that cave. I answered both your questions honestly, so do I get to keep my backbone?" Luke told him, "Just one more, and we're done. Who's the boss of this sorry outfit?"

The man chuckled again and said, "You're holding him right now."

Luke called out, "Paddy, you and the others come tie up these yahoos and tie them tight!" When all the men had been tied up, Luke stepped away from the man and said, "Stand up and face me." The man stood up and turned around, and Paddy blurted out, "By all the angels and saints! The man's a Bailey! I'll swear to it!" The man grunted and said, "You know me? I'm sure I ain't seen you before." Paddy asked him, "What's your name?" The man shrugged and said, "They call me Declan Bailey, and again I say that I don't know you." Paddy shook his head and told him, "I don't know you either, but look at the man in front of you and see the resemblance; that's a Bailey, and I know two more." Declan looked at Luke and then said laconically, "I don't know about resemblance; I'm sure that I'm much more good-looking." Luke stared at him for a moment and then said, "First time I've heard of a Bailey being a hired gun." Declan shrugged and said, "A man's gotta make a living. I don't always hire out my gun, but at times..." He shrugged again and then asked Luke, "Irish here said that you got brothers; you wouldn't be four brothers and a sister, now would you?"

Luke nodded his head, and Declan exclaimed, "Well, how's old Nolan doing these days!" Luke frowned and asked him, "Which part of the clan do you belong to?" Declan laughed and told him, "Your Dad and your brother Mike will know me. We lived on the far side of the hill, but we did our fair share of killing Hawkes boys; until your Dad fell in love and married Katie Hawkes. I was just about three years old, I reckon, at the time, so I missed out on the feuding, but my Dad and his brother did their share. His name was Emmett, and he was Nolan's first cousin; their fathers were brothers. He died when I was thirteen, and I been drifting ever since. Tried to settle down but failed each time, and so by accident I started hiring out my gun. Got a reputation now as a bad man, I reckon, so sometimes people come searching for me." Luke asked him, "So how did you come to be here? Who sent for you?"

Declan scratched his head and said, "Now that's a funny thing, and I been wondering about it, but seeing you here now clears it up; they wanted a Bailey to fight a Bailey. I was way over in Montana working as a ranch hand when a man came to find me. He said that someone wanted me in particular 'cause of my name, and he offered me more than a fighting wage. I was just about to quit because the ranch was laying off men, but I still said no; so he kept upping the amount until I said yes. I been wondering why he wanted me in particular, but now I know." Luke asked him, "So what you going to do now?" Declan shrugged and said, "Can't fight cousins, so I reckon I'll quit. If the man who paid me wants his money back, he can come find me. I did take his money, but he wasn't straight with me when he hired me, so I can quit with a clear conscience." Luke said, "There's a snake in this here woodpile, and I'm trying to find it, so tell me who hired you."

Declan told him, "He paid the money, but he wasn't the one doing the hiring. I was told to meet up with the rest of this crowd in Phoenix and then come down here to settle a mining fight over some claims. I got my orders from that gambler Drake Manning." Luke scratched his chin and asked him, "You saying that Drake is the one calling the shots here? He hired you?" Declan shook his head and said, "No, I spoke to him, but I don't think that he's the one in charge. When he told me what to do, it sounded like he was just relaying instructions." Luke looked disappointed and said, "So you don't know who hired you." Declan said, "Yeah, I don't. But there's one thing that I can tell you; the man who paid me said that Black Bob was in this and running the show." Luke stared at him and exclaimed, "You mean Black Bob the gunslinger? The Iowa gunman?" Declan said, "That's the one. I've heard it said that he's the fastest gun alive, but I never met anyone who actually knew him or could describe him."

Luke asked Rock, "You been here since this started; you seen anyone who could be Black Bob?" Rock shook his head and said, "Drake Manning is fast, but I know him and he ain't Black Bob. Hans, Rupert, Max, Burt? I don't know, but maybe he came after and is laying low using Drake as a front." Declan offered to stay and fight alongside Luke and Mark, but Luke told him, "You took his money so it wouldn't be right. We're good here, got a lot of guns, so you just go your way for now." But when Declan was leaving, Luke told him, "Mike is on the ranch in Cedar Creek, and I got me a ranch near the Red River in Texas. Brian and Mark are ranching up in Colorado near the San Juan Mountains. Come visit sometime, and if you're in need, just holler or send us word." Declan raised his hand in acknowledgement, then turned his horse and rode away. Paddy asked Luke, "So what we gonna do with these men? Four of them are dead, but there's still twenty-three left." Luke looked at the line of tied-up men and remarked, "I reckon the best thing to do would be to just shoot them." One of the men said, "Mister, you let Declan go, so why not let us go as well? We would ride right out of this state and we wouldn't ever come back."

Luke scratched his chin and appeared to ponder the question, but then he shook his head and said, "Declan is different and I can trust him. But you boys got paid, so if I were to set you free you would just turn right around and come back with guns blazing." He paused as though in thought and then added, "No, I think the safest thing to do would be to just shoot the lot of you." Rudy came up leading the man that Luke had left bound and gagged. Luke told him, "I forgot all about you; how's the head, by the way." The man grimaced and replied, "Like I got the world's worst hangover ever!" Another man told Luke, "Mister, you could take our guns and let us go. Like Wes here just said, we'd keep riding and wouldn't ever come back." Luke asked him, "What's your name?" The man replied, "Billy Cassidy, and I'm a man of my word. If any of these men don't keep their word, then they'll answer to me." Luke looked at the others and they chorused, "We ain't coming back!" Wes said, "If Billy says we ain't coming back, then I reckon we ain't coming back."

CHAPTER 23

MARK AND LUKE

LUKE SENT THE REST OF THE HIRED GUNS ON THEIR way with a warning that they would be shot on sight if they returned. He gave them their guns as they were leaving and told Billy, "I like a man who keeps his word, so you get to keep your guns; but break your word and I'll shoot you on sight." When he was back in town, he told Mark about Declan and what he had said. Mark shook his head and said, "We were too young, but Mike will remember him. So he thinks that Black Bob, that Iowa gunman, is here?" Luke shrugged and replied, "That's what he said, so I'm taking the boys to check every single building in this town, and then I'm sending everyone out to search the countryside for any hiding place. If the man's here, he's got to sleep somewhere!"

Luke made it a point to see every man in town, but as he did not know how Black Bob looked, he didn't get anywhere. They searched every building and they searched the countryside, but they came up empty. Mark was on his feet in a week and sent the miners back to their mines. He and Luke went to see Drake, and Mark told him, "One of the hired guns said that he reported to you." Drake gave him a level look and said, "Hired guns can say many things; maybe he was protecting the man who hired him." Luke asked him, "So you're saying that you did not hire those men?" Drake told him with a small smile, "I do all right where money is concerned, but I sure don't have the kind of money it would take to hire so many men." Mark told him, "That bill of sale for Pat Simpson's mine won't hold. I have sent word to his relatives for a specimen of his signature, but until then the mine remains in the hands of his partner Kelly Proctor." Drake shrugged and told him, "Big Red came to me and said that Simpson wanted to sell and that he could get the mine for me, but it would cost. I paid him and he came back with the bill of sale; and that's all I know about it. You check it out and I'll wait to see what you find out."

They next went to Hans, and Mark told him, "That bill of sale for Harvey Kline's mine won't hold up. I've sent word to his relatives for a specimen of his signature, but until then the mine will remain in the possession of Butch Brady." Hans and Rupert just stared at them, and Luke said bluntly, "Those bills of sale are fake and you know it. If you want to make something of it, now's the time. Remember, Mark has sent word to their families to get someone who knows their sign or to get a sample of their signature. Once we have that proof, then we'll just naturally have to arrest you." Hans said blandly, "Big Red came to me and said that Kline wanted to sell out. He told me that he would get the mine for me if I paid, so I did and he got me the bill of sale. But if you have doubts about it, then go ahead and check it out and let me know what you find." Luke told him, "One of the hired guns that we sent packing told me that he reported to you. Did you hire them?" He was watching both of them as he spoke, but their expressions did not change. Hans told him, "Hired guns can say many things, but it doesn't mean that it's true. I fight my own battles and I don't need to hire others for that."

A week went by and nothing happened. Mark, Luke, Paddy, Dewey, Trent, and Joe went over everything in the Marshal's office. Mark told Trent, "Things have settled down for now, so you and your boys can head back to the Box T. Thanks to Sally, you came just in time to help me out, but now that we got things under control, you got to think about the ranch." Trent said, "If you're sure, then I'll be on my way, because we surely left the Box T shorthanded." Mark told him, "You and the boys leave tonight, one by one, and meet up outside of town. No need to advertise that you're leaving." Trent told him, "That's smart; leave them guessing!" He shook hands with Luke and the others, and that night the Box T riders left town quietly.

The next day Mark asked Luke, "You brought thirteen of your boys with you, so who's running the ranch?" Luke shrugged and said, "Mike Holden runs the place as always, but I did leave him shorthanded. I'll keep Rudy, Jake, and Hardy with me, and I'll send the rest of the boys back home." He paused and then said, "That's a good idea that you have; keep the enemy guessing as to our strength. My boys will leave one by one, and no one will be sure if they're gone or not." Mark smiled at him and said, "You're keeping those three boys with you. I noticed that they seem mighty attached to you." Luke grinned and told him, "If I told them that they had to go back without me, I reckon they would just quit and stay here. When I first got to the Rafter C after I had found Gina's father shot dead, these three boys came with me to track down his killer. They're good boys, and so I started teaching them about tracking, the fast draw, and a few of Jack's fighting tricks. They're fast learners, and they're good men to have at your side in a fight." Mark said, "There's you, me, Joe, Dewey, Paddy, and your three boys; that makes eight, and let's not forget Rock and Rusty." Paddy said, "When those riders hit town, I was holed up in the Gold Mine Saloon. Those two are very cool under pressure; Rock picked his targets and took down two of the riders, while Rusty held a shotgun in case they tried to charge the saloon. I reckon they're good men to have on your side in a fight."

Luke had his head down and appeared to be deep in thought, and Mark asked him, "What you thinking about, boy?" Luke looked up and said, "You were talking about Big Red and about how big and tough he was." Joe said, "Oh, he was big and tough all right. They say he was fast with a gun, but that he preferred to rely on his strength." Mark told him, "When he tried to pull me or throw me over this here desk, I wasn't about to find out if that was true or not, so I shot him." Luke shook his head and told them, "I ain't doubting what you say, but have you two had a look at that Max Shultz and Hans Kruger?" Mark looked suddenly thoughtful and said, "Yeah! When he walked up and took a swing at me in the Silver Rock that day, I realized that he was very big and looked hard and tough. I reckon, being in the shadow of Big Red, no one really noticed how big he was. But Kruger now..."

Joe said, "Now that you mention it, I think he's even bigger than Big Red." He frowned and then said, "How come we didn't notice that?" Mark told Luke, "I think we never even thought about it because he doesn't push his weight around. He acts like a legitimate businessman, and he talks softly without any bluster. But now that I think about it, I do believe that Joe is right, and the man is bigger than Big Red was. He wears that loose, long, shabby-looking coat, so you don't get to see any muscle or anything." He paused and then added, "Now I wonder why that is so; unless he doesn't want to attract any attention. Everyone knows Drake, and everyone talks about his fast draw, so he's a natural to be the ringleader of any gang. But what if he isn't? What if the leader is that big man who is always in the shadows?"

Luke told him, "Now that you're thinking about Hans, think about Rupert as well. I was watching him when you were talking to Hans, and his face had no expression. But when I called them out about the fake bill of sale, I saw his fingers twitch. His face was the same, no expression at all, but those fingers did give a sudden twitch." Mark frowned and said, "He does wear his gun slung low and tied down, but so do many others in this land. Folks from the east think that a tied-down holster means a gunslinger, but you tie down the holster so that it doesn't bounce around when you're riding hard and fast. Same thing with the thong around the trigger, which is just to hold the gun in place when you're riding." He pondered for a while and then remarked, "But that twitch of the fingers now, when you called them out; that's the sign of someone keeping an iron grip on themselves. So you think he's a gunslinger." Joe said, "That could well be, because I did notice that the gun butt looked like it had seen a lot of use."

Luke smiled grimly and told them, "But I'm thinking more than that; much more than that." He paused for effect and then said, "I think Rupert Schwartz is Black Bob!" Mark looked thoughtful and Joe exclaimed, "How did you come up with that!" Luke said, "I just remembered that 'Schwartz' means 'black' in German. Both of them have German names, so maybe they grew up together." Mark said slowly, "Bob is short for Robert, and if I remember correctly, Rupert is the equivalent of Robert. You might have something there, boy." Suddenly Dewey exclaimed, "Damn me if I ain't real stupid!" Joe retorted, "Okay, you're stupid! Now tell us why." Dewey told them about the two men who tried to stop him in Oneida. "The barkeep told me that they were asking if anyone who seemed to be in a mighty big hurry had passed through the town," he told them. "I was in a hurry and I didn't stop to think about it, but now that I do..."

Joe interrupted and said, "They were watching for us." Mark exclaimed, "Those three men who tried to stop us!" Paddy grunted and said, "I reckon Dewey's got something there." He told them about Fast Buck, and Luke said, "Declan said that they wanted him because his name was Bailey, so they knew that Tally had sent for us. Which also means that they already knew about Tally and his connection to you and Brian; and they also found out about me." He paused and then said, "They sent men to watch the trails, with orders to kill us or somehow prevent us from coming here. Black Bob would have all the necessary connections to find out about us and to hire the men to kill us." Mark told him, "If you're right and Rupert is Black Bob, then he's the leader and not Hans Kruger."

Luke got up, stretched, and then said, "I'm feeling a mite tired, and seeing that everything is quiet now, I reckon I'll go to the hotel and get me some sleep." He started for the door, and Mark said sternly, "Sit down! If we're going to tackle Black Bob and Hans Kruger, then we do it together." Luke gave him an innocent look and said, "I ain't going to do nothing; I just want to catch up on some sleep." Mark's face was grim as he again said, "Sit down!" Luke sighed, and sitting back down, he told Mark, "After you and Brian left, Jack started training me because he saw how restless I was. He trained me with gun and fist, and before I left, he told me that I was as fast as he was; so let me take Black Bob." Mark asked him, "How much did you learn about Jack's way of fist-fighting?" Luke said, "A good bit, I reckon." Then he told them about the town of Shackelford and the fight with Harry the Ape. Mark told him, "I've just recovered from the wound through my chest, so I can't fist-fight; but it doesn't affect my ability to draw a gun. So you deal with Hans and I'll deal with Rupert." Dewey asked him, "Want me to deal with Hans?" Mark shook his head and said, "There's still Max Shultz, so he's yours."

CHAPTER 24
BLACK BOB

HANS KRUGER AND RUPERT SCHWARTZ WERE BORN IN Iowa before it became a state. Their families were neighbors, and the boys grew up together. Their families were farmers, as were all their other neighbors; and all of them were German settlers in the region. Farming at that time was a struggle, and everyone lived from harvest to harvest. By the time the boys were eight, they were working the whole day on the family farms except for three hours when they attended the community school, which was held in the open under a tree. Mothers of the community took turns teaching the children daily until they turned twelve; then they became full-time workers on their farms.

Hans was a big lad right from his childhood; not just in height but in bulk as well. He and Rupert were always together; they played together and they fought against others together. Because Hans was the bigger of the two and the more outspoken, everyone assumed that he was the leader. But in actual fact, it was the silent Rupert who was the leader of the two. Rupert was thin but extremely strong as a boy, and there was a ruthless streak in him which Hans discovered when they were just ten years old. Two big-made boys from an outlying farm, who were two years older than Hans and Rupert, used to torment them during the harvest, when everyone joined together and harvested farm by farm to make the work easier. Rupert took their bullying for two years, and Hans took a beating or two from them during that time.

When Rupert and Hans were ten years old, they were working on the outskirts of a farm during the harvest, and the two older boys attacked them. Hans was using a pitchfork, and Rupert snatched it from his hand. He stabbed one of the boys in the leg with it and hit the other on his head. Both boys fell to the ground, and Rupert tried to impale them on the pitchfork, but Hans stopped him and took it away. That did not stop Rupert because he proceeded to kick them viciously as they lay moaning on the ground. Finally, Hans was able to stop him and dragged him away. The two boys complained, but Hans told everyone that it was the boys who had attacked Rupert and him and they had injured themselves when Hans held out the pitchfork as a defense. The two boys were bigger and older by two years, so no one believed that thin Rupert had beaten them up. But from that day, Rupert was the leader and Hans the follower.

By the time they were sixteen, they were fed up with the dull farm life that they lived, and they ran away from home. They worked their way slowly to Omaha, in the Territory of Nebraska, which was along the Missouri River. It took them two years to make it to Omaha, and then the Civil War between the states started. But the conflict did not reach Nebraska, and the two young men, now eighteen years old, worked hard at the docks, on the ferry, and at whatever odd jobs came their way, and they saved their money. When they were twenty, they joined up with a group of settlers who were heading west to seek their fortunes. Rupert had told Hans, "Hard work alone is not going to give us what we want. Everyone says that there is a golden land out west, so we're going there." Hans never argued much with Rupert because he was a bit scared of him. He knew that Rupert kept an iron control over his emotions, but he also knew that when that control slipped, then Rupert could go berserk.

They were making their way to Omaha, doing odd jobs wherever they could find them to earn eating money, but many times they went hungry. It was one of those times when they hadn't eaten all day. They were passing by a farm, and a man was walking back to the house with a spade and a bag slung over his shoulder. Hans stopped and told him, "Mister, we haven't eaten all day, and we would be indebted to you if you could spare us a little food. We would work for it as we're not lazy." The man regarded them for a moment and then said rudely, "I don't have food or anything else for vagabonds like you. Get off my land or by all the gods I will beat you to within an inch of your life!" Rupert had been standing silently as usual, letting Hans do all the talking, but now he snapped. He took two quick steps towards the man and kicked him viciously with his heavy boot on his shin. The man lost his balance, and Rupert grabbed the spade from his hand. The man lifted his hand to defend himself, and Rupert hit it with the blade of the spade, almost cutting his hand in half. Hans shouted at him to stop, but in a frenzy of rage, Rupert hit the man across his neck, almost severing his head from his body. They took the man's bag and ran for two miles before stopping. The bag was filled with vegetables, and they made it last for three days.

They travelled with the group of men across the north of Kansas, headed for Colorado and the gold mines. When they were introducing themselves, Rupert said his name was Black Bob. It was during their travel that they were introduced to the art of the fast draw by a man from Texas, and they started wearing gun belts and holsters. Hans was just average in speed, but Rupert took to the fast draw as though he was born to it; the fact that he had dexterous hands and practiced for more than four hours every day also helped. By the time they turned twenty-two, they had made a lot of money out of the goldmines, but not by working in them; and Black Bob had killed six men in straight-up gunfights. They had worked in the mines for about six months when Rupert told Hans, "This is a fool's game, and it isn't going to make us rich." Hans asked him, "So what else is there?"

Rupert told him his plan about becoming partners with a miner and then killing him. Hans protested and said, "I can just beat them up and they will sign." But Rupert sneered at him, saying, "And what if they beat you up? No, we have saved enough money now to buy into a partnership, and there are many miners who are in need of hard cash to start mining." They found a miner who claimed to have a mine with good prospects but needed money to outfit himself. Hans and Rupert inspected the mine and decided that it was a fifty-fifty chance. They were alone with the miner on the hillside, and Rupert drew his gun and shot him in the leg. He then gagged the miner and proceeded to break his fingers one by one until the miner signed a paper that stated he was selling the mine to Hans. Rupert then killed him and they buried the body in a shallow grave, caving in a slide of sand and rubble to cover it.

They sold the mine and then became partners in another two mines with Hans doing all the talking and negotiating. But after they became partners, Black Bob forced the owners into gunfights and killed them. The word soon spread, and Hans and Rupert found that they weren't welcome in Colorado anymore. They now had money, and they moved to Kansas and opened a general store. But before they left Colorado, the story of Black Bob and the speed of his draw had already started. When the cattle drives started from Texas to Kansas, the two took advantage and preyed on the smaller herds. They formed a gang of rustlers, and many a head of cattle was robbed on the trail from Texas to Kansas. By the time he was twenty-five, Rupert was famous, or infamous, using the name Black Bob, because he had killed a total of twelve men in gunfights. He was spoken of as the fastest gun in the West. But whenever they moved on, he used his own name of Rupert until they settled in another town. Since it was always Hans who was the front man and Rupert stayed in the background until he killed someone, Black Bob became a shadowy figure, and no one could really describe him.

They were in Phoenix running a general store when Tally and the others rode into town with the silver ore. They had heard of Tally, who was a legend among miners, and Rupert sensed an opportunity to seize the great wealth that he had always wanted. He left Hans in Phoenix and went travelling to meet with some of the rough crowd that he had worked with before. When he returned to Phoenix, he had all the information he needed about Tally and the Baileys, and he told Hans about his plan. They knew Drake Manning, who was gambling in a saloon in the city, and they sold him on the idea of taking over the gold and silver mines. Drake's nerves were getting frazzled because Rock and Rusty were always following him now. He was tempted many a time to finally shoot it out with them, but he knew that he could never take both of them together. Rupert had also heard about Drake's story, and he told him, "If you come with us and front the operation, we will take care of everything else. Before we're done, I'll take care of those two men for you; or if you prefer, then we could do it together." Drake said, "They're both very fast on the draw, although Rock Masters is the faster of the two. But as fast as I am, it would take more than speed on the draw to kill a man like Masters; which is why I have been holding back. How good are you with a gun?" Rupert told him bluntly, "I'm also known as Black Bob, and I'll take care of Masters for you." Drake joined them and took along Big Red and the others when they followed Tally to Two Forks.

CHAPTER 25
ATTACKING THE MINES

JOE, DEWEY, PADDY, AND HARDY WENT TO THE SILVER Rock Saloon to keep an eye on Drake and to stop anyone from interfering in what was going to take place at Hans' general store. Mark and Luke went to the store while Rudy and Jake kept an eye on the street. The door was shut and Luke pushed it open and then stepped to the side, but nothing happened; no shots were fired. He took a quick glance around the corner of the door, but the store seemed empty. He beckoned to Mark, and they walked in, but no one was there. Mark looked puzzled, and he said slowly, "Now why would they just leave the store empty and walk away? Unless they didn't want anyone to know that they're gone..." Luke suddenly exclaimed, "The mines! They're attacking the mines!" Both of them rushed out of the store and called out to Paddy and Joe. The others came running up, and Mark told them, "No gold has been shipped since before we came here, so there must be a lot of gold up in them hills. These two are not here, so their plan must have changed, and they're going after the gold." Luke said, "With all that's been happening, with their failure to take control of the mines, and the routing of their hired guns, they must have figured that their long term plan won't work anymore."

Joe was skeptical, and he said, "Just the two of them? That man may be Black Bob, but to attack mines..." His voice trailed off, and then he almost shouted, "They must have brought in more men!" Luke nodded and said, "Black Bob must have known when the men were coming in, and he's gone to meet them outside town. I figure he's going to attack the mines for the gold while we sit here planning to take him down." He told Paddy, "Go tell Rock and Rusty that we're riding to the mines; ask them to hold down the town until we're back." Paddy swung into his saddle and raced to the Gold Mine Saloon, while the others mounted up and rode from town.

By the time Paddy caught up with the others, they were halfway to Tally's mine. Mark figured that Tally would have the most gold, and so he decided to head there first. They were nearing the mountain when they heard the shots, and Mark shouted out, "Don't stay bunched up, keep at least a ten-foot gap between each of you." They raced to the mountain but slowed down while riding up the slope. They stopped once they had cleared the trees on the foothills and looked up towards Tally's mine. They could see four men on horses making their way slowly to the mine. Mark said, "Everyone off your horses! Hardy, loosely tether the horses a few feet back in the trees so they won't get shot up. The rest of you find cover and then start shooting." There was cover enough for everyone; trees and boulders were all over the place. They began shooting, and the men above glanced back and then urged their horses faster up the slope towards the mine.

It is not easy shooting uphill or downhill, and most of the shots missed except for Mark, Luke, and Rudy, who scored hits. The man Luke shot tumbled off his horse and lay still. Mark's target took the bullet in his shoulder, but he rode on. Rudy's bullet hit the horse in the rump, and the horse reared violently, throwing the rider, who landed hard and rolled down the slope. Mark immediately told Jake, "Try and get to him; if he's alive, find out how many men they have and whether they're attacking all the mines." Jake darted from cover to cover and asked Mark as he ran, "What if he refuses to talk?" Mark said with exasperation, "Break his fingers, burn his toes! Just get it done, boy!" Jake kept moving, but muttered to himself, "That was a damn fool question to ask a Bailey!"

The shots fired by Mark and the others had alerted Tally, and they heard scattered shots from the mine as the last two attackers hunted for cover. Mark told the others, "Move up slowly, but keep to cover and keep shooting when you see a target." He and Luke began moving up, and when Luke saw a boot protruding from the shelter of a tree, he took aim and squeezed off a shot. There was a loud yell, and the boot disappeared. The others also began moving up, and soon there were scattered shots from below and from the mine. The two attackers were caught in crossfire, and they led their horses across the mountain face using the trees as cover and soon disappeared from sight.

Paddy started to go after them, but Mark stopped him, saying, "First go and see if Jake got that man to talk. We need to know what we're up against." He told Luke, "You hold the others here while I go up and talk to Tally." Luke whistled twice, and in a minute, Hardy came riding up leading the horses. Mark smiled at his brother and said, "You got them trained really well." He caught up his horse and swung into the saddle. Over his shoulder, he told Luke, "Maybe you ought to go and talk to that man with Jake."

When Mark neared the mine, he shouted out, "Hey Tally! Don't shoot! I'm coming in!" He rode closer, and Tally's head popped up from behind some rocks. Seeing Mark, he jumped over the rocks and walked forward. "Thanks for the warning," he told Mark. "They brought in more men?" Mark shrugged and said, “Looks like it, although it was pure luck that we came to know of it. We figured they had changed their plans and decided to take the gold from the mines, so we came riding as fast as we could.” Tally cursed, and Mark told him, “No point in that. How many men have you got with you?” Tally said, “Clayton, Harry, Sam, and Wayne. Pete Ford and Mason are at their mine, and Butch and Kelly are at Harvey’s mine. They’re working together on both mines, and today they’re at Harvey’s mine. You go help them; now that we know the score, we’ll be okay. Hugh Benton and his boys are now working one mine at a time, so don’t worry about them. They would have heard the shooting, and they’ll be under cover by now.”

CHAPTER 26

SHOOTOUT ON THE MOUNTAIN

LUKE SCRAMBLED DOWN THE SLOPE AND FOUND JAKE and Paddy still talking to the man who had been thrown from his horse. He was lying there with a broken leg, and Paddy was telling him, "Be smart, Reuben; when Jake here says that he's gonna break your fingers, that's exactly what he'll do." The man shrugged and said, "I already got a broken leg, and the pain is killing me, so what's a broken finger gonna do." Luke came up to them and told Jake, "Light a small fire and be quick about it; we ain't got a lot of time to save the other miners." Reuben looked at him and said, "What you gonna do to make me talk; whatever it is, it won't work, so don't waste your time." Luke shrugged and said bluntly, "I don't have time to waste, so either you'll talk or you'll be dead." He caught hold of the broken leg that was bent at an angle and slowly straightened it out. Reuben screamed and fainted, and Luke remarked, "Not as tough as he claims to be." He told Paddy, "Get a canteen of water from one of the horses." Paddy ran to a horse and came back with a canteen. Luke had slapped the man until he came around, and now Luke told him, "Each time you faint, I'm gonna bring you back by splashing water on your face." He told Paddy, "Get his boots and socks off."

Reuben stared at him for a moment, and then as Paddy started pulling off his boot from the uninjured leg, he asked him, "What's the idea of removing my boots?" Luke shrugged and said casually, "It's an old Indian trick; I'm gonna set fire to your toes." He turned around and told Jake, "A small fire is enough; I just need some burning sticks." Jake came up with two thick sticks that were burning nicely, and Luke took one and held it to Reuben's toes. Reuben screamed and shouted, "I'll talk! I'll talk!" Luke threw away the stick and asked him, "How many men are there, and what's the plan of action?" Reuben stared at him and said bitterly, "No white man would do such a thing!" Luke said, "Pass me that burning stick, Jake. I've got no time to waste, so maybe I'll burn his eyes first."

Reuben spoke fast and told him, "There are twelve of us, and we came in two groups. We did as we were told and hid outside the town until Black Bob came to us. Now we're attacking the mines to get the gold that's been sacked and kept ready for shipment. Four men each to attack the three mines, and I don't know which mine Black Bob is attacking. That's the truth, Mister, so just let me be!" Luke said mildly, "You're not as tough as you think. The fire hardly touched you, and your toes aren't even singed." He stood up and told the others, "Mount up and give Mark a shout to come down." He told Jake, "Round up Hardy and Rudy; you three are coming with me. We'll go to Harvey's mine, and Mark and the others can go to Pete Ford's mine." He told Paddy, "You tell Mark where we're going and say I said for him to go to Pete's mine."

He rode off with his boys without waiting for Mark to come back down. When Mark came down, Paddy told him what Luke had said. Mark slapped his thigh and declared, "Damn that kid!" Paddy looked confused, and Mark explained, "He thinks that Black Bob will be at Harvey's mine, and that's why he's going there. He's trying to protect me." Joe remarked, "Figures; he's a Bailey after all." Mark told him, "There's nothing we can do about it now because we need to get to Pete's mine first." They rode away at an angle up the slope because Pete's mine was higher than all the others. They were about fifty feet from the mine when Mark called a halt and said, "Tether the horses here; we'll move in on foot."

He started forward and then stopped with a frown on his face. "I would have thought that the attack would have started by now," he said. Joe told him, "Maybe Pete and Mason were taken by surprise, and the attackers are already in the mine." Mark abruptly said, "You all wait here, but come running if you hear anything." He loosened the gun in his holster and checked the action of his Winchester. He moved forward fast but with his eyes scanning everything in front and to the sides of him. There was the trunk of a huge tree that had fallen on the trail a long time ago, and Mark climbed over it and dropped to the other side.

He dropped right into trouble because, as he dropped, he saw four men who were moving forward stealthily towards the mine. The four men spun around with their guns blazing, and bullets sang a song around Mark. When Mark saw the four men, he knew that a shootout was inevitable; so as he dropped to the ground, he shifted his rifle to his left hand and palmed his pistol with his right. By the time the four men spun around shooting, Mark's pistol was speaking. He shot his targets from left to right, and before you could count to five, the four men lay dead or dying. Paddy and the others jumped down from the tree trunk, and Joe said laconically, "Always the showoff. You could have at least left one for me."

Mark gave him a grim smile and said, "Wasn't no time to pick and choose; it was root hog or die!" They went forward and hallooed the mine, and John Mason's head popped up from behind a bulwark of rubble and rock. Mark told him about the attackers and said, "You two stay forted up here until someone gets back to you." They rode as fast as they could to the Harvey mine because Mark was worried about Luke, although he never mentioned it. He knew why Luke figured that Black Bob would take Harvey's mine; because they had called him out on the bill of sale.

CHAPTER 27
THE SNIPER

LUKE AND HIS BOYS MADE GOOD TIME TO HARVEY'S mine, which was located halfway up another mountain slope about a mile from Tally's mine. They slowed down and proceeded cautiously when they were about five hundred yards from the mine. They spread out, keeping a distance of five yards from each other. Luke kept his eyes moving all around as he rode, and it was his alertness that saved him. He caught a flash of sunlight from the top of an escarpment about a hundred yards to his right, and he threw himself from his saddle to his left. As he fell, he heard the sound of the rifle shot and actually heard the buzz of the bullet passing over his head. He caught up the reins and ran towards the nearest tree cover, leading his horse. He shouted out to Rudy, who was the closest to him, "You three keep going to the mine; I'll take care of this!"

Once he was behind the trees, he scanned the area around the escarpment from where the shot had been fired, searching for a safe way to get there. He swung into the saddle and made his way through the tree cover to where he had spotted a shallow ravine running across the face of the mountain. He entered the ravine, and bending forward to lie flat on his horse, he rode fast towards the escarpment. When the ravine started to slope upwards, he raised his head and saw that he was behind the escarpment. He straightened up in the saddle and rode out of the ravine, scanning the land ahead on all sides. He found an old trail that led in a circle around the escarpment, and he made it in good time. He looked down at the escarpment, but no one was there. Riding straight down without hesitating, he reached the spot and saw the bullet casing and the marks where the sniper had knelt down to shoot. He figured that the sniper must have left in a hurry because the tracks were clear and had not been rubbed out; which also meant that the sniper had known that he was circling around to get behind him. Luke again did not hesitate but turned his horse and followed the tracks; but he was wary and kept scanning the area ahead and to the sides with only a glance now and then at the tracks to make sure that he was headed in the right direction.

He came to a tree where the grass had been cropped around it, and he figured that the sniper had tied his horse there. The tracks of the horse led straight to a well-defined trail, and Luke urged his horse into a gallop and went in pursuit. He was determined that this time the sniper wasn't going to get away. There was a score to settle as the sniper had nearly killed Mark. Half a mile down the trail, he saw that the tracks had veered off the trail to the left about fifty feet ahead of him. Luke was an expert tracker and hunter, and he had been keeping an eye on the tracks far ahead of him and not looking down at the tracks; which was what saved him a second time that day. When he saw the tracks veer off the trail, he immediately pulled on the reins, bringing his horse to a sudden stop, and then, turning on a dime, he swung his horse to the left and with a jump he left the trail. A bullet sang its song past his head as his horse jumped off the trail, and then he was racing around to get behind the sniper again. He slid his Winchester from the sheath and began triggering shots at the small knoll from where the shot had come.

Then he was behind a few trees, and he could see the sniper swinging around to aim at him. Luke halted his horse and triggered a shot at the sniper, not with any hope of hitting him but just to distract him until he could find some better cover; but the bullet hit the frame of the rifle, and it dropped from the sniper's hands. Luke immediately spurred his horse and raced up the slope to the sniper. He halted a few yards away and gave Hans Kruger a grim look. Hans dropped his hand to his pistol, and Luke said conversationally, "Now that's a mighty good way to get killed. Loosen the belt and let it drop or take a Winchester bullet in your gut; your choice." Hans glared at him but unbuckled and let the belt drop to the ground. Luke said, "Take two steps forward." Hans complied and then growled, "If only I could get my hands on you, I'd tear you apart!" Luke regarded him for a moment and then said, "For a man who wants to use his fists, you killed a few men with that rifle instead; bushwhacked them actually." Hans turned red and he said, "I wanted to use my fists, but Rupert thought otherwise." Luke asked him, "You mean Black Bob; and speaking of the devil, where is he?"

Hans gave him an evil look and said, "He's waiting down the trail for your brother. He wanted the two of you, but you're here now, and if you put down the gun, I'll show you how I killed men with my bare hands." Luke gave him a look of disgust and said, "I'm supposed to give a yellow bushwhacker a fair chance? Okay then, strap on your gun belt and you'll get your chance." He sheathed the rifle and swung down from the saddle. He took two steps forward, and Hans charged him; but Luke knew men, and he was waiting for the move. When Hans was a foot away, he swung his big fist, but Luke stepped inside the swing and hit Hans hard on the lip just below his nose with a straight jab that had all the power of his shoulder behind it. He did not hit him with a closed fist but with a half-closed fist that had the knuckle of the center finger extended; but the effect of the blow was stunning.

Hans came to a halt as though he had run into a brick wall, and his eyes closed in pain. Luke stepped forward and hit him with the same knuckle-extended fist in the center of his throat, and Hans' eyes opened wide in shock. His mouth opened and closed like a fish out of water as he struggled to take a breath, and he slowly sank down until he was kneeling in the dust. There was a cold, implacable look in Luke's eyes as he walked behind Hans and caught hold of his head with both his hands. "This is for shooting Mark," he said coldly. Then with a swift jerk, using all his strength, he twisted Hans' head to the side. There was a dry snapping sound as he broke Hans' neck. Luke stood back as Hans' neck flopped loosely on his shoulders, and then slowly Hans' body toppled over, and he lay sprawled in the dusty trail. Luke walked over to his horse and swung into the saddle. He rode away down the trail without looking back.

Rudy watched Luke ride off after the sniper, and he waved to the others to come to him. When Jake and Hardy came up, he told them, "Luke's gone after the sniper, and I reckon this time that bushwhacker won't get away. There's the three of us, and we got to save those two miners; keep a five-foot gap between us, and let's move in." They moved forward slowly for another two hundred yards until Rudy held up his hand. He had seen movement ahead, and now he swung his hand downward as he dropped to the ground, and the other two followed suit. Carefully, he sighted his rifle at a small boulder and a shrub growing next to it, and waited. The top of a head slowly appeared at the side of the boulder, half hidden by the shrub, and then a forehead followed. Rudy squeezed the trigger, and the head jerked backwards with a hole in the forehead. As soon as he squeezed the trigger, Rudy rolled his body to the side. Two shots sounded, and two bullets hit the place where his body had been a second before. Jake and

Hardy had their targets now, and they fired together. The echo of the shots died away, and they heard a groan from above. Then there came a fusillade of firing from above, and then silence descended on the mountainside. After a while, there came a shout from above, "This is Kelly! I think we got them all, and I figure you must be friends, so I'm coming down. Don't shoot!" None of the three young men moved from their cover until Kelly Proctor appeared at the side of the small boulder; then they stood up and moved to him. Kelly was staring at the body of the man with a hole in his forehead, and he remarked, "Now that's shooting!"

CHAPTER 28
END GAME

MARK AND THE OTHERS CAME DOWN TO HARVEY'S mine minutes after the shooting ended. Rudy told him about the bushwhacker, and Mark just said, "Luke will get him; let's ride to town." They rode into Two Forks, tired and dusty, and Mark swung down in front of the Marshal's office. He told the others, "You boys go ahead and have a drink at the Gold Mine; you've earned it!" He stretched his body and then adjusted his gun belt. For no reason, and without thinking about it, he slipped the thong off his six-shooter and loosened the gun in the holster. He saw that the boys had entered the Gold Mine Saloon, and he turned to enter the Marshal's office. He had taken two steps when he saw someone in his peripheral vision coming from the Silver Rock Saloon. He stopped and turned around, and sighed when he saw Rupert Schwartz walking fast towards him. Mark stood and waited with his hands hanging limply until Rupert was ten feet away; then he called out, "That's far enough, Black Bob!"

Rupert's eyes opened wide, but then he smiled as he stopped and said, "So you know about me, Marshal. That's good, because now you know the man who will kill the Marshal of Two Forks. This is the killing that I will enjoy the most. You ruined a perfectly good plan of mine, and because of that, you will die." His hand hovered over his gun, and he became still. Suddenly there was the sound of a running horse and a wild yell; just for a second, Rupert threw a glance towards the sound, and Mark shot him. Rupert, or Black Bob, stood swaying for a few seconds with a smoking gun in his hand, and Mark shot him again. Black Bob crumpled to the ground, and the gun fell from his hand. Luke came racing up on his horse and skidded to a halt. He was off the horse and running before the horse came to a stop. He knelt down by Black Bob, who whispered something to him and then died. Luke stood up and went to Mark, who was still standing with the gun in his hand. He told Luke, "He was fast, real fast! You distracted him for a second, and I shot him, but he still got off a shot at the same time. I think he hit me."

Luke saw the blood slowly seeping from Mark's side just above his belt, and he pulled out the shirt and checked the wound. He told Mark, "Your bullet must have hit him just as he fired, and it deflected his aim. This is just a flesh wound to your side above your hip; you'll be fine." The others, including Rock Masters, came running up, and Luke told Paddy, "Get him inside the office and patch him up; he'll be okay." Mark asked him, "What about the bushwhacker?" Luke said shortly, "He's dead; it was Hans." Mark put his arm around Paddy's shoulder and turned to limp away, but then asked Luke, "Black Bob say something to you just before he died?" But Luke waved him away, saying, "Nothing much; just go and tend to that wound."

Luke waited until Mark walked into the Marshal's office, and then he told Rock, "Black Bob did say something, but it was about your sister." Rock's face turned grim, but he just said, "Tell me." Luke gave him a compassionate look and said softly,

"He told me that once, when Drake had had a little too much to drink in Phoenix, Hans asked him why you were following him around the country. Drake wouldn't say, but they pressed him, and finally he told them that in a fit of rage, he had accidentally killed your sister; broke her neck, was what he said." Rock Masters stood still as though he had turned to stone, but after a moment, he asked softly, "He say anything else?" Luke sighed and told him, "He said that Drake's men took the body to Mexico and buried it deep." Rock said as though he was speaking to himself, "I knew she was dead; I could feel it, but ole Rusty hung on to hope all this time." He turned to look at the Gold Mine Saloon and muttered, "Maybe now the kid can get on with his life."

He sighed deeply and turned to go, but Luke stopped him, saying, "There was one more thing that Black Bob said, Rock." He stopped and asked, "And that was?" Luke told him, "He told me, and I'll quote him, 'I hate a woman killer, but tell Rock that Drake is faster and meaner than he ever was.'" Rock stood there for a moment, and then he said, "Send someone to the Gold Mine to keep Rusty there. I'll deal with this." Luke told Joe, "Take Rudy and go to the Gold Mine." He told Jake, "Go tell Mark what's about to happen so he won't come charging out." Rudy asked him, "Where you gonna be, boss?" Luke said grimly, "Right here! If Rock falls, then I'll settle the score for him." He paused and then added, "I hate a woman killer too."

Joe and Rudy walked fast to the Gold Mine Saloon, and Rock Masters went to the Silver Rock saloon. He stood outside and called out, "Drake Manning! Your time has come!" Rusty heard Rock calling out, and he started for the door, but Rudy put his arms around him from the back and held him tight. Joe removed his gun from the holster and told him, "I'm sorry, Rusty, but this was Rock's call. He said to keep you off the street." Rusty struggled, but Rudy was too strong. Finally, he almost sobbed out, "Let me at least watch from the door." Joe nodded and caught hold of one of his hands while Rudy released his hold and caught hold of his other hand. The three of them moved to the door and watched the ending of a long and sad story.

CHAPTER 29

THE FINAL SHOWDOWN

ALL SOUNDS DIED OUT FROM INSIDE THE SALOON when Rock called out and then Drake came walking out the door. He stepped down into the street and faced Rock. There was an expression on his face that almost looked like relief as he said, "Let's get this over with." He drew with such lightning speed that it made Rock Master's draw look real slow; and Rock's draw was the fastest he had ever made. His gun was out and lifting when Drake's first bullet hit him in the side of his chest. Rock's body just jerked slightly as he aligned the barrel and squeezed the trigger. His bullet hit Drake right in the center of his chest just as Drake's second bullet hit him in the left thigh and knocked his leg out from under him. Rock dropped to his right knee and Drake's third bullet sailed over his head. Rock held his gun steady and squeezed off his second shot, which took Drake in the stomach, and Drake's fourth bullet hit Rock in his left shoulder. Rock's body again jerked, but he held his gun level again and squeezed off his last shot, which took Drake right in the head and threw him back, dead before he hit the ground.

Rusty and the others came running from the Gold Mine

Saloon as Luke ran over to Rock. He picked him up bodily and walked fast to Homer's hotel just as Rusty and the others came up. Rusty asked Luke, "How is he? He was hit more than once!" Luke said, "He was hit three times, but I think he'll live. Rudy, run and tell Homer that he's got another patient. Joe, get the bark and leaves from my saddlebags." He reached the hotel and went in just as Homer came out with Rudy. They trooped in, and Homer said, "He's losing a lot of blood; just lay him here on the floor." Joe came running in with the bark and leaves just as one of Homer's men came in with a bucket of hot water and some clean cloths.

Homer told him, "Get some beef broth going and put a kettle on to boil the bark that Joe will give you." Joe said, "I'll take care of it." Luke took the leaves from Joe and ran to the kitchen, where he pounded the leaves into a thick paste. Homer cut away Rock's shirt and bared his chest. He sucked in his breath when he saw the two wounds, but then he muttered, "No air bubbles, so the bullet missed the lung. The shoulder is nothing much for a man like you." Rock told him, "He got me in the left thigh as well." Homer cut away the pant leg and pressed the wound slightly. "Well," he told Rock. "The blood ain't pumping out, so I guess it's mainly a flesh wound." He stared at Rock and remarked, "Three bullets in you, but you still killed your man." He shook his head and muttered, "This land makes tough men for sure!"

Luke came in with the paste, and Joe brought the bark water. They cleaned up the wounds, applied the paste, and then bandaged all three wounds. Homer remarked, "He's lucky the bullets all went right through and didn't lodge inside." Luke said soberly, "They were less than ten feet apart. By rights, they should both be dead!" Then he told Rock, "They sure named you right! You took a bullet to the chest before you got off your first shot and yet you stood there. You took three bullets, and yet you got your man; it takes a lot to kill you, I reckon." Rusty said, "He's a rock all right. He's been my rock for the past two years; but now it's over, and we can get on with our lives." Rock told him, "We have a lot of money saved, so go buy a gold mine from Tally. I reckon this is as good a place as any to make a new start."

The next day, Mark told Luke, "Go home, boy; we're all done here. I should be ready to ride in a week, and then we're all going home." Luke asked him, "So who will be the Marshal of Two Forks?" A voice from the door said, "That's what I want to know too!" Phil Barnaby, Homer Lee, Fat Fred, and Bret Hogan walked into the room, and Phil said again, "That's what I want to know too." Mark took off his badge and handed it to Phil. He told him, "Pin that on Harry Moss and don't take no for an answer. Clayton told me that that boy's got the itch to travel again. Clayton wants him to stay put in one place, and a town Marshal's job would be just the thing for a man like Harry Moss. I reckon he'll make a good Marshal for the town of Two Forks!"

ABOUT THE AUTHOR

Terence Newnes was born in south India. He dropped out of college and during the 70s and 80s he worked in fabrication, machine shops, and tool rooms. He then worked a short stint in Ethiopia. At the age of 43 he became a certified medical transcriptionist and worked in Toledo, Ohio as a medical transcriptionist, editor, and finally shift team lead. He started his own business of call center and data entry in 2006. During the pandemic and lock-down he lost his business and went broke, but he never lost hope. He started writing, which was a childhood dream, and he has never stopped.

To learn more about Terence Newnes and discover more Next Chapter authors, visit our website at www.nextchapter.pub.

Printed in Dunstable, United Kingdom

63749365R00088